A Patent on Murder

For Becky and Kevin
With Love
Uncle Charles Kaplan

A Patent on Murder

Charles Kaplan

Dedication

To my wife, Sara.

Table of Contents

Chapter 1   Revenge

"I WANT TO get a patent on murder," said Arnold Hamilton. The 59-year-old inventor sat in a chair across the desk from Lemont Levy, a patent attorney.

Levy laughed out loud and shook his head. "You can't. Murder's been done too many times already. You've got to know that."

Hamilton frowned. "Yes, of course I know that. But not murder the way I want it done." The look on Levy's face changed from amusement to a serious stare. "And I want my patent to say my invention's a death ray gun that'll be used for murdering Arabs. Because one of their terrorists murdered my son."

"Hold on a second," Levy said. "Have you ever tried to get a patent before?"

"No. This is the first one."

"Well, before you tell me the details. I mean, before you tell me about your invention and how it   works, we've got to deal with the *murdering Arabs* concept. The Patent Office won't let you get a patent on something that isn't legal."

Hamilton rolled his eyes in frustration. "My gun's no more illegal than any firearm you can use to do legal things like hunting or illegal things like robbing stores. But I want everyone to know I invented the ray gun so it can be used to kill Arabs. I want the Army and Marines to use it kill those raghead murderers."

"Look," Levy said. "I'm a Jew and I think I'm as patriotic as anyone. But I don't believe all Arabs deserve to be murdered. All Arabs aren't terrorists. Anyway, I think you mean Muslim terrorists, don't you? So what's your reason for having your own personal crusade against just Arabs? Why not include Muslims? And I can tell you right now the Patent Office won't let you get a patent with the word 'murder' in the title. I can prove it to you right now with an Internet search of their data base."

Hamilton didn't respond. He stood up and put his palms flat on the desk. He leaned over, jutting his chin as close to the lawyer's face as he could. Levy pushed against his desk and rolled his chair back a foot.

"I know all Muslims aren't Arabs. But all terrorists I know about are Arabs. An Arab murdered my son, my only child. A good man who was trying to help their people…to help the Arabs. And the killer snuck up on him from behind and murdered him. He never had a chance to defend himself. And that's why I have a jihad of my own. The Arabs don't have a monopoly on jihads."

Levy rose and walked around his desk. At age 64 he was five foot eight with a distance runner's build. His hair was completely white with some brown color still in his eyebrows. Blue eyes were spaced wide apart in his thin face that tapered to a rounded chin. He was wearing gray flannel pants, a pale blue button down oxford cloth shirt with a solid red tie, and a tweed jacket. His black loafers badly needed a shine. Levy put his hand on Hamilton's shoulder. "If it's not too upsetting, I'd like to hear about your son."

Hamilton sat down again with his head bowed while he massaged his eyebrows with the thumb and middle finger of his left hand. After a minute or so of rubbing he looked up. "To understand this tragedy, I've got to tell you what a great man and leader Allan was on the way to becoming. He was a champion soccer player, good enough to play on a pro team. But he never tried out with the pros. He got a soccer scholarship at FSU, and captained the Seminoles to their championship in '99. But he chose to fight for his country, and he joined the Marines a year after he graduated from college. Allan was always popular with his schoolmates. He was elected to several student government offices in high school and college. He wanted to go into national politics and believed a tour of duty in the Marines would help him.

Levy gestured with open hands. "If Allan was good enough to be a pro, why didn't he just do it? That'd make him famous enough to run for public office."

Hamilton's face beamed. "Well, one day a scout from the Orlando Pirates did come over to him. He was practicing at Percy Beard Stadium. The scout offered him a tryout with their team. But he wasn't interested in being a pro. Allan knew he wasn't good enough to be a star player as a soccer pro. He thought being a great amateur athlete would be better for his political career than being an average professional.

Allan's ambition was to be elected to the US Senate or even the White House. Look at how many of the men we elect to national office are war veterans. He was just as popular as a Marine as he'd been in school. Because of his soccer skills, they gave him assignments working for their public relations officers. Soon they promoted him to sergeant. In 2003 his division was sent to Iraq, and he fought on the ground in that war." Hamilton rose from his chair and stood with his hands clinched into fists. He pressed his knuckles down against the desktop.

Levy was on the verge of becoming alarmed by the increasing rage in Hamilton's tone. He narrowed his eyes and stared into those of his client. Then he shifted his gaze and noted Hamilton's well muscled, lean frame that indicated he was in good physical shape. His brown hair was about forty percent gray, and his receding hairline made his rectangular face appear even longer. He had light blue eyes, and his short straight nose had tiny nostrils. Under a navy blue sport coat, he wore a yellow short-sleeved shirt and dark gray chinos. On his feet were top of the line Nike running shoes.

Hamilton continued, "After our troops defeated Saddam's army and occupied Baghdad, they assigned Allan back to the public relations staff. His job was to set up and run soccer teams for the Iraqi kids. He was always very patient with kids. He could figure out what any particular kid needed to do to improve his performance on the soccer filed. The kids loved him. He was giving our Marines a good name with their parents. That must be why the terrorist murdered him. On February 22, of '03 he was refereeing a soccer game between two teams in a league he'd set up. He was standing in the middle of the field with the kids running around him."

Hamilton began to slowly rise on his toes. "An Arab walked out of the crowd of parents and other spectators on the sidelines. He came up behind Allan. No one shouted a warning or tried to stop the assassin. That Arab was holding a Colt 45 the whole time in plain sight of everyone in the crowd, but no one warned Allan. The Arab shot him three times in the back. Then he walked….he didn't run. He just walked back through the crowd and disappeared. But before he left the field, that Arab murderer held the 45 up in the air for everyone to see and he yelled at them. That crowd of Arab spectators just parted to let him walk through. No one tried to stop him."

"What'd the Arab yell?" Levy asked.

Hamilton ignored him and started rocking back and forth as he moved up and down on his toes. "Allan's coaching assistant was a corporal and he ran on the field to help Allan. But my boy was already dead. One of the 45 slugs hit his heart. The corporal got up from where Allan fell and went after the murderer. But he was gone. He asked for help identifying the killer. No one admitted knowing who the killer was. But several people remembered the murderer raising the 45 he above his head and turning around so everyone could see the gun. They said the assassin yelled a couple of times, *al Khanjar yaqtil, al Khanjar yaqtil.*"

"Do you know what it means?" Levy asked.

Again Hamilton ignored him and rose to his tiptoes and stayed there. Levy pushed with his feet to inch his chair back further from his desk.

"Allan was helping their children and those Arabs didn't even try to warn him, or help him, or try to catch his murderer. And that's why I invented the death ray gun. And that's why I want my patent to say my invention'll be used to murder Arabs. I want everyone to know I avenged my son's murder." His eyes glistened and he wiped a tear from his cheek with the back of his hand.

The date was January 9, 2004.

Chapter 2   Sami

EIGHT YEARS EARLIER Sami Insien, a boy who would gain the power to have Allan Hamilton assassinated and to spread terror into the United States, removed his sandals and walked into the Mosque of Gentle Peace. The mosque was an unadorned building coated with blue stained cement having a two-story ceiling and high windows just below the ceiling. It was located in Zatoon, a small town of farmers and herdsmen in the Kerman Province of Iran.

Yassan Bieheiri, a white-bearded, middle-aged Imam, controlled everything going on in this mosque and many things in the town it served. When he was in the mosque attending to prayers or the village's business, the Imam wore a traditional ankle length gown having a buttoned collar and sleeves, and a matching ornamented skullcap. On this winter day his garments were made from emerald green wool.

Sixteen-year-old Sami looked frail for a teen of his age. His clothes were hand-me-down gowns given to his mother by prosperous townspeople for whom she cleaned and cooked. The harsh washing they endured over the years leached out their color. That day he wore a gray gown that hung loosely from his body, as it would from a scarecrow made of sticks. In his sunken-cheeked face, his piercing black eyes matched his jet-black hair, which was cut short, high above his skinny neck. He had received only the minimum schooling available to children of his low status, learning how to read and write Arabic and little else.

The Imam stood in the doorway of his office. Sami grabbed the Imam's sleeve in his fingers and said, "Allah spoke to me, and He told me to—"

The Imam glared at him and growled, "Allah does not speak to mortals."

But Sami moved into the Imam's space and stared into his face. His eyes intimidated the Imam while he insisted he could prove Allah spoke to him many times. At this, the Imam broke eye contact and moved back angrily. He cuffed Sami on the side of the head with the back of his hand and had him thrown out of the mosque.

Some people standing outside of the mosque witnessed the commotion when the Imam's deacons ejected the struggling boy. They gathered around as Sami stood in their midst and yelled, "I'll come back here and prove Allah spoke to me."

Two elderly men in the gathering nodded to each other. Then they moved toward Sami and reached out for him. Before they could catch hold of him, he fled toward the shack where he lived on the outskirts of the town with his widowed mother, Amina Insien.

At dawn the next, Sami burst into the Imam's office and blurted, "Allah told me to read the Qur'an one time from beginning to end, and He will seal the words of the Holy Book in my memory."

The Imam looked up from papers on the desk where he was sitting, and fumed: *The only way I can get rid of this pest is to let him read the Qur'an and that will expose him as a liar when he can't recite it from memory.*

He stood and motioned to Sami, "Follow me." The Imam walked to a low table in a corner of the mosque where he placed a copy of the Holy Book. He looked at Sami and inclined his head toward the Qur'an.

Sami knelt down on the floor with his legs straight out under him. He put his left hand on the floor supporting himself above the table with his face slightly more than a foot above the Qur'an. He slowly read the text, running the index finger of his right hand across each verse, and turning the page with that hand when he came to its end. His head bobbed up and down and his lips moved, but he uttered no sounds as he spoke each word silently to himself.

After Sami was thus occupied for about three hours, Deacon Abduhl Ariann walked over to him and said, "Do you needed to stop for food or water?" The boy kept running his finger across and then down a page as if the deacon hadn't spoken. Shaking his head, the deacon walked away and told the Imam what the boy was doing.

The Imam said, "Leave him alone. He'll soon tire and give up his pretense."

As the day progressed, nothing changed. In the late afternoon after Sami was bent over the Qur'an for at least ten hours, the Imam came to investigate. He grabbed hold of the boy's shoulder, but Sami didn't look up or stop moving his finger across a page. In irritation he bent down to where his mouth was next to the boy's ear and hissed, "Stop this nonsense and go home for your supper."

But Sami didn't stir or remove his gaze from the Holy Book. His concentration was so intense that he didn't bother to brush away flies that lit on his face from time to time. Again the Imam decided to leave him alone, although now he was becoming concerned for his health. He hadn't consumed food or drink and hadn't risen from the awkward position he'd assumed shortly after the day dawned.

Imam Bieheiri dispatched a lesser deacon to summon Amina Insien. The Imam met her on the steps of his mosque and told her what her son had been doing since the day began. She said, "Sami often kneels with his forehead touching the floor in a trance mumbling words of obedience to Allah. When he wakes up he tells me Allah's been speaking to him."

Now the Imam was alarmed. He turned to deacon Ariann and said, "Go, rouse the boy and take him outside to his mother. It's time for him to go home."

Deacon Ariann was a squat 25 year old having great physical strength gained from manual labor he'd performed during his youth. He came up to Sami and placed his hands under the boy's armpits. Ariann bent his knees as if he were going to lift a heavy sack of flour and started to pull the boy up from his position bent over the desk. Suddenly Sami's body lunged upwardly. He said in a voice as deep as that of a grown man, "Allah commands you…. leave me." He pivoted with his left arm extended and rammed the arm into the deacon's chest with strength that was amazing for an emaciated boy. Ariann was lifted and flung over backward against a nearby wall of the mosque.

Momentarily Sami's eyes caught those of Ariann, and a vision was seared into the deacon's brain through his eyes. The black pupils of the boy's black eyes projected the image of a bottomless abyss of infinite power. Sami resumed his position bent over the Qur'an, silently talking to himself and running his fingers across and down the page as he'd been doing all day.

Ariann was so surprised by the boy's phenomenal strength he remained crouched on his hands and knees in the position into which he was thrown. He stared at Sami in awe. Slowly he rose to standing position while he continued to stare at the boy. Then he turned and walked in a daze out of the Mosque to where Mrs. Insien and the Imam were waiting. The shaken deacon told the Imam, "With one arm that frail lad lifted me and hurled me across the room when I tried to stand him up. Surely he's supernatural …or possessed."

The Imam could see Ariann was rattled. He said, "Leave him be until he gives up his hopeless efforts. No one ever read the Qur'an one time and then knew it by heart. From now on we'll ignore him until he comes to us and admits he's failed."

"I know he'll succeed," Ariann said. "I'll be his protector."

The Imam shook his head in amazement at the attitude of his previously down to earth deacon. He dismissed Mrs. Insien and returned to his office to conclude his routine for that day. He ignored Sami as best he could.

Ariann walked back into the mosque and sat on the floor behind Sami. There he stayed for the remainder of the day, leaving only for his evening prayers, food and to relieve himself. There the deacon also stayed through the night, dozing frequently, as Sami continued his reading marathon.

The next day dawned bright with none of the brisk winter winds that plagued the village by blowing sand into every opening and unshielded eye. The sunny sky lifted everyone's spirits and made them want to rejoice for reasons they could not articulate. Shortly before the noon hour, Sami moved his finger to the end of verse 6 of Chapter 114 at the end of the Qur'an. He looked up for the first time since Ariann interrupted him the previous afternoon and closed the cover of the Holy Book. Ariann jumped up from where he maintained his vigil. He moved to where he could look at the Sami's face, which was flushed and had grey circles under the eyes.

"You want food and water," Ariann inquired.

Sami merely shook his head and continued to kneel next to the table where the Qur'an lay closed. Ariann went to the Imam's office where the cleric sat attending to business matters. Twenty-nine hours had passed since Sami began his quest. Now the Imam was sure he could shame Sami. No one could memorize the Qur'an in so short a time, more absurdly claiming he did it in one continuous sitting. "Bring that boy to my office at once," he said.

"But he hasn't eaten, drank or slept or urinated for over a day," Ariann protested.

"Never mind that. Fetch some strong coffee and bread with honey for him. Also some dates or figs. But bring him here immediately," the Imam directed.

Ariann left and ordered a subordinate to bring the food and drink to the Imam's office. He went into the mosque where he found Sami kneeling beside the desk with his head up and his eyes staring at a wall in front of him. Ariann approached and stood where he was sure the boy saw him. Sami fixed his weary eyes on the deacon. Then his face lit up with a smile when recognized the observer who was his companion through the previous night.

"I'm ready," he whispered. "Allah has sealed the words of Muhammad and other holy men in my brain."

"Come with me. The Imam's waiting for you in his office. We'll give you something to eat and drink. Do you need to go?" he said motioning in the direction of a lavatory.

Sami shook his head. He stood but swooned as the blood rushed from his brain toward his feet, which tingled with sleep. Ariann placed his hands under the boy's armpits. He supported Sami for a minute or two until the blood flow adjusted to his standing position and his feet regained their feeling.

"I can walk now," he said, and gave Ariann a smile on his fatigued face.

Ariann removed his hands from under Sami's arms, but kept one hand under his elbow. Together they walked into the Imam's office, which was in one of several small rooms built against the exterior wall of the mosque beneath the high windows.

The Imam pointed to a chair across from his desk, and Sami sat down. The smile remained on the boy's face, and he stared into the Imam's eyes. Unnerved by the vision he saw in those eyes, the Imam looked down at a copy of the Qur'an lying open on the desk in front of him. The Imam piled other volumes on the side of the Holy Book nearest to where Sami sat, in case the boy could read upside down text. Before the Imam spoke, a woman entered carrying a tray bearing a pot of coffee, a loaf of bread and a jar of honey.

The Imam nodded toward the food. "Do you want to eat and drink before we begin?"

"Not yet. Allah gives me strength," Sami said and moved his face to look into the Imam's eyes.

"Enough of your blasphemy," the Imam scolded. To avoid the of risk eye contact, he continued to look down at the Qur'an on his desk. "Recite the first verse of Chapter 96." The Imam decided to make Sami's task more difficult by using the chapter numbers instead of their titles.

"Read in the name of your Lord Who created," Sami said without hesitation.

"Verse 5 of Chapter 60," the Imam said.

Again the reply was instant, "Our Lord do not make us a trial for those who disbelieve, and forgive us, our Lord surely Thou art the Mighty, the Wise."

"Verse 15 of Chapter 49," the Imam barked angrily.

Sami thought a moment, then said merrily, "The believers are only those who believe in Allah and His Apostle then they doubt not and struggle hard with their wealth and their lives in the way of Allah; they are the truthful ones."

The Imam seemed perplexed. He paused for a minute to search through the Holy Book for a lengthy passage. Then his face lit up with a sly grin. "Verse 5 of Chapter 22."

Sami shut his eyes for a moment, opened them and tried to establish eye contact, but the Imam refused to look at his face. Then the boy began in a melodious voice, "O people. If you are in doubt about the raising, then surely We created you from dust, then from a small seed, then from a clot, then from a lump of flesh, complete in make and incomplete, that We may make clear to you; and We cause what We please to stay in the wombs till an appointed time, then We bring you forth as babies..."

"Enough," the Imam thundered. "What is your trickery?"

But Sami continued the long passage, almost singing, until he concluded it with a smirk on his face.

Visibly shaken, the Imam said, "Take a break. Eat and drink. We'll continue later."

The Imam motioned to Ariann indicating he wanted the deacon to follow him out of his office. Sami pulled his chair closer to the desk, put honey on a slice of bread and began to eat. He sipped sweetened coffee between bites.

"Do you know how he deceives us?" the Imam implored eagerly.

"I believe he speaks the truth. Allah bestowed a gift on him," Ariann murmured meekly.

"Fool!" the Imam raged. "You're either in league with the brat, assisting him in his deception, or else you're too gullible to be trusted. Go bring Haifein. I can trust him. You stay away from my office until I learn the method of this deception. His arrogance is infuriating."

Ariann bowed to the Imam. Then he turned away and strode off in search of Haifein, a lower level deacon. The Imam returned to his office and stared at Sami while the lad ate and drank everything on the tray. Sami pointed toward the lavatory, and the Imam nodded his head. He returned five minutes later looking refreshed and energized.

While Sami was gone, Haifein entered the Imam's office. The Imam moved next to him and exploded, "Sami Insien is pulling some kind of stunt. He says Allah put the complete Qur'an inside of his head. He pretends to recite from memory any passage I ask him. I want you to watch closely. Help me expose his trick. First, you must look into his ears and frisk him to make sure he's not receiving signals by radio. Next I want you to put a blindfold over his eyes. Then you sit beside him and face the same way he is. He won't get away with this fraud any longer."

Haifein did as he was instructed. Sami submitted to the frisking and examination without protest. He even helped Haifein adjust the blindfold. He didn't flinch when having a knife thrust at his face tested his obscured vision. The Imam indicated with a nod he was satisfied with these preparations. Haifein led Sami back to his chair and pulled another next to it. The deacon sat at his chair's edge so his left arm touched Sami's right shoulder.

"Now we will find out if you've really memorized the Qur'an," the Imam said. "Speak Chapter 4, verse 168."

Sami thought a moment, and his face lit with a smile as he recited cheerfully, "Surely those who disbelieve and act unjustly Allah will not forgive them nor guide them to a path."

"Chapter 9, verse 193."

Sami said, "It is not for the Prophet and those who believe that they should ask forgiveness for the polytheists, even—"

"Enough of that one," the Imam interrupted, and Sami stopped reciting the requested passage. "From now on, just tell me the first five words or the last five words. I'll tell you which I want. Do you understand?"

Sami laughed and bragged, "I can start in the middle or with any word you choose." Since he fasted for the entire previous day, the influx of sugar from the sweet coffee and honeyed bread he'd eaten caused his insulin to spike, which gave him a surge of energy and self confidence.

And so it continued for almost an hour, with Sami correctly reciting the first five words or the last five words of dozens of passages whose numbers the Imam fired at him without let up. When the last five words were requested Sami paused to recall the entire passage before he recited them, but he never made a mistake. Sami was wired; he bounced up and down on his chair and hummed a tune when he waited for the Imam to select a passage.

The Imam's mood went from anger to bewilderment. He could not believe what he was hearing. His confidence faltered. He wondered if he were witnessing a miracle. He intended to continue with the inquisition for hours longer, but without a warning, Sami collapsed against Haifein.

The surge in Sami's insulin was only temporary so eventually it plummeted. When this loss of energy was combined with his lack of sleep and intense mental exertions, Sami passed out. Haifein laid him down on his back on the floor beside the Imam's desk. Slapping his face and dousing him with cold water didn't arouse him. The Imam decided to let him sleep and to continue questioning him the next day. Perhaps his memory of the Qur'an would fade with the passage of time. In the mean time the Imam pondered what he'd just witnessed. Had the boy actually did memorized the entire Qur'an? He admonished Haifein and Ariann to say nothing of what they witnessed, until the mystery of the boy's memory or his trickery was solved.

Chapter 3   Diagnosis

IMAM BIEHERI LEFT his office to conduct business and prayers in the mosque. The rest of the afternoon passed, and Sami continued to sleep on the floor in the Imam's office. The Imam returned after evening prayers and found the boy still asleep exactly where he'd been left. Efforts to wake him were unsuccessful. The Imam said, "Ariann, you stay and watch him until he wakes up. I'll send Haifein to tell his mother he'll be sleeping in my office, perhaps for the entire night."

The Imam returned to his office the next day right after morning prayers were concluded. Ariann was extremely upset. He said, "I fear Sami is dying. He didn't stir during the entire night. He hasn't changed his position and he barely breathes. His muscles are stiff and his joints are locked."

The Imam took a magnifying glass from his desk drawer and put it under the Sami's nostrils. When the moisture of his breath fogged the glass, the Imam said, "See, he breaths. He's not dead. But something's wrong. Go get Haifein and bring a stretcher. We'll take him to Dr. Quadi. I'll go with you. Maybe the doctor can help us solve this riddle."

The two deacons carried Sami into the doctor's office and laid him face up on an examination table. His mother, who joined them on the way, stood by his side. She rubbed his wrists and forehead with her calloused hands. The Imam told the doctor what happened during the previous two days.

Dr. Amil Quadi was the town's only resident with formal medical training. The 55-year-old physician and his staff of two nurses and one midwife handled the medical needs of the townspeople, including minor surgeries. He examined Sami with his stethoscope and blood pressure monitor. He took his pulse rate. He lifted his eyelids and shined the beam of a small flashlight into them. Then he moved his hands over the boy's body probing his internal organs and trying to flex his muscles and joints. He tried unsuccessfully to open Sami's mouth.

The doctor said, "This boy is undergoing a catatonic episode. His blood pressure, pulse and breathing are all normal, and I don't detect any visible sign of damage to his body. From what you've told me about his behavior, I'm going to guess he's bipolar, and his catatonic trance is a form of depression that's following a manic episode. I'll send a copy of my report of this examination and a summary of what you told me of his behavior to my friend, Dr. Saleem. He's a psychiatrist at the Shiraz Psychiatric Hospital. Saleem may ask to see the boy to recommend treatment. For now, I want you to leave him here. He's undoubtedly dehydrated and looks undernourished. We'll give him fluids and glucose intravenously until he comes out of the catatonia."

The next day Sami awoke feeling weak but happy. His muscles were sore but they relaxed during the night. The doctor released him into his mother's care after she promised to make him eat heartily.

A week later, a car drove up to the Insien home. Out stepped Dr. Saleem, a stooped, 52 year old man with a fat round face that showed through a trimmed, sparse, grey beard. He examined Sami's body and read his vital signs. He concluded the boy was in sound physical health. He asked Sami to tell him about his conversations with Allah. He repeated for the doctor what he told the Imam. Then Dr. Saleem opened a copy of the Qur'an. He asked him to repeat his performance by reciting the verses the doctor identified by number. With great pride in his accomplishment, and smiling all the while, Sami recited every requested verse without error. The doctor questioned his mother. She confirmed what Dr. Quadi said about her son's psychotic episodes.

Finally Dr. Saleem kept an appointment with Imam Bieheiri. The cleric confirmed the boy's performance in reciting the Qur'an, and asked for a diagnosis.

"I can confirm Quadi's speculations," Saleem said. "I believe Sami Insien is a delusional manic-depressive teenager with a photographic memory. Also, he's probably a borderline schizophrenic. I recommend treatment with anti psychotic drugs."

"His mother is too poor to afford those medications," the Imam said.

"Then I must warn you the boy should be watched closely. These psychotic personalities sometimes turned violent or suicidal."

Only his mother, the doctors, the Imam and the two deacons knew of Sami's affliction and mental ability. Everyone except the doctors was under strict instructions from the Imam not to talk about what happened.

Dr. Saleem was an agent of Murtazan bin Nazamunde, a forty-year-old Saudi Arabian multibillionaire with the announced dream of ridding Islamic people of western influences. In truth he had a much more sinister secret agenda. Bin Nazamunde possessed ample funds to finance his schemes. But at that time only a few followers worked for and with him toward his goal of organizing his own jihad against the West.

Dr. Saleem's assignment was to identify Arabs with uncommon mental skills who might be able to think creatively and originate new strategies and plans of attack against those who stood in bin Nazamunde's way. In Saleem's opinion, this delusional teenager with a photographic memory had the potential of becoming a living, breathing, human computer. If he were motivated and his exceptional mind channeled to the task, he could spew out unique schemes and plots for the jihad. His hunch that Sami might be a good candidate for bin Nazamunde's jihad was the reason he journeyed to the Insien home in Zatoon. Dr. Saleem telephoned bin Nazamunde and told him about the boy's memorization feat.

Bin Nazamunde recognized the value to his schemes of having a human computer in his service that he'd be able to manipulate and control. He dispatched a plane to fly Kahdir abu Wagdy, his trusted assistant, to an airport in Kerman Province near the town where Sami lived. A chauffeured Land Rover picked up abu Wagdy at the airport and drove him to Zatoon.

Bin Nazamunde had instructed abu Wagdy, "Interview the boy to verify Dr. Saleem's report. If you confirm what I've been told about his memory, bring him and his mother to my resort hotel in Jubail for an interview."

Abu Wagdy began working for bin Nazamunde as one of his bodyguards. He was six foot one with wide shoulders and strong arms. His heavy lidded brown eyes shift back and forth under black eyebrows above his severely curved nose. A close-cropped black beard covered his fleshy face. Bin Nazamunde sensed the man was ruthless and first tested him by assigning him to intimidate rivals and officials reluctant to take baksheesh. He carried out these tasks with an intelligent aggressiveness, earning him his employer's confidence. Bin Nazamunde tested him further with the responsibility for eliminating those who were in bin Nazamunde's way and could not be bought or scared off. This he accomplished by hiring known thugs when possible, but by taking a gun, knife or garrote wire into his own hands when no one else could be found to finish the job in time to meet bin Nazamunde's expectations. His intelligence and perseverance in carrying out every order eventually earned him the post of bin Nazamunde right hand man.

Abu Wagdy met with Sami, his mother and Imam Bieheiri. He telephoned his report to bin Nazamunde, confirming the boy's memory feat. He arranged for mother and boy to be flown to King Khalid International Airport in Riyadh. Then they were driven in a stretch Mercedes limousine to bin Nazamunde's high-rise, luxury resort, The Apricot Hotel. They were ensconced on an upper floor in a suite having a large tub with air jets and a balcony over looking the Gulf of Oman. The hotel staff treated Amina Insien and her son like royalty.

Amina stayed in their suite and had their food brought in by room service. Their concierge taught her how to use a remote to control the large TV in the living room. Not having to cook or clean was the treat of her life. Sami ate large omelets, toast, orange juice, dates and figs for breakfast. For lunch and dinner he ate beef, lamb and potato dishes, and cake and pie with ice cream for dessert. Also, he discovered bottled juices and carried a glass of ice cubes filled with sweet juice wherever he went.

The concierge looked Sami over carefully. A short time later, a bellman brought him three new colorful cotton robes to wear over new pairs of matching shorts. They also gave him three pair of canvas soled leather sandals. He told Sami to go to the resort barbershop to get a hair cut and shampoo.

Sami learned that the people he met became uncomfortable when he stared at their faces. He realized his eyes intimidated others when he made direct eye contact. So he kept his gaze lowered, and asked the concierge for a pair of sunglasses because the sun bothered his eyes. But the real reason was to hide his eyes from the people he encountered. The bellman brought two pair of wrap around, polarized sunglasses to his room.

Their life of luxury at the resort continued for four more days. Bin Nazamunde wanted Amina Insien and her son to have a taste of the life of ease he could bestow on them before he asked them to move under his control. He brought two of his wives with him to his resort so they could enjoy a short vacation while he interviewed the boy. The bin Nazamunde family took over the entire pent house floor.

The next morning, the concierge knocked on the door of Sami's room. He told the boy "You must bathe and put on fresh clothes. Murtazan bin Nazamunde wants to interview you this morning. Possibly, he has important work for you to do."

"What work can he do for a rich man?" Amina Insien asked skeptically.

"You'll find out in due time if bin Nazamunde can use the boy," she was told.

In the two weeks since his ordeal with the Imam, Sami exercised regularly, was fed well and slept soundly, with no psychotic episodes. His body began to fill out, and he no longer looked undernourished. He was well groomed and his new clothes fit him properly. He looked like a healthy teenager.

At 11:00 that morning the concierge escorted Sami to a room furnished like an office in bin Nazamunde's pent house suite. There he was introduced to a lean man, six foot five in height, with a neatly trimmed black beard that left his upper lip exposed. He had cold eyes the color of tarnished stainless steel and a long nose that curved downwardly toward his wide lips. He was wearing an amber, ankle length robe encircled by a wide belt woven from solid gold strands. Bin Nazamunde wore either traditional Arab or European clothes, depending on where he was and who he would be with. All of his clothes were hand crafted by his own personal tailor from the finest silks. A full turban that matched the robe adorned his head and hid his hair and ears from view. A gold headband encircled the middle of the turban. Bin Nazamunde remained seated behind his teak desk and beamed a smile at Sami. He pointed to the chair where he wanted the boy to sit.

Sami sat up straight on the edge of his chair and twisted his fingers around each other. He stared directly into bin Nazamunde's eyes from the moment he entered the office. The black pupils of his black eyes were all but invisible to the older man. Sami's stare was so intense bin Nazamunde felt like his own gaze was being captured by the energy the lad's eyes gave off. Sami was controlling their eye contact. Bin Nazamunde was not intimidated and wondered momentarily if Sami achieved his feats of memory by somehow hypnotizing those who questioned him.

"I've been told you talk to Allah," bin Nazamunde said.

Shyly Sami answered, "No, sire. He speaks and I listen to what he says."

"And he told you to memorize the Qur'an."

"Yes, because that way I could prove to the doubters that he speaks to me." Sami's nervousness began to fade.

"And can you recite from the Holy Book now if I question you?"

"Yes, sir, I can." Sami continued to hold the man's eyes captive to his stare.

Bin Nazamunde swiveled his chair around toward a bookcase behind his desk, from which he picked out a copy of the Qur'an. He was happy to have a reason to break eye contact with the boy. He kept his gaze on the Holy Book, which he placed in the center of his desk. Continuing to look down, he opened it and began turning its pages. "Recite verse 116 of The Believers."

Sami said, "So exalted be Allah, the True King; no god is there but He, the Lord of the honorable dominion."

"Very good. Now tell me verse 5 of The Cleaving."

"Every soul shall know what it has sent before and held back," his nervousness now replaced by confidence as he demonstrated his accomplishment.

Bin Nazamunde turned to a page marked with paperclip. "One more, and this is my favorite. Recite verse 33 of The Dinner Table."

"The punishment of those who wage war against Allah and His apostle and strive to make mischief in the land is only this, that they should be murdered or crucified—"

"Stop right there," bin Nazamunde ordered. "I'm convinced you know the Qur'an by heart. Will you do as Allah commanded in the verse you just recited to me? Will you murder someone who wages war against Allah or strives to make mischief in Allah's land?" Bin Nazamunde looked up from the book and once again felt the power of Sami's eyes.

"What Allah commands me to. Yes, I will do anything He commands."

"Will you convince other boys and men that Allah wants them to kill those who strive to make mischief in his lands?"

"Yes, I will do what Allah has commanded."

Bin Nazamunde took pride in being able to quickly assess the value to his schemes of everyone he encountered. He didn't believe for a moment that Allah spoke to Sami, but he was impressed by his feat of memory. He surmised what Imam Bieheiri judged to be arrogance was charisma. He thought Sami possessed leadership potential that he could nurture and use to gain followers and enlist agents for his ventures. And the boy might also have undemonstrated creative abilities. So bin Nazamunde decided to take over his education and ensure he was well fed and obtained any needed medical care. He guessed Sami might be of the most value when he was in a delusional state, so he decided not to let any doctors prescribe the medication Dr. Saleem recommended.

Few words were required to convince Amina Insien that she and her son would be well taken care of if they moved to Saudi Arabia with bin Nazamunde as their benefactor. She agreed to let his agent sell their belongings in Zatoon. They stayed at the hotel for three additional days until abu Wagdy located and furnished a two-bedroom apartment in Shallael, a working class suburb of Riyadh. Sami continued to eat like a starving lion.

Amina and Sami were delighted with the small third floor apartment abu Wagdy leased for them. Their unit was in a blue and silver colored, eight story concrete building having thirty units; it was one of five identical buildings in a complex of dwellings, shops and offices. Sami took the larger of the unit's two bedrooms because he needed space for a desk and bookcase, in addition to a bed and wardrobe. Pale, lime colored paint coated the cement block walls, and new hemp throw rugs partially covered the tile floors in the living room and bedrooms. The indoor bathroom with a shower in the tub and the air conditioning were luxuries the members of the Insien family never before enjoyed.

To earn their keep and obtain spending money, Amina was expected to perform day care and chaperone services for families in the complex. Sami was not expected to work. Bin Nazamunde told him to devote all of his time to completing his education, to building his body and to acquiring physical skills assigned to him. Sami happily complied.

Bin Nazamunde hired a physician and a nutritionist to monitor Sami's health and physical development. Every six months the physician gave him a complete examination, and a dentist checked his teeth. A nutritionist studied the physician's reports and prescribed vitamin and nutrient supplements for him to take each day. Sami was eager to increase his height and strength. He gratefully ate the prescribed foods his mother prepared for him. To determine if his mental state changed, Dr. Saleem interviewed Sami whenever he was in Riyadh.

Bin Nazamunde decreed that his ward should have contact with as few people as possible. He wanted Sami's mental abilities kept secret until he needed to use the boy to perform some task to further his intrigues. So Sami did not participate in sports or social activities with his contemporaries. His sheltered lifestyle all but eliminated the opportunity for interaction or conflict with other teens. This was not a hardship for Sami because his mental illness caused him to obsess about what he was studying and to deeply focus on himself and whatever he was doing.

Professional trainers, acting individually, oversaw Sami's physical education and development, and his acquisition of skills. His supervising trainer, Osman Rukon, a muscled, thirty-five year old physical therapist appraised the boy's body and watched as he worked out on the stations of a home gym. He taught Sami exercise routines for strengthening his muscles. Except when his physical activities required some particular wearing apparel, Sami always wore a simple, but colorful, traditional robe, skullcap and sandals.

Bin Nazamunde wanted his ward exposed to as many sports as possible without having him compete with other boys. He believed this would help him understand the western enemies and competitors of his enterprises. Experts taught him karate, judo and Tae Kwon Do. He learned to fence and box with his instructors. They taught to him throw and catch baseballs, footballs, basketballs and to kick and header a soccer ball. He took a golf lesson, and learned how to play snooker and billiards.

Chapter 4   The Death Ray

LEVY REFLECTED ON Hamilton's first statements about having invented a death ray gun. He didn't know if he was talking to a crackpot, or if the inventor had brought a real weapon into the office. He said, "I'll help you avenge your son's murder if I can. But first you've got to show me that your invention actually works. What you call a death ray gun must kill living things, if you expect to get a patent on it."

At this, Hamilton bent over and reached down beside Levy's desk. He picked up a medium sized leather suitcase, stood and put the suitcase on the attorney's desk. The clasps unsnapped with a pair of audible metallic pops. The suitcase shined with a gloss like you expect to see on the boots of a Marine standing guard at the Tomb of the Unknowns. Hamilton reached into the suitcase and removed a cardboard box that once contained a pair of New Balance running shoes. He put the shoebox down near one corner of Levy's desk, and carefully lined up a corner and sides of the box with a corner and the edges of the desk.

"What's in there?" Levy asked.

"A big ugly Florida roach, and I'll prove my ray gun works by using it to kill the roach."

"OK, do it. No. Wait. First show me your ray gun."

Hamilton reached into the suitcase and removed a weapon that was larger than any gun Levy had ever seen that is intended to be held in one hand.

Levy chuckled, "It looks to me like some of the futuristic water pistols the toy stores sell to my grandchildren."

Hamilton laughed along with him. "I know it looks crude but I modeled my gun to look like a ray gun I saw Buck Rogers use in an old movie. The body is a hollow plastic shell. Inside is a shiny plastic tube covered with aluminum foil. There's a small hole centered in the front end of the gun barrel, and the tip of the tube extends out of the hole. A piece of purplish glass covers the protruding end of the plastic tube. This button on the top of the grip fires the death ray." Hamilton touched the button with his thumb. "And this laser light pointer on the top of the gun barrel is for aiming the death ray."

Hamilton gripped his gun by the handle and waved it around as if he were John Wayne standing erect on Iwo Jima firing a browning automatic rifle at charging Japanese soldiers.

Levy ducked away instinctively and said, "Don't point that weapon at me if it's loaded."

"Don't worry. Today it doesn't have enough of a punch to hurt anyone, except maybe for a direct hit in the eye."

"Well, do me a favor and just point your deadly gun toward the floor from now on." Levy frowned. He was still unsure if he was wasting his time talking to a crackpot. "You said you can prove your gun will kill a roach. OK, let's have a demonstration right now before I spend any time talking about how to protect your invention. I'll call in Rosalind Katz and you can show us how it works. Better yet, let's have Rosalind use it and you and I'll watch. Can she make the thing, uh, your gun, work?"

Hamilton nodded his head.

"Good, I'll call in Rosalind right now." Levy hit some keys on the keyboard of the closer of the two iMacs on his desk.

In less than a minute Rosalind, his paralegal assistant, opened the door and walked into his office. She was 62 with a matronly figure and a head of straight, gray hair she kept close cropped around her neck. She had a short curved nose, and her blue eyes twinkled out of a round face that always seemed to have a smile, as she sent forth a stream of wisecracks to make light of most situations. She wore the Levy law office's standard uniform of running shoes, jeans and a sweatshirt or colorful T-shirt, depending on the Florida weather.

Levy said, "Rosalind, Mr. Hamilton invented a gun that sends out a death ray. You and I are going to be his witnesses. He's going to use the ray gun to kill a cockroach."

"Not with me around." She turned and headed toward the door. "I hate roaches and don't want to be anywhere near them."

"We have a solution," Levy said, "You'll be the one who uses the death ray on the roach. You'll kill the critter without touching it."

She stopped at the door. "Yuk. I hate them so much I have the bug guy come out every two weeks. That's twice as often as he recommends. I won't do it if it's going to squish him. I can't stand it when you step on one and that custardy stuff squishes out."

Hamilton took the lid off of the shoebox, and they all peered in. The sudden influx of light into the box agitated a large reddish brown roach, which scampered around the box and tried desperately to climb up the sides.

Rosalind jumped back and said, "Oh, no, don't you dare let it get out. Where'd you get such a big roach anyway?"

"You already know the answer to that one," Hamilton replied. "In central Florida, all we have to do is leave some old food on the ground and the roaches will find it. Yesterday evening I turned that shoebox on its side and put some orange peels, bread crusts and eggs shells in it. Before I went to bed last night, I crept up to it and turned it right side up. That trapped three roaches inside of it, and I kept the biggest one for today's demonstration. It's a Florida Woods roach. Don't worry about it getting out. That kind of roach can't fly."

Hamilton raised the ray gun and pointed it at a pencil on Levy's desk. "You use this laser pointer beam to aim the ray." He pressed the small button on the end of the laser pointer that turned it on. A red beam shot on to the desk, and he moved the beam until there was a red spot on the pencil. "Now it's aimed so the ray'd hit the pencil if I pressed this button." He touched the large button on the top of the gun with the tip of his thumb. "You wanna try aiming it Ms. Katz."

Hamilton held the gun out with the handle toward Rosalind. She took hold of the handle with her right hand and placed her left hand underneath the barrel, as if she were holding a rifle. Her hands trembled slightly.

"Sure, but how many bullets are in it in case I miss him," she said and waved the gun toward the shoebox.

"One ray uses up all the power stored in the gun, so you only get one shot today," Hamilton said.

She shook her head. "Uh uh, not me. If I miss the bug the whole demonstration is a failure, and you won't have a reduction to practice that two people witnessed."

"Now you're sounding like the attorney in charge," Levy joshed with mocked indignation.

"Well, I ought to. I've heard your spiels so many times. Here, you take it and you shoot the roach," She thrust the gun at Levy with the barrel pointing toward his chest.

"Hey, point it down," he said and jumped to his left and banged his hip into one side of his desk.

Rosalind reached over and gingerly placed the ray gun on Levy's desk with obvious relief at not having to use it to kill the roach. Levy moved back to the desk where the gun lay, picked it up and leaned over the box containing the roach. He held the gun with the grip in his right hand and his thumb on the firing button. By now the roach was tired out from scampering around the shoebox. It backed into one corner with its long antennae slowly twitching back and forth as if it sensed something was about to happen and it wanted to be ready to spring out of the way.

Levy pointed the gun toward the roach and pressed the button activating the laser beam. When the red beam hit the bottom of the box near the roach, the bug started frantically running at the sides trying to climb out. In a half minute it was tired again and stopped to rest with its hind legs on the bottom of the box and its front legs part way up one side of the box. Levy quickly moved the gun so the red spot from the laser light was in the middle of the roach's back. With his thumb he pressed the button on the top of the gun, releasing the death ray. The gun made no sound, but a faint purple shadow flashed for an instant in the shoebox as the death ray hit the roach. The ray bent the large bug back on itself as if someone took it in his hands, placed the thumbs in the middle of its back, and bent it double. The creamy fluid of the bug's innards oozed from its underside, which was split open by the backward distortion of its body. It twitched for a few seconds and then lay motionless.

Rosalind had moved away from the desk where the shoebox was sitting. Now she came back and looked into the box. "Gross!" she said. "I knew this was going to make a gooey mess."

Chapter 5   Education

BIN NAZAMUNDE WANTED to control Sami's education and emotional development, so he did not enroll him in a school with other children. He hired the best available tutors, professors and professionals for each academic subject he wanted his ward taught. He was betting Sami possessed a creative mind capable of producing a cornucopia of original ideas he could use to increase his wealth.

Sami turned out to be intelligent, and eager to master every subject and acquire every skill his benefactor assigned to him. He studied all day and sometimes into the night without wanting to spend time with other teens. On some days Sami worked at his desk by himself on previously assigned lessons. On other days he rode his bicycle or was driven by car to an office where he met with a tutor. At other times he spent a week at a university with an expert, immersed in some topic he needed to learn quickly to pave the way for more advanced subjects.

He worked on his assigned tasks and prayed five times every day. On Friday, his Sabbath, he went for the evening prayer at the mosque closest to wherever he happened to be at the time the muezzin called. He spent the earlier part of the Sabbath day listening to music native to the Arab cultures on a short wave radio Bin Nazamunde gave to him

He progressed quickly through arithmetic, algebra, plane and solid geometry and trigonometry. By the end of his first year under bin Nazamunde's sponsorship, he was ready to learn calculus, and a year later to move on to differential equations. His progress in high school physics and chemistry was equally swift during the second year. By the end of that year he was permitted to conduct college freshman level experiments in the labs at the King Fahd University of Petroleum and Minerals, when the students enrolled there were away on vacation.

About a year later Sami had learned all he needed to know about Arabic usage and grammar. Bin Nazamunde took the boy aside one day and emphasized to him his need to learn English. He said, "Use that short wave radio to hear what spoken English sounds like."

Sami's stored enough English words in his photographic memory to enable him to understand what he read and what was spoken to him. Learning English grammar was his most difficult challenge.

Bin Nazamunde gave an IBM and a Macintosh computer to Sami, and told him to learn to use them. Sami plunged into the world of computers with a fanaticism he hadn't shown for any other activity. First he mastered Cobol and Fortran. Then he moved on to C, C+ and C+++. Eventually he devoured Java and JavaScript, aided by his photographic memory.

When the service became available in Riyadh, he connected his computers to the Internet. Sami studied the sites teaching how to roam the net. Soon he discovered the hackers and crackers. He joined them to learn all he could about penetrating computers belonging to others. He discovered how to invade computer networks connected to the Internet and how to peruse their data. Sami wrote a variety of programs that concealed his identity, so even if a system's security detected penetration by an outsider, they did not learn his identity. Sami was cracking into other computers for the sheer fun of being able to get away with it. He did no damage to any machine, data or system. He was not yet corrupted into an instrument of bin Nazamunde's destructive schemes.

Next Sami studied world and Middle Eastern history, with emphasis on politics. He was intrigued by the ways in which political power, which he understood to mean the power to rule, could be gained and lost. Studying history gave him his first contact with the influence of economics on political power. He was fascinated by the ways in which events, such as the invention of the steam engine, the propagation of potatoes in Europe, and the use of electricity led to changes in the economy of a country, which resulted in changes in its politics. He tried to imagine what changes in world politics the Internet was going to make.

This led to the first turning point in his education. While he was indifferent about the study of English, he enjoyed learning science and math, and he was enthusiastic about mastering computer science and programming. But Sami was fanatic about learning all he could about economics, and about the interplay of economics and politics. This led to his first urge for independence, which is not surprising for a young man with his mental malady. Sami ignored his other assignments and spent all of his time studying economics, economic history, and political economics. After a week of failing to show up for tutoring sessions, Sami's truancies were reported to bin Nazamunde, who ordered Sami to come to one of his offices.

When Sami entered, bin Nazamunde stood up so he towered over the boy. Sami walked uneasily up to the tall man's rosewood desk, and stood there looking up into his regent's eyes. Bin Nazamunde was wearing a beige European style business suit. No turban adorned his head, so the boy saw his patron's full head of black hair flecked with many gray strands. He had a broad high forehead and large ears lying close to his scalp. His eyebrows were separated by a wide space.

Bin Nazamunde expected his orders to be carried out to the letter, and would've been furious if anyone else disobeyed him. However, he knew he wasn't dealing with an ordinary human being. His innate shrewdness induced him to proceed cautiously. He didn't smile down at Sami, but he didn't use his icy glare either. Also, he was looking into the boy's bottomless black eyes, and again he felt they were holding his eyes captive. In measured tones indicating neither approval nor disapproval, he demanded, "Tell me why you are not attending to your studies."

"Oh but I am, Sire," Sami protested anxiously. "I am studying as hard and for as many hours every day as I ever have. I'm more concerned about learning economics and about how new things, new technologies, new inventions can change history, than anything I've ever studied before."

Bin Nazamunde continued his deadpan stare. "But what makes you so concerned with economics and technology that you abandon everything else you have been studying?"

"Because Allah spoke to me." His face beamed. "He told me I would learn how to recover from the infidels the wealth they've

stolen from our lands and from our people. He told me I'd learn how
to use their own technologies to destroy the heathens and the
infidels."

Bin Nazamunde was glad he'd been cautious. Sami was heading
in the right direction. "Do you remember Allah's exact words?"

"Only a few of them. But His message was clear. The key to
destroying the infidels is by turning their technologies against them.
And He told me I would learn how to become the instrument He used
to take their wealth away from them." Sami paused and thought a
moment, then spoke confidently. "Those were His exact words. That I
would learn to become His instrument." He walked up, put his hands
on the desk and leaned forward. "I must do as He commands. And,
Sire, every day I do read, as best I can, the English language
newspapers like I promised you."

Encouraged by what he was hearing, bin Nazamunde asked,
"When did Allah tell you these things?"

"One night while I slept."

Bin Nazamunde felt trapped. He knew Allah hadn't spoken to
the boy. But he didn't know whether he was lying. Saying he was
obeying instructions from Allah could be Sami's excuse for doing
anything he wanted to do. But bin Nazamunde decided to give him
the benefit of the doubt for the time being. So he didn't challenge
Sami for telling him he was obeying a command from Allah. Also it
really wasn't important if he shifted the emphasis of his studies to
economics.

However bin Nazamunde was reluctant to give up control and
have the schedule he selected replaced by what his ward wanted to
do. So he made Sami stand in front of him for a few minutes while he
wrote on a legal pad and pretended to ponder the matter. Finally, he
said, " I approve the change of emphasis in your studies. I will permit
you to spend almost all of your study time on economics, with an
emphasis on the importance of technology and technological change.
But you must keep abreast of current political events everywhere in
the world. And you must spend one day each week studying science
and math."

"And I'll continue to spend some of my time learning English," Sami volunteered, "especially reading *The Wall Street Journal*."

Sami's disobedience left bin Nazamunde perplexed. He wasn't sure whether he was creating an Islamic super hero, or a monster, or whether he was wasting time and money on a lunatic. His instincts told him he'd get the super hero for his own personal jihad. But he needed to talk to someone who could reassure him he was on the right track. So he telephoned Dr. Saleem at his office at Schiraz Psychiatric Hospital.

Bin Nazamunde said, "Sami has been insubordinate. He did not attend his tutoring sessions or do his assigned lessons. The excuse the boy used was Allah told him he should study something else, something involving economics. Are there were any medical tests for verifying when he is having a psychiatric episode?"

"There aren't any physiological tests, such as electroencephalograms and blood chemistry analysis, for confirming my diagnosis of his condition," Saleem said. "The only thing I can think of is to give him lithium and see if the episodes stop."

"What if he is lying about hearing voices and uses commands from Allah as an excuse for doing whatever he wants?"

Saleem was tempted to laugh, but suppressed the urge, remembering bin Nazamunde dour visage. "You'll have to figure that one out by yourself. I've told you before he actually thinks Allah is talking to him when he lapses into schizophrenia. If he justifies something trivial as a command from Allah, you might surmise he's lying. We don't expect Allah to be concerned with trifling matters, and the boy wouldn't think that either.

It just occurred to me that when he's having a depressive episode, he might be highly receptive to verbal instructions, maybe even brain washing. If he goes catatonic and blacks out like he did in the episode reported by Dr. Quadi, find some man with a deep voice, like you'd expect Allah to have. Station this man next to the boy while he's unconscious, and have the man repeat over and over what ever you want him to do. It may work or it may not. And don't let his mother or anyone else know you're doing this."

"I'll experiment with your suggestion," bin Nazamunde said, "because when I figure out what I want him to use him for, I might need some technique like you suggest to get him to comply. I still do not want him on lithium. I doubt he'd be of any use to me if he were cured of his mental illness."

Abu Wagdy had a deep, resonant voice. Bin Nazamunde explained Dr. Saleem's suggestion to him, and assigned him the task of conducting experiments to determine if speaking to Sami when the boy blacked out might influence his behavior. Abu Wagdy asked Amina Insien to tell him whenever her son experienced an episode of unconsciousness. One morning she called and said, "Sami passed out during the night. I have to leave him because I've been hired to take care of a neighbor's children and to prepare the day's meals for the family."

"Don't worry," Abu Wagdy said. "I'll come over right now and look after him."

She thanked him and left for her job. He drove to the Insien apartment and entered Sami's bedroom. He pulled up a chair next to the bed, leaned over with his mouth close to the boy's ear, and said over and over in an even voice slightly louder than he used for conversation, "Drink nothing except water with no ice for seven days." He knew this was a valid test because Sami loved to carry around a glass of ice cubes filled with one of the sweet bottled juices

After about three hours when Sami began to stir and awake from his torpor, abu Wagdy stood and walked out of his bedroom and drove away. The next day he phoned Amina and asked about her son.

She said, "Sami is acting crazy. He won't drink his milk, or his tea. Or even the cold juices he loves. He told me Allah ordered him to drink nothing except unchilled water for a week."

Abu Wagdy chuckled and said, "Don't worry. Drinking only water for a week won't hurt him. And he'll feel good because he thinks he's obeying a command from Allah." He reported the success of his experiment to bin Nazamunde, and was praised for his creativeness. On two subsequent occasions, abu Wagdy repeated the experiment giving Sami different commands. Both times he obeyed the commands, telling his mother they came from Allah.

On hearing him report the success of his latest brain bending experiments, bin Nazamunde said to abu Wagdy, "We have a human computer that is unique in all the world, and you have learned how to program our living computer." Then he indulged in a rare action by laughing out loud. So seldom did bin Nazamunde reveal any human emotion, other than greed or rage, that abu Wagdy was startled. But he quickly recovered, nodded his head vigorously in agreement and laughed loudly along with his boss.

Chapter 6   Godfather

MARIO PUZO'S *Godfather* fascinated bin Nazamunde when the film and book arrived in Saudi Arabia several years earlier. This led him to read every book written by Puzo. He kept them on a shelf in the bookcase behind his desk. Bin Nazamunde imagined he was like the cold, calculating Michael Corleone. Carrying his *Godfather* fantasy a step farther, he regarded abu Wagdy as his *consiglieri*. The two of them, he figured, could devise ways to turn a jihad against western democracies into a profitable enterprise.

Though strict in his observance of Islam's rituals, three times he made the Hadj pilgrimage and he always fasted during Ramadan, bin Nazamunde easily rationalized the sanctity of his criminal ambitions.

Puzo's story gave him the idea of running the Corleone mob's strategy in reverse. Instead of using the profits from criminal enterprises to start or take over legitimate businesses, as Michael Corleone planned on doing, bin Nazamunde decided to use the profits from his legitimate business to start, or gain control of, illegal activities and enterprises. The bribes used by the Corleones to control government and law enforcement officials had their counter part in Arab countries, where baksheesh has been a way of life for as long as anyone can remember.

Like the Corleones, he'd exact a tribute from those criminal activities he chose to leave for others to run. And a jihad against the West would give cover to almost any kind of violence he used to achieve his goals. The jihad's fighters were his enforcers; he could send them against other criminal organizations he sought to replace or to take over with his own. To motivate his private army, bin Nazamunde needed someone to convince the troops that his rivals were infidels or the dupes and lackeys of the infidels.

Bin Nazamunde's first goal was to skim profits off the trade in heroin made from poppies grown in Afghanistan. Baksheesh was his primary strategy. Abu Wagdy sent agents to bribe the Afghani warlords and corruptible Taliban clerics into giving bin Nazamunde's organization a monopoly for distributing the dope. And he was pleased with their progress. His goal was to gain control as many of the Afghan poppy fields as possible and to destroy the others.

His Afghan endeavors came to an end on September 11, 2001.

Abu Wagdy reported the raid by bin Laden's followers to bin Nazamunde, and he turned on the TV in his office. He could not believe what he was seeing.

Bin Nazamunde shot to his feet and exclaimed, "Those idiots. They had the Americans at their mercy outside of the United States. They got away with every bombing and murder they undertook. Now look what bin Laden's done with this publicity stunt. And that's all it is. A publicity stunt to make him famous. And that's all it will accomplish for him." He stomped back and forth behind his desk.

"Knocking down some buildings and killing a few thousand Americans is not going to make them leave Saudi Arabia or any other Islamic country. That's what he says he wants them to do. But it will have the opposite effect. The Americans will come after him with every weapon they have. And their troops will be in Afghanistan too. And they'll probably stay there for as long as any of us are alive. And the American public will become suspicious of all Muslims. I should have sent you to eliminate that fool, bin Laden, the last time he was here in Riyadh." Bin Nazamunde pounded his desk with his fist and continued to fume.

"My program to control the heroin trade in Afghanistan is obviously over now. Soon there will be too many American troops there for us to operate effectively. We have to find another way to increase our profits. What do you think we should do now?" He turned and shifted his gaze from the TV to abu Wagdy.

"Thank you for the compliment of asking me what to do now," abu Wagdy said. "But you know I'm not an idea man. I'm a doer, an operator. I make other people's ideas happen. We need to get your employees thinking about new ventures. How about putting Sami Insien to work giving out his ideas. Considering all of the information and training pumped into his head, maybe now we can mine something useful out of his photographic memory."

"Maybe so." Bin Nazamunde looked solemn as he thought for a moment. "You're right. It is time for me to start cashing in on my investment in him. I believe Sami has a superior intellect that we can channel to serve our goal of creating new sources of profits. I'll appeal to his religiosity to get him to work for our ends. Bring him in here first thing tomorrow morning, and let's get him started on this." He dismissed abu Wagdy with a jerk of his head toward the door.

Sami's routine of study, bodybuilding and the acquisition of physical skills continued. He matured into a muscular young man just under six feet tall with strong arms and legs, and a compact, agile body with narrow shoulders and tiny hips and buttocks. Both his manic and his depressive episodes occurred less frequently and both were of shorter duration. Bin Nazamunde continued to have abu Wagdy brainwash him during his depressive blackouts. So by the time Sami was twenty-one, he was indoctrinated with bin Nazamunde's anti western schemes, thinking he was receiving instructions from Allah.

Abu Wagdy and Sami entered bin Nazamunde's office and seated themselves on the same side of his desk. When he was in bin Nazamunde's presence, Sami usually assumed the persona of the young lad he'd been when his benefactor first undertook his education. He moved his chair back from the desk and sat on its edge.

Bin Nazamunde turned toward Sami and said, "Infidels are roaming the lands of Islam. The Wahhabi Imam's have told us how they corrupt our people with ideas of individualism. Their global companies suck out our resources to prop up their consumer driven economies. American consumerism has especially damaging effects; these are visible where pure Islam once flourished. Our youngsters are seduced away from the holy teachings of the Qur'an by American cinemas, broadcasts, publications and advertising. The Wahhabi Imams have launched a jihad against western ways. I am giving financial assistance to their jihad. I want you to join the jihad. I want you to think of new ways to drive out the infidels. I want you to motivate warriors to fight against the infidels. Help me raise funds to pay for these worthy goals."

Sami leaned forward and tried to make eye contact. "I've already been given instructions by Allah to destroy the infidels and heathens." He pointed heavenward with an extended index finger. "He told me that modern Muslims must revert to the pure Islam of the Prophet Muhammad's generation. Only after the very last infidel and the very last heathen have converted to Islam, or have been killed for refusing to convert, will Allah's final objective for mankind be reached.

The holy Prophet Muhammad started this jihad, and his jihad has never stopped for over a thousand years. With his own hands Prophet Muhammad killed many infidels. His works teach us that the righteous end of Allah's jihad justifies any means we use to achieve its end. Every form of deception and killing we use against our enemies has been sanctioned by Allah." He pointed upwardly again.

With increasing enthusiasm, Sami stood and looked down at the seated bin Nazamunde. "The infidels and heathens have escaped the will of Allah because they developed superior technology. When our enemies had only horsemen with swords and arrows, Allah's warriors defeated them. Their conquests extended the domain of Allah to the gates of Vienna and almost to Paris, to the borderlands of China and India, and far into Africa. But when Satan taught the infidels technologies using explosives, and machinery, our brave fighters were never given the weapons or training they needed."

Bin Nazamunde stood now so he did not have to look up at Sami, who continued, "That has all changed now. Allah has instructed me to use the technologies developed by the infidels against them. We have unlimited access to computers. We can use them as weapons in which information and destructive programs are the ammunition. The Internet will be the delivery system for those weapons. And when we need them, the heathen Orientals will sell us explosives. And human beings will be our delivery systems for the explosives."

In a jubilant voice, Sami intoned, "We no longer need the metals and factories to process them into large machines of destruction that have been used to subjugate we true believers and to defy Allah's will. I will gladly join the Wahhabi jihad to bring about the conversion or the death of every one of the infidels and heathens roaming the earth. Allah will help me to discover new ways to

37

deceive and kill the blasphemers." Sami sat down again and beamed as he leaned back in his chair.

Bin Nazamunde was taken aback by the scope of his ward's ambition. This went far beyond what abu Wagdy pumped into Sami's ears during his blackouts. Bin Nazamunde wanted to oust the westerners and their influences from the lands of Islam to make way for his plans to expand his profits from legitimate businesses and gain the power to control illegal commerce. The conversion of every infidel and heathen to Islam was not on his agenda.

Bin Nazamunde sat down again. "I know Allah will be pleased with your zeal to carry out his will," he said and smiled at Sami. "We must find a way to pay for Allah's jihad. Concentrate your thinking on this goal and come back to me with your recommendations."

Several days later Sami asked for a meeting with bin Nazamunde and abu Wagdy. Sami pulled his chair up next to bin Nazamunde's desk and spoke in a self-assured, mature voice. "Here are the first two parts of Allah's plan," he said pointing up to heaven with his index finger. "The first part is to organize fighting forces of infantry, guerrilla bands, tribes, armies, and as many men as we can enlist and train. These foot soldiers will distract the infidels, especially the Americans, into sending large numbers of their troops to foreign lands where they can be engaged and tied up for years by small numbers of our recruits, and what ever local fighters we can convince to fight with us."

Holding up two fingers, he said, "The second part of Allah's plan is to drain the infidel's wealth into our hands where we can use it to finance other parts of His plan that He has not yet revealed to me. That is why Allah told me to study markets," he said thumping his heart with his closed right hand. "I know how to plan events for causing commodity prices to rise and fall. This will let us invest in the futures markets and profit from the rising or falling prices. These profits will be great enough to make the jihad financially self-supporting."

Abu Wagdy stood, held his arms out to his sides with the palms up and said, "What're you talking about? We will be training fighters, not stock brokers."

"Let him finish," bin Nazamunde said impatiently. "Tell us how you plan to control commodity prices."

Sami smiled and spoke with confidence, "The history of commodities proves their prices skyrocket when a catastrophe disrupts the supply of the commodity. The key to making profits in the futures market is to know when such a catastrophe is going to happen. The best way of knowing when a catastrophe is going to happen is to have the power to make the catastrophe happen when you want it to happen.

By commanding our fighters to destroy stores of a commodity, or to destroy the facilities used to make or harvest or transport it, we can disrupt the supply. Knowing when this disruption will happen will let us buy large numbers of futures contracts before the catastrophe occurs."

Sami stood and thrust both of his hands toward the ceiling while saying, "When the commodity's price shoots up, we can sell our contracts at a handsome profit. We can perform acts of sabotage and destruction causing the price of crude oil to rise. Gold and gasoline futures will follow oil upwardly. Agricultural commodities, like coconut oil, coffee and copra, are vulnerable to raids on the plantations where they are grown or where they are stored.

Bin Nazamunde stood and smiled down at his ward. "I believe this will work and generate the profits to pay for the jihad. We must begin by building a camp for training the warriors. Then we will organize a staff of experts and recruit and train the fighters and terrorists to carry the jihad to the infidels. Write me a plan for creating the camp." He sat down and looked at papers on his desk.

Two days later Sami returned with a typed report. He named the enterprise *al Khanjar* (the Dagger). He advised against building a terrorist training camp in Saudi Arabia because of the American influence and presence, which he predicted would increase during the years ahead. The Saudi government would give in to American pressure and close or destroy such a camp.

Sami recommended building the camp in Iran because it had a theocratic government, and pursued development of nuclear weapons. The western infidels were consuming their influence in Iran trying to shut down its nuclear weapons program. The infidels would not risk incurring Iran's ill will by complaining about or attacking a conventional military training camp. Finally he advised locating the camp in the mountains east of Beheshti near the coast and near the border with Pakistan. That way personnel and supplies could enter and leave by way of the waters of the Persian Gulf or over the mountains and across the border of another Islamic country.

Bin Nazamunde was amazed at his ward's astute recommendations and at how quickly he'd arrived at them. He ordered Sami to proceed and abu Wagdy to guide him.

During the next month, Sami located and took over an ideal site for the training camp in the southeast corner of Iran. He deployed engineers and workers from bin Nazamunde's construction company, and began erecting buildings and setting up a firing range began. The structures for housing and feeding the troops were nothing more than aluminum roofed sheds with dirt floors and no amenities. The quarters for the instructors and other camp cadre were more complete having wood floors and individual rooms. A landing strip long enough for a small passenger jet was one of the first completed projects. They built a suite of deluxe rooms for the camp director at one end of the jet hanger, and put up a small concrete block mosque as the construction project came to an end.

Sami learned organizational techniques and obtained management experience by working with abu Wagdy on the project. He took on the persona of an executive in a construction company. Bin Nazamunde recognized his administrative skills and gave him increased executive responsibility. By the time construction of the camp was nearing completion, abu Wagdy returned to Saudi Arabia and bin Nazamunde passed responsibility for finishing the facility to Sami. He had the name *al Khanjar* painted in red letters on the outside of the mess shed above its door.

When the time came to hire the staff and recruit fighters for *al Khanjar*, Sami asked for another meeting with bin Nazamunde and abu Wagdy. He told them Allah had given him two more parts to His plan for ridding the earth of infidels and heathens. Again they sat in the office of Bin Nazamunde, who began the meeting by saying, "So far your strategy has made sense to me. Tell us about the new parts."

"The next part will begin execution several weeks before the final part. I'll set up and carry this part out myself with a few experienced computer programmers who I'll supervise. They'll be the expert code writers we call hackers or crackers. We will infect important infidel computers with a variety of diseases that will disrupt their operations and erase information stored in them. We will create thousands of cascading viruses, Trojan horses and other malware we can release one after another for weeks." Sami beamed as he anticipated his direct role in creating weapons to inflict damage on the infidels.

"The objective of the final part is to deprive the Americans of electricity," he continued. "Almost everything they do and use requires electricity. Without it almost nothing in America works. Electricity is the lifeblood of their civilization. Their transmission lines and transformers are especially vulnerable. Some well-placed bombs exploding at the same time at critical choke points will shut down their three electric grids.

Chaos will result. There won't be any light or heat or air conditioning for most of the people. Cash registers won't run. People won't receive mail. Banks won't be able to cash checks or honor withdrawal requests. Gasoline can't be pumped. Communication will only be possible with battery-powered devices, and only until the batteries run out. And all of this will be going on while they are trying to escape from the viruses we'll still be sending into their computer systems."

Bin Nazamunde turned toward abu Wagdy, nodded his approval, smiled and said, "These conditions will be similar to what happens when a hurricane hits an area in America."

"Yes," Sami said, "But the weather service gives the American people several days warning before a hurricane arrives so they can stock up on water, food and batteries. Blowing up critical parts of the electric grid will take them by surprise, and almost all of the country will be affected. The people won't have stored the supplies they need."

Abu Wagdy interjected, "Most of the Americans have firearms. Gunfights will break out in their cities when people run out of the supplies needed for their family's survival. They might have to declare marshal law."

"Their stock and bond markets will plummet, and we'll reap the profit because we'll sell short massively before we execute the final part," Sami said. "We'll also be able to profit from rising commodity prices, especially by buying gold, silver and platinum futures."

"But how do you plan on shutting down their electric system?" bin Nazamunde said.

"There are two possible ways. The first way is the most devastating. It is called an Electro Magnetic Pulse (EMP) attack. We'd execute the EMP attack by detonating nuclear explosions high up in the planet's atmosphere in a suicide jet plane. The electromagnetic pulse generated by the nuclear blast will destroy all of the electronics and satellites within its field of vision. The pulse wipes out electronics and telecommunications, and this will shut down the power grid. It could take years to restore the entire system. We'd need three nuclear bombs to shut down their power grids.

But it probably won't be possible set off an EMP because it will require the cooperation of a government having nuclear bombs. The Iranians, Iraqis and North Koreans are trying to develop these bombs. But they may give up under pressure from the United Nations. Or Israel or the United States might destroy their reactors preemptively to stop them; like the Israelis destroyed Saddam's Osiraq reactor. So the EMP attack is a possibility, but we can't count on it."

"That is a good plan if we could execute it. But I'm sure we will never get hold of nuclear bombs," bin Nazamunde said. "What's the other way you think we could shut down their electric grids?"

"This way will require many secret agents of the jihad infiltrating America. These agents will find jobs and live close to the critical locations of the power grid. Also, they must be willing to blow themselves up with bombs if it becomes necessary. We'll supply them with explosives. We can buy all of the C4 we'll need from the

Russians, Iranians and North Koreans. When we have an agent in place near every choke point of the three power grids and every critical transmission component, we'll give the signal for them to set off their bombs at the same time."

Sami gave a thumbs down with both hands as he said, "This'll cause the chaos I described before and the stock markets will crash. Also the infidels will consume their wealth trying to recover and rebuild. They'll have to bring back their soldiers from overseas. The American form of government might not survive marshal law for very long. They may turn into a dictatorship or oligarchy like the Russians. And we'll profit when the stock markets around the world crash. Allah told me that our profits will be large enough to recruit, equip and train a great army that can invade and conquer our neighbors."

Bin Nazamunde stood and beamed a small smile of approval at his ward. "These last two plans are so startling that I need to think about them. Come back next Thursday," he said.

Sami jumped to his feet. "They're not my plans. They're His." Again he pointed upwardly. "I'll need to have funds available to invest in the futures markets. All of the profits will go to whatever account you choose. Put a billion US dollars in several accounts that I can control."

"We can discuss the details when you come back next week. You may leave now," bin Nazamunde said. He turned to abu Wagdy. "You stay here."

After the door closed behind Sami, abu Wagdy stood up and began to pace back and forth in front of the desk where his boss remained seated with a smile on his face. "These plans are the ravings of a mad man," he said. "Allah didn't tell him what to do. Allah doesn't speak to mortals. And I didn't plant those schemes in his head when he was having psychotic episodes."

Bin Nazamunde nodded. "I know you are correct in everything you say. But just because the plan came out of an insane mind doesn't mean that it's not a good plan. And Sami opened my eyes to another weapon we have against the infidels. International commerce—our ability to make exorbitant profits from our businesses at the infidels' expense. If he is correct and can cause commodity prices to go up or down, the jihad can destroy, or at least disrupt, American civilization at no cost to me. The profits he makes from disrupting the commodity futures markets will pay for our jihad. And we can profit from using our businesses to rebuild America and other countries that we'll damage. And the profits from the rebuilding work will finance recruiting, arming and training armies of terrorists. The cycle of destroying and rebuilding the infidel's countries can be repeated for our benefit.

It will be like what happens in America when a hurricane devastates part of Florida. The insurance companies pay to rebuild, and businesses from other states rush in to make the profits. Yes, the cycle of destroying, rebuilding and rearming can go on and on. Michael Corleone never would have had a better plan if he'd really existed." He clapped his hands together and laughed.

"We'll never get control of nuclear bombs. So we have to turn men into bombs. The question for you to answer, abu Wagdy, is whether we can recruit and train agents capable of infiltrating and working in America without being discovered. And, these secret agents must be trained to retain their zeal for years until we have enough of them in place to destroy the power grids. Then we'll tell them to blow themselves up along with specific targets in the grids. If we can find and train the agents, I believe the chaos Sami predicted will occur."

"I think—"Abu Wagdy began.

But bin Nazamunde held up his hand to silence him, and continued, "With an army of terrorists at our disposal, we can continue to manipulate commodity prices to pay the army's expenses. And the cost of setting up the agents in America is within my means. The question is whether we can find men who can be trained to die, but who will wait for years to die until we tell them to." He pointed at abu Wagdy indicating it was now permissible for him to speak.

Abu Wagdy said, "Finding men willing to kill themselves and innocent bystanders for the jihad will be easy. Arafat already proved that. But I don't know if we can find men who'll not arouse suspicion in America because of their appearance. Also, they must have the intellect to learn to speak American. I just don't know how to do this."

"Good enough. I appreciate your frankness." Bin Nazamunde nodded approvingly. "I've heard of a Russian agent in Teheran who might be able to help us. Have a jet plane fueled and ready to go if he's willing to talk to me," He dismissed abu Wagdy by waving his hand toward his office door.

The date was March 20, 2002.

Chapter 7   Spymaster

VLADIMAR URIE GURTENKOV was a fifty-three year old, former KGB Colonel who astutely foresaw the demise of the Soviet state. He had a flabby five foot seven body that was once muscular and hard. His short, narrow face came to a point at his chin below thick lips that always seemed on the verge of puckering. His thin brown hair receded halfway up his scalp, and his light blue eyes slanted slightly upwardly at their corners beneath thin accurate brows. He was an ethnic Russian whose ancestors were nobles of high rank in the Czar's court. Most of them lost their lives, and all lost their power, in the Communist revolution.

Gurtenkov was well aware of the privileged lives his forbearers lived, and he was determined to regain a status and power equal to theirs. This he did by rising to his rank of Colonel, first by ruthless cunning in climbing past his superiors, and by capitalizing on his ability to predict which agents would fail and which would succeed in carrying out the spy agency's plots against the Americans and other democracies. When he was just a teenager, he realized that learning to speak American English like a native and understanding the culture of this enemy were vital to his achieving success.

He anticipated that dissolution of the KGB gave a Russian with his background no choice but to organize a gang of cutthroats for hire. But he didn't think being an outlaw in a nation with a crumbling economy was going to be profitable enough to satisfy his hunger for power and beautiful women. Also, he liked to get drunk on expensive single malt scotches. And the top killer in a band of murderers needed to watch his back at all times—could not afford to let his guard down and carouse as much as Gurtenkov desired. So he decided to find an employer willing to pay handsomely for his skills as a teacher of agents and a trainer of murderers and assassins. The Iranians were more than willing to do just this.

Gurtenkov maintained his contacts with current and former KGB operatives around the world. The operatives were like the alumni of a small college who threw business to each other whenever the opportunity arose. He recruited his staff from among these contacts.

For two years Gurtenkov had been in charge of selection and training of what was in all but its name, the Iranian secret police. But he chaffed at living in a country run by austere Imams and an Ayatollah who made it difficult for him to find the scotch he loved and amiable companions to carouse with. Also, beautiful women were kept out of sight, and those beauties he did discover were afraid to be seen with him. So he was reduced to paying for female consorts.

When the call came from bin Nazamunde, Gurtenkov was willing to be flown to Riyadh to hear what he had to say. He walked into bin Nazamunde's office wearing a tailored brown wool suit that fit him well, a white shirt and an aggressive red and black tie. His black tassel loafers were highly polished.

Bin Nazamunde wore a red silk, ankle length gown held together by a wide belt woven from solid gold strands. A full turban that matched the garment adorned his head and hid his hair and ears from view. A gold headband encircled the middle of the turban. He stood up and looked down at the Russian from his full height. Without offering a greeting or to shake his visitor's hand, he pointed to a chair covered in soft brown calfskin.

"I know your background. You may be able to help me," bin Nazamunde said. "Here's what I need. Someone who can train guerrilla fighters. Also, someone who can train agents that will blend in...in America. Secret agents who will be willing to blow themselves up when ordered to do so. Agents who will be willing to blow themselves up years after they've been trained here. Can you select and train these fighters and agents? If you can, you'll be richly rewarded for the rest of your life." Bin Nazamunde sat down in the chair behind his desk, momentarily looking distractedly at some papers.

"I have some questions," Gurtenkov said. "First, when you say 'America' I assume you mean the continental United States." Bin Nazamunde simply nodded, and stared impassively into the Russian's face. "Second, how long between when I train them and when you order the agents to die? Third, how much will you pay me, and fourth what restrictions will be placed on me...what I drink...how I live?"

Bin Nazamunde focused his iciest stare on Gurtenkov's face. "You will spend your time here in Riyadh and at a remote training camp in the mountains of southern Iran. You will be given all of any kind of alcohol you ask for, so long as it does not impair you effectiveness in doing your job. No clergy of any persuasion will know what you're doing unless you put yourself on display in public. Whatever the Iranians are paying you, I will increase it by fifty percent. And the delay between when you train the agents and when they will be told to die will depend on how long it takes you to train between fifty and a hundred of them, and to deploy them in America. At this time we don't know exactly how many agents we will need."

"What do you want the agents to blow up, besides themselves? Will this be plain ordinary terrorism like Arafat's?"

"You don't need to know their target today. You will learn of that if we make a deal."

Showing his uneven stained teeth in a wide grin, Gurtenkov said, "If you agree to pay me double what I'm getting from the Iranians, four thousand US dollars a week, plus all my living expenses. And to make it possible for me to meet attractive women...tourists and western women who work here, I'll stay here today and never return to Teheran."

Bin Nazamunde nodded his head slowly. "Those parts I agree to, but we do not have a deal until you outline for me how you can train, deploy and motivate the secret agents."

Whenever bin Nazamunde was talking, Gurtenkov perused the books on shelves in the bookcase behind his desk in an effort to obtain information about the man with whom he was negotiating his compensation. He quickly noted that all were non-fiction works relating to business, history, economics and construction. All, that is, except for a cluster of about a dozen books in bright dust covers directly behind the Arab's turbaned head: *The Dark Arena, The Fortunate Pilgrim, The Godfather, Fools Die, The Sicilian, The Fourth K, The Last Don, Omerta, The Family, The Godfather Papers & other Confessions,* and *Inside Las Vegas.* He noticed Puzo's name in large letters on most of the volumes and deduced that his prospective employer was a fan of crime novels and the Sicilian mafia. In particular, he made a mental note of two titles including the word Godfather. Gurtenkov had read both of them.

Gurtenkov mused: *I understand this Arab. He already has immense wealth. But the more he has the more he wants. I'd feel the same if I were him. I also understand what I am to him. A heathen who'll have a limited usefulness. When this greedy megalomaniac decides I'm no longer useful to him, he'll try to have someone put me away, unless, of course, I kill him first. You live by the sword, in his case the scimitar, and you die by the scimitar. I've lived in a corrupt, cutthroat world all my life. I can survive here among these Muslim fanatics. I expect to die of old age in my own bed.* He said "Show me how well I'll be treated today while I think about this and prepare a report for you. I'll need a word processor, a bottle of single malt scotch, and tonight, a beautiful girl."

Bin Nazamunde masked his revulsion by turning away and pointing out of his window toward another tall building. He said, "I maintain a suite for business guests across the court yard at the other Oil King Tower." Thinking to himself: *For scum like you who will never be allowed to enter my home.* He buzzed abu Wagdy's office, and told him to take care of Gurtenkov. "Get him anything he asks for." He stood and nodded curtly at Gurtenkov, who also stood, turned and walked out of the office without another word being exchanged.

As the Russian emerged from bin Nazamunde's office, he saw abu Wagdy, who was dressed in a black robe embroidered in red, a matching skullcap, and sandals. He introduced himself as bin Nazamunde's administrative assistant when the two men shook hands. As they rode down the elevator, Gurtenkov told abu Wagdy he needed a computer with a word processor, Windows or Macintosh, it did not matter which, since he used both kinds; a bottle of single malt scotch by night fall; and, by midnight, a slim, not heavy, woman under thirty.

Even though it was only a short walk across the park that separated the twin towers, Abu Wagdy ordered the stretch Mercedes limousine to transport them there. About an hour after Gurtenkov was checked in and escorted to an opulent suite of rooms on the fourteenth floor, abu Wagdy provided everything the Russian asked for, the girl coming from a gallery of women who could be sent to a visitor on short notice.

Between glasses of scotch and romps in bed with the girl, Gurtenkov scribbled notes on a yellow legal pad and typed into the word processor well into the night. He developed an outline of his recommendations to bin Nazamunde. He slept until noon, then ordered room service to bring a meal of rare prime rib and mashed potatoes to his suite. By sundown he had finished his outline.

Gurtenkov phoned abu Wagdy and said "I'm ready for an audience with bin Nazamunde."

Abu Wagdy said "He's left for the day to attend his evening prayers and he told me not to contact him at his home."

The Russian was used to being put off by his patrons, so he enjoyed the night drinking scotch, and bedding a different girl in his room.

The next day bin Nazamunde summoned Gurtenkov to his office after the noon meal. Before he arrived he requested that his recommendations be recorded by a stenographer or on a tape recorder, or both. Abu Wagdy brought a tape recorder in with him and placed it in front of the Russian on the desk behind which bin Nazamunde sat impassively.

Without a word being spoken in greeting, Gurtenkov sat down in a chair directly across the desk from bin Nazamunde, looked down at his notes, hand written on the yellow legal pad, and began, "The first requirement is that your agents blend into the American society for years without arousing suspicion." Bin Nazamunde nodded holding the Russian in an icy stare. "Since agents willing to commit suicide will undoubtedly be Muslims, and most likely will be Arabs, skin color will be a factor. Another factor will be the absence of striking physical appearance. The agents won't be exceptionally good looking or bad looking according to American taste. They won't be so tall or so short they attract attention. They won't be so heavy or so thin that they're easy to remember. In other words the agents should be plain looking with skin as light as possible." He looked up from his notes into bin Nazamunde's eyes for the first time.

Bin Nazamunde glared at him, "This is so obvious. I've read about espionage and crime so I don't need you to tell me what an agent in America should look like. Stop wasting my time. Get on with it."

"Don't jump down my throat. I have no idea how much you know about recruiting and training agents. Today I'll give you an outline of everything I think is important. Whatever you accept...agree to...will be in a written report. I'll stay and work for you only if I believe you've approved of a plan that'll work. I won't undertake anything I think might fail."

Not changing his expression or saying a word, bin Nazamunde pointed to the legal pad Gurtenkov was holding indicating for him to continue his report, as he cogitated, *And well you shouldn't. If you fail, your head will be cut off.*

"The secret agents will pose as Cubans in America. There're several reasons for choosing Cubans. First, their skin color is about the same as Arabs. Second, there're already lots of Cubans in America, so they won't be regarded as exotic. Third, it'll be easy to smuggle them into the US. We can transport them into the Straits of Florida in a small Cuban boat and transfer them to a sport fishing boat from a southern Florida port. Sport fishing boats aren't monitored, so the agents will be able to come ashore when the boat lands." Gurtenkov looked up from his notes. Bin Nazamunde nodded approvingly, but did not change the hostile look on his face.

Gurtenkov continued, "It won't be easy to find men who can become these agents. They'll have to know English when they're first enlisted in the training program. They'll only have to know enough Spanish to pass as someone who used to speak Spanish, but only wants to speak English in America. I know a Cuban who can teach them some Spanish so that any dialect they pick up will be authentic."

Bin Nazamunde said, "Many men here and in other Arab countries are taught English as their second language." He motioned for Gurtenkov to go on with his report.

"Each agent will be trained and paired with one other agent. Only one other agent. No agent will know the identity of any agent except the one he's paired with. And they won't be told their real targets until it's time for them to act. Initially we'll give them false targets, like bridges and Government buildings. That way if an agent defects to the other side, or if one is caught and tortured, he'll only be able to identify one other agent and he won't reveal the actual targets."

"What are you saying about torture?" bin Nazamunde interrupted. "I know you Russians tortured your prisoners and we torture ours. But the Americans will consider themselves bound by the Geneva Convention. They won't—"

"No one knows what the Americans will do if they feel desperate. And the Geneva Convention won't cover your agents. They won't be wearing uniforms and they'll be preparing to attack civilian targets. And they won't be representing any country in a declared war with the US. So they won't be entitled to the protections given to prisoners of war under Geneva.

Who knows what the Americas will do. We always believed their CIA secretly tortured some of our spies they caught during the Cold War. But the Americans have many weak-minded politicians and news editors, so these days they may not use all of the persuasion techniques available to them. But we've got to be prepared in case the Americans decide that preventing terrorist attacks within their borders is sufficiently important to authorize the use of torture."

"Why must they work in pairs?" bin Nazamunde asked. "Why can't they work alone? That way no agent can give up the identity of any other one. We'll have too much invested in every one of them to risk losing any of them if someone is captured. I assure you that any Arab Muslim we train will never defect to the Americans."

Gurtenkov sat back in his chair a put his hands behind his head. "I wouldn't be too sure of that. The Americans turned several KGB agents against us. Life's so easy in that country that it's possible for an agent to be lured into becoming one of them after he's caught. And even if an agent isn't caught he may be seduced by their luxurious way of life.

But the reason I recommend they work in pairs is because it'll be so difficult for a devout Muslim willing to blow himself up to live alone in America. He'll need a companion who shares his devotion to your jihad. Someone he can talk to without fear he'll slip up and reveal his true identity. Someone he can curse with about the Americans infidels. Someone he can consult and gain strength from when the time comes to blow himself up."

Bin Nazamunde shook his head emphatically. "Your experience has been with non-believing Russians." *Heathen pigs*, he mused. "No Muslim will ever be seduced by the Americans."

Laying the yellow pad on bin Nazamunde's desk, Gurtenkov stood up and said, "I believe this is so important we can stop now, and I'll return to Teheran, if you don't accept my recommendation to work the secret agents in pairs."

Bin Nazamunde deliberated, *He may be correct. I won't risk the entire enterprise on this detail.* He said, "Very well, Gurtenkov, you shall have your way. But I want you to try sending in at least one agent alone...not paired with anyone else."

The Russian sat down again and frowned disapprovingly. "It'll be an experiment in loneliness. How much stress can a man endure on his own in a place he despises, living with people he hates, with no one to talk honestly to. Perhaps we can find a sociopath or mentally deranged person to do this."

Abu Wagdy lifted his palm and said, "I think we may know of—"

Bin Nazamunde interjected sternly, "Silence, he is much to valuable for this kind of assignment."

Gurtenkov looked from one to the other with the glimmer of a smile on his face. "If you have someone in mind I'd like to meet him." Bin Nazamunde shook his head and gestured impatiently with his left hand for the Russian to continue.

"Actually, I've been thinking of assigning one agent to infiltrate some branch of the American government. I haven't decided which agency to try yet. Just to give us information. Not to blow up himself or anything else. And to learn how easy or difficult it'll be today to get an agent into their government. That agent'll have a different level of commitment. He won't have to agree to blow himself up, and might be able to function alone...by himself."

Bin Nazamunde nodded and twirled his right index finger in a gesture for Gurtenkov to continue.

"The first pair of agents I'll train and send to America will be our assassins. They'll already be there when the rest of the agents arrive. We'll tell the agents that assassins will be available if they run into anyone making it impossible for them to carry out their mission. After first getting my permission, an agent can call on the assassins to kill whoever is in his way. But this is only part of the reason for having assassins."

Gurtenkov looked from one to the other of his listeners. "We'll also tell the agents that if they think anyone has learned of their identity or mission, the agent should call for the assassins to eliminate the threat. The unspoken message from this will be the assassins are there to kill our own agents if they try to escape from their mission or defect to the Americans. I doubt if we'll ever have to use the assassins against our own agents. The threat from the knowledge the assassins are there should be enough to keep everyone in line." Bin Nazamunde nodded in agreement.

"The assassins won't be committed to martyrdom like the suicide bombers. They won't be able to look forward to the heavenly rewards promised to the jihad's martyrs. The assassin's rewards will have to be different. The assassins will expect to be rewarded in this lifetime. Obviously they'll be violent and brutal men, and maybe cruel too. The rewards that motivate this type of killer are money and sex, and sometimes a thrill from the power to kill."

"You can forget about providing them with sex," bin Nazamunde proclaimed. "I will not take on the role of international pimp."

"You're attaching more importance to this particular expense than it deserves. And to keep you from being involved, I'll conceal it when I account to abu Wagdy for what's being spent. No one'll be able to connect you to it." Looking up from his yellow pad and into bin Nazamunde's eyes, the Russian said, "Michael and Vito Corleone never gave a second thought to paying for their agent's sex needs."

This startled bin Nazamunde. He scowled and pondered for a moment. *How did he know I've read The Godfather? He must have seen it on the bookshelf behind my desk. This heathen is shrewd. He must know what he's talking about.* Bin Nazamunde nodded his assent and lifted his chin quickly, indicating for Gurtenkov to continue.

"Now we come to the most difficult part. Keeping the agents motivated for years before they carry out their suicide assignments. You've already indicated that you believe Muslim agents will stay motivated because they hate the infidel Americans so much. But a few of our KGB agents who believed in communism and hated America were eventually worn down by the stress, or seduced by bribes, into turning to the other side. I recommend keeping the agents motivated by bringing them back here for a short visit to a mosque that we control. We'll only do this if they ask for relief from the stress of living among the infidels. We'll need an Imam they'll respect as a holy man to spend time with them and bolster their enthusiasm for their mission. Can we find a holy Imam who'll cooperate?"

"I have someone in mind. With some preparation, I'm sure he will be more than you hoped for," bin Nazamunde said. He smiled for the first time.

Gurtenkov flipped closed the pages of his pad, "That's an outline of my plans. As you requested, I've told you how I'd train, deploy and motivate the agents. Tell me you agree to it, and you'll pay me what I asked for, and I'll stay here and type the full report."

"I agree. We have a deal. Abu Wagdy will be your contact. Come to me only if you want to change the plan. Give your full written report to abu Wagdy. He will review it and pass it on to me with his comments. He will make a $20,000 down payment to whatever bank you choose, and for the time being, you may stay in the suite where you are now. Goodbye."

"Kahdir, come back after you've seen Gurtenkov out." Bin Nazamunde stood and nodded toward the office door.

Gurtenkov rose, did an about-face, and walked out.

Chapter 8   Muhamed

WHEN ABU WAGDY returned to his boss's office, bin Nazamunde looked up from papers on his desk and said, "We can have Sami trained to be the Grand Imam Gurtenkov wants to use. His ability to recite anything in the sacred Qur'an will impress our recruits. And his eyes can intimidate anyone who is not accustomed to him. These two talents will convince young agents he's a holy man. You must speak into his ear the next time he has a depression blackout. Have Allah tell him he must become a holy Imam when it's necessary to motivate agents to perform the plans that Allah's already told Sami about. Find a dramatics coach who can teach him to play the part of the Imam."

Bin Nazamunde summoned Sami to office several days later. As Sami stood in front of his master's desk, bin Nazamunde said, "I approve of the last two parts of the plan Allah gave to you." He turned and faced abu Wagdy. "You begin by helping Gurtenkov train terrorists to fight with guns and rockets."

Turning back to Sami, "You plan the raids to bring us profits from your futures investments in the commodity markets. You have control of one hundred million in US funds in a numbered account. Contact Caspare Ouiment at AraSuz, the bank I own in Zurich. He will give you the details and instructions on how to trade in this account. Also, go and set up the computer hacking and virus creating operation for the jihad. Before you do anything, think about the importance of your assignments to the success of the plan Allah gave to you and the tremendous responsibilities you have."

Sami did not say anything in response to bin Nazamunde's orders. Instead, he asked, "Who's this Gurtenkov you speak of to abu Wagdy?"

"You will meet him soon. He's a heathen from Russia who I hired to train secret agents and to teach men to kill with modern weapons."

"I've never met a heathen. Let this Russian be the first blasphemer I kill with my own hands to achieve Allah's goals." Sami thrust out his arms and clenched his fingers into claws, as if he had them around someone's throat.

"No," bin Nazamunde exclaimed. He stood quickly and glared down from his full height at the young man. "Do you fail to understand what I just told you? You will never be used to kill anyone. You are too valuable to the jihad's most important operations. And this Russian's also very valuable to us at this time. He knows how to do things that none of the rest of us know. When he is no longer useful to us, someone else will kill him. This reminds me. It's time for you to have bodyguards. Abu Wagdy will assign men from our security staff to protect you."

"Sire, I'd like to recommend someone I believe will become devoted to my safety."

"And who is that?"

"His name is Abduhl Ariann. He was a deacon at the mosque in Zatoon when I lived there. He's very strong. He looked after me when I needed a friend."

Bin Nazamunde nodded his assent. "Bring him here, Kahdir, and have him trained by our security guards."

Except for his mother, Sami never experienced anything that could be called a normal human relationship. In a short time Abduhl Ariann became like an older brother to him. He was a constant companion and mentored Sami in matters a sane person learned from his daily experiences with other human beings. The two men even shared the same call girls.

During Sami's next depression blackout, abu Wagdy spoke into his ear declaring Allah forbids him to engage in any activity risking his life, like fighting or killing infidels and heathens. And he must cooperate with the Russian to achieve the jihad's goals. Allah appointed him as the holy Imam for inspiring and motivating the fighters and also the secret agents they trained and sent to America.

Abduhl Ariann was sitting beside the bed while abu Wagdy was brainwashing the unconscious Sami. He was furious at the manipulation and deceit being practiced on the person whose safety was entrusted to him. But he acquiesced to the brainwashing when abu Wagdy explained to why it was necessary for Sami's protection.

"You've heard his ravings," abu Wagdy said. "I needed to bend his mind back toward normal thinking because he wanted to kill Gurtenkov and other infidels with his bare hands. That'd get him killed for sure. And you'll see. He'll gladly become the Grand Imam of the mosque at the *al Khanjar* camp. His role as Imam will fulfill his religious passions and make him happy."

As abu Wagdy predicted, Sami was flattered and gladly assumed the persona of a Grand Imam. Soon after he awoke Sami announced his name would be Muhamed Allah Yatakalan (Muhamed to Whom God speaks) when he was performing the role of a Grand Imam.

Abu Wagdy hired a dramatics teacher to give Sami lessons on how to play the holy Imam. He learned to speak in different voices. He learned how to portray different emotions, like anger, compassion, fear, hatred and divine inspiration. Sami was measured and outfitted in the robes and turbans befitting a Grand Imam. A makeup specialist taught him how to augment his beard and how to put gray color into his facial hair to make him look older. He mastered using cosmetics to make his eyes look sympathetic or fierce or sad or angry. When in the role of Muhamed Allah Yatakalan, Sami took on the persona of a slow moving, slow speaking, dignified zealot whose primary interest was pursuing the jihad against infidels.

Chapter 9   *Al Khanjar*

ABU WAGDY HIRED the staff to provide the services, consumables and nonmilitary equipment required by *al Khanjar* terrorists. Gurtenkov selected the weapons and the instructors to train the recruits. He chose them from the ranks of experienced Russian mercenaries and a few professional terrorists who had fought for Islamic causes. By the middle of the year 2002, they were ready to start training terrorists to do the dirty work for bin Nazamunde's jihad.

A call from bin Nazamunde went out to Wahhabi Imams throughout the Arab speaking countries to find recruits willing to fight as guerillas or terrorists. Many of those who volunteered were Saudi males in their late teens or early twenties. The rest were mainly Palestinian, Afghani, Pakistani, Iranian, Iraqi, Syrian and Egyptians in the same age bracket. Those who were trained as regular fighters or soldiers were a mixed group that came from a cross section of the population of the country that sent them. They traveled to the *al Khanjar* camp in Iran alone or in groups of two or three.

Gurtenkov was confident his subordinates could meld them into fighting units where their loyalty to their peer group was more important to them than their own lives. The trainees latched on to the *al Khanjar* symbol of a dagger. One of them came up with the motto *al Khanjar yaqtil* (the dagger kills). The Russian soon learned that training fighters motivated to fulfill their duty to Allah was not very different from training idealistic communists and Russian youth to fight for Mother Russia.

But those willing to become suicide bombers were of a different sort. Gurtenkov was surprised when he found them to be the elite of their Muslim countries. They were not poor, uneducated, socially estranged or psychologically deranged street scum or crazies as he expected. They were idealistic and irrational. These suicides-in-the-making thought that by sacrificing themselves they could change the world and make it into an Islamic paradise. And gain extravagant rewards in heaven.

Gurtenkov knew how to get in touch with an independent, computer genius, known only as Ganges, who stole business information and sold it to the KGB and other spy agencies. He left a message for Ganges to contact Sami Insien. After a brief conversation with Ganges, Sami paid five thousand dollars into Ganges' Swiss bank account.

After the payment cleared, Ganges sent an email message giving Sami the telephone number of Rajan Hiresh, a Muslim computer hacker living in Bombay. Hiresh was a multi lingual twenty-eight year old who spoke Hindi, Tamil, Arabic, and English. He was eager to leave over-crowded Bombay for a well paying job in an opulent country like Saudi Arabia. As a practicing Muslim, he was used to the customs and obligations of Islam he was expected to observe in Riyadh. And he could speak their language.

Sami, reverting easily to his confident business executive persona, leased an entire one story building on the outskirts of Riyadh for the *al Khanjar* Computer Department, as he called it. Eight spacious, sunny rooms sat empty except for the numerous electrical outlets and high speed DSL Internet wiring sockets. He planned on having in each room, a Muslim devoted to creating the viruses and doing the hacking and cracking for the jihad. Hiresh persuaded him this was not realistic. Sami would be lucky to have three expert Muslim computer hackers willing to dedicate their efforts to the jihad.

Hiresh told him, "Hackers in general are too free spirited to be tied down to the long-range goals of the jihad. And they won't tolerate the strictures of life in Saudi Arabia. If you want to attract and retain several non-Muslim hackers, you'll have to move this Computer Department to an ultra attractive location, like Nice, France."

Sami decided to stay where he was and to farm out the tedious segments of their work to software factories in India where Hiresh had contacts. "I'll keep the lease on this building," Sami said, "There'll be a complete computer set up in each room. So every member of our Department will have two rooms he can decorate to his own tastes. Each can choose the flooring he prefers, and the type of desk, bookcases, blackboard, executive swivel chair and wall decorations he wants. I'll buy any computer and software program that each of our team members wants. Both of his rooms will be fully equipped. Maybe the ability to move from one room to another will promote the creativity we will need."

"If we end up attracting only two more computer literate Muslims," said Hiresh, "there'll be two extra rooms. What'll you do with them?"

Sami laughed and replied, "I'm the first member of the Computer Department. They'll be my rooms. I ordered G5 Dual Processor Apple computers with 30 inch cinema display screens. They've already been shipped and will get here any day now."

Hiresh was able to attract one of his cousins from an Indian software factory. His cousin knew a Muslim coworker who was ready for a change, so within a month the *al Khanjar* Computer Department was up and running with four programmers. They began turning out viruses to unleash against the computers of infidels.

Sami spent most of his time in the Computer Department. Acting the part of Grand Imam Muhamed Allah Yatakalan also briefly required his attention. During his manic phases he spewed out the architecture for virus after virus. The other members of the Computer Department used his designs for the viruses as the blue prints to guide them to the final scrip and activation codes. His photographic memory enabled Sami to memorize the activation code for each of the viruses, so these codes were never recorded anywhere. This gave Sami complete control over release of the viruses.

Chapter 10   Provisional

"OK," LEVY SAID after he dumped the dead roach into his wastebasket, "I'm convinced you've invented something that'll actually kill a living creature. If we end up applying for a patent I'll be able to include a description of how the death ray smashed the roach as an example of its ability to kill. But now, I need a few more answers from you, please. Do you know about the timing restrictions on the deadline when a patent application has to be filed?"

"I think so...maybe. No. I'm not so sure. You better tell me to make sure," Hamilton stammered while looking down at the desktop and rubbing its smooth surface with his left palm.

Levy said, "Your patent application will have to be on file, that is, the patent application papers have to be inside of the Patent Office, before the invention has been used in public or offered for sale, or sold in the US or described in a printed publication anywhere for one year. What is the invention's state of development, and what marketing efforts have you made?"

Hamilton looked up from the desktop and thought for a moment before answering. "I've made several prototypes, but not shown them to anyone, or made any effort to sell or publicize them. However, I've got an appointment late tomorrow afternoon with an Air Force Colonel at the Pentagon who claims he can speak for all of the armed forces if they are interested in my death ray. The name death ray really got their attention, in particular when I told them I can demonstrate the gun by killing living fauna. I haven't told them yet that the fauna are roaches."

Levy grinned, imagining the Colonel's surprise when Hamilton first showed him a box of live roaches. "So far so good," he said. "Let me make sure I have this straight. No one but you, Rosalind and me have ever seen the ray gun work."

"Right, I've never shown it to anyone else, except, of course, the roaches," Hamilton said laughing softly.

Levy grinned at him. "Did you make drawings of the gun and have witnesses sign the drawings?"

"No, nothing like that. Like I said, I made several prototypes of the gun itself, but never anything like a complete set of drawings."

"We'll have to take care of the lack of witnesses right now."

Levy turned toward Rosalind and said, "Now that we know Mr. Hamilton's invention works, here's what I want you to do. Write up what happened at this demonstration of the ray gun as a witness statement for each of the three of us to sign. You'll notarize my statement and Mr. Hamilton's statement, and I'll notarize yours."

Rosalind gave Levy a two-finger salute with her right hand. "Aye, aye, Skipper," she said.

"You're both notaries." Hamilton said.

"Yeah. It makes formalizing documents a lot easier when every one who works in the office is a notary. And here's what I'm advising you to do today. You've convinced me you have an invention worth protecting with a patent. So you need to be protected from the Pentagon officer you're meeting with tomorrow."

"How come. Can't a military officer be trusted?"

"Maybe, and maybe not," Levy said as he moved his head from side to side. "But why take a chance. I heard rumors about bad experiences inventors've had with the Pentagon that make me paranoid about dealing with them. Now I don't know whether the rumors are true or not. But there's no reason to take a chance when it's so easy to protect yourself one hundred percent. So I recommend we get a provisional patent application on file for you today. That way you'll be completely protected before you tell anyone else about your death ray gun."

"What's a Provisional patent application?" Hamilton asked as he gave Levy a sideways glance.

Levy laced his fingers together and leaned back in his chair. "A Provisional application is not a permanent patent application. This type of patent application will secure the earliest possible date for the filing of a patent application covering your invention. The date the Provisional is filed can be used later as the date of a complete Utility patent application. Getting your invention covered by a Provisional will protect you from anyone you tell about the invention who tries to steal it from you. But to get a patent you can enforce against infringers, you have to file a complete Utility patent application within one year after you file the Provisional application."

Hamilton was squinting at Levy as he tried to absorb all the fine points of patent law he was being peppered with. His face relaxed and he inquired, "Why don't we just file a complete Utility application now? Why waste time with a Provisional?"

"Time," Levy said. "We can't prepare a Utility application in one afternoon. Also, we'd need a complete set of drawings, and there just isn't time for that. All of the details of the invention have to be shown and described in the Utility application. You can't add anything new to a patent application after it's been filed. The Provisional application has to disclose the most important features of the invention, but it doesn't require a formal drawing or claims like a Utility application."

Levy sat up straight and put his elbows on his desk. "We can get a Provisional on file for you today. So you'll be protected tomorrow when you meet with them at the Pentagon. You'll need to tell'em you have a patent application on file already. But don't tell'em it's a Provisional application, and don't tell'em the date it was filed. And never tell anyone the serial number of your patent application without first checking that it's OK with your lawyer. Anyone who knows your application serial number can write to the Patent Office and put derogatory information about your invention in the Patent Office's file."

"What's all this going to cost me?"

"Okay, good question. Now is the right time to talk about what I'm going to charge for the work I do for you. My billing rate is $200 per hour plus any out of pocket expenses and Patent Office fees. My rate covers Ms. Katz's time, except when she can work completely independently of me. Then I bill for her time at $75 per hour, plus, of course, out of pocket expenses and government fees. Bills are due and payable when sent to you, and I'll give you a bill at the end of today for what we do today getting the Provisional application on file."

"So what will it amount to today?"

"Let's see, we started half-hour ago, and it'll take most of the rest of the day. About five to six hours plus fees and associate attorney expenses, so it'll be roughly $1500 to get the Provisional application on file today."

"Sounds reasonable, if you're sure they can't steal my invention. Oh, who's the associate attorney, and why do I need one?" Hamilton glanced around the office impatiently.

"After we get the invention sketched and written up, Rosalind'll fax all the papers to Ed Winters. He's an attorney with an office next door to the Patent Office. He'll put the papers in an envelope and drop them into the Patent Office's incoming mailbox before they close up today. That way your Provisional application will have today's date on it. The Utility application that we'll file in a few weeks will also have the benefit of today's date."

The office door swung open, and Rosalind Katz walked in holding three sheets of paper. "Here are the witness statements describing how the death ray killed the roach." She handed copies to Levy and Hamilton. They both read their statements.

"Sounds right to me," Hamilton said.

"I wouldn't change a word," Levy agreed.

Rosalind smiled and handed them pens. Each signed his statement, and handed it back to Rosalind. She had already signed her statement, so she handed it to Levy. He took out his Notary seal and notarized her statement. She turned to walk out of the office with the Levy and Hamilton statements for her to notarize.

Levy stood and said to her, "Just a minute please, Rosalind. We're going to file a Provisional this afternoon. So you need to phone Winters and alert him that we'll fax it to him, and we'll need to have someone in his firm to file it at the Patent Office before they close today. You go prepare the formal papers. Mr. Hamilton and I will start writing it up right now."

Levy sat down again and spoke to Hamilton. "You'll be involved as much as we are in getting this done. First, you have to show me the parts of your ray gun and tell me about them so I can write up a rough description of it. While I'm doing that, you need to make me a sketch of the gun. We'll need two views. One view will be what you see when you look at the gun. The other will be a cross sectional view from the side showing every part and component of the gun. Do you know what I'm talking about? Can you do that?"

"Ha. Sure can. I'm an engineer just like you," the inventor replied.

Levy pointed toward the gun, which Hamilton was now holding in his hand. "Before you start drawing it, show me what the gun's made of."

Hamilton lifted a hinged side of the gun body to reveal what was in it. A shiny, conical, clear plastic tube slightly under a foot long was inside of the barrel. At the large end of the cone, a pair of insulated copper wires were attached to the opposite sides of the clear plastic. A purplish glass lens was attached to the smaller, opposite end of the plastic tube. The copper wires connected a 300 volt battery in the handle through the firing button.

Hamilton pointed with a pencil to the parts of his invention as he spoke, "The death ray gets its energy from an electric spark that arcs across the large end of the plastic cone where you see the two wire ends spaced apart from each other. The cone is covered with wrinkle free aluminum foil so the light energy from the spark can't escape. It's important for the foil to be wrinkle free or else the light energy gets dissipated as it travels down the cone from the large end to its small end. A double convex glass lens covers the small end of the cone. The color of the lens is important. It has to concentrate the energy from the spark into pinpoint beam in a violet wave spectrum of about 400 nanometers. Any waves much above 400 nm won't have any punch." Levy rubbed his chin with his fingers as he concentrated on the details of the ray gun's construction.

Hamilton continued, "The battery produces a 300-volt sparking flash, and you only get one shot from each battery. More voltage might give a bigger punch, but I don't know how much'll be needed to kill an Arab. I don't know why this gun works. It seems to defy the laws of physics because light energy is turned into a physical force, instead of vice versa."

Levy nodded his head in agreement. "I was thinking the same thing about the laws of physics. But from the point of view of patent law that's good because you get an unexpected result, and something that's not expected almost always gets you a patent. Of course, when an invention is as radical as this one, we'll have to demonstrate to a Patent Examiner that it actually works. And I know we can do that because we just killed a roach with it a few minutes ago. What you just told me was almost a complete explanation of everything I need to describe your invention. But I have a couple more questions." He reached out, took the gun from Hamilton and pointed to the purple glass on its front end. "First, where did you get the lens, and second, what holds the aluminum foil on the plastic cone?"

"I made the lens myself. I have a workshop in my garage with lots of machines and power tools. I do a lot of tinkering and fixing things. But I never made anything I wanted to patent until now. Anyway, I bought some different colored glass things to make into lenses to try out. None of the light or bright colors worked. Finally, I found a purple ash tray at Ginsberg's; it was already curved a little bit like a convex lens."

"Do you mean Ginsberg's art and gift shop on the square at Bay Walk across from the Cineplex?"

"Yep, that's where I got it. I cut out a piece of the ashtray the size I needed, shaped it and polished it up, and voila, it worked. It took several tries before I found something to hold the foil on the cone without absorbing most of the light energy. It has to be a glue that dries crystal clear."

Levy asked, "What variations or modifications are you considering now?"

Hamilton gestured toward the ray gun still in Levy's hand. "I'm concentrating on giving it more energy so it'll kill animals larger than cockroaches. I don't want to kill anything I don't have to. But I imagine the Pentagon will try more powerful versions of the ray gun out on mice and rabbits, and then will move up the food chain as far as they can, until they're convinced the ray can be made to kill men...err...Arabs."

Levy said, "I'd like to keep the gun here with me to look at while I write. I think I'm ready to start writing the Provisional application right now." He pointed to the small desk at an angle to the one where he worked. "You need to pull a chair up to this desk and start drawing the views I asked you for."

Levy's desks, somewhat resembling Parson's tables, were made from a pair of matching cherry flush doors that were customized to his specifications. One desk was about twice the size of the other. The desks abutted each other at right angles with the smaller desk facing the office door and the larger one facing a window. His chair was positioned at the intersection between the desks, where he could swivel from the iMac computer on one desk to the matching computer on the other desk.

Levy opened a drawer and removed some drawing instruments. He handed them to Hamilton. "Here's some paper, a draftsman's plastic triangle, a compass and French curve template to help you. Can you do the drawing for me right now?"

"Sure. Will you be insulted if I take off my coat and tie?" Hamilton took off his sport coat and moved the chair he was sitting in up to the desk.

"Of course not. Mine are coming off too." Levy stood up and walked to the door of his office. He removed the garments and draped them on a coat hanger he took from a hook on the back of the door. He returned to his large desk, opened a new file on the screen of the iMac, and started typing with only a nod to Hamilton. The inventor was bent over the smaller desk moving the triangle over a sheet of typing paper as he sketched a drawing of his ray gun. The two worked at their tasks for over two hours with few words being spoken.

Rosalind pushed the office door open and peeked in. "Hey guys, its 2:30. Does anybody want to eat lunch today?"

"I'm not sure we have time to go to a cafe," Levy said.

"For a change, I'll be your gofer today." Walking into the office and approaching Hamilton, she said, "Three G's deli is just across the street and they have—"

Hamilton looked up from his drawing and interrupted. "I've been to Three G's a few times. Please get me a pastrami on rye with hot mustard and lettuce, and iced tea with a lime slice and no sugar."

"How about you, Chief, the usual?"

"Yeah," said Levy. He put his hands behind his head and leaned back in his chair until his spine made an audible crack. "That felt good," he sighed. "When Rosalind gets back, let's take a break and go outside and eat in the little garden on the south side of the building. I can see the light at the end of the tunnel on this draft, so I'm sure I'll finish in time for you to read it over to correct any mistakes or omissions I made. This 75 degree January weather is too wonderful not to go outside and enjoy it."

"OK by me. I think I'm finished with the sketches. Look'em over now and let me know if you need more views?" Hamilton handed two sheets of paper to Levy.

"These two views are just what we need," Levy said. "But now that I think about it, you need to draw the shape of the purple lens. Draw a cross section through the center of the lens and draw another at right angles to the first cross section. Make those two views about five times greater in scale than these." He waved the sketches and handed them back to Hamilton.

"Got it," Hamilton said. He bent back down over a sheet of paper on the desk and began sketching with a French curve. Levy turned back to the iMac on his desk and continued typing.

Chapter 11   Assassins

AFTER THE *AL Khanjar* camp was staffed and running smoothly in the summer of 2002, Gurtenkov was ready to concentrate on selecting, recruiting and training the volunteers capable of becoming secret agents, and eventually suicide bombers, in America. But first he needed to have his assassins already established there.

Gurtenkov disliked Chechens. He blamed the fallout from the Russian failures in Afghanistan and Chechnya for the decline in importance of the KGB. His associates in the organization predicted an easy victory in Chechnya. And the KGB decline forced him into his self-imposed exile in the lands of these idiotic Muslim zealots. But he also respected the Chechen doggedness in fighting for their own independence, which Gurtenkov believed was loosing cause for the Russians. He read the reports on how Chechens did not hesitate to murder innocent non-combatants, women and children. This made them ideal for assignment as the first secret agents Gurtenkov wanted settled in America—the assassins.

Gurtenkov circulated among the Russian intelligence officers in Chechnya, the terms of a bounty he'd pay for the identities of two ruthless men willing and capable of operating as assassins in America. Soon he was told about two Chechen brothers, Zaindin and Ruslan Khilmadof, respectively, twenty-nine and twenty-seven years old. The Russian military authorities imprisoned the men for a brutal murder. They were awaiting their execution for cutting the throat of a Russian officer. When he learned that they spoke Russian and some English, Gurtenkov agreed to pay baksheesh to the prison director to talk to the prisoners on the jailer's phone.

The brothers could not have been more unlike if they had different parents. The elder, Zaindin, was slender and lanky with light blond hair and fair skin. His face was round and handsome with a short straight nose and wide set blue eyes. His facial hair was soft, thin and light colored like the hair on his head. He had a sunny disposition and always seemed to be smiling and laughing at whatever was going on around him. His younger brother, Ruslan, was his opposite in disposition and appearance. He was sullen, withdrawn and easily angered. His moods were frequently so dark and pessimistic that he might be called paranoid in the United States. Curly black hair and thick wiry facial hair made his appearance match his somber moods. He was shorter than his brother having an angular, bony face with a sharp, curved nose, and deep, close-set brown eyes. His skin had a light brown hue, and his ears stuck out like handles on teacups. Both men were muscular, strong and well coordinated.

When Gurtenkov placed the call, the jailer put Ruslan on the line. Gurtenkov spoke to him in English. He said, "Your lives will be spared if you agree to learn to talk like Americans, and learn how to assassinate infidels who stand in the way of a holy Muslim jihad. You'll live a life in America of what I'm sure for you will be luxury." He believed their positive answers were a foregone conclusion.

Ruslan quickly understood the gist of what the caller had in mind. It was an offer the condemned brothers could hardly refuse. He conned Gurtenkov shrewdly. Glancing around to make sure he was out of earshot from any guards, he replied haltingly in broken English, "My brother and me...we was guerrilla fighters. We kill lot of people...men...and women too. We kill them lot of ways. Our father made us to learn to talk American." He assured the Russian he and his brother knew enough of the language to get by in the US.

Gurtenkov was delighted to find what he thought were experienced murderers who could be passed off in America as Cubans. He told Ruslan he'd arrange for him and his brother to be released into his custody. Then they'd be flown to a training camp.

Gurtenkov forbade the brothers from contacting their parents after their escape or to reveal they were alive to anyone who knew them. When Ruslan asked how long they might have to stay in America, Gurtenkov told him their assignment might be more than five years. The Russian assured him that if they completed all of their assignments as ordered, they'd be allowed to stay in America, or they'd be brought back to Chechnya. The choice was theirs.

Ruslan asked, "Can my parents come stay in America if I stay there?"

Gurtenkov said, "That might be possible, but it'll be expensive. And you have to pay all the baksheesh that's required." He knew this wouldn't happen because he planned to have the two brothers murdered on a mafia contract when he no longer needed them.

Gurtenkov paid an enormous baksheesh to have two fire blackened bodies photographed and put on display the next day to support the story of the captive brothers being burned to death in a car hit by a rocket as they tried to escape. The charred bodies were buried in an unmarked grave.

The previous night the two brothers were awakened, handcuffed, hustled into the back of a truck, and covered with a tarpaulin. The truck drove over paved roads for about an hour, then turned and bounced over rough terrain into an open field. The driver uncovered Ruslan and Zaindin and yanked them to their feet. A sleek, jet-black civilian helicopter was whirling its blades nearby. He marched the brothers up to the chopper, and as each put one foot inside its door, his handcuffs were removed. The door slammed behind them and the craft rose into the black sky.

Tawfik Wasaeem, a rail thin, bearded, olive skinned guard wearing baggy camouflage fatigues and a sweat stained turban sat in the back of the craft. He held a 9mm Glock 18 machine pistol and pointed it at the backs of the brothers. They sat between him and a dark skinned pilot, who wore a tan leather flight jacket and a black skullcap. When the pilot started speaking to the guard in Russian, the brother's tension eased. Zaindin started jabbering about how good it felt to be with friends again. Even the scowling Ruslan gave a sigh of relief. Wasaeem pointed his weapon at a thermos and offered them coffee, which they gladly accepted. Zaindin filled cups and passed them out.

Ruslan asked, "Where we going?"

The pilot said, "I don't know beyond the jet landing strip at Makhachkala. That's the capitol of Dagestan." As the sun began to rise in the direction they were heading, the shape of a city became visible on the distant horizon. "There's your next ride." The chopper circled once and put down on a thin strip of tarmac next to a sleek Model 25 Learjet.

The brothers were awestruck. Neither was ever before in an aircraft of any kind. The helicopter ride was a unique and thrilling experience for them. Now the upcoming ride in a luxurious jet was something neither ever expected to experience. Even the usually moody Ruslan had a smile on his face as they said goodbye to their guard and 'copter pilot and stepped out into the emerging daylight. But Wasaeem came out with them and gestured with his Glock toward the jet. A door on its side opened as they approached, and steps were lowered for them. Once they were inside and the door closed, the jet's engines came to life, and they were soon flying low in the sky just above a broken layer of widely spaced clouds.

Ruslan noticed the sun rising on the left side of the jet. "We fly south into trouble, and only Allah knows how bad it is," he said to Zaindin.

When he contacted abu Wagdy to arrange for the baksheesh and the jet to fly Zaindin and Ruslan out of Chechnya, Gurtenkov asked him to find a secure, barren location where the brothers could be isolated and tested.

"They'll be murdered if they fail my tests, and their bodies disposed of," the Russian said.

"What!" abu Wagdy exclaimed. "After paying all those bribes and risking a helicopter and jet to fly them out, how can you even consider murdering them."

"We might have to do it. We can't take the risk the assassins will be cowards or fools. Also, we've got to know how resourceful and creative they are," replied the Russian.

"How can you question whether they are cowards? Haven't they committed many murders?

"Murderers are often the most cowardly killers. It all depends on how and why they kill. Oh, also we will need to watch them while they're being tested. Can you have a video camera and audio transmitter installed there?"

"Maybe. I'll see if we've got a place with electricity and running water."

"No. Neither of those. No modern facilities of any kind," insisted Gurtenkov.

"Then forget about using video or audio equipment."

Late in the afternoon the jet landed at a private airstrip in the desert fifty-five miles north of Riyadh. A Land Rover with tinted windows drove up to the plane, and their gun carrying guard ushered the brothers into the vehicle. The Rover drove several miles over a roadless expanse of sand. It stopped at a small, flat roofed concrete building located in a featureless expanse of desert waste with no other structure or sign of human habitation in sight. The driver ordered bruskly, "Go in there and sit inside until you get further instructions." Then he sped off. Their guard remained with him in the vehicle.

After the Rover disappeared, Zaindin looked around and said, "Let's get out of here and find some way to get back home. Maybe we can find a way back at that landing strip."

Ruslan shook his head. "Don't you understand we're someone's prisoners, and they want to find out if we'll try to escape. This is some kind of test. And we better pass it if we want to be allowed to live."

"You told me we'd have a cushy life in America if we pretended we knew how to kill people."

"I don't think we'll get away with pretending. We're going to have to prove we can do it to get out of here and go to America. After we get to America, we can decide what we want to do."

The building where they were left had one room with a bare concrete floor, a sagging wood door, and two grime encrusted windows that were sealed shut. It was completely empty except for an open topped pail containing about two gallons of warm water, and sitting on the floor, a loaf of moldy bread. They walked in, felt the 120 plus degree temperature, picked up the bucket and bread and walked out into the broiling afternoon sun.

During their fighting with the Chechen guerrillas, the brothers were hungry and thirsty many times. And they lived out of doors for weeks at a time. But they were never in danger of death from heat and dehydration. Ruslan figured out how to cope with their life-threatening situation. From the lowering sun in the west, he knew which side of the building was on the north. There the sand was the coolest because it had been in the shade for the longest time.

They walked around the building to its north side. With their bare hands, they began scooping away the sand next to the building's north wall until they excavated two elongated pits. They dug down to a level where the sand felt cool to their bodies. Zaindin made a pit in the cool sand for the water bucket. They lay down in the long pits and waited for the sun to set. At sunset, Ruslan stood up, walked around the building and opened the door to let in the rapidly cooling night air. He returned to his pit and stretched out in it again.

"Can we get out of these graves now?" Zaindin asked.

"Not yet. Still too hot in there."

Several hours after sunset, the cool desert air made the brothers shiver, so they filled in the pits, picked up the water bucket, and went inside the building. The concrete floor was cool enough to make lying on it tolerable. They thought about breaking the sealed windows, but decided enough cool air came in at night in through the open door.

They left the bucket of water just outside the door where the night air might cool it off more, and they could guard it in case some animal came around. Each brother dipped a hand into the bucket twice for a mouthful of water, then licked the wet hand for any remaining drops and finally dried it on his hair to wring every possible cooling effect from the available moisture. They decided not to eat the moldy bread yet, hoping to be rescued before they got so hungry they wanted it. They slept on the floor in their clothes with their shoes stacked under their heads for pillows. At dawn they walked out into the desert about two hundred yards from the building, scooped holes in the sand with their hands, and relieved themselves. They buried their waste in the sand, so as not to attract flies or other insects

They did nothing all the next day except lie around and sleep, and they became restless. So the second night after the desert cooled down, they walked around hoping to find some animal they could catch and eat. But they did not see another living creature.

The brothers existed like this for two days. Just before sundown at the end of the second day, they brushed the mold off the bread, broke it in half and ate it while resting in the shade in their shallow pits. They each required two big mouths full of water to wash down the vile mass.

Sometime after dark that night, after they fell asleep on the floor, the lights of the Land Rover shinning through the open door of the building woke them up. When they sat up, they saw in the lights of the car, the outline of their guard striding toward the building with his machine pistol in his hand. He stopped short of the door and shouted at them, "Come out here and get in the Rover."

The length of their test was determined in part by how many more days it took to complete the training of the class of recruits at the *al Khanjar* camp. Gurtenkov did not want any of the recruits to learn the identity of the assassins and vice versa.

Believing their ordeal in the desert was over, the two brothers hastily took turns gulping down the rest of the water they had been carefully doling out.

When Zaindin put his mouth on the bucket, Ruslan ordered, "You shut up. I'll do all our talking." The older brother nodded his head in assent. They picked up their shoes and ran out to the vehicle in their socks. When they climbed into the center seats ahead of Tawfik Wasaeem, they saw a squat figure sitting in the passenger seat next to the driver.

The seated figure in the front seat turned half way around and glared at them in the dim light from the bulb in the vehicle ceiling. Gurtenkov was wearing a billed fatigue hat and camouflage fatigues immaculately tailored to fit his lumpy body. He turned to the driver and motioned with his hand for him to turn the Rover around and drive away. "You do not follow orders," he thundered in Russian.

"What orders," the brothers asked almost simultaneously, after which Ruslan stomped on Zaindin's foot and glared at him.

"You were ordered to sit in that building until we gave you other commands."

"We weren't given any orders. Things a car driver says to us are not orders," Ruslan protested. "You need to tell us the chain of command if we've got to follow orders from a driver. If all we did was sit in that building, we'd be dead now from the heat. You didn't fly us all the way here to have us die for no good reason"

Zaindin rolled down a window and looked out. "Where are we anyway?"

"I'm your commander now, and I'll ask the questions. You'll follow my orders even if you die carrying them out. Do you understand that?"

The brothers nodded glumly. They drove back to the desert landing strip, where the Learjet was waiting for them. Everyone climbed up the already lowered steps, the door was closed, and the jet took off. The guard sat behind the brothers with his weapon in his lap.

After the plane leveled off, everyone removed their seat belts, Wasaeem looked at Gurtenkov and raised his eyebrows. The Russian nodded his head, reached under his left arm and removed a banker's special snub-nosed Colt 38 from a holster. He pointed the pistol in the general direction of where the brothers were sitting. The guard stood and went to a refrigerator in the jet's galley kitchen. He reached in and brought out a paper sack containing ice-cold fried chicken parts. He handed the sack to Zaindin, who looked in, smiled and showed its contents to Ruslan.

Ruslan took the sack from his brother, and tore it into two pieces. He wrapped half the chicken parts in one piece of the sack and handed the food to Zaindin. Without offering any chicken to Wasaeem or to Gurtenkov, the brothers quickly wolfed down every morsel of meat. Then they bit the bones in half, sucked out the marrow and licked their fingers. Zaindin smiled, gulped in air and belched loudly, intending it as an Arab's compliment to Gurtenkov for providing food.

"Your training starts right now," the Russian said. "In America, you'd be disgraced by that noise. Never do that again."

"Commander...do I call you commander? We need something to drink," Ruslan said.

Again the Russian nodded to the guard, who stood and went to the kitchen. Wasaeem brought back a gallon thermos jug filled with warm coffee and put down it down with four plastic cups. He filled one cup and gave it to Gurtenkov, and he filled one for himself. The brothers helped themselves, drank a cupful of black coffee, helped themselves to another, and settled down in the jet's bucket seats for the ride to they knew not where. Despite having just drunk two cups of coffee, the brothers soon fell asleep in their comfortable seats. They slept until the jet bumped down on the landing strip at the *al Khanjar* camp. This woke the brothers, and they stared out the windows at the dreary scene.

In the pale morning light, the clouds hung low over the seemingly deserted buildings. Gurtenkov timed things so that no jihad fighters were at the camp. Only a skeleton crew of cooks, armed guards and maintenance workers remained there. But they stayed out of sight. The plane taxied into a large hanger. A rectangular enclosure took up part of one sidewall at the far end of the hanger. Gurtenkov enjoyed a sealed, luxury suite of air-conditioned rooms in the enclosure only he was allowed to use.

Before deplaning Gurtenkov said to Wasaeem, "Take these two to the barracks. We no longer need you as a guard so go practice at the firing range after you eat breakfast" Turning to the brothers, he said, "You bathe, put on the uniforms waiting for you there, and meet me in the mess hall."

Gurtenkov strode to the only door to his suite, punched a code into the keypad of its lock, and went inside. He noticed the blinking light on his answering machine and knew the call came from bin Nazamunde. He had orders to call when he arrived, regardless of the time. So he punched the return call button on his answering machine and sat down on the edge of his bed.

Bin Nazamunde picked up on the third ring and said, "Did you have to murder the two murderers."

"No," Gurtenkov said. "They behaved as well as we could've expected. They didn't try to escape. They saved their energy during the heat of the day and stayed cool by digging pits in the sand down to the cool level. At night they roamed around, presumably looking for food. And they conserved their water and didn't fight over it. They even had a supply of water left when we came for them. I decided it was time to rescue them when they ate the rancid bread. There was no need to risk—"

"How do you know all of this?" bin Nazamunde interrupted.

"They were under surveillance from helicopters we flew near them during the day. At night a squad with night vision binoculars roamed around the concrete hovel."

"How did you know when they ate the bread?"

"The transmitter bug we planted in it stopped broadcasting. That meant someone swallowed the bug and had it in his stomach, or else he ruined it when he chewed it in a piece of the bread. Eating the bread indicated they were becoming desperate, so I decided there was no need to risk harming them. Also, this camp was clear of other trainees by the time we brought them here. The younger one even had enough energy left to argue with me when we first got them into the Rover. I'm optimistic I can develop them into the assassins your jihad needs."

"Keep me informed," the Saudi said as he abruptly ended the call.

Someone knocked on Gurtenkov's door. He opened it, and a corpulent cook in a clean white uniform and white chef's hat came in. He placed a tray on a small table covered with a smooth red tablecloth. Gurtenkov jerked his thumb toward the door, and the cook bowed his head and backed out of the room. He sat down and started eating the crisp bacon and blueberry filled pancakes he drenched with butter and maple syrup. He washed them down with mug of strong American coffee he diluted with fresh cream and two heaping teaspoons of sugar.

Zaindin and Ruslan showered, donned clean, but ill-fitting fatigues, and walked to the mess hall. There they found serving plates loaded with toast, scrambled eggs and orange slices waiting for them on a wooden table having a worn and scratched top. They ate all the food before them and each drank three mugs of black coffee. The brothers were used to military protocol, so they stood up and waited for orders from Gurtenkov when he appeared at the door. He sat down on one side of the table and motioned for them to sit facing him on the opposite side.

"This is what I'll teach you," he said. "You'll learn to defeat locks so you can enter anyone's home or office. I'll show you how to make bombs you can explode by dialing a telephone number. You'll learn American customs and your English will improve. I'll tell you how to live in America without revealing who you really are. I'll teach you how to disguise your appearance so witnesses won't remember what you look like."

He pointed to Ruslan, and said, "Your ears stick out so much they're noticeable. Let your hair grow over them and wear soft caps you can pull down on them."

"Your next assignment will be to Cuba, where you will learn how to earn money to pay some of your living costs, and to prevent appearing suspicious because you'll live too well to be unemployed. We'll pay you much more than you earn so you can live better than you ever have lived before."

Zaindin turned toward his brother and grinned. Ruslan scowled at him and shook his head.

Gurtenkov continued, "When you're in America, you mustn't do anything that'll call attention to you. If we order you to shoot someone, you'll only use cheap hunting rifles you'll throw away after you use them once. The booby traps the Chechen guerillas set are crude compared to what I'll teach you.

Whenever possible, you'll inject sex into the crime scenes you leave behind after you kill. I'll teach you to kill in ways that make your target's deaths look like kinky sex acts that went too far."

Ruslan raised his hand and stood, indicating he wished to speak. Gurtenkov nodded his head. "Why do we have to learn to kill like sex perverts?"

"Most American law enforcement agencies have detective units specializing in sex crimes. For them the sex aspect of a crime will outweigh other factors. So these special units of sex detectives won't be looking for clues leading them to the jihad or our other agents. They won't be able to detect any pattern linking the victims. How many men have you killed with your own bare hands?"

Zaindin grimaced and turned his head to look away. Ruslan looked down at the tabletop and shrugged his shoulders.

"I was afraid of that. So I've bought from the Iranian secret police, three criminals the Khomeini regime has condemned to die. Next week I'll fly them here by helicopter. I'll teach you about the deviate sex techniques that can result in death. You'll practice disguising their deaths as sex accidents by killing each of them with your own hands."

At this, Zaindin stood and rushed into the lavatory. He barely reached a toilet before he threw up everything he ate that morning. He washed his face, gargled with water from the sink, and returned to the table. When the Russian quizzically eyed his now pale face, he said, "I'm sorry. I regret eating too much rich food. I won't make such a pig of myself again."

Gurtenkov knew he was lying. He stood and said, "Let's get to work." He turned his back on the brothers and strode out of the mess hall. And during the next two weeks he taught them every thing he said he would.

Ruslan stoically accomplished his role in the heartless killings with his usual sullen indifference. Zaindin dreaded killing their victims with his own hands. But when he actually killed the first prisoner, he learned it turned him on sexually. And the more his victim suffered the more aroused he became. So by the time the two brothers murdered the third prisoner, Zaindin was eager to get to work in America. In two weeks, Gurtenkov turned a happy-go-lucky, exuberant young man into a sadistic killer. Or did he merely uncage the beast that always lurked in Zaindin's heart and mind. Was it nature or nurture? Or some of both.

When their training at the *al Khanjar* camp was completed, Gurtenkov handed each of them a death button. "We use these tokens to control who your assassination targets'll be. Unless I personally gave you other instructions, I forbid you to kill anyone unless you receive a death button together with a photograph of your target."

The death tokens were uniquely shaped wooden buttons made from solid ebony by a factory in Israel. Gurtenkov purchased their entire production run of ebony buttons in return for the promise not to ever again make identical buttons. He ordered the brothers not to show the buttons to anyone or to reveal for what or how they were used. He shook their hands and told them they'd be flown to Cuba to finish their training.

As he entered the jet to fly back to Riyadh, Gurtenkov said, "You must not speak one word of Russian or any other language except English or Spanish after you leave this training camp."

As a graduation present, Gurtenkov let the brothers spend their last night at the camp with a tall, red headed Scandinavian girl who slept with him during the previous week. He promised the brothers they'd have such rewards on a routine basis when they completed their training in Cuba.

Originally Zaindin dreaded his assignment as a killer in America. But he was so turned on by the murders he participated in and by having sex with the red head, who was for him an exotic creature, that he eagerly looked forward to the pleasures coming with his life in America. Ruslan remained his same morose self, and brooded pessimistically about their new life.

Chapter 12   Cuban

THE DAY FOLLOWING Gurtenkov's departure a truck with the two brothers in the back drove across the eastern border of Iran into Pakistan. They were let out of the truck at an unpaved landing strip in a barren landscape surrounded by low brown hills. They sat on the packed clay strip until a jet cargo plane landed and bounced to a stop near them. The pilot got out and urinated in dirt. He told them to get in and find a place to sit or lie down among the boxes of goods inside the hold. During the next two days, they were transferred from one plane to another until one finally landed at Cayo Coco, Cuba.

In the small, thatched-roof airport terminal building, a short, stocky, man wearing a Cuban army Major's insignia came up to them. "Follow me," he said in English. They walked out to a waiting Jeep. The uniformed customs agents never even looked in their direction.

The Major drove the brothers over the 17 kilometer stone causeway from the island to the Cuban mainland. Then he drove down A4 through the interior of the island to the outskirts of Pinar del Rio City in the westernmost province having the same name. He motioned for them to get out, and the Major drove off in the Jeep without ever having given his name or asked for theirs.

A new mentor, Alont O'Durea, waited for them with three bicycles. He was a forty one year old native Cuban with a slim body and no facial hair. He had a wide deep forehead beneath his abundant and curly black hair. His nose was flat and his brown eyes close set. He was the same height as Ruslan, and his skin was a shade lighter. He wore faded denim shorts, a soiled Miami Dolphins tee shirt, and dirty, worn canvas topped shoes. He once worked for the KGB in the United States under Gurtenkov's control until the FBI began to follow him. Then he fled back to his native land.

He pointed to two of the bicycles and said, "I'll be your trainer while you're in Cuba. Get on the bikes; follow me."

"Who are you?" Zaindin asked.

"I just told you. My name's O'Durea, and that's what you'll call me."

They followed him, peddling through the city and out of its northern side into the foothills of the Sierra del Rosario Mountains. After going up and down many hills, they finally arrived at a large wooden building in a poor state of repair. The structure looked as if it might have been a hotel in its better days. O'Durea told them they'd learn skills useful in America when they helped him fix the building up. And working as repairmen was part of their cover story.

The brothers were exhausted from their journey, and wanted only to sleep after eating a meal of black beans and rice they washed down with ice-cold Cuban beer. But before he took them to their room, O'Durea made them sign several papers he said were required to get them a bank account and credit cards at a Miami bank that did not ask its Cuban customers any questions. O'Durea said, "I've bought fake social security cards, Alabama driver's licenses, and Florida birth certificates for your new identities. Zaindin, now you're name's Juan Alveraze. Ruslan, now you're Pedro Ganzolez. Those are the only names you'll use from now on. And we'll work on smoothing the way you speak American."

Gurtenkov didn't want the brothers doing any kind of work requiring getting their fingerprints on file. So during the next week O'Durea taught them how to use lawn and ground maintenance equipment. "Both legal and illegal dark skinned immigrants who don't speak English well are often hired for that type of work. But the outdoor work won't be available for you during the winter months in most parts of the country. So I'll teach you how house painters work in America." He used sets of modern tools and brushes, and five-gallon cans of paints and stains he'd brought back from a trip he made to Florida. But ground maintenance was going to be their main work. And they could get a few jobs painting for homeowners because painters didn't have to be licensed in America.

Their ground maintenance and painting chores were interspersed with Spanish and English lessons, and they learned to drive American cars and trucks. The brothers sometimes dressed as tourists, and O'Durea guided them into nearby hotels and resorts where they observed how the wealthy behaved. After their credit cards and bank checks arrived in Cuba, they used the credit card to rent a room for a night, eat at a restaurant, and buy new shoes. Pedro continued as the leader of the two brothers.

One evening Gurtenkov phoned. "How well do the brothers blended in with the foreign tourists?"

O'Durea said, "Excellent. I've told them whenever anyone in America speaks to them in Spanish, to say they're Americans now, and Americans should speak only American. Besides, speaking Spanish reminds them of how bad their lives were in Cuba. I think they'll be able to pass as Cubans."

Gurtenkov said, "Good. Take them to Florida, and get them established in Chicago. I'll decide whether to let them live or die, depending on how well they eliminate their first target. You still have the Mafia connections, don't you, for when I decide we don't need them any more?"

"Of course."

"Buy them a couple of days with some girls as a reward for completing their training. I want them to get hooked enjoying a better life than they had before, so they'll have to depend on me to pay their bills. Tell them not to become friends with any one. Tell them not to date any girls. The jihad will pay for their sex needs. We'll pay for one woman every other week. Tell them not to use any of those women more than once. We'll do the same thing for all our agents. We don't want them to be friends with or to become attached to anyone except the agent they're paired with. That's it for now."

After two days of enjoying their graduation present with four different girls, O'Durea told Juan and Pedro to dress like tourists for the trip to Florida. They donned colorful open necked shirts, khaki pants and Chicago Bulls caps. O'Durea was similarly dressed, and he gave them blue plastic windbreakers like the one he was wearing.

O'Durea said, "A cab'll drive us to the coast. We'll cross the Straights of Florida in an open boat tonight, and it'll be colder on the water than it is here."

Late that afternoon a dented Ford of some unknown ancient vintage drove up to the entrance of the now partially refurbished hotel. It shuddered to a stop and belched a plume of blue smoke out of its tailpipe. The shabbily dressed driver got out and with a pair of rusty pliers unwired the trunk lid so they could stow the canvas gym bags containing their clothes. Then he wired the trunk shut again, the three men got in and the cabbie drove north through the mountains to the wharf at Puerto Esperanza.

There they boarded a beautiful Express Cruiser as the sun set behind a bank of low clouds. The boat's captain was tall, deeply tanned, and European looking. He wore a black, custom fitted jacket with "Captain Clint" embroidered on its breast pocket. The moment his passengers were all on board, Captain Clint pressed forward the throttle of the idling engine, and the sleek boat roared into the Straights of Florida.

The clouds hid the moon and stars as they sped over the black water. A slight breeze produced a light chop the passengers hardly felt. About two hours after they left Cuba, the boat's captain slowed and stopped his craft. He took out a cell phone and made a call. He jotted numbers down on a tablet, and turned on his GPS receiver. He changed course and headed toward a rendezvous with another boat.

An hour later he slowed the boat and blinked a flashlight five times. No one answered. He turned and blinked his light again in a slightly different direction. Still no answer. He stopped the boat and climbed up on to the cowling covering the bow. He blinked his light again and this time an answering light flickered in the blackness a mile or more to the starboard. He motored cautiously toward where the light had answered. The running lights of a smaller sport fishing boat soon came into view, and he edged his boat toward them. The two captains were trying to get their boats to touch each other in the choppy water. They finally succeeded in holding the vessels against each other momentarily at intervals by engaging the gunwales with boat hooks.

O'Durea uttered a hasty, "C'mon," as he tumbled head first over the side into the bouncing fishing boat. He waved his arm gesturing for Juan and Pedro to follow him. They easily jumped aboard over the gunwales. The boat hooks were disengaged, and the two vessels took off in opposite directions.

There were no seats in the open cockpit of the Grady White Islander they boarded. Oren Finney, the captain, pointed to folding chairs stacked against the port gunwale. "Open those up and have a seat," he said. "We'll get there before the sun comes up." Finney was a short white haired man with a neatly trimmed beard of the same color. Only his tanned face was visible from under the dingy, crinkled oilskin slicker and pants he wore over his clothes.

They motored in silence into the Gulf of Mexico. Juan and Pedro dozed off and on while sitting slumped in their chairs. Finally, before there was any hint of the approaching sunrise, lights shining from a distant shore of Marco Island appeared on their starboard side. Finney spun the wheel, and the boat veered toward the lights. He slowed to a crawl when they entered a no wake zone near shore, and made a wide turn bringing the boat to a short private dock jutting into the water from a large, two-story house on S. Barfield Drive.

"Jump out and throw me those lines," Finney said to Juan and Pedro, who quickly obeyed. Turning to O'Durea, he said, "Pay me and I'll give you the keys to the car. I paid four thousand dollars for it and registered the title in your name."

O'Durea stepped on to the dock, and opened his gym bag. He counted out seventy, one hundred dollar bills, and handed them to Finney.

"Your three big is in here," he said handing the wad to Finney. "I'll need you again for the trip back. I'll let you know when. I'll be alone, so you'll only get a thousand."

"At your service," Finney said. He saluted with one hand and held out a ring of car keys with the other. "It's the blue 1993 Pontiac Grand AM parked on the street in front of my house." Chuckling to himself, he turned away from them and started his routine for putting his boat to bed. The other three walked around his house and got into their car as the first glimmer of sunlight began to penetrate the darkness.

O'Durea drove up Barfield Drive to state route 951, which he took north to I-75, where he turned east toward Miami. A few miles past Golden Gate, he stopped the car and told Juan to start driving. Reassured of Juan's ability to drive on an American highway, at the first rest stop on Alligator Alley, he told him to pull in and stop the car. He woke Pedro, who was sleeping in the back seat, and told him to drive. Pedro's driving showed he too was a capable driver, so at the last rest stop on the Alley he told Pedro to pull in and stop. Pedro slid over to the passenger seat, lowered it all the way back and slept again.

O'Durea drove the rest of the way. He exited the Alley on to I-595 and turned south at Davie on to I-95, which he followed to US 1. This took him into South Miami, where he turned east at Pinecrest. He drove down the street to a small house coated with fresh white stucco having a neatly trimmed, deep green lawn. He removed a garage door opener from his gym bag, pressed its button and drove up the driveway into the garage as the door moved out of his way. He pressed the button lowering the door and woke up Juan and Pedro.

During the next week O'Durea taught the brothers how to find work and live inconspicuously in the United States. He transferred the Pontiac's title to Pedro, and obtained insurance from an agent who did not ask Cubans any questions. They opened separate bank accounts, and learned to use ATM cards to get cash from their accounts. O'Durea assured them they'd always have a balance of about one thousand dollars in each account. He bought them a supply of prepaid cell phones they had to use when they needed to talk to him or Gurtenkov. He also bought them a small laptop computer and taught them how to get on the Internet at rentable WIFI access locations, from which they could communicate with him.

O'Durea knew many of their victims were going to be Midwesterners. So he told Pedro to drive them to Chicago to find a place to live. They packed their clothes and possessions, and loaded them into the Pontiac's trunk. Pedro bought a map of the United States, and the three men got in after O'Durea closed up the house. Without any assistance from O'Durea, the two brothers took turns driving and successfully followed the map to Chicago by staying on the interstate highways. There they rented a one-bedroom apartment in a four flat brick building on Archer Avenue in a Hispanic neighborhood in the 25th ward.

The Cuban wished them good luck and told them to call him on his cell phone whenever they needed advice or help. Then he cautioned, "A few final words of advice. If you carry out your assignments successfully, you'll be rewarded well, like I am. But never forget you're working for the most ruthless people on this earth. If you double cross them or betray them to the Americans, they'll hunt you down and kill you in a cruel way. And there's nowhere in the world for you to hide. They have connections to the underworld and crime syndicates in every country." He took a taxi to Midway Airport and flew back to Naples to arrange his return trip to Cuba.

No sooner was O'Durea's taxi out of sight than the two brothers began talking to each other in their native dialect of Russian. They drove to a Starbucks Coffee shop providing wireless Internet access and set up the required T-Mobile HotSpot account. They remembered their cousin, Dikalue Nashkoev, used his full name for his internet address, so they sent him an email revealing they were alive and well in America. They asked Dikalue to tell this to their parents but not to anyone else. Their lives might be in danger if the Russians found out they were still alive. They said they'd send their parents more information in the future. Then they looked for a girl to buy for the night with some of the cash O'Durea left with them.

Chapter 13   Agents

GURTENKOV RECRUITED CANDIDATES for assignment as secret agents in America from among the English-speaking terrorists training at the *al Khanjar* camp. These were intelligent, educated men who volunteered to become suicide bombers. He kept them at the camp after they completed their basic training.

One at a time, they were scheduled for a motivation interview with Muhamed Allah Yatakalan. Abduhl Ariann, wearing a white robe and turban trimmed in gold, ushered each of them into a small, windowless, high ceilinged room at one end of the white stucco building used as the camp mosque. He told the candidate to sit in the chair facing away from the door; it was upholstered in leather soft enough to feel like velvet. Thick white, odorless animal skins completely covered the floor. The door, walls and ceiling were painted with shiny gold enamel. An empty chair identical to the one on which the candidate was sitting faced him across a pedistalled ebony table inlayed with abstract geometrical patterns. An inlaid flange extended downwardly for about six inches from the flat top of the table.

A copy of the Qur'an lay open on the table. Gas flames effused from jets high in the walls illuminating the room. The flickering flames reflecting off the walls and ceiling gave the room a heavenly glow. When the heavy door was closed, the room was completely sound proof. All the candidate could hear was the beating of his own heart and the sound of his own breathing.

Each candidate was kept waiting for ten minutes, and then Abduhl Ariann entered and placed an ornately decorated coffee urn and two matching cups on the ebony table. The sweet scent of strong Arabian coffee in the urn quickly filled the room. A hidden camera showed the candidate's every movement on a TV monitor located in Muhamed Allah Yatakalan's office. Any candidate reaching for the coffee was dismissed from the program. Ten to twenty minutes later, after the candidate appeared to show signs of stress, the door opened.

Muhamed Allah Yatakalan entered, closed the door, and glided past the candidate. He stood beside the empty chair facing the candidate.

Muhamed Allah Yatakalan appeared as a Grand Imam dressed in a gold brocade robe extending from his chin to the top of his sandals. The outline of a dagger was embroidered with thick black threads in the center of his chest. A four-inch wide sash woven from gold threads cinched the robe. On his head he wore a matching gold turban fringed in bright red. The flickering light and his grey beard made his jet black eyes seem enormous. The candidate usually jumped to his feet and stared at the imposing figure before him. The Imam smiled at the candidate, sat and motioned with his hand for him to also sit. He poured them each a cup of coffee, and pointed to the Qur'an of the table between them.

"Allah has put every word in the Qur'an into my head," he said. "Find verses you like and we will recite them together." Muhamed Allah Yatakalan demonstrated his mastery of the words in the holy book. He captured the candidate's eyes in his gaze; few ever looked away once this Imam locked on to their eyes with his.

"You have special talents making you a candidate eligible for carrying out a mission for the jihad that is much more important than merely blowing up infidels and heathens. As the Wahhabi Imams have already told you, the jihad you have entered was started by the holy profit Muhammad over a thousand years ago, and his jihad has never stopped. The infidels and heathens have escaped the will of Allah because the devil taught them how to develop accursed technologies. When the infidels had only horsemen with swords and arrows, Allah's jihadists defeated them. But when they developed technologies using explosives and engines, our brave men never obtained the weapons or training they needed to prevail.

That has all changed now. Allah has revealed to me how to use technologies developed by the infidels against them. Only after the very last infidel and the very last heathen have been converted to Islam, or have been killed for refusing to convert, will Allah's final objective be reached. Successful completion of your mission will bring that glorious day closer. You will learn how to destroy structures vital to the fundamental workings of the cursed American society that has infected the rest of the world with its greed and individualism."

The Grand Imam paused and lifted his coffee cup to judge the impact of his words. He nodded permitting the candidate to drink. If he deemed the candidate's reactions acceptable, he continued, "You have pledged your life to the fulfillment of your mission. You know the rewards that await you in paradise after you give your life for the jihad. The questions I must ask you now are the most difficult you will ever have to answer."

Muhamed Allah Yatakalan would rise from his chair and stared down at the seated candidate. "The questions are these. Are you are willing to delay receiving your rewards in paradise for at least a year, or maybe for many years, and are you willing to live among the infidels during the time you delay your entry into heaven? And are you willing to pretend you are an infidel during the time your entry into paradise is being delayed?"

He raised his hand and silenced any candidate who started to speak at this point. "What you will be assigned to do for the jihad will be much more difficult than merely using your body to deliver a bomb. You will have to live a life of frustration until the time is right for you to explode a bomb and enter paradise." No candidate ever answered "no" at this time. The spell binding eyes and visage of the imposing Imam standing before him captured the mind of each of them.

Before leaving the camp each agent candidate had another session with Muhamed Allah Yatakalan. The Imam affirmed for them that when they were in America, they were fighting the enemies of Islam and their efforts were as important as those of any terrorist firing a gun or rocket launcher. Consequently when the agents were in America disguised as its citizens, he relieved them of their duty to perform the rituals of Islam whenever doing so might reveal their true identity or compromise their mission. They were told to dress and to groom themselves, and to behave like Americans. Those candidates who continued to profess their willingness to postpone their entry into paradise to accomplish their mission were flown to Cuba for further training by O'Durea.

Each was paired with a compatible agent candidate. Those candidates O'Durea thought unsuitable were flown back to the *al Khanjar* camp and sent on a suicide mission. He taught each pair of successful candidates the things they needed to know in order to work as under cover agents in the United States.

O'Durea showed them the death button they could use to call on the assassins to eliminate anyone who deduced their agent identity or stood in the way of completion of their mission. He told them, "The procedure is first to contact me with an explanation of who and why someone should be killed. I will contact Gurtenkov and obtain his approval of the killing. If he approves your death request, I will send you a death button together with instructions on how to call in the assassins. Muhamed Allah Yatakalan sanctioned the use of death buttons as a fatwa for the benefit of the jihad."

Each pair of agents was transported to Florida in Oren Finney's fishing boat together with O'Durea, who set them up with cars, bank accounts and cell phones in a medium sized city near their ultimate target. The agents did not know their targets at this time. They only knew they had to place explosive charges on their bodies and also hide other bombs somewhere to blow up structures important to the American economy. To throw any investigation off the track in the event an agent was apprehended and unmasked, O'Durea hinted their targets were bridges.

After the program for selecting, training and dispatching secret agents to America was successfully operating for more than a year, bin Nazamunde summoned Gurtenkov to his office. Sami Insien, garbed as a computer programmer in jeans and a tee shirt, was already seated at one end of his desk. Bin Nazamunde started speaking as soon as the Russian passed through the door. "I see from the reports that you have sent several pairs of agents to America, but you have not sent any that will be alone. I told you to send in some single agents to reduce the cost."

Gurtenkov strode slowly to a one of the plush chairs directly across from where bin Nazamunde sat, but the Russian remained standing. "And I told you it is asking too much of men willing to die for your jihad to live alone as infidels. Anyone sufficiently committed to your jihad to blow himself up along with innocent bystanders will go insane from loneliness, frustration and guilt if he doesn't have someone he can talk to who has the same motivation. But I didn't forget my promise to you that I'd send in one lone agent."

The Russian sat down and stared at his employer, with hostility in his eyes. "I finally found a young engineer at the camp who speaks English almost as if it were his native language. He has a withdrawn personality. He seldom if ever seeks the company of other young men or women. And he's deeply committed to and observant of the practice of Islam. He volunteered for a suicide mission. So we'll have to convince him he can serve the jihad better by staying alive.

We need to find out how difficult it will be to assign some agents to infiltrate the United States government. Some day I want to have agents working in the Pentagon and at the FBI. But first we need an easier target. I read that the United States Patent Office is having difficulty in its attempts to recruit engineers and scientist because a government agency can't compete with the wages and glamour of working for private industry or a law firm. So the Patent Office will be our first target for getting an agent into the American Government."

Bin Nazamunde shook his head and scowled, "This sounds like a foolish waste of a skilled terrorist and a waste of the money required to establish him in America."

"Give me some credit for knowing what I am doing," Gurtenkov's anger evident from his tone. "We'll learn if our agents can qualify for advanced security clearance in a Government agency. Also, we'll have our agent in the Patent Office assigned to study weapons and weapon systems. Maybe we'll find out about weapon developments before they can be used against our men. Maybe we'll shorten the time needed to learn to use the latest weapons. And maybe we'll get information about American weapons we can trade to the Chinese or Iranians for something we want from them."

Bin Nazamunde nodded imperceptibly indicating his grudging approval.

"I've always told you I believe there's a great risk of loosing any agent who works alone. This agent will be told his assignment will be to gather information about weapons. He will not know anything about the network of human bombers we're setting up. So if this agent is discovered, it won't jeopardize your basic objective of destroying the American economy by shutting down their electricity grids. I'm only sending him in by himself because you insist on having an agent who works alone." Gurtenkov squirmed slightly in his chair.

Noting the Russian's discomfort, Nazamunde smiled inwardly to himself. "How will he be able to get a security clearance without the Americans detecting he's in the country illegally?"

"He'll enter the US via the Cuban route like all the rest of our agents. But he'll be the only one with O'Durea at the time. He won't know there are any other agents in America, and no other agent will know he exists."

Sami Insien broke in, "My hackers are cracking into the records identifying engineering graduates at large American universities. We'll find one who's about the same age and size as our agent and who has no family…no parents or brothers or sisters or wife."

"O'Durea and the assassins will make the engineer we choose disappear," Gurtenkov said. "They'll kill him and bury his body where it will never be found. No one will report him as a missing person. Our agent will take over his identity. The records backing up our agent will already be in place when he arrives in America. We'll take the dead engineer's driver's license, credit cards, bank checks and other forms of identification, and we'll replace any required photos with forgeries." He turned and grinned at Sami, revealing his crooked teeth.

Bin Nazamunde showed impatience as he asked, "Doesn't the FBI send investigators to interview references when an American seeks a high security clearance, and what if the dead engineer's fingerprints are on file?"

Gurtenkov turned back toward bin Nazamunde and his nodding head affirmed the relevance of the questions. "The fingerprint files in America have been collected in the FBI's Integrated Automated

Fingerprint Identification System. They call it their IAFIS. Other information on criminals is collected in what the Americans call a National Agency Check." Gurtenkov rubbed two fingers with his thumb. "We'll pay someone baksheesh to search IAFIS and do a National Agency Check so we can screen out any engineers whose fingerprints are on file or who are named in any criminal records. Our agent will seek an intermediate security clearance that only requires IAFIS and National Agency Check investigations. When our agent is fingerprinted, his prints will be the ones entered under the name he's taken from the dead engineer. After he's been cleared for an intermediate security position, we'll find a way to get him moved up to a higher security status."

Sami moved to where he could look at bin Nazamunde face, trying to capture his eyes. "I insist that our agent get the Top Secret security clearance," he said. "Information he'll send me will give my hackers what they need to crack the US Patent Office files. I want him to have access to all of their files, so I'll have the codes that'll let me to open all their files too. They use software which has no defenses my hackers can't get passed. I'll be able to make millions for the jihad with the information I get out of the so called secret Patent Office files."

"That is wonderful news, Sami," bin Nazamunde said, turning toward him and smiling for the first time. "I agree we should find a way to move up this agent's security clearance. Keep me informed on what he does and how many dollars you make off the information he gets for you." Facing Gurtenkov he said impatiently, "And you find a way to use more single agents for assignments like that one. Now, both of you...get out."

As he walked through the office door, Gurtenkov just shook his head and marveled at how naive bin Nazamunde and Sami were in relying on a young, inexperienced agent to perform a mission from which they expected to earn millions.

The date was August 20, 2003.

Chapter 14   Receipt

ABOUT FORTY MINUTES after Levy and Hamilton decided to eat their lunch outside, Rosalind returned with sandwiches. "One pastrami on rye with lettuce and hot mustard for you," she said gesturing toward Hamilton. "And one turkey on whole wheat with lettuce and tomatoes and ketchup for the Skipper." She put the bag and drink cups from Three G's down on the smaller of the desks.

"Come on, let's go eat these out in the garden," Levy said. He picked up the bag of sandwiches. "I think I've got a solution to the murdering Arabs problem."

Hamilton picked up the cups.

The two men left the office, walked down the stairs to the outside door, which opened into a garden where a round, redwood picnic table was partially sheltered from the sun by the overhanging branches of a Ficus tree. The garden is a square oasis of green foliage with red and yellow impatiens in the concrete and asphalt covering downtown St. Petersburg. They sat facing each other on benches on opposite sides of the table. Levy took his sandwich from the bag, and handed to other one to Hamilton. Both were hungry. They removed the wrappers, and both put their elbows on the table and leaned into their food. They chewed in silence for a couple of minutes.

Levy put down his sandwich, took a drink of water and said, "I want to help you accomplish your goal of letting everyone know you've revenged your son's murder. Will you be satisfied if the archives of the United States, in other words in a permanent record maintained by the US government, if it said Arnold Hamilton invented a death ray gun he wanted to be used to murder Arabs?"

Hamilton finished chewing a bite and washed it down with a sip of his iced tea. "Yes. That's exactly what I want my patent to say."

Levy nodded slowly, "Let's talk...just talk...right now about the Provisional patent application   we're going to file this afternoon. You can instruct me to have Rosalind type in the title 'A Death Ray for Murdering Arabs.' And Arnold Hamilton will appear as the name of the inventor of the death ray in your Provisional patent application. So, after the Patent Office processes the Provisional application, the records of the United Sates will contain the statement that Arnold Hamilton invented a death ray for murdering Arabs. Will that accomplish your objective?" Levy picked up his sandwich and took another bite.

"Will I be able to show my friends a record certified by the government saying I want my death ray gun used to murder Arabs?"

Levy wiped his mouth with a paper napkin. "The Patent Office will send us an Official Filing Receipt having your name, Arnold Hamilton, printed on it, as the inventor of A Death Ray for Murdering Arabs. You can do what ever you want to with the Filing Receipt. But now we need to talk about the Utility patent the Patent Office will issue to you sometime in the future, about a year or two from now."

Hamilton looked confused and muttered, "I thought we were talking about my patent."

"No," said Levy shaking his head. "We were talking about the Provisional patent application, we're going to file in the Patent Office today so no one can steal your invention after you tell them about it. We'll file the complete, regular Utility patent application a few weeks from now. And you need to understand that the title of the Utility patent application and the title of the final patent issued to you will not have the words murder, or murdering or killing or Arab or Arabs in it."

Hamilton still looked confused, so Levy paused to let what he just said sink in. He continued, "The Official Rules of Practice of the Patent Office won't permit use of inflammatory words, and the Rules of the Patent Office have the same force as a law passed by Congress and signed by the President. They simply will not let anything get out implying the Government is condoning or giving someone the right to murder anyone, an Arab or not. Does that make sense to you?"

Hamilton slowly inclined his head. "But I'll always have the Official Filing Receipt saying Arnold Hamilton invented a death ray for murdering Arabs. Is that right?" His doubt evident from his tone.

"Yes, you will." Levy affirmed enthusiastically. "But I need for you say to me you understand the final Utility patent, not an application, but the final patent describing our invention in detail will not say anything about killing or murdering anyone, and it will not have the words Arab or Arabs in it. Will you please tell me that is clear to you." Levy stared inquiringly at Hamilton.

Hamilton smiled back at him. "I'll have one Official record from the Patent Office saying what I want it to, and I can show it to anyone I choose, but the final patent I'll get won't say anything about Arabs, or murder. Yes, I understand that."

Both men resumed eating, and when they were done, Levy said, "O.K., lets get back to my office and finish this thing off." He stood up from the table, crumpled his paper napkin in his hands and brushed the sandwich crumbs from his lap.

Levy took a key from his pocket and unlocked an exit door in the office building. The two men entered and walked up the flight of stairs to the second floor where the attorney's office was located. They entered the outer room where Rosalind sat at her desk. She stood and handed a draft of the provisional patent application papers to each of them.

"While we read these over, you prepare the Cover Sheet for the Provisional," Levy said to her. "Mr. Hamilton will sign the Cover Sheet as the inventor. Put in his home address, but use our box number at the private mail forwarding service as the return mailing address. My name and the address of this office will not appear in this Provisional application. Prepare a power of attorney for me, but we won't mail it in to the Patent Office unless something comes up and I have to act for Mr. Hamilton."

She raised her eyebrows. "What's up, Chief?"

"I'll explain it all later, Rosalind."

Pointing toward the open door, Levy said to Hamilton, "Now let's go into my office and give this a final read before it's faxed to Winters for filing today." He handed a copy of the application to Hamilton. They each pulled out a chair and sat down, Levy at the larger desk and Hamilton at the smaller one. They looked down and concentrated on proof reading the application draft. Thirty minutes later the two men walked into the outer room and each handed Rosalind his copy of the draft with a few words changed.

"Is this one O.K. by you?" she said to Levy as she held up the draft with Hamilton's changes.

"Yes. I've read it over."

Levy picked up two typed pages from Rosalind's desk and walked back into his office. He hand the papers to Hamilton. "Here are the documents for you to sign. One is the Cover Sheet every Provisional patent application's got to have. The other is a Power of Attorney for me, in case I have to do something else after the Provisional is filed."

Hamilton sat down and read the papers Levy handed to him. "I don't see your name anywhere on this paper," he said holding up the Cover Sheet.

Levy remained standing. "My name doesn't have to be on it, only your name and residence address, and a mailing address. My name and address'll be on the complete Utility patent application when we file it in about a month. In the mean time you'll have a copy of the Provisional patent application you can show the Pentagon officers or anyone else you want involved in developing your death ray gun. You'll be protected because the Provisional patent application will already be on file in the Patent Office by the end of today."

Hamilton signed the two documents and stood up. "What about that official Filing Receipt that says I invented a death ray for murdering Arabs. When'll I get that?"

"The Patent Office will mail it to us in about four to six weeks, and I'll send it to you after it arrives. In the mean time I'll prepare the Utility application, and we can meet again to go over it and have you sign the formal papers."

Hamilton handed the signed papers to his attorney. "So we're through here for today. What do I owe you for this work?"

"I'll prepare a bill at the end of the day with all of the charges, the Patent Office fee and Winter's charge for hand carrying the Provisional application in for filing. Also, I'll include an estimated charge for preparing Utility application, including the draftsman's charges and the Patent Office filing fee."

"Gimme a ball park estimate."

"About five thousand."

Hamilton plucked a silver pen from the chest pocket of his shirt. "I'll just write you a check for that amount right now, and you can deduct the charges from it as we go along."

"Wonderful, it's a pleasure doing business with you."

Hamilton bent over and removed a checkbook from his shiny leather suitcase. He made out the check and handed it to Levy.

"I'll let you know how the meeting goes tomorrow at the Pentagon."

"Good," Levy said. "I'll send your sketches of the death ray gun to a draftsman and begin writing the Utility application when the formal drawings come back from him."

The two men walked from Levy's office into Rosalind's outer office, where Levy put the two papers Hamilton signed on her desk and motioned toward the fax machine. She picked the Cover Sheet up and began faxing the Provisional patent application papers to Winter's office in Crystal City, Virginia.

Levy picked up two copies of the Provisional patent application from Rosalind's desk and handed them to Hamilton. He put them into his suitcase.

Hamilton hooked the forefinger of his left hand into the collar of his sport coat and slung it over his shoulder. He held out his right hand, which Levy took, and the men shook hands. Hamilton waved to Rosalind and said, "Seeya," as he walked through the door and out of the office.

When Hamilton was gone long enough to be out of hearing range, she looked up from the fax machine and said to Levy, "What's gong on with this business about murdering Arabs, and why don't you want to file this Provisional application naming you as the attorney of record?"

Levy walked over to where each of them could see the other's face as Rosalind continued at the fax machine.

"First about being named as attorney, it's the title that bothers me," he said. "I don't want my name associated with a title having the words murder and Arabs in it. It isn't required for any Patent Examiner to look at this Provisional, so probably no one will pay attention to the title. I'll have to put the official serial number of the Provisional application and today's date in the file of the Utility patent application, but I can leave out the Provisional title. This way Hamilton gets a piece of paper he can use to show his friends he's avenging his son's murder, but I don't get identified as the attorney who wrote up an application with an illegal title."

Levy held out hands in a gesture of helplessness. "Second, about why he insists on that title saying he's murdering Arabs, it's a long sad story, and I'll tell you all about it tomorrow. The short version is an Arab terrorist shot his son in the back and killed him."

Rosalind opened her mouth and looked up at him. "Oh my God. That poor man. I am so sorry to hear that."

Levy touched her shoulder with one finger. "After Winters acknowledges he's got everything he needs to get the Provisional application on file today, let's get out of here. I can still get in half an hour hitting chip shots and putting on the practice green before Susan'll expect me to get home."

Chapter 15   Unique

AS SOON AS he entered elementary school in Saudi Arabia, Hamde Jawade was recognized as a precocious boy with exceptional intelligence and learning ability. His teachers and relatives held high expectations for what the unique youngster should accomplish. They gave Hamde extra assignments and moved him to a higher grade as soon as he covered the curricula at each grade level.

This brought Hamde into contact with boys who were older, larger and more mature. And they tormented Hamde both mentally and physically. Even his parents criticized him when he was not the top student in any subject. This changed him from the happy, laughing, exuberant child he was before he started school, into a withdrawn loner who avoided other children and seldom spoke unless someone spoke to him first.

He learned English before any of his classmates, and vented his frustration by cursing his tormentors in it. They just laughed at him and the unknown words. Hamde stopped this way of releasing his anger when he moved ahead to a grade where the other boys knew enough English to understand him. Although he was well coordinated and strong for his size, he refused to compete in soccer against the larger boys in his classes. He exercised alone in his room with hand weights, and ran for miles by himself in the Arabian heat.

The practice of Islam was not an important factor in Hamde's upbringing. His parents, Jenni and Raule Jawade, were wealthy intellectuals who gave lip service to their adherence to the religion. Only when it made them look good to someone they wanted to impress did Raule attend services at a mosque. Raule and Jenni dressed in western garb except when to do so offended someone important to them.

The family traveled frequently to Spain and England. And once, when he was nine, they took Hamde with them on a cruise ship sailing from Tangier to New York City. The family stayed for a week in a hotel overlooking Central Park, before flying back to Riyadh, with stops in London and Paris.

They spent their days in New York at its museums: MOMA, Guggenheim, Natural History, Metropolitan, and Hall of Science. At night they went to Broadway shows and the opera. They ate at the most expensive restaurants in the city. The crowds of people everywhere they went appalled Hamde, and the taxi rides terrified him. The ways in which the American ladies revealed their bodies shocked him. He was glad when they left, and eager to get back to Saudi Arabia, even though there was no joy in his life of loneliness there.

When Hamde finished college preparatory academy at age fourteen, his father gave him his first sexual experience as a graduation present. He drove to a run down building in a part of the capitol city where immigrant workers lived. They walked up the drab stairway and entered a small two-room apartment.

Most Arab men regard obese women as the most sexually attractive. So some Arab parents subject their daughters to gavage, a force-feed technique similar to the process used by the French to fatten geese to make foie gras. Raule Jawade introduced Hamde to his favorite call girl, who was an obese 150 kilograms. Her nickname was the Vase. She motioned for Hamde to follow as she waddled into a windowless room carpeted in bright red with matching red walls. The ceiling was completely covered with abutting mirrors.

The Vase dropped the flimsy robe barely covering her bulk, and lay face up on a large round bed with her short arms and legs extended outwardly to the side like a giant turtle beached on its back. Her undersized breasts looked like pimples on the bloated mass of her body. Hamde was through in less than five minutes.

The only thing she said was, "Wonderful, wonderful, wonderful," as he finished, but he knew she was faking satisfaction.

The experience reminded Hamde of the times when, as a small child, he climbed up on top of a large beach ball and bounced up and down. He was intrigued by the way the woman's rolls of fat jiggled.

He lingered beside her creating ripples by poking her belly with his fingers.

Soon she scolded, "That's enough of your finger jabs. Pull up your pants and leave."

After Hamde left her room, his father entered and stayed for about half an hour. Hamde wondered what was taking him so long. The boy passed the time by looking at photographs of naked women in books stacked on a low table in the waiting room. All of the women were as obese as the Vase, and some looked twice her size. He came away from the experience with the imprint that sexual satisfaction required a fat woman.

After leaving the preparatory academy, Hamde enrolled as a student in the Physics Department of King Fahd University, located in Dharan near the coast on the Persian Gulf. There the other students treated him with respect and even awe. He moved quickly to graduate studies in the medical physics unit, where he worked on their most advanced projects. But Hamde still felt lonely.

He matured physically into a well-proportioned and muscled young man five foot ten in height having unruly, wavy brown hair. His unblemished, light tan complexion turned the color of pale sherry when he spent several days exposed to the sun. He had deep set, dark brown eyes in his rectangular, exceptionally handsome, face that sometimes broke out in a smile at some thought known only to him, revealing his perfect white teeth. He trimmed his brown beard, completely exposing his tiny lips, and his nose was short and straight. Hamde still kept to himself and seldom had a conversation not involving his work. The gloom of a deepening depression began to engulf him.

In August, 2003, when he was twenty-seven and a member of the faculty of the Physics department, Hamde walked into the office of dean Magazi. He handed the dean his written resignation, and said, "I intend to return to the first principles of the Qur'an and the *Hadith* (the sayings of the prophet Mohammed). I will join the Wahhabi jihad against infidels. I will dedicate my life to the ascendancy of Islam over all other ways of life on earth."

The dean was dumbfounded. He reached out and grasped Hamde's arm firmly with his hand. "Hamde, you've never been strict in your practice of our faith. You've always possessed the skepticism of a scientist. You seldom went to a mosque and never observed the fast of Ramadan. In fact I recall several times when you made fun of the fundamentalist preachings. And I remember you drank whisky cocktails with a visiting pediatrician from England."

Hamde jerked his arm from the dean's fingers. "That was all before I found meaning for my life in Allah's jihad."

Magazi persisted, putting his face close to Hamde and staring inquisitively into his eyes. "The European women who visit the lab are always chasing you. Something must have happened to you. What was it?"

Hamde recoiled and turned his face away. "Those infidel women are blasphemers. They revolt me," he replied.

Then he remembered the time when he was twenty and a visiting French physicist seduced him. In France she was admired as curvaceous and sexy, but Hamde regarded her as scrawny and unattractive. One day at lunch she spiked his lemonade with vodka, and shuffled him into her dormitory room. He came to his senses with her naked body on top of him...she was on top...pumping up and down. She strained forward and swayed from side to side attempting to rub her bare nipples back and forth across his beard. He couldn't prevent his own climax, and the experience left him with a deep sense of guilt. At this moment the memory of her ascendant body, which to him was revoltingly skinny, made his flesh creep.

Returning his thoughts to the present and moving to face the dean, Hamde said, "My life has always seemed empty to me. I've worked and studied hard to please others. But I don't enjoy what I do. I've always been told I have great intelligence. It must be a gift from Allah because I did nothing to earn it. I have a debt to pay to Allah."

The dean countered, "But you've worked many hard hours for years at your studies. You've earned everything coming to you now."

"I've listened to the Wahhabi Imams preaching in our mosques. They tell of the glorious rewards waiting in heaven for those who martyr themselves for Allah's jihad. There is no joy in my life here on earth. The Imams promise me I will be happy when I earn my right to enter heaven."

"You're a highly educated and uniquely skilled member of the University's research team. Your work will teach others and enable them to advance our medical research. What you are doing will eventually lead to the discovery of treatments and machines that'll save countless lives. Continue what you're doing." The dean moved toward Hamde and reached out to touch him again. "You can repay the debt you believe you owe Allah by continuing to do exactly what you're doing now. You probably have a temporary case of depression. Please go talk to Doctor Fermond in Psychiatry. He'll prescribe pills for combating your depression. Other researchers here have been depressed. In time, with treatment, it always goes away."

Hamde backed away and shook his head. "No. I'm lonely and miserable in this life on earth. I want the happiness and rewards given to a martyr in heaven."

Dean Magazi put his head back and laughed. With a wide smile on his face he said, "Are you talking about the nonsense they preach about a harem of virgins welcoming the jihad's martyrs when they get to heaven? If it'll make you happy, we can arrange for sex right here at the University."

Hamde Jawade's jaw dropped in astonishment, and he stared at the Dean for a moment. Then, again remembering his seduction by the skinny French scientist, his face turned red, and he walked out of the room and off the campus without another word or glance at anyone.

Hamde drove his BMW convertible to the Mosque of the Sea, where he was swayed by the sermons of Imam Razaque. When he told the Imam he wanted to become a martyr in Allah's jihad, the Imam gave him a telephone number to call. He dialed the number and answered some basic questions about who he was. The next day the phone in his apartment rang; the caller told Hamde he had three days to wind up his affairs before being flown the *al Khanjar* camp for his training.

When he arrived at the camp, Hamde filled out a lengthy questionnaire. His scientific education and ability to speak English were recognized as qualifying Hamde for a unique assignment.

The next day they withdrew Hamde from the training routine, and told him to go to the Gold Room, as the camp cadre called it. Abduhl Ariann, wearing the white embroidered robe of a priestly attendant, led Hamde into the camp mosque. Without any forewarning or explanation, Ariann ushered Hamde into the windowless room at one end of the mosque and told him to sit in the soft leather chair. He noticed the thick white animal skins covering the floor and wondered why there was no odor. They did not subject Hamde to the waiting test like the other secret agent candidates. His qualifications were extraordinary.

Right after Hamde was seated, Abduhl Ariann returned and placed the ornately decorated coffee urn and two matching cups on the ebony table. Ariann left the room, and Muhamed Allah Yatakalan, garbed as a Grand Imam in his gold brocade robe and matching turban fringed in bright red, entered and closed the door. Hamde jumped to his feet and stared at the imposing figure before him. The Imam smiled and told him to be seated. He poured a cup of coffee and handed it to Hamde. The Imam attempted to capture Hamde's eyes with his, but the young man did not look at his face. He stared at the dagger outlined in the center of the Imam's chest.

The Imam said, "You have unique talents and a unique physical appearance, and a sophistication making you the only soldier we've ever found who can carry out a vital mission for the jihad. Surely Allah had you in His mind for this mission from the time you were born. Your mission is much more important than merely blowing up infidels and heathens. Your mission is to enter the American infidel's government and to supply the jihad with intelligence...information we can't get in any other way."

The Imam picked up his cup of coffee and took several slow sips, letting the impact of his words sink in. Hamde glanced into the Imam's eyes for the first time and then quickly looked back down at the dagger outline.

"As the Wahhabi Imam has already told you, the jihad you have entered was started by the holy prophet Muhammad over a thousand years ago, and his jihad has never stopped. Only after the very last infidel and the very last heathen have been converted to Islam or have been killed for refusing to convert will Allah's final objective be reached on earth."

Muhamed Allah Yatakalan smiled warmly at Hamde and made hand motions urging him to drink some coffee.

"Successful completion of your mission will bring that glorious day closer by giving us vital information about American weapons we can use to destroy the fundamental workings of the cursed American society, which pollutes the rest of the world with its greediness and glorification of individuals.

You pledged your life as a fighter in the jihad. You know the rewards awaiting you in paradise after you give your life for the jihad. The questions I must ask you now are the most difficult you will ever have to answer."

Rising from his chair Muhamed Allah Yatakalan looked down at Hamde and said, "The questions are these. Are you are willing to delay receiving your rewards in paradise for many years, and are you willing to live among the infidels during the time you delay your rewards?" Hamde stood up but he continued to stare at the outline of a dagger. He frowned and shook his head while the Imam spoke.

"You have already been among the infidel Americans, so you know what it will be like. Are you willing to pretend you are an infidel during the time your entry into paradise is delayed? What you are being assigned to do for the jihad is much more difficult than merely giving your life as a fighter. You will have to live a life of frustration all by yourself. Answer now if you can."

Hamde shook his head more vigorously. He intended to die for the jihad the first chance he got. Life on earth was a boring misery for him. He wanted the happiness of paradise. When an opportunity arose, he intended to volunteer to become a suicide bomber. If he was sent into combat before a suicide mission was offered to him, Hamde intended to commit suicide by the reckless way he attacked the enemy. He planned to charge against the infidels in the first firefight he was in, to ensure they killed him. He could not believe he was being asked to continue for years the unhappy ordeal of living his life.

"Your eminence," Hamde muttered, "I don't think I can do what you ask of me. I want to give my life to the jihad. I want to be in heaven."

"Look at my face," Muhamed Allah Yatakalan said sternly.

For the first time, Hamde fixed his gaze on the Imam's bottomless black eyes. He felt his will power being sucked into the eyes of the Imam, as black holes suck in the energy and matter around them. It felt like his mind was being captured by the Imam.

"Maybe I can do this...maybe...for a while...maybe," Hamde stammered.

Continuing to lock on to the young man's eyes with his, the Imam pointed to the copy of the Qur'an on the table between them. "Turn to verse 16 of Chapter 48. There The Profit says 'you shall be summoned (to fight) against a people given to vehement war: then shall you fight, or they shall submit. Then if you show obedience, Allah will grant you a goodly reward, but if you turn back as you did before, He will punish you with a grievous penalty.' "

Hamde read the words in the Qur'an to himself as the Imam spoke them. He looked up again into the Imam's eyes.

The Imam reached over the small table, put one of his hands on each of Hamde's shoulders, and preached with authority, "You have the choice of earning Allah's reward or suffering his penalty. I've already told you we've been searching all over the world for a warrior with your special qualifications. If you don't accept this assignment, you will betray all of your fellow warriors who will die because we lacked the intelligence about American weapons you could have given us. You will betray the jihad. You will prolong the time before the jihad is completed. It is Allah's will that you do this. You will betray Him by not using the gifts he bestowed on you to perform this mission in America."

Hamde succeeded in breaking contact with the Imam's mind-paralyzing eyes. He dropped his chin against his chest and cast his gaze to the floor in shame.

The Imam pleaded, gently intoning, "Any imbecile can strap explosives on his body and blow up a few infidels. Only you have the talent to enter the land of the infidels and appropriate information about their weapons and other inventions for the jihad to use. Your task on earth will be difficult, but your rewards in paradise will be immense. Your family and your ancestors will bask eternally in the glory you'll bring to your family's name."

As a heavy fog of guilt engulfed him blurring his vision, Hamde drew his elbows against his ribs and hunched his shoulders. "I will submit to Allah's will. I will do as you ask," he mumbled with tears shining in his eyes.

"Excellent. While you're in America disguised as one of its citizens, by the power Allah has bestowed on me, I relieve you of your duty to perform the rituals of Islam whenever doing so might reveal your true identity or compromise your mission. You must dress and groom yourself, and behave like an American, even if doing so is blasphemy if you were not a warrior in Allah's jihad.

You will be given the identity of a dead American engineer. Report to the camp office to have your picture taken. Then pack your belongings. We'll send you to Cuba to complete your training. You are very good looking. While you are in Cuba, you might have to undergo facial surgery or some other blasphemous procedure to achieve your disguise."

Then the Imam picked up his coffee cup, finished his drink, and walked out of the room, leaving the distraught Hamde Jawade standing there alone to deal with his feelings of frustration and despair.

Chapter 16　　Tailoren

AFTER BRAINWASHING HAMDE Jawade, Muhamed Allah Yatakalan flew back to Riyadh. His persona changed to Sami Insien. He went to the *al Khanjar* Computer Department with Hamde Jawade's photos and a copy of the questionnaire the young scientist filled out. His hackers cracked into the alumni records of major engineering schools in the United States searching for a match. They found three possibilities whose names passed an initial screening by not being entered in the records of the FBI's NCIC (National Crime Information Center) or the SCIC (State Crime Information Center) of any state. Sami chose one, Bennie Tailoren, because he was from the Midwest and appeared to have no living relatives.

Bennie was the only child of a farm couple who postponed having a family until they felt secure financially. He was twenty-six years old and always looked like he had a tan, even during the long winter in Appleton, Wisconsin, where he was born and raised. His mother was from somewhere in Minnesota, and his father told him his own grandparents were born in Germany. None of this explained Bennie's dusky complexion. Both of his parents died by the time he graduated from the University of Illinois at Urbana with a Bachelor of Science degree in Mechanical engineering. He was about the same height and build as Hamde Jawade and also had brown eyes and hair.

The hackers succeeded in getting an application for employment Tailoren left in the University's file. Where he was asked for his next of kin, he wrote "none." That made him the ideal person for Hamde to replace. The only problem was he worked in Waukegan as a low level engineer for Railleko, a manufacturer of replacement parts for railroad cars. He almost never left the area. And despite the legends persisting since the era of Al Capone, it would be difficult to make his body disappear in Chicagoland.

By now Juan Alveraze and Pedro Ganzolez were experienced killers. They expertly executed the targeted victims who hindered or threatened the jihad's secret agents. But the assassins were not capable of planning a disappearance without arousing suspicion. So Gurtenkov told O'Durea to go to Chicago and set up the hit, and to instruct his assassins how to make Tailoren vanish. Gurtenkov personally phoned the assassins and told them no death button was required for this hit. He ordered them to do whatever O'Durea instructed them to do.

The assassins met O'Durea's flight from Miami at O'Hare and drove him to Waukegan. There the three of them staked out Tailoren's apartment. Pedro took photos of him with a long-range camera lens when he came home from work. Then the assassins dropped O'Durea off at a Hertz rental station and drove back to Chicago awaiting his further instructions.

After observing Tailoren over a weekend, O'Durea learned his target liked to dress up in a suit and tie, wear sunglasses with barely darkened lenses, and play low stakes blackjack at the Ho-Chunk Casino in the Wisconsin Dells. He ordered the two assassins to fly to Las Vegas, rent a limousine and chauffeurs uniforms. He told them what he planned for them to do to Tailoren. They needed to find a remote place on a side road in the desert where they could bury his corpse.

The next Wednesday when Tailoren went to the casino, O'Durea followed him and posed as a representative of the Mill of Gold Casino in Las Vegas. The Cuban wore a checkered sport coat and a flashy tie with the Mill of Gold's logo prominently displayed on it. He handed his target a business card identifying him as the Director of Promotions for the Las Vegas casino. When Tailoren acted suspicious, O'Durea produced an employee identification badge having his photo and a picture of the casino.

He handed Tailoren a round trip plane ticket to Las Vegas, and told him the number of the space in the parking lot where he parked his Dodge pickup had been drawn in the Mill of Gold's lottery. A room was reserved for Tailoren at the Casino's hotel, and all of his expenses were being paid for the coming week. He was also getting a thousand dollars in casino chips to gamble in any way he chose, or to redeem for cash. But he needed to leave that same night to claim his prize.

O'Durea said, "You can phone your boss in the morning from Las Vegas. Just tell him you won a trip and will be on vacation for a week. A limousine driver'll meet your plane at the Las Vegas airport. The limousine will take you to our hotel. So you need to get back to where ever it is you live. Pack a bag and drive to O'Hare in time to catch a late night flight to Las Vegas. Here're your tickets. You'll fly first class."

When Tailoren put out his right hand reaching for the plane tickets, O'Durea noticed a tattoo on his wrist. It was the letters PAM surrounded by a wreath of roses in the shape of a heart.

"I've been thinking about getting one of those," O'Durea said, pointing to the tattoo. "Does it hurt when they do it?"

"Uh. Well it stings a little," Tailoren said. "It's a good idea to get drunk or high before he starts on you."

"I was thinking about getting one on my back. Does it hurt more somewhere else? Do you have any more on other places?"

"Naw, I wouldn't know. Only on my wrist."

"What does PAM stand for?"

"It was my girl's name. I mean…it's still her name, but she's not my girl any more. Yuh know, she was Pamella Brown then. Yuh know like in the song. Yuh know…all the good times with Pamella Brown. Man did we have good times for a while. Then one day she walked out." Tailoren shifted from one leg to the other, impatient to be on his way.

"How come?"

"Said she was bored with Waukegan. Told me I didn't make enough money. Married some navy guy, an officer that teaches at the academy. Yuh know…Annapolis."

"You remember her married name?"

"Not sure. Something like Hunter, Huntley, maybe Hundly. Begins with a H. Turned me off when she walked out. Never wanted to hear about her again." He eyed O'Durea suspiciously. "Say why're you asking all these questions, anyhow?"

"Human interest story about you. The Las Vegas papers'll be curious about you. You won a big prize. Anything else interesting I need to tell them about you?"

"Nope." Tailoren turned and walked out of the casino toward his truck.

When Tailoren was out of his sight, O'Durea flipped open his small leather bound notebook, sketched the tattoo and wrote down the information about Pamella H. He hoped the assassins would never have to make a professional call on her.

When Tailoren's flight landed in Las Vegas, Juan, wearing a driver's uniform and cap, met him at the gate. He escorted his mark to a shiny black Mercedes limousine having darkened windows. Pedro, also dressed as a limousine driver, was sitting on the passenger side of the front seat. When Tailoren hesitated as he stuck his head in the vehicle's door, Pedro said they sent him in case the driver needed help with the luggage. Tailoren entered and sat down in the back seat. His head nodded and he was dozing quietly by the time they exited the airport. The limousine drove into the desert and Tailoren disappeared.

Late that night O'Durea picked the lock on Tailoren's apartment and removed all of his personal possessions, clothes, medicines, compact discs, bills, financial records and papers. The only photo he found was a black and white 4x6 of an elderly looking couple in a frame with chipped white enamel. On the back was written, "Mom and Dad. 1990." The next day he phoned the landlord and arranged to pay what was demanded to break the lease. He told he landlord to keep everything left in the apartment. He filled out a change of address card and mailed it to the Waukegan post office directing the forwarding of Tailoren's mail to a P. O. Box he had rented in Las Vegas.

O'Durea planted a homing bug in Tailoren's pickup, so he was able to locate the Dodge in the parking lot at O'Hare. The next day he broke into the vehicle and drove it to a chop shop, and it too disappeared.

A day later O'Durea sent a letter of resignation with Tailoren's signature forged on it to Railleko. The letter said Tailoren took a higher paying job offered to him by a foreign executive he met at a blackjack table in the Mill of Gold Casino. He was working for Societe du Metallas, a French mining company having a branch office in Nevada. O'Durea set up dummy corporation, and fabricated records evidencing Tailoren's employment.

It was now possible for Hamde Jawade to take over the identity of Bennie Tailoren, and for the new Bennie Tailoren to apply for employment as a Patent Examiner at the United States Patent Office.

The date was September 21, 2003.

Chapter 17   Examiner

HAMDE JAWADE FLEW on Saudi Arabian Airlines from Riyadh to Orly in Paris, and from Paris on Air France to Havana, using his Saudi passport. His instructions were to hire a cab at the airport, and pay the driver to take him to the La Molaken Hotel in Pinar del Rio City. He was told to enjoy the hotel pool and restaurant, and the local sights like any other tourist, and to wait for someone to contact him.

Hamde shaved off his beard, revealing his broad cleft chin, and got a western style hair cut, as he had been ordered. He concealed his prayer rug, and his Muslim identity. Three days after Hamde checked into the hotel, O'Durea knocked on his door. It was late in the afternoon of a warm sunny day. Hamde had dressed to go out to dinner at a fine restaurant. O'Durea wore cutoff jeans, a clean yellow tee shirt and sneakers.

O'Durea introduced himself, and handed Hamde the missing half of a torn Saudi riyal note to verify the Cuban's identity as his contact. O'Durea said, "Change into shorts and a comfortable shirt. Pack your stuff, and meet me in front of the hotel. I paid your bill already."

When Hamde emerged blinking in the late afternoon sunlight, O'Durea pointed to one of two bicycles and said, "Strap on your suitcase and that leather case you're carrying, and get on the bike and follow me."

Hamde followed him, peddling easily through the streets of Pinar del Rio City and out of its northern side into the foothills of the Sierra del Rosario Mountains. The peddling became more difficult. After going up and down many hills, they finally arrived at the old wooden hotel being refurbished by the agents who O'Durea was teaching skills useable when they were on their own in America. The bike ride enabled O'Durea to evaluate Hamde's state of physical conditioning. The young man was exhausted by the exercise. But O'Durea decided it didn't matter because the original Bennie Tailoren had a sedentary job, and the new Bennie Tailoren would have the same type of employment.

Hamde's task was to learn everything he could about the real Bennie Tailoren from the papers and records O'Durea brought back to Cuba. O'Durea ordered him to assume the identity of Bennie Tailoren and to answer only to that name. He practiced getting used to his new American identity by shopping for new clothes and mingling with the tourists in Pinar del Rio City.

If he was ever asked to join someone for an alcoholic drink, O'Durea advised him to say he was allergic to alcohol; it made him feel like he had a head cold, and to order an alcohol free beer. If offered pork, he should say it is too greasy and upsets his stomach. O'Durea rented a Dodge, and taught Bennie to drive like a young American.

They both thought it might look suspicious if Bennie Tailoren turned up in Washington, D. C., looking for a job soon after he quit at Railleko. So the new Tailoren sat around in the old hotel for two weeks reading American magazines and newspapers, and watching American channels on satellite TV, so he could talk about current events in the United States. He read an American history textbook, and several books on the history of weapons. His instructions were to learn about America's newest weapons, so he needed to have knowledge of weapons development to understand the field. He also studied the US Patent Office web site (uspto.gov) to find out as much as he could about his new job as a Patent Examiner.

O'Durea told him one of Patent Examiner Tailoren's daily jobs was to forward the Patent Office's internal access codes to a new email address he'd be given each working day.

"What does the jihad need the codes for?" the new Bennie Tailoren asked.

"How should I know," O'Durea said. "Here's the first email address you're to use." He handed a business card with writing on it to Bennie. "They told me after you make contact with this web address, a message will appear on your computer monitor every day from a different address. You reply by typing in all of Patent Office access codes for the day."

Bennie paced about nervously. "They'll be on my neck for giving away the access codes. I'll be fired the first day I do this."

O'Durea moved in front of Bennie and confronted him. "Look, I don't know how they think they can get away with this," he said. "I hear there're some computer geniuses working for the jihad. And you've got to get one thing straight right now. You're a soldier and you don't question your orders. You obey your orders, even if you don't like them. Got that."

Bennie looked down at his shoes, nodded and put the business card into his wallet.

During the time the new Bennie Tailoren was in Cuba, O'Durea obtained a copy of the original Bennie Tailoren's birth certificate and social security card. He also had the new Tailoren's picture substituted on a forged copy of the original Tailoren's drivers license.

O'Durea contacted Caspare Ouiment at bin Nazamunde's AraSuz bank in Switzerland. The bank does not follow the Sharia Law forbidding paying or receiving interest. He set up in Bennie Tailoren's name another of the security trading accounts used by the jihad to funnel money into the bank accounts of its agents in the United States.

O'Durea told Bennie, "There'll always be a balance of between three and four thousand dollars in your US bank account. Use the money to make your life comfortable and pleasurable in that alien country where you've been stationed. But don't indulge in extravagances that'll put you in the limelight. The account'll be monitored on a daily basis. Every January AraSuz will mail a record of bogus security trades to a small accounting firm in New York City. They'll prepare the Federal and state income tax papers for you to file as Bennie Tailoren."

O'Durea told Bennie the jihad stationed assassins in America to eliminate anyone keeping an agent from accomplishing his mission, or to eliminate anyone who gave information about the jihad to the Americans. O'Durea showed him a death button and told Hamde to contact him if he needed help from the assassins.

One day O'Durea handed Bennie a color picture of the Tailoren tattoo.

Bennie stared at the picture a few moments. "What's this?" he asked.

"The other Tailoren had this tattooed on the back of his right wrist, so you'll have to have one put on yours. We'll make an appointment and get it done tomorrow."

Bennie stamped his feet as he walked up and stood in O'Durea's face. "Never. No way, as the Americans say. It's blasphemy for me to adorn my body with a true likeness of living things like roses," he said, with a flash of hope exploding in his mind. He looked away and prayed silently to himself that the odious tattoo was his excuse for getting out of this undercover assignment and joining a band of fighters. Then he could get a suicide mission or fight in a way that was sure to get him killed.

O'Durea stood his ground and glared at Bennie. "Don't put on an act for me. I know your Imam released you from the strict practice of Islam while you're serving the jihad."

Bennie stared at his right wrist as if it were already tattooed. "But this desecration of my body will remain on me for eternity after I enter paradise. It'll be a shameful disfigurement marking me as profane for the rest of time. I won't let you do it. Send me back to the *al Khanjar* camp if there's no other way for me to perform this mission in America. And what about my accent. This man form Waukegan...this Tailoren...he didn't speak the way I do."

"We've already thought about your accent. If anybody asks about how you talk, you say you had a stuttering speech impediment when you were a kid. You took lessons and got rid of it, but it makes you talk differently. Now, you keep on learning about Bennie Tailoren. I'll arrange for you to talk to the Grand Imam about the tattoo."

The next day an iSight call came through for Bennie on O'Durea's computer. He recognized the voice and face of Muhamed Allah Yatakalan appearing on the monitor. The Imam said, "He told me you refused to have the tattoo. Your horror at having your body desecrated with a profane image is understandable. We are asking you to make a great sacrifice for the jihad. But your sacrifice will be no greater than that of the warriors who become human bombs."

Bennie leaned toward the computer screen. "Yes it will. I'll be marked forever as a blasphemer. Look at this, your holiness," he pleaded as he held a drawing of the tattoo in front of the iSight camera mounted on top of the computer.

"Yes I see the drawing is blasphemous. But, the opposite of what you say is the truth." The Imam's bottomless eyes stared from the computer screen capturing Bennie's mind even from eight thousand miles away. "You will be marked. But your mark will be of a warrior of the jihad who made a sacrifice as great as giving his life. Allah bestows justice on His warriors. He will ensure the image on your wrist is recognized and celebrated as a badge of your courage and devotion to His jihad. You must have it done. And you will be proud of yourself for all of eternity for doing this for Allah's jihad."

The next day Bennie fasted and prayed almost continuously not to be tattooed, but for Allah to forgive him if he was tattooed. Consequently he was lightheaded when a man with a stringy grey beard rode up to the old hotel on a scarred and dented motorbike. Aron LaPedez wore a soiled shirt and shorts, and carried a black bag of the kind doctors used to carry when they made house calls.

Sensing Bennie's tension, the tattooist made him lie down on a couch and close his eyes. He left the room and returned with a shot glass, which he filled to the brim with a clear liquid. He told Bennie to sit up. He handed him the glass and told him to drink the clear liquid quickly to make the tattooing easier. The 190 proof alcohol felt like fire going down his throat. But because of his body's unfamiliarity with liquor and because his stomach was empty, Bennie was sleeping soundly soon after he put his head back down.

The tattoo artist worked quickly and expertly. By the time the sun was setting, the job was done and LaPedez was back on his motorbike speeding away.

Bennie slept on the couch all night, but awoke before dawn the next morning ravenously hungry and with only a mild headache from his encounter with alcohol. His hunger and headache masked the pain from the tattoo, so he didn't complain about it to O'Durea. He went into the kitchen and fixed what for him was a big breakfast of fresh melon, three scrambled eggs, two bagels, a slice of smoked mullet, and two cups of heavily sugared coffee with cream.

O'Durea awoke to the smell of the coffee, and ambled, eyes blinking, into the kitchen while Bennie was still eating. "We're going to leave for the United States at sunset," he said.

Bennie went into a state of shock. He was aware his training in Cuba was over, but somehow he never accepted that he actually had to change his identity and live among the infidels.

O'Durea sat down and poured himself a cup of coffee. "Before we leave here I'll have a girl come over to take care of your sexual needs. It'll be your graduation present."

Bennie stood up and shook his head vigorously. "That won't help me at this time."

It puzzled O'Durea to have one of his trainees turn down sex. He pondered whether Bennie's good looks made him so attractive to women he was very choosy. It didn't make any sense, based on his own life's experience with men of all ages. It occurred to him that maybe Bennie was gay. *The best looking guys sometimes were*, he thought to himself.

O'Durea said, "The jihad will buy you sex with a girl twice a month. But don't use any one of them more than once. Like the Imam must have told you, it might compromise your mission if any infidel gets to know very much about you."

"I don't need that kind of woman." Bennie rushed from the kitchen without eating all of the food on the table in front of him. He stomped out of the house and walked into the trees surrounding the old hotel.

O'Durea smiled and moved to where Bennie had been sitting, picked up his fork and finished off the rest of the uneaten breakfast.

Late in the afternoon the same dented Ford O'Durea always hired drove up to the hotel entrance. The driver unwired and rewired the trunk lid shut, after their duffle bags were stowed inside. Bennie held on to his leather case. O'Durea said, "Remember, from now on you're Bennie Tailoren and that's the only name you answer to." They got in and were driven north through the mountains to the wharf at Puerto Esperanza.

There they boarded an idling Solara as a fresh breeze made the waters of the bay slap against the wharf. Ramond Esterito, the boat's captain, was a stocky Cuban with a full head of slick, raven black hair. He wore an orange windbreaker and grease stained blue jeans. Once O'Durea and Bennie were on board, he started the engine, and the sleek boat shot away from the wharf into the blackening water. A swift breeze caused a moderate chop on the water, so the boat bounced up and down as its speed increased.

Bennie was seasick before they were out of sight of land. He leaned over the side and gripped the gunwale. It felt like everything he ate for a week came up. After the initial spasm of nausea had passed, he pleaded with O'Durea to have the boat turned around so they could go back to shore and he could get off. But there could be no turning back now. O'Durea knew he needed to get Bennie established in the United States before the young man could renege on his commitment to bin Nazamunde's jihad.

It didn't help the situation when Esterito began mimicking Bennie's plight and laughing. O'Durea walked up behind the captain, punched him in the back of the neck with the extended knuckle of his middle finger, and yelled, *"Cállate!"* (shut up) in his ear. Esterito winced as the pain from the blow caused his vision to blur momentarily. He made a mental note to get even with O'Durea, but he stopped mocking Bennie, who lay limply on his back on the deck with his eyes closed.

Their rendezvous with Oren Finney's Grady White Islander was quick and easy despite the choppy waters at the center of the Gulf of Mexico. O'Durea helped the limp Bennie up and over the side into the Islander. As he started over the side, Esterito engaged his motor, so O'Durea had to jump across an open space to avoid falling into the water. When he regained his balance and turned to shoot a vicious look at Esterito, O'Durea saw he was laughing and flipping him the bird as he turned his boat back toward Cuba.

Finney had experience with seasick patrons of his charter fishing service, so he was empathetic toward Bennie. He told O'Durea to take the wheel, and he pointed out the window and said, "Hold this northeast heading on the compass the dashboard. I think I've got something that'll help this kid get out of his misery. It usually works."

He opened a locker and took out a bottle of clear liquid and two vials of pills. He poured about two ounces of the liquid into a paper cup and took one anti seasickness pill out of each vial. He handed to pills to Bennie and said, "Bite down on these. They'll taste terrible, but they'll help you faster if you chew 'em. At the same time you chew 'em, wash 'em down in one gulp with this." He handed him the cup. "It'll burn like hell going down, but it'll make the pills work faster."

Bennie did as he was told, but barely avoided upchucking the bitter, throat burning mixture. He lay down on the hard deck and soon fell asleep with a life preserver under his head.

"What was that stuff?" O'Durea said pointing to the empty paper cup.

"Two different kinds of seasickness pills. They work better together than they work alone. And he washed 'em down with pure high proof alcohol. This isn't the first time one of your customers got sick on my boat. Why don't you give'em anti sickness pills or patches before you leave Cuba."

"The boat ride is part of a test. Their employer needs to know if they can tolerate being on the water so he'll know if there are any limitations on their works assignments.'

"Oh," Finney said and to himself mused: *I thought he was just smuggling in Cuban refugees who can afford to pay the freight. If this is part of some illegal employment scheme, or if he's pulling an employment scam, I can charge more for the boat ride.*

They motored swiftly up the Gulf of Mexico and were at Finney's short private dock jutting into the water from his house on S. Barfield Drive on Marco Island before there was any light from the dawn. O'Durea stepped on to the dock and threw lines to Finney. Then he woke Bennie, who looked greenish in the beams from their flashlights.

"Welcome to the United States," O'Durea said.

Bennie just looked at him and scowled.

"How much for the car this time? And I assume its registered in my name like before."

"Seven thou," Finney said, "an' you've got title in Georgia, like you asked for. It's another old Pontiac... black... an' it's out front as usual." Turning to Bennie, he asked, " Is that a fancy fishing rod in that leather cylinder you're carrying? I'd like to see it if it's a rod. Better not be drugs. What kind a work you'll be doing here, kid?"

"Never mind that," O'Durea said. He handed a wad of hundreds from his bag to Finney and grabbed the keys to the car. And to himself he thought, *This guy knows too much now. If I can find another runner, I'll ask Gurtenkov to send Juan and Pedro to pay him a visit.*

Finney turned away from them and started his routine for putting his boat to bed.

O'Durea helped the unsteady Bennie walk around Finney's house to his car before there was the first glimmer of sunlight. He drove up Barfield Drive to state route 951, which he took north to I-75, where he turned west toward Naples, and drove without stopping until they reached Sarasota. There he exited and motored up to a diner with an unrememberale name advertising pancakes.

Bennie slept on the back seat for the entire trip. O'Durea woke him up, handed him a bottle of mouthwash.

"Put your hands over your mouth and breath into them. See. Your breath smells like a garbage dump. In America bad breath is a no no. Now go into the restroom and gargle."

Bennie did as he was told. He came back, sat down, and ordered a large glass of fresh squeezed orange juice, which he gulped down. He ordered another large glass of the juice to go with his pancakes, scrambled eggs and caffeinated coffee, which he drank black. After he finished breakfast and went to the restroom, he went outside into the bright sunlight of the warm, humid March day. He did a few yoga stretches, and told O'Durea he felt like a live human being again and was ready to begin his mission in America. He didn't mention the guilt and depression descending on him for having to live a dead man's life in the land of infidels he despised.

They drove on I-75 north to Tampa. There they got sidetracked briefly to go to the Apple Store at the International Mall to buy a top of the line Powerbook laptop and an iSight camera for Bennie. They headed east on I-4 across central Florida to I-95, which they stayed on all the way to the outskirts of the nation's capitol. O'Durea and Bennie took turns driving and sleeping. Except for gas, food and toilet, they made no stops until they reached Arlington, Virginia, shortly after noon on their second day. There they checked into the Qurtyard Motel at one end of Crystal City, where the US Patent Office was located.

They showered, shaved and relaxed by the hotel's indoor pool for the rest of the day. O'Durea sipped bourbon, read *USA Today* and dozed. Bennie drank iced tea and ogled in amazement at the scanty bathing suits worn by the girls enjoying the pool.

All except one was so skinny in Bennie's eyes, they repulsed him. One heavy woman entered wearing a skimpy two-piece, red bathing suit of the type that usually evoked smiles or laughter when a woman of her size appeared in it. He stared at her through his sunglasses, and put a towel in his lap to hide his erection. He went back to his room for a cold shower when he could no longer stand it as the woman paraded her corpulent body around the pool. O'Durea was perceptive enough to realize what was going on, and he reassured himself that Bennie was heterosexual.

The two men spent the next day driving and walking around in Crystal City. They found a furnished ground floor apartment that Bennie could rent in the Butlarian Arms Condo. The building was within easy walking distance of the Patent Office. His apartment rental lease did not include a parking space.

O'Durea coached him through having telephone and DSL lines installed. At a nearby Circuit City, they got four prepaid cell phones. Bennie set up an Internet address. The Cuban said, " Give out your email address to everyone and to every web site showing any interest in you. This will create traffic so the messages involving jihad business won't be conspicuous. The same for your apartment phone.

Give the number out to everyone. The more calls you get on it the better."

They made duplicates of Bennie's apartment key, and O'Durea slipped one of the extra keys into his own pocket. He might need it if this neophyte screwed up badly and turned out to be a liability.

O'Durea gave him his own cell phone number, and mailing and Internet addresses. He said to Bennie, "Don't use your apartment phone for any jihad business. If you have to call me or anyone else working for the jihad, you must use one of the prepaid cell phones. In an emergency, you can send an email message. But avoid everything except the cell phones if at all possible. And don't get an answering machine."

After spending two more days checking out the surrounding area, Bennie said, "I have everything I need close by and don't want to bother with owning and parking a car. When I want a car, I'll rent one."

O'Durea told him goodbye and wished Bennie luck in his assignment. His parting advice was, "It's clear to me you're not happy here. You're what the Americans call a sourpuss. Americans smile a lot, even when they're not particularly happy. I'm telling you in the strongest way to smile at people. And when a woman smiles at you, it doesn't mean she's a streetwalker, like it does in your country. And don't forget to send them the computer access codes." Then he got into the black Pontiac and drove off for the Canadian border, pursuing some errand Gurtenkov assigned to him.

Bennie's feelings of guilt and depression deepened. The damp, chilly spring weather of the Potomac basin didn't help. He was used to the dry sunny days of the Arabian desert.

Bennie Tailoren applied for a job as a beginning Patent Examiner at the GS-12 level. His qualifications and experience were just what the Patent Office was seeking. He was hired on the spot, subject to his passing the AIFIS and National Agency Check inquiries. Bennie started work the following week, and entered the Patent Examiner Training Program where they taught him the procedures for examining and processing patent applications. Adam Elmanni, the short, bald Supervisory Examiner conducting the training sessions attended by Bennie, recognized his exceptional mental abilities, and told him he was going to be assigned to an examining group dealing with complicated mechanisms.

"My hobby has been studying the weapons used by ancient and modern armies," Bennie said. "I guess you could say I'm a weapons history buff. I'd really like to work on the patent applications for new weapons."

"Good," Elmanni said. "That'd be class 89, Ordinance, in Examining Group 3300. And they have a lot of big, complex patent applications going through that group all the time. I'll see if they have an opening, and if they do that's where you'll go. And you'll have to apply for Top Secret security clearance to work on anything that's classified higher than Secret."

There was an opening for him in Group 3300, and they furnished Bennie with a greenish grey metal desk and swivel chair in a small, glass-sided cubicle, in a line of identical cubicles in Building 4 of the Crystal City complex. A computer terminal, keyboard and mouse sat on his desk. After he returned home from his first day at work, he entered the web address from the business card O'Durea had given him, and typed in the access codes he was authorized to use. It became his daily routine to send the access codes to the new email address appearing on his terminal.

To get a Top Secret clearance, Bennie needed to fill out form SF-86 (National Security Questionnaire) and bring it back with all of the supporting documents it required. He called O'Durea and asked him what to do about the SF-86.

"Fill it out, and I'll get you a copy of any additional supporting papers you need. You already have a copy of Tailoren's birth certificate and social security card. But don't turn any papers in yet. You'll never survive a background check by FBI field agents. The people you give as references are sure to tell the agents things exposing you as an impostor. So we'll have to use baksheesh or blackmail or intimidation to get falsified approval papers into the Patent Office personnel files. Look around. Find out who handles these papers. I mean who actually gets their hands on the security clearance papers.

I can get a fake approval signature and fake approval stamp on your papers. We'll get to one of the paper handlers, and we can get the bogus, approved papers into the personnel file where they belong at the Patent Office. Call me back when you find out who works on this. Get as much information as you can about these people without actually asking them questions."

"Not ask questions," Bennie said. "Do you expect me to read minds?"

"OK, ask questions. But be careful to conceal what you're trying to find out."

And that is why Bennie Tailoren met Carmina Burneta.

Chapter 18   Carmina

LATE ON HIS first Friday afternoon in Group 3300 of the Patent Office when everyone was eager to put away the papers and files for the weekend, Bennie Tailoren walked up to the desk where Carmina Burneta was sitting, looked into her eyes and gave her the biggest smile she'd received since arriving in the nation's capitol.

Ordinarily, no one paid much attention to Carmina as she sat at her desk in the pool of clerks and typists located outside of the cubicles occupied by the patent examiners of Group 3300. None of the other Patent Office employees related to her unless they were directly involved in the clerical work she was doing. She didn't have any close friends among the people with whom she worked. Only the chief clerk, Lilly Amber, ever talked to her about anything other than what they were working on. Sometimes Carmina felt invisible. But she didn't feel invisible in the radiance from the smile of this handsome young man with deeply tanned skin.

Carmina was a full-blooded Coeur d'Alene Native American, or at least as full blooded as any Native American is at this time in their history. She was born and raised on the tribe's reservation in Idaho. Once she had a well-paying job dealing blackjack at the Coeur d'Alene Casino in Worley, Idaho. She saved every cent from the tips winning players gave her. When she accumulated enough money to go out on her own, she defied her parents, and moved to the nation's capital.

Carmina was not in any sense ordinary looking. Her straight nose separated her almond shaped eyes, the right one of which slants slightly upwardly from her high cheekbones as is common in the orient. Full plump lips surrounded her small mouth, and her oval face ended in a protruding rounded chin. She wore her shiny, jet-black hair in straight bangs stopping just below her ears in back, revealing her short, thick neck. Her bangs in front extended past her eyebrows, which draw attention to her strikingly large chocolate brown eyes.

She had expected her Native American looks to be considered exotic and to make her stand out in the nation's capitol. And eventually she expected to attract an intelligent, ambitious man to marry her and father her children. But no one took special notice of her. There are too many other exotic looking people walking the streets for her to attract any attention. And her physical appearance didn't help matters. She was short and fleshy—thick bodied— with heavy legs and large calves. Her breasts were too large for the rest of her body and made her look top heavy.

Carmina dressed better than her coworkers in clothes from Saks and Neiman Marcus. She was able to afford expensive clothing because she supplemented her government salary with winnings from playing blackjack at tables in Trump's Taj Mahal casino in Atlantic City. When she was dealing blackjack at the Coeur d'Alene Casino, she studied the players who won consistently. She applied the lessons she learned from watching them to her own gaming strategy. And she always won enough to pay the expenses of her trip, and most of the time she was able to take some winnings home with her to apply to her clothing allowance.

"What do I have to do to get a higher security clearance, higher than I have now?" Bennie asked Carmina.

"Let me see," she said. "What's your name?"

"Bennie Tailoren, and I work in that cubicle over there." He took a step over to the door and pointed down the hallway separating the clerks from the patent examiners.

Carmina rose from her desk and walked up next to Bennie. "Over where?"

"There," he said pointing to the farthest cubicle.

"I see." She grazed him with her breasts as she turned and walked toward her desk. "Sorry." Her big smile revealed her tiny rounded teeth and indicated she made physical contact with him on purpose.

Bennie would be repulsed by such obvious flirtation by any American woman he considered skinny and unattractive. But as she walked away from him, he noticed her full, heavy figure. He was amused by her forwardness, and did not experience the distaste he ordinarily felt when an infidel woman came on to him.

Carmina returned to her desk and sat down. She opened a drawer, pulled out a file and removed a form. He continued to stand against to her desk where he could look down at her cleavage.

"This is a SF-86 National Security Questionnaire." Carmina waved the form. "You have to fill it out and attach all the confirming documents they ask for. Then bring it back to me. Everybody here already has a security clearance for Secret. You must've passed the AIFES and National Agency Checks already or you wouldn't have your examiner job." She handed Bennie the form.

Bennie waved it back at her. "Then where do the papers go? How long does it take? When will I know if I'm cleared?"

"I send the forms by the inter agency mail over to the FBI. When they're through investigating your background and talking to your references and everyone else they can find who might have some dirt on you, they'll send the SF-86 back to me. It'll say whether you're cleared for Top Secret or not."

Bennie glanced over the form and then looked into Carmina's eyes. "Who else handles my papers? I'm concerned about identity theft. You hear a lot about it on the TV these days."

"I don't know who works on this at the FBI." Carmina jabbed herself in the chest with her thumb, making her breasts undulate. "But I'm the only person here that gets their hands on the papers. When everything's approved and we're finished, I send the SF-86 to Personnel. I guess it goes into the file with your name on it. I guess the folks down in Personnel can see it, if they need to. Of course, if the FBI finds out something really bad about you, you might loose the job you have now. It happened once to an examiner."

"Ouch." Bennie grimaced. "I'll have to think about this security clearance business. I'll see you later." He turned to leave, but first he lingered to eye her body and again to give her his biggest smile.

Carmina beamed at the approval she felt she was getting from this handsome young man. A hot flash ran down from her lips to the inside of her thighs. Her dusky complexion must have turned crimson because the women sitting at adjacent desks who saw and heard what transpired started to giggle. The head clerk, Lilly Amber heard it all too. She came over, gave Carmina a high five, and said, "Go for it, girl. I think that gentleman likes what you showed him."

Carmina felt light as a feather when she stood and walked away from her desk as the workweek ended. On the way home she went into a drug store and dropped off the prescription for birth control pills she had carried in her purse for months. She also bought a package of condoms for use in case of an emergency.

Chapter 19   Trap

BENNIE TAILOREN BENT forward as he walked the three blocks back to his apartment. He felt as if a heavy weight were tied around his neck and pulling his head down toward his feet. He expected he might have to become involved with the infidel woman, and he dreaded the thought.

That evening Bennie was sitting at his kitchen table eating a corned beef sandwich from a deli when he phoned O'Durea. "A woman in my work unit told me she was the only person at the Patent Office who had to handle my form SF-86 until after the FBI finished interviewing my references and sends it back to her."

"Only one person," O'Durea said. "That might make things easy for us. Tell me about her. Oh, first, be sure to mail that SF-86 to the PO Box I gave you. Now tell me about her."

"She looks like she's a few years older than I am. Maybe she's thirty, but I don't know. It's hard to tell. She sort of looks oriental, but not definitely so. Dark skin. Sort of reddish. No, that can't be right. I'm not sure I remember accurately. Maybe her mother and father are different races. She's short and heavy. Not skinny like most American girls, but she's not as round and plump as a really attractive Arab girl. But she's not bad. Jet black hair, and brown eyes. Really pretty big brown eyes." Bennie took a bite of his sandwich.

"I don't know either," O'Durea paused to think. "I was going to guess she's an American Indian but I'm really not sure. And it doesn't matter any way what race she is. Could you tell if she's married? Did you see a picture of a man or any children on her desk? A wedding ring on her left hand? If she's married or attached to some guy already, we'll have to use baksheesh to buy her or someone else off. But if she's single and unattached, we can set a honey trap."

"Honey trap," Bennie managed to mumble with food still in his mouth. "What's that?"

"That's when an agent uses sex in some way to trap a target, another person. To entice the target, or to force the target, to do something for the agent. In this case, you'd seduce the woman into thinking you're in love with her, and ask her to do you a small favor that'll make you love her even more. You ask her to accept the already approved SF-86 from you and to put it into the inter office mail addressed to the Personnel Department. Or wherever else an approved form ends up. After that's done, we eliminate the target."

Bennie gulped a drink of coffee to wash down the remaining food in his mouth. "I don't think I can do this," he protested. "I've only had two sex experiences with women, so I don't know how to seduce her. And, she's an infidel. What can we talk about? My instructions were not to get personally or emotionally close to any infidels. You told me that yourself. The Grand Imam didn't say anything about seducing women when he convinced me to come to America. I did not agree to seduce women. And then what? What will happen to her after she accepts the SF-86? Will I have to keep on pretending I love her? I will not marry an infidel."

"Don't worry about afterwards. After the approved form is where it belongs in the Patent Office files, we'll issue a fatwa. She'll be killed. No one'll ever know where she is or what she did for you. That's all you'll ever need to know about the fatwa."

Bennie was too stunned to speak. There was an uncomfortable silence before O'Durea continued, "Say, is the fact she's a woman what's upsetting you? Is it men you're attracted to? When you said you've only had two sex experiences, sex experiences with women, did you leave out having sex experiences with men? In short, Bennie, are you a queer?"

Bennie held his cell phone out at arm's length and glared at the device as if it were alive and had insulted him. "That's disgusting," he shouted at the phone and slammed it shut. He reflected a moment on what O'Durea said, and felt a surge of guilt as he pondered that if the woman helped him, she'd be murdered under a fatwa.

Bennie hurried into his bedroom and removed his cylindrical leather tube from under the bed. He pulled the zipper open and took out a hand woven three by five foot prayer rug rolled up inside the tube. The multicolored rug was embellished with a design depicting the interior of the mosque he attended as Hamde Jawade during his last days in Dharan. This design now comforted him somewhat by reminding him of how peaceful he felt when he was praying in that mosque. In a way, he felt as if he had brought his mosque with him to America. One end of the rug had as its prayer niche, a pointed figure resembling a spear flanked on both sides by ascending steps.

He unrolled his rug and laid it on the floor of the bedroom. Then he oriented the end of the rug so   the prayer niche pointed toward a travel poster showing a desert oasis hanging on the Eastern wall of the room. This assured him his prayer niche pointed toward Mecca. Bennie knelt down on the rug and wept as he prayed aloud to Allah for guidance, and for relief from the gloom from his feelings of loneliness and guilt for what he feared he had to do.

After having the phone call end with Bennie's shout, O'Durea called Gurtenkov to report the crisis he believed was brewing. "I doubt that the new kid is going to make it in America."

"You mean the one we call Tailoren now?"

"Yeah. Looks like we'll have to use him in a honey trap to get him a Top Secret clearance. He thinks only one girl'll handle his papers at the Patent Office. You already know he didn't want to be in America until the Grand Imam laid a special guilt trip on him. And I had to sic the Imam on him again to get him to have his wrist tattooed."

"I hadn't heard about the tattoo," Gurtenkov said.

"Well I'm not going to bother you with every detail of every agent's troubles. I've been able to handle everything that's come up so far. But this one looks like it may explode in our faces, and I want to make sure the goal is worth the risk."

"Explain," the Russian interjected.

"Here's the question. Is it worth risking Tailoren breaking down, and either insisting we return him to Saudi Arabia? Or, worse, him flipping on us and revealing we have agents in America. Is it worth any of these risks to get him the higher security clearance?"

"He doesn't know anything about the other agents, unless you told him," Gurtenkov said accusingly.

O'Durea replied with unconcealed resentment, "I'd never breach our security like that."

"I'll think about it and call back later today," Gurtenkov said and hung up.

Gurtenkov angrily pushed the phone across his desk and mused: *I knew sending a young, inexperienced agent in solo wouldn't work. It's too much to ask from even these crazy Arab zealots. If Tailoren fails, it'll prove my point and get bin Nazamunde off my back about using solo agents instead of pairs of agents. So what's to loose? Tailoren thinks he's the only secret agent in America, so al he can give up is the fact the al Khanjar camp exists, and the existence of O'Durea and our Cuba connection.*

He opened his desk drawer, took out and lit a short, thin cigar. *Sooner or later the Americans are going to find out about the camp anyway. Too many people are involved with it. Loosing O'Durea and his contacts, especially the boats, would be big. In order to prevent that loss, we'll have to kill the kid if he gets close to cracking. But I'll have to deal with bin Nazamunde if I call the kid back now. He'll be insulted and say I didn't give the solo agent enough time. No I won't do that. We'll continue with the honey trap.*

Gurtenkov waited an hour in case he had any second thoughts. Then he picked up the phone and called O'Durea. "Go ahead with the honey trap if the target is available. But stay close to Tailoren. Coach him before every contact with the girl and debrief him after every liaison. Go to America and stay with him if you think necessary. If you think he's going to crack, you can call in the assassins without getting my approval."

"OK," O'Durea said. "I'll take it from here. If things go real bad or real good, I'll let you know. Otherwise I won't be in touch." He silently deliberated: *Does the Russian think I'd be foolish enough to risk giving up my identity by staying with an amateur while he screws up. And if Tailoren flipped, the Americans'd find out about me and my operations. Gurtenkov has to know that. I'll alert Juan and Pedro right now, and tell 'em to get ready for an assignment in D.C. I'll have 'em rent a place in Baltimore until this caper is over.*

O'Durea gave Bennie two days to calm down, before calling him back on Sunday night. Bennie was sitting in an easy chair reading the *Washington Times*. "You've got a job to do. And my job is to help you. Espionage is a rough trade. It's too bad if some of the rough things we do upset you. But you'll have to get used to them to get your job done. I have to ask a lot of questions to be able to help you. Your orders are to find out if this woman... what's her name anyway?"

"Carmina Burneta."

"Tell me again what you think of her looks?"

Bennie contemplated a moment. "She's not repulsive looking to me...not too skinny, like other American women I've seen. But she doesn't turn me on either."

"Can you make love with her and act sincere?"

Bennie pondered longer. "I don't know," he said finally and wagged his head.

O'Durea continued, "OK, her name is Carmina Burneta. You've got to find out if she's already committed to some man. I'm going to assume she's not because of the way she flirted with you. So you just walk up to her desk tomorrow and ask her to go to lunch on Tuesday or Wednesday, or whatever day she's free next week. Take a cab, and go to lunch at the rooftop restaurant in the Hihat Hotel."

"But it's only a short walk from here," Bennie interrupted.

"Don't you think I remembered the hotel's walking distance from where the two of you work," O'Durea said with irritation. "You need to impress her; convince her you're willing to spend money on her. And get her to talk about herself. Ask a lot of questions. Everything she says should suggest the next question. You understand what I'm talking about?"

"Let me see, if she says she's from Texas, I ask where in Texas. When she says where, I ask what the weather's like down there this time of year. Where did she go to school? What did she study? What movies did she like? Who did she vote for?"

"You've got the right idea, but leave out politics and religion. Try to show a sincere interest in everything about her, where's she's been and what she's done. In contrast, you've led a dull life in

Waukegan and never been hardly anywhere else. And remember to smile at her all the time."

"OK, O'Durea, I get your point."

"Listen up, this is most important. She needs to believe she can mold you into her ideal of a man. That's what women always want to do."

"And how do I do that?" Bennie asked with exasperation.

"Convince her you're eager to have her teach you new things. New places to go. New places to eat. New experiences. Be sure to take a cab back to work after lunch. If she seems happy after your first date, ask her out again for lunch or dinner the next day. Then report back to me."

"OK, OK, already."

"Hey, I'm glad to hear you talk like an American," O'Durea said with obvious amusement. "While I'm waiting to hear back from you, I'll go over my copies of the original Bennie Tailoren's records and figure out something he might want to hide from the FBI field agents. Like a drunk driving or drug possession charge, or skipping out on his debts. There's probably nothing serious because his prints weren't in AIFES."

"So what good will finding out about his non serious mischief do us," Bennie said sarcastically.

"Because you'll need a reason to not want your papers to go through normal FBI channels. I'll find something you'd be ashamed of. But not a word about your papers to her now. You understand?"

"Yeah, yeah, can I go now?"

"Go, already, yourself," O'Durea said, chuckling to himself.

Bennie slept very little that night. He dreaded having any further contact with the infidel woman, but he rehearsed over and over what to say to her the next day. When the time came, he walked up to Carmina's desk, smiled broadly and said, "Let's go to lunch together tomorrow. I will take you to the place at the top of the Hihat. Can you leave at twelve sharp?" It was difficult for him to make eye contact.

"Yes and I'd be delighted to go with you," Carmina beamed at him.

"OK, I will be back here at noon tomorrow." Bennie's smile weakened and he walked away without looking back.

When he was out of earshot, Carmina and the other women smirked at Bennie's obvious embarrassment.

After work Bennie walked to a bookstore and bought two sex manuals. He started reading one, which was mainly text, and then switched to the other, which was liberally sprinkled with drawings. Some of the things people were shown doing amazed him. And he was surprised they did not revolt him. In fact once his curiosity was awakened, he eagerly paged through the book looking at every drawing. He vowed to be a good warrior in Allah's jihad, and do as ordered. Even if he needed to perform those astonishing acts the men in the book were shown doing.

As the minute hand on the wall clock swept past twelve, Bennie walked through the door. Carmina was already standing by her desk, purse in hand. She was wearing a navy blue wool skirt that extended below her knees, a grey cotton long sleeved blouse from the reservation gift shop decorated with multicolored Coeur d'Alene animal motifs, panty hose and high heeled blue leather shoes. Although it was sunny outside, the wind was brisk and damp. So Bennie helped her put on a medium weight, blue coat that reached almost to Carmina's ankles. He wore tan chinos. A black leather biker's jacket covered a long sleeved, heavy wool, black shirt extending past his wrists and concealing the hated tattoo. On his feet he wore fleece lined, over the ankle, leather after ski boots.

Bennie put his hand on Carmina's elbow and walked with her toward the elevator. They smiled at each other but said nothing as they descended to ground level, and walked outside into the bright noon sunlight. A cab waited opposite the door. He gently guided her toward the cab, and opened a rear door for her to get in. She was relieved she didn't have to walk the two blocks to the Hihat in her high heels. She only wore them when she was trying to impress someone. She believed Bennie sensed her discomfort from the heels, and hired the cab out of consideration for her. He left a five-dollar bill for the two minute ride. In return he received a smile and a concealed thumbs up in return from the cab driver, who figured they were another couple hurrying in for a noontime quickie in the hotel.

They entered the hotel and took an elevator up to the Chesapeake Grill on the rooftop level. Bennie had a reservation, so the hostess gave them a table at a window overlooking the rooftops of Old Town Alexandria and the Potomac River beyond Washington National Airport. The view was enhanced by swaying trees, which appeared to be energized into dancing a samba by the wind and cheery sunshine.

A waiter appeared when they were seated and asked for their drink order. Carmina felt naughty and wanted a Martini or Margarita, or two of them, but she waited for Bennie to order first.

"I am allergic to alcohol," he said. "It stops up my nose, like when I have a cold. But don't let me stop you from having whatever you want. I like alcohol free beer. Coors is my favorite brand. Bring me one now. Please do not pour it. I want to pour it myself so it will have a big foamy head."

"Oh, I almost never drink during working hours," Carmina lied. "But this is such a beautiful view." She pointed out the window. "I feel like celebrating just from being up here. I'd like a Margarita."

"With salt on the rim?" the waiter asked.

She nodded her head. "Yes, please."

The waiter left and they both stared out the window for half a minute without speaking. Then, as if it were rehearsed, they turned simultaneously toward each other and started to say, "Where were you born?" They stopped talking and laughed.

"You first," she insisted.

Bennie put on a big smile. "OK. Here's my whole life story. I was born near Appleton, Wisconsin, and raised on my parent's farm there. My mother was from Minnesota, and my father from Wisconsin. Dad told me his grandparents were from Germany. That's where we got the name. I think it means someone was once a tailor. My dad was born on our farm. Both of them died by the time I graduated from the University of Illinois at Urbana. I got a BS in Mechanical engineering. I worked as an engineer in Waukegan, but it was a dead end job. So I decided to make something of myself and came here to be a patent examiner. That's it for me."

The waiter arrived with their drinks, and asked if they were ready to order lunch. They told him to come back. She raised her glass and said, "To our beautiful view." He clinked her glass with his beer bottle, and held it high and poured into a frosted mug until the head foamed over the rim. He saw an actor do this on an American TV show, so he figured it must be a cool way to pour beer. They perused the menu in silence for a minute or two.

Bennie looked up and beckoned to the waiter. "I'd like the strip steak, medium, with a baked potato, and salad with Roquefort dressing," he said.

She said, "I'd like the same thing, except I want bacon bits on my baked potato and Russian dressing on the salad."

The waiter looked quizzically at Bennie. "No bacon bits for me, just sour cream on the potato." He turned to Carmina, "Now it's your turn. Tell me all about yourself."

"I'm a Native American and was born and raised on a reservation in Idaho."

Bennie forced himself to smile. "Are you a tribe member?"

"Yes, the people in my tribe call themselves *Schitsu'umsh*. It means *The Discovered People.* Everyone else calls us the Coeur D'Alene. I bought this blouse at the reservation store," she pushed forward her more than ample breasts. "These animal figures are traditional tribal designs." She pressed her finger successively against several animals making her breasts undulate when her hand moved from one design to the next.

Bennie was surprised that seeing her breasts jiggle caused an incipient erection. He repositioned himself on his chair. "That sounds French. How did they get the name?"

"You're right. The Frenchmen trading for the skins gathered from the animals we trapped gave us the name. And it stuck. I guess it stuck because it's less of a mouthful than Schitsu'umsh," she said laughing.

"I'd like to know what the French name means." He smiled earnestly at her.

"The tribe name means Heart of the Awl. Our name refers to the sharpness of the trading skills of those old tribal members. I like to think I inherited some of those sharp trading skills, so watch out." She batted her big brown eyes at him.

Bennie felt his erection grow.

"I used to deal blackjack at the tribe's casino, but there wasn't any future in it. So I left Idaho and came here. I'm going to night school two evenings a week at George Washington. I wanna get a degree and become a Trademark Examining Attorney at the Trademark Office."

Bennie asked about what living on a reservation was like, and she answered talking mainly about the Idaho weather.

"Where do you live now?" Bennie asked.

"I've got a one bedroom apartment on the fifth floor of the Nobility Apartments in Rosslyn. It's close enough for me to walk to the subway entrance. So I can take the Blue line to work and back. And then on nights when I go to GW, I still take the Blue line from Crystal City to the GW stop in Foggy Bottom. Then back to the Rosslyn stop when I'm done."

"Do you have a car?" he asked

"Yes. It's an old Toyota. I don't use it much, except to go shopping. Or to go to Atlantic City to play blackjack at one of the casinos." Carmina shifted the burden of conversation to Bennie by asking him where he lived.

"I have a one bedroom apartment on the ground floor of the Butlarian Arms," he said. "I rented it already furnished, so there's not much of me in it. I do not have a car. I figured it will be less expensive if I mainly use cabs. I can rent a car when I want to travel somewhere. The cars I can rent will be fancier than any car I can afford to buy now."

By the time they discussed these topics, the waiter returned with their meals. Carmina finished her first Margarita and ordered another. She was starting to feel light headed from the drink, so she decided to talk as little as possible until she had some food in her stomach. They both concentrated on their lunches and discussed the food they were eating and other dishes they liked. Bennie only mentioned the American cuisine he'd already eaten. He was relieved he didn't have to keep a smile on his face while he was chewing his food.

Carmina was already infatuated with Bennie. He was by far the handsomest man ever to pay any attention to her. She knew he had an engineering degree, and a good job as a patent examiner. And a furnished apartment at the Butlarian Arms was not inexpensive. The second Margarita dulled her natural wariness to the point that she believed she was finally getting the attention she deserved from a man of quality. She was ready to hop into the sack with him at her first opportunity.

Bennie was putting on an admirable performance for a novice secret agent. He just smiled and tried to concentrate on maintaining eye contact and talking about something…anything. But his mind was buzzing with confusion and apprehension.

He avoided talking about religion, as O'Durea instructed him. But his curiosity prompted him to muse: *Weren't Native American heathens? Is being a heathen worse than being an infidel? Is it worse to be a heathen and deny the existence of Allah, and not to worship Him at all? Or is it worse to believe He exists, but to worship Him in the wrong way like an infidel?* Bennie closed his eyes for a moment to clear his head. He opened them and glanced cautiously at Carmina. He felt secure when he realized she'd been so intent on what she was saying she hadn't noticed his distraction.

So Bennie continued to ponder, not paying attention to what Carmina said: *What difference does any of this make to my mission. I need the higher security clearance to obtain valuable information for the jihad, and my orders are to seduce this woman into helping me get it. And it's all that matters now. Having a carnal relationship with this woman no matter what she believes will not contaminate my soul. So I need to get on with my work.*

He forced his attention back to what Carmina was saying. Fortunately she hadn't asked a question requiring an answer from him. Suddenly a plan flashed into his mind he believed O'Durea would be proud of.

"Let me change the subject," he said excitedly. "I have a kitchen full of brand new machines I have no idea how to use. I can heat water in the microwave for a cup of instant coffee, but every thing else I eat comes from a restaurant or the deli counter at the grocery store. Oh, also, I can heat up the deli food in the microwave if it gets cold before I want to eat it. Some evening when you're not too busy with your school work, maybe you could come by and teach me how to use those kitchen things."

Carmina was so tipsy she was ready to say lets go now, but her good sense suppressed her libido. "Sure. I can teach you cooking. After we get back to the office, I'll look at my school work schedule, and we can find time that's good for both of us." She knew every detail of her schedule, but she didn't want to reveal how eager she was to make their next date.

They finished eating and skipped desert. He ordered a cup of coffee with cream and sugar. She drank two cups, black. Bennie paid the check with cash and left a bigger than called for gratuity he was sure Carmina noticed. The coffee restored her almost back to full sobriety, so she barely wobbled on her high heals as they walked to the elevator and out to a cab in front of the Hihat. During the brief ride back to their office building, she held his arm in her two hands and laid her head against his shoulder. Bennie laughed nervously but said nothing. He avoided looking at her brown eyes and swaying breasts because he was afraid his erection was growing to where the bulge in his pants was going be noticeable. When the cab stopped, they got out and she thanked him for the lunch. She excused herself and hurried into the ground floor ladies room to relieve her distended bladder.

Bennie went into his office, having forgotten for the moment they were supposed to schedule a cooking lesson in his apartment.

Back at her desk with the pressure out of her bladder, those uncomfortable shoes off her feet, and her sobriety almost completely restored, Carmina's inborn wariness made her suspicious this was just too good to be true. She began to speculate about what she was getting herself into. *This handsome hunk might want something instead of, or in addition, to just getting into my pants. But so what. I'm sure I'll enjoy the sex as much as he will. I've almost always gotten as much pleasure out of it as any of my partners. So what do I have to lose? I can always say no to anything beyond our relationship, whatever the relationship turns out to be. And there's always the possibility this one's the mister right. The man I'll marry and raise a family with.*

Carmina stood up, picked up her monthly planner, and walked down the hall to Bennie's cubicle. He was sitting at his desk sorting through a list of patents relating to a machine shown in an application he was examining. "Still want a cooking lesson?" she asked.

Looking up, startled out of his deep concentration, Bennie said, "Sure I do. Forgive me for not coming right back to your desk. I get so wrapped up in what I'm doing here." He pointed toward his computer. "The image of this apparatus was on my monitor when I walked back in here after lunch. It grabbed my attention and made me forget. I am sorry." He stood and walked up to her. "I am free every evening, so you choose the day and time."

Carmina looked at her planner. "I have a class tomorrow night, but Friday is good for me."

To himself Bennie thought, *Friday at sundown my Sabbath will be over. So if I have sex with this heathen I won't sin. But I've been forgiven for everything I do for the jihad. So why do I even think these things.* "Friday is great. What time?"

"I'll go with you right after work, unless you need to do some grocery shopping."

"Uh. I forgot." Bennie waved his hands apologetically. "I'll need to buy food if we're going to cook. My pantry and refrigerator are empty, except for coffee. And some left over Chinese take out cartons I should throw out. Make a list of what you want to cook, and I'll try to find it all at the store. And if I can't find it myself, we can go after it together after work on Friday."

She said, "What do you like to eat? No the question should be what do want to learn how to cook?"

Bennie licked his lips. "I love lamb chops. Teach me how to cook lamb chops and wild rice and how to make lettuce salad. And how to bake a potato."

"Wild rice is my specialty. Lamb chops aren't always available. How about pork chops if we can't get lamb."

"No. I do not like pork chops. They're too greasy. They upset my stomach." He patted his middle. "How about veal chops, if we cannot find lamb. And if we cannot find veal or lamb, we can fix a big thick beefsteak. Please make a list and give it to me tomorrow. No, better give it to me today, so   I can shop tonight. And tomorrow I will be able to tell you if there's anything on the list I didn't find tonight."

A few minutes later Carmina returned with her shopping list. She put it on Bennie's desk and leaned over his shoulder as she pointed to items on the list and explained where those foods ordinarily could be found in a supermarket. Her breasts pushed against him as she bent down and brushed him as she straightened up. He looked up at her and she was smiling broadly as if to say, "Wasn't that nice." She gave him her phone number and told him to call if he had any questions. She asked for his phone number in case she wanted to add anything to the list. He gave her his apartment phone number, and asked if she wanted his email address too. She did, and she gave hers to him.

After work Bennie walked out into the street and called O'Durea on one of his prepaid cell phones. The sidewalk was crowded with people hurrying away from where they worked. He explained in detail what happened at lunch and afterwards, and what was planned for Friday. Then he asked what to do.

"You're doin' great," O'Durea said. "First, you go to one of the grocery stores we saw. I think I remember a Safesome and something else. Buy the expensive things on the list. But don't buy everything. Leave something off so she'll have to bring it. That way she'll feel more involved. Are potatoes on the list?"

Bennie removed the list from his pocket and glanced at it. "Yes."

"Don't you buy 'em. Tell her there were too many choices and you couldn't make up your mind. She can bring some potatoes to work with her. They won't spoil. And buy a bottle of good wine and some non-alcohol beer for you. Do you have any wine glasses?"

"I do not know," Bennie said impatiently.

"Well find out and buy four of them if you don't have any. Oh, yeah. Buy an inexpensive wine bottle opener. Go to the ABC state liquor store. The clerk'll help you. Tell him what you're eating and ask him to select a wine for you. They probably have some wine glasses there too."

"OK, I'll do all that. But Friday when we go to my apartment after work. What do I do?" Bennie looked around to see if any of the passersby could hear him talking. "Do we eat first or have sex first?" he asked softly.

O'Durea laughed heartily. "Ah, the universal question." He paused a moment to think. "You do what she wants to do. Pour her a glass of wine and see what happens. If she moves against you and kisses you, that's your signal for sex. If she goes into the kitchen and starts fixing the food, it's your signal to eat first. And some people don't have sex on their first date. But from what you've told me about how often she bumps into you, I think she'll be ready on Friday."

Bennie shielded his mouth with his hand. "So when I get the sex signal, what do I do then?"

"You take her hand and lead her into your bedroom. You start taking off your clothes. If she helps you take yours off, then you help her take hers off. When you're both naked, if she starts rubbing on you, you start rubbing on her. Follow her lead. Soon enough you'll be lying on top of her. You know what to do next. In and out until she's had enough. Don't do anything kinky unless she leads you to it or asks you to do it. And do it as often as she wants it. That's your assignment...your mission. Remember you're doing it for the jihad and for Allah." O'Durea put his hand over the cell phone while he laughed out loud.

"Wait a minute." Bennie forgot where he was and blurted loudly. "I thought the male of the species was supposed to be in charge...to dominate the female." Some women walking nearby gave him angry looks.

"You're right. That's the way it usually works out. But not always. From the way she's behaved, I think this gal has a lot more experience in the sack than you have. So use your head. If she just lays down, you take charge. If she grabs you or moves you or herself around, follow her lead."

Regaining his awareness of being in a crowd, Bennie whispered, "I'll do my best."

"I...am...sure...you...will." O'Durea hung up his phone feeling a glimmer of confidence his neophyte agent could handle the next phase of his assignment.

Chapter 20   Tryst

THEY WALKED HAND in hand to his condo after the workweek ended on Friday. She brought a valise, which she said contained the baking potatoes for their dinner and a few condiments and ingredients she didn't expect him to have. She didn't reveal that underneath the food were tooth and hairbrushes and a change of underwear. If she succeeded in spending the night, she planned on sleeping in one of his tee shirts. But she drew the line at using someone else's toothbrush.

Bennie was meticulously clean and tidy, so there was little for him to do in getting the place ready. The guy at the wine store told him not to put the bottle of merlot in the refrigerator, to serve it at room temperature. Room temperature for Bennie was as high as he could make it go— seventy-seven degrees. He was uncomfortably cold from the moment he arrived in the Capitol area and always wore a sweater or jacket. But he did like his own drinks cold, so he put the entire six-pack of alcohol-free beer in the refrigerator.

He took Carmina's coat when they walked in, hung it up, and asked "How about a glass of wine?" She nodded and went over to the refrigerator to inspect its contents. She smiled in satisfaction at his purchases and closed the door. He struggled with the corkscrew.

"Here give it to me," she said and took the corkscrew from him.

They both laughed when extraction of the cork made a pop. He poured her a glass of wine and pulled the tab to open his can of beer. He removed a frosted mug from the freezer and poured a foamy draft. The guy at the liquor store told him to dampen the mug he bought and put it into the freezer.

Carmina removed a wedge of Gruyere from the fridge, put it on a plate and set the plate on a table. She opened a package of wheat crackers, cut a slice of cheese and put it on a cracker. When he reached for the snack, she shook her head and stood next to him moving her hand toward his mouth. He opened his mouth, and she slid in the cracker and cheese. Bennie lifted his eyebrows; he was amazed at how erotic being hand fed was for him. Then she took a sip of wine and put another slice of the cheese on a cracker. She removed her hand and let the snack sit on the plate. She just stared at it. It took Bennie a moment to get the message. He held the cracker between his thumb and forefinger and moved it toward her mouth. She opened up and he slowly inserted in the snack, letting his fingers press against her lips. Bennie was even more amazed at the aphrodisiac effect of hand feeding someone else. They fed each other that way two more times and became sufficiently aroused to forget about food. He took her hand as O'Durea instructed and started for his bedroom. But she stopped and put her arms around him and held her face up for a kiss. He obliged and again was surprised by how good it felt.

They almost ran into the bedroom and fell down on top of a green wool blanket covering his queen-sized bed. She started kissing his neck, his cheeks, his chin, his eyes, his nose and each corner of his mouth. He started taking his clothes off and she helped him. Soon he was completely naked. He realized the tattoo on his wrist was visible now, so he turned his arm palm up to try to hide it. Then he noticed she was still fully dressed. Sitting there on the bed with no clothes on aroused him even further. She could see he was ready.

Carmina stood up and slowly dropped her skirt. But she restrained the urge to undress as quickly as possible. Slowly she started unbuttoning her blouse. Bennie jumped up and tried to pull it over her head. She was not used to being in such a hot room and knew the wool blanket was going to feel scratchy. So when he was out of bed, she snatched off the blanket and tossed it into a corner. She just laughed and continued slowly unbuttoning her blouse. Finally the blouse came off and she reached down to unfasten her bra. She pretended to be having trouble with the frontal clasp, so Bennie grabbed hold of the recalcitrant fitting and almost ripped it off the garment. His jaw dropped when her melon sized breasts spilled out. He had no idea they looked so enormous.

She thrust her chest toward him. "Taaa...dummm. They're real. All me," now oscillating her shoulders up and down, making her breasts bounce like a pair of miniature basketballs dribbled simultaneously by a Harlem Globetrotter showing off.

Bennie could take no more. He grabbed her arm and pulled her on to the bed. His hands moved over her body and he thrilled to the soft feel of her flesh. He kissed her throat and felt the throbbing of her heart. Her erotic teasing had aroused her also. She knew so little about him. And she feared he was going to try to use her in some way. But when she looked at this handsome man, much more handsome than any other she ever slept with, she was swept away with desire. They made love hastily and often. When it was finally over he lay on his back trembling and aching in a pool of sweat. His brain was so fogged he felt as if he were drugged. He had experienced three orgasms. Each felt as if electrodes were clamped to the tips of his ears and the tips of his toes and a jolt of current discharged between them. There was no way he could count the number of times she climaxed.

Carmina fell asleep on top of him with her arms and legs splayed out spread eagle fashion and her cheek on his chest. Her warm breath flowed down his side and against his arm. He lay motionless enjoying the heat her body radiated and soon was asleep himself.

About an hour later Bennie awoke first and was ready to go at it again. He rolled her off of him and was positioning himself above Carmina when she woke up. "Uh, uh. I'm too sore inside." She wiggled out from under him.

"Aren't you hungry? I'm starved. Say, is it always so hot in here? I'm not sure I need to put on any clothes. Do you have a tee shirt I can wear? No, better make that big a loose-fitting dress shirt," she said envisioning the effect her breasts bobbing under a tee shirt might have on him. He obliged, reaching out to hand her a heavy, long-sleeved flannel shirt that buttoned down the front.

Bennie realized he was still naked and she could see the tattoo on his wrist. He resisted the temptation to cover it up. That only called attention to it. And Carmina did see it. And what the girl's name and the heart design signified finally registered with her. But this was not the time to ask for an explanation.

"Don't you have any lighter clothes? Let me look for myself." She turned her back on him and opened the door of the only closet in the room. "Ah, this'll feel cooler." She took out a canary yellow, short-sleeved cotton shirt Bennie hadn't worn since leaving Cuba. "I'll start dinner while you take a shower. Then you can set the table and make the salad while I shower." She padded out of the room, still naked, holding his shirt in her hand.

Bennie was gratified at how confidently she took charge. He liked having her tell him what to do in this unfamiliar situation. After showering he put on a heavy, navy blue, terrycloth robe and matching over the heel slippers. He found Carmina, still naked, working in the kitchen.

He reached out as if to grab her bobbing breasts as she pranced past him toward the bathroom. While she showered, he cut a head of lettuce into wedges, and opened a bottle of prepared blue cheese salad dressing she brought in her valise. She returned from the shower, barefoot, and dressed only in his loose fitting shirt, which ended half way between her crotch and knees.

They prepared and ate the lamb chops, wild rice and baked potatoes. Then, exhausted, they went straight to bed. It never occurred to either of them that Carmina should return home and sleep in her own bed. The room was too hot for her, so she removed his shirt before she got into the bed. Although there was ample room on the queen sized bed for them to sleep apart, they lay snuggled on their sides with his back to her, one of her arms under his and down his chest, her legs tucked under his and her naked breasts pressed into his back.

They both slept through the night. Soon after the sun rose and was shining in the bedroom window, he woke up and started lazily to make love to her. She responded languidly, and after it was over they both went back to sleep. The noise of a motorcycle roaring down the street out side broke their torpor. They got out of bed, attended to their morning rituals, ate a breakfast of toast, scrambled eggs and coffee, and tumbled back into bed for one more round of tranquil lovemaking.

After a nap lasting almost until noon, Carmina got up and announced, "I'd like to stay but I've got to go home and study, and run errands. It's my time to prepare for the week ahead."

Bennie was still drowsy and didn't know what to say. All he came up with was, "I enjoyed my cooking lesson and want to learn how to do other foods, and soon."

Carmina laughed at this and hurriedly dressed herself. She gathered her things into her valise, bent over him, still lying in bed, and planted a sisterly kiss on his grinning lips. "See ya soon, and we'll do this again," she said as she walked out the bedroom door.

Chapter 21   Afterglow

BENNIE THOUGHT HE'D competently carried out his mission, but he wasn't sure. He knew she'd enjoyed the lovemaking, but he didn't know what Carmina's final thoughts about him were. He wondered if sight of the tattoo turned her off. He needed to talk to O'Durea for guidance on what to do next.

He took one of the prepaid cell phones off a bedside table and dialed the Cuban's number. O'Durea didn't have an answering machine and always let the phone ring six times before he picked up. As Bennie expected, O'Durea answered on the sixth ring with a, "Yeah." He was sitting on the shaded veranda of the old hotel drinking iced coffee.

"I had a date, and I need some advice." Bennie told him in abbreviated but graphic detail what happened. O'Durea laughed from time to time. "I'm not sure where I stand with her now. She saw the PAM tattoo. Maybe it made her mad. I really like being with her. I want to do it as often as she will."

"Stop right there," O'Durea said. "You're a soldier on a mission. What you want or don't want to do isn't important. What's important is that you follow orders and accomplish your mission. Tell me what your mission is with this girl."

Bennie delayed answering for a moment. "To get her to help me get a Top Secret security clearance."

"That's right. You understand your mission. I hope you're wrong about her being offended by the tattoo. Because the tattoo is going to be your excuse for asking for her help."

"What! How can it be." Bennie got out of bed and paced about his bedroom.

"Be quiet and listen. Your story is you're ashamed about what happened between you and Pam. You were gullible back then. Pam led you on. She told you she loved you. Pam asked you to show your love for her by getting the tattoo. You did, and it hurt like hell. Then, and this is more or less what Tailoren told me, you say she told you

you're lazy and not ambitious enough for her. So she dumped you and moved on."

"You're making me sound like a fool," Bennie said. "I'd never fall for a girl like that."

"Stop interrupting me. Then you say you got high and lost your temper. You went to a bar Pam liked and waited for her. When she came in with some of her girl friends you pushed her down and cussed her out in front of them."

"I've never been high and I'd never do anything that stupid," Bennie insisted, as he stomped around impatiently.

O'Durea ignored him and continued, "You embarrassed Pam by showing her friends the tattoo and telling them how she led you on. She wasn't injured, but she was very upset. Pam called and told you she'd get even with you one way or another. Now you're afraid an FBI field agent will interview her, and she'll make up some story. Tell some lies that'll keep you from getting the security clearance you need."

"OK. Finally this makes sense to me. What do I say next."

"Tell Carmina you have a friend at the FBI. A classmate from college who owes you a favor. A big favor. Say you took an exam for him in a course he needed to pass in order to graduate on time but he'd flunk it if he took the exam himself."

"That's cheating. I never cheated in school," Bennie said indignantly.

O'Durea took a sip of the iced coffee and reflected: *This poor sucker was willing to blow up himself and innocent bystanders, but now he's giving me a hard time about pretending he cheated to help a friend.*

He continued, "Will you just shut up and listen. The rest of your story is that your friend moved up in the Bureau. No one knows about what you did for him, and he wants to keep it that way because it might put his career in jeopardy if they found out he cheated to get his degree. So he's willing to guide your SF-86 through the FBI and get the necessary signatures and stamps on it, without submitting it to a full audit by field agents.

But tell her your SF-86 can't come into the Bureau or leave through the interagency mail. All those interagency security clearance documents get entered into a log he can't control. So say you have to hand your SF-86 directly to him. And he'll hand it directly back to you, when it has all the signatures and stamps it needs."

"Is any of this true? Would a FBI officer suppress a field audit for a friend?" Bennie stopped pacing around and sat on his bed.

"Of course not. Don't be naive. No one at the FBI ever does something like this. They're incorruptible, but Carmina doesn't know that. This is your cover story for her. The SF-86 I'm going to send back to you will be a complete forgery. All the girl has to do is to put it into a Patent Office mail envelope, log it in or whatever they do when it comes from the Bureau, and pass the form on so it gets into your personnel file. Think she'll do it?"

"Yeah, I do. She really liked what we did. And told me she wants to spend more time with me," Bennie said with pride. "Now that I have the story you just gave me, I can tell her about the tattoo."

"No! Don't you bring it up. It'll be better if she brings it up. Act guilty about the tattoo. If she asks about it, apologize, and tell her the story about Pam dumping you. But if she doesn't say anything for a week or two, you'll have to bring the tattoo up. And when you tell her about it act like you're embarrassed and are confessing something you're ashamed of."

"But I am the victim here. Why should I feel ashamed?" Bennie jumped off the bed and started pacing around again.

"OK. Don't act ashamed. Act angry, or however you think a victim should act. That'll set the stage for telling her the story about Pam threatening to get even with you. It'll be too much for you to ask her to accept the bogus SF-86 any time soon. Let the affair go on for at least a month before you ask her. And check with me before you do." O'Durea paused to take another drink of iced coffee.

"You have any more orders to give me now," Bennie said, suddenly resentful.

"Have a good time. Spend money entertaining her as often as you can. Take her out to lunch and dinner a lot. Rent a fancy car, and take her away for a couple of weekends. Somewhere she wants to go but can't afford. Buy her some sexy nighties. But don't buy her anything really expensive. You don't want her to feel like you're paying her, like her body is for sale. If she's the independent type, let her spend some of her own money when you go out."

"OK. Thanks for those orders," Bennie said now in a friendlier tone. "And I almost forgot. Your hunch was right. She's an American Indian." And they ended the call.

Bennie lay back on his bed thought about their lovemaking. Carmina looked sexy enough for him. Sure, she'd be more erotic if she was obese, but she was heavy enough to turn him on. And maybe he could fatten her up by taking her out to restaurants where she'd eat rich food.

His feeling of depression from still being alive and being lonely ebbed. Bennie felt happy for the first time in as far back as he could remember. He thought about how good it was to have the feeling Carmina might care about him. But guilt from thinking about what was going to happen to her remained.

This time he didn't unroll his prayer rug and pray for guidance. He picked up the bottle of Merlot, put the open end in his mouth, and drank the last few ounces left in its bottom. His former scientific skepticism about the validity of his religion was creeping back into the edge of his consciousness. Bennie decided not to initiate any further contact with O'Durea.

When Carmina walked up to her desk on Monday and took off her coat, the clerks at the adjacent desks uttered amused titters and give each other knowing winks.

"What," she asked, looking astonished. "What is it?"

Hearing the commotion, Lilly Amber leaned out of the door to her office, pointed a finger at Carmina, and ordered, "Girl, move your scalp collecting, Native American fanny in here."

Carmina got up, went into her boss's office and sat down on the only chair available for visitors. "What." she implored. "What has got into everyone this morning?"

Lilly bellowed with laughter. She stood up and stuck her head out of her office door and said, "Did you hear that girls. She wants to know what's got into you all." Everyone within earshot laughed. Returning to her chair, Lilly faced Carmina and, pretending to be serious, said, sternly "The question, young lady, is not what's got into them now. The question should be who got into you, and was it really that good?" Then she shook with laughter.

Carmina was embarrassed. But she was also happy to be the subject of so much attention, and proud to be credited with having the scalp of the best looking man in their work unit. "How do any of you know what happened. I'm sure he didn't talk."

"You sashay in here like you just won the lottery," Lilly admonished. "Your body language, your red complexion and the look on your face all say you had the best sex of your life. Now close that door, girl, and tell me all of the details you dare to admit." And so Carmina and Bennie became an item of gossip that spread to everyone who knew anything about them.

Their life together settled into a relaxed routine. He usually slept at her apartment on Wednesday and Thursday nights when she went to night classes at George Washington, and she usually slept at his apartment on Monday and Tuesday nights. Friday night and the weekend nights varied and were the subject of negotiation. Some weeks either or both of them wanted Friday night off. On most of the weekends he convinced her to find some place for them to go and stay: at a resort, or just a hotel away from the Capitol area. On other weekends they didn't see each other at all, especially when Carmina needed to catch up on her class work.

Their lovemaking cooled from incandescent to torrid to heated. Both were always eager for it and ready to give their time in bed top priority when they were with each other. Carmina could always turn him on by baring her breasts. One weekend they drove to Atlantic City so   Carmina could play blackjack. But she only spent three hours at the gambling table. They spent the rest of their time lovemaking, or sleeping and otherwise recovering from the act.

Bennie tried to apply his scientific training to analysis of why he felt so much better. But the best he could come up with was that his previous feelings of depression probably were caused by excess testosterone in his body. He no longer wanted to end his life and receive the rewards the Wahhabi Imams promised for martyrs in heaven. His life on earth was good enough the way it was right now. But the hatred of infidels the Imams instilled in him raged on unabated. So he was determined to continue his work supplying vital Patent Office codes and information to the jihad. He needed to compartmentalize his relationship with Carmina, and banish thoughts about infidels and the jihad from his consciousness when he was with her.

Chapter 22   Favor

BENNIE WAS NOT a good actor. But his clumsy attempts at trying to look like he felt guilty about the tattoo, and to conceal it caused the result O'Durea hopped for. One evening Carmina could take it no more. As the two of them lay naked on his bed having napped after lovemaking, he turned his right arm so his wrist was down as he always did when they were together.

"I can't stand it any more. Who is she?" Carmina grabbed his hand and turned it over so the wrist tattoo was visible.

"I am so ashamed. I hoped you would never want to know."

"Well it can't be all that bad. You didn't murder her did you? When her man has something as obvious as that," pointing to the tattoo, "a woman has to be told all about it. Now tell me." She faced him and propped herself up on one elbow so her nipples pointed accusingly at his face.

"I am hungry," he said eyeing her disapproving mammaries while licking his lips and advancing his mouth toward them.

She pushed his head away. "No you don't. Nothing more until I have the whole story."

Bennie turned to lie on his back and raised his right wrist to his face. "I've often thought of having this thing removed. But it hurt so much when I got it. And they say it hurts even more to get one removed. So I chickened out. But if it really offends you, I will get it taken off."

"Will you please stop beating around the bush and tell me about it. How do I know if I'm offended if I don't know what happened?"

"Ok, here goes, but promise you won't hate me."

"I'm beginning to hate you right now, and I really will hate you if you don't get on with the story." She grabbed his arm and held the tattoo in front of her face.

"I'm ashamed about what happened between me and Pam. Her name was Pamella Brown."

Carmina laughed. "You mean like in the old song about all the good times and fooling around."

"I don't know about any song, but Pam and I did fool around. Not like you and me. It was different. Nothing was ever even close to being as good for me as it is now. I was gullible back then. Pam said she loved me and asked me to show my love by getting the tattoo with her name. She sat there with me while the guy in the dingy parlor did it. Nobody told me how much it hurt." He snatched his hand from her and shook it vigorously, as if trying to relieve pain. "If I knew, I do not think I'd have done it. And it seemed to excite her…watching me in all that pain. She was very passionate for a while. It turned her on to look at her name in the tattoo. She held on to my arm so she could see her name when we made love. One day about two or three months later, out of the blue, she tells me I'm lazy and not ambitious enough for her. She says she is going to dump me and move on to someone better."

Bennie shifted on to his side and faced Carmina. "I was crushed. I was younger then, of course. But she really led me on. One weekend I got high and lost my temper. I went to a bar she liked and waited for her. When she came in with some of her girl friends I pushed her down and cussed her out in front of them. I embarrassed her. I showed her friends the tattoo and told them she lied and led me on. She wasn't injured physically, but I think someone called the police. I left in a hurry, and they never charged me with anything. But I do not know if my name is in the police records."

He rubbed his wrist as if he were washing off dirt.

"Pam was so upset and scared of me afterward that she left Waukegan. She moved to Annapolis. One day she called me and said she was going to get even with me one way or another. I heard from one of her friends that she married some naval officer. I don't know what her name is now or where she is now. I want to forget about her completely, but I keep seeing this thing." Again he rubbed at his wrist.

"I don't care," Carmina said. "Now that I know the whole story, the tattoo's no more important to me than the mole on your shoulder. It's a minor blemish on your otherwise beautiful body. I'm not offended by it. Now love me again." She pulled him on top of her supine body.

Afterward when Carmina swung her feet off the bed and started to walk to the bathroom for a shower, she stubbed her toe on something protruding from under the bed. She reached down and rubbed her toe. Then she noticed the end of the cylindrical case in which Bennie kept his prayer rug. She pulled it part way out from under the bed and asked, "What's in this beautiful leather tube?"

"It is my fishing rod case," Bennie lied, remembering the question by charter boat captain Finney asking if his tube contained fishing rods.

"Oh you like to fish. We haven't talked about that. There's a lake full of trout on our reservation. Let's fly up there when the weather gets nice. I know all the tribe's secret fishing holes. I can guarantee we'll catch more fish than you ever have before. And I'd like for you to meet my parents."

"Sounds like fun. We can go there after I earn enough vacation time to go for at least a week." The thought of meeting her parents filled him with dread.

With her curiosity aroused, when it was Bennie's turn to shower, Carmina took the leather tube out from under the bed and pulled the zipper half way down its length. What she saw inside was not fishing rods, but instead, a rolled up piece of fabric. She folded out one of its edges and saw an intricate design woven into the fabric. She was stunned. Bennie had lied to her. He didn't have any fishing rods. She began to wonder what else he'd lied about. Maybe what he'd told her about Pam was also a lie. She wound back the end of the fabric she'd folded out, pulled the zipper closed and pushed the tube back under the bed.

Carmina didn't know what she should believe. She smiled as the thought entered her mind that maybe the piece of fabric was a present for her. Maybe Bennie told her a little white lie so he could surprise her later with a gift. She decided for the time being to give him the benefit of the doubt. She fantasized receiving the present and decided she'd act surprised when he revealed he'd been hiding in the leather tube a tapestry he'd bought for her.

Three weeks later O'Durea telephoned Bennie. "It's time to ask Carmina for the favor. The counterfeit SF-86 is on its way to you. When it gets there you tell the girl the story I gave you about having a friend at the FBI."

An envelope addressed to Bennie arrived in the mail. He opened it and took out the SF-86. It had signatures and stamps in all of the required places. He postponed showing it to Carmina. He enjoyed her company, and the sex, too much to risk alienating her by asking her to do something dishonest. So he put the SF-86 in his desk and tried to forget about it. A week later O'Durea called and asked what happened.

"She is not going to go along with this," Bennie complained.

"What did she say when you asked her?"

"I did not ask her," Bennie muttered.

"Your orders were to ask her!"

"Yes, I know but I'm afraid it'll compromise my entire mission."

"That's not your decision to make. I say it's worth the risk. Now do it," O'Durea ordered.

The next night when Carmina and Bennie walked into his apartment after work, the SF-86 was in the middle of his kitchen table. He didn't say anything.

Carmina saw it and picked it up. "Where'd this come from?"

"I have a friend at the FBI. He's pretty high up over there. Anyway, he chaperoned this through for me."

"Isn't that unusual. I don't remember getting this back from you. Did you give it to someone else at the Patent Office to send over to the Bureau?" she asked suspiciously.

"No. I handed it directly to him and he handed it directly back to me." Bennie avoided eye contact.

"How come you got the special treatment? It usually takes months before we get these back from the Bureau," her skepticism obvious from the frown on her face.

"Remember I told you Pam said she was going to get even with me. Well I talked to Rog… never mind his name. I talked to my friend and he said if she lied and told a field agent something bad about me, it might get my application rejected. I asked him if there was anything he could do to help. You see he was my classmate at college, and I did him a real big favor."

Carmina stared at the form, also avoiding eye contact. She asked, "What kind of favor?"

"I took the final exam in thermodynamics for him. He needed to pass the exam in order to graduate on time. He would flunk it if he took the exam himself. Now he's moved up in the Bureau. No one knows about what I did for him. It will be considered cheating, and he wants to keep it secret. So he was willing to guide my SF-86 through the FBI and get the necessary signatures and stamps on it, without submitting it to audit by field agents."

Bennie reached out and took the form from Carmina. "But this particular SF-86 couldn't come into the Bureau or leave through the interagency mail. All these security forms get entered into a log he can't control. So we have to get this SF-86 into my personnel file some other way." He waved the form at her. "Got any ideas."

"I don't know about this. Sounds illegal to me. And they get real nasty at personnel when you screw up anything concerning national defense. I don't know," she shook her head reproachfully.

"What happens if you just put this SF-86 in an interoffice envelope addressed to personnel. Who cares where it came from? Who has to know it came from you. I don't think there's anything illegal going on here. My friend will not risk his career for me. He acted as if all he was doing was cutting corners, something that goes on all the time over there. They expect to do favors for their friends to speed things up. So how about it. If you don't help, I will have to tell him he wasted the time he spent getting this approved or me."

"OK, let me have it. I'll send it on down to personnel."

Bennie handed the form back to Carmina. She walked to the entry hall, put it in her purse and reflected: *I was afraid this affair was too good to be true. I always expected he had some ulterior motive in addition to the sex. But my instincts tell me he genuinely likes me. My lumpy body really turns him on. He's so good looking he could make out with any of the other single girls. They're always flirting with him. And some have really great figures. And he could ask one of them to send this form down to Personnel for him. But he's stayed with me. I'll decide what to do after I have a chance to think about this some more when I'm alone. I won't risk ending it with him right now by saying no. And he might surprise me with the present he's hiding under the bed in that leather tube.*

The next day Carmina put the SF-86 in an unmarked manila folder in her desk. She decided to hold on to it for a week, but to tell Bennie she sent on to Personnel. During the week she'd see if his attitude toward her changed. If he lost interest in her, she'd give the form back to him and break off their relationship. But the exact opposite happened. Bennie became more attentive to her and more considerate of her wants and moods. He was suffering from guilt for what he feared was to be a fatwa of death placed on Carmina by O'Durea.

Bennie made a momentous decision sealing his destiny. *I no longer want to die for the jihad. I am content to keep on living. If I have to cause others to die in order to do the jihad's work, I will be the one who decides to make them die. But I will not be told who I must make die. And I choose not to make Carmina die.*

During the next four days Bennie resisted advances by two attractive girls. When she saw Bennie giving those women a cold shoulder while at the same time doting over her, it made Carmina feel so good she removed the SF-86 from the manila folder and sent it on its way to the Personnel Office.

Two weeks passed and there were no repercussions. The SF-86 was accepted as legitimate. A clerk from Personnel phoned Bennie and told him he now had a Top Secret clearance and was permitted to examine patent applications with that security classification. From now on he was going to get the access codes to patent applications classified Top Secret. He could pass these codes on to the computer hackers working for the jihad.

Bennie reported to O'Durea what he hoped was good news. A week later a padded envelope arrived containing a death button and instructions to take a photograph of Carmina Burneta and send it with the death button to a designated post office box in Baltimore. Since he was spending so much time with the girl, his instructions also said

O'Durea was going to contact him to schedule her fatwa at a time when he'd have an alibi. Bennie did not expect the fatwa to be set up so soon after he was cleared for Top Secret. He decided to ignore his orders.

Chapter 23   Utility

FIVE WEEKS AFTER their initial meeting in Levy's office, Rosalind phoned Hamilton. "The formal drawings and papers for your Utility Patent Application are ready for you to read. Also, the Official Filing Receipt for the Provisional patent application arrived from the Patent Office. The Receipt verifies Allan Hamilton has invented a death ray for murdering Arabs."

Hamilton was so delighted he put down the brush he was using to paint the gutters on his house, and without changing clothes, drove directly to Levy's office. Smelling of turpentine, he burst into the office with a big smile on his face.

Rosalind anticipated their client's enthusiasm and made twenty copies of the official Patent Office Filing Receipt naming Hamilton as the inventor of a death ray for murdering Arabs. She handed a manila folder containing those copies to him the moment he came up to her desk. Hamilton looked at the form having his name on it and noted all of the copies she prepared for him. He walked around her desk and gave the still seated, and startled, Rosalind a hug.

Levy heard the commotion, and opened the door from his office. Hamilton was standing in the doorway grinning at him. "C'mon in and sit down," the attorney said pointing to the same chair Hamilton used previously.

"Here's your copy of the final draft of the Utility patent application," he said and handed an envelope to Hamilton. "The formal drawings from a patent draftsman are clipped to the back. Read the draft carefully to make sure the best mode for practicing your invention is completely and accurately described. And also correctly shown in the drawings."

Hamilton pulled the papers out of the envelope and quickly flipped through them. He looked at Levy expectantly. "We can't change anything in the descriptive part of your application or the drawings after it's been filed," Levy said. "The only way we can change any of those details is to start from scratch by filing a new application. That's expensive to do." Hamilton nodded his head.

"The last eight pages are the claims," Levy continued. "The claims are the legal definitions of your invention. But we are allowed to change the claims. And we usually have to make changes in the claims when we negotiate the final legal definition of your invention with a patent examiner."

Hamilton turned to the claims and casually studied them. A frown spread across his face.

Levy resumed his lecture, "Claims have to be in a peculiar form that's evolved over the years. So don't worry if you don't understand what they mean. Interpreting patent claims is a job for patent lawyers and judges. We're always accused of making the claims mysterious to keep the work from going to ordinary lawyers," he joked.

Hamilton's frown was replaced by a smirk. "You want me to read it now…here?" he asked.

"No. Take this draft home where you can study it carefully. Then come back and we'll talk about anything you think needs to be changed. When we're both satisfied with what the specification says, you can sign the formal papers, and I'll mail the application to the Patent Office.

Did you notice the title of your invention is now 'Methods and Apparatus For Creating A Death Ray.' There's not one word in it about murder or Arabs."

Hamilton looked at the title page, which was on top. He opened his mouth as if to speak, but then just closed it and nodded.

Levy said, "Now, I'd like to change the subject and hear about your meeting at the Pentagon." Levy got up and opened his office door open because he knew Rosalind was as curious as he was about Hamilton's encounter with the military brass.

Hamilton tipped his chair back and said, "I drove my Buick to Washington because I didn't want the hassle of going through airport security carrying live roaches in a shoe box."

Both of his listeners burst out laughing as they envisioned a security guard's expressions of dismay when he opening a box containing roaches scurrying around as they tried to escape.

"I phoned the Colonel I was scheduled to meet with and told him about what I'd be bringing. His name is Elron Bench, and I guess he's in his fifties. Bench must have passed word of the roaches down the line because the MP who inspected me was able keep a straight face when he opened the box and the roaches jumped up at him. I don't know where he was from, but he whistled. So, I don't think he'd ever seen Florida sized roaches before."

Again the attorney and paralegal started laughing.

"When we first got together, I didn't tell Colonel Bench we'd filed any kind of patent application. I just handed him a copy of the drawing sheets with the sketches I made for you. Those copies of the sketches he was looking at were the ones Rosalind made for me before you two signed on them as witnesses. So there was no indication anyone else ever saw the sketches. And I took out the prototype of the death ray gun and laid it on his desk. The desk was light oak, the only decent looking furniture in the office. The rest was Government Issue grey metal.

Bench called in two lieutenants, and everyone took a turn zapping a roach with the ray gun. After the demonstration convinced them it worked, I told him I wanted my death ray to be used by the infantry. I said I wanted my death ray to be used to kill Arabs because an Arab murdered my son, shot him in the back when he was a Marine helping their children. He said he was sorry to hear of my loss, but the final use of the ray gun could not be determined until they established the ultimate power or force wave it shot out."

Levy picked up a pen and started taking notes on a yellow legal pad.

"The Colonel had what seemed like dozens of questions I couldn't answer. Like measurements of the force the ray exerted, and over what distances was it effective, and what happens if you lengthen the tube, or increase the voltage. I told him I was investigating those last things but only had limited equipment available to me. And I was hoping for a contract from the Pentagon to finance the research. He suggested I turn all of the development work over to the Defense Department."

Levy interrupted, asking, "Did any of those officers sign the drawings as witnesses?"

Hamilton shook his head.

"Did they give you a write up of your death ray demonstration?" Levy asked.

"No, but Colonel Bench did hand me a piece of paper, and he asked me to sign it."

Levy looked down at his legal pad and continued writing.

"I told him before I signed anything, I'd like to show it to the patent attorney who filed my patent application. Bench said I'd have to come back the next day and talk to a legal officer to work out the Defense Department's rights to develop my ray gun.

You know the rest of the story. I faxed you the form they wanted me to sign. You said it was a standard Confidential Disclosure form similar to ones you used yourself dozens of times. You changed a few words to add my recommendation for the death ray being developed to kill Arab terrorists, and giving the defense department a royalty-free license for any weapon used against Arab terrorists. And you faxed it back to me. Major Olsan from their legal department accepted your changes. I signed on the dotted line. Colonel Bench and his secretary witnessed my signature."

Levy looked up from his notes and interrupted, "I need to have a copy of the form you signed in my file. Anything else I should know about?"

"Yes. I think there is. Colonel Bench said to let him know the serial number and filing date, and he'd have Major Olson pull some strings over at the Patent Office to have my patent application made Special. But he didn't explain to me the advantage of having it made Special."

Levy put down his pen and raised a finger to signal he had another question. "Did you get the names of the two lieutenants who shot the roaches?"

"No, I didn't even think about it."

"Too bad. We never know when we'll need living witnesses to testify about a successful reduction to practice of an invention." Levy sat back and rested his hands on his belly.

The pleasant expression on Hamilton's face vanished as he realized he lost potentially beneficial information, so he changed the subject.

"Remember I told you about the terrorist yelling to the crowd after he murdered my son."

Levy nodded.

"Well, I tried to look it up in an Internet dictionary. It's not easy to go from Arabic to English. Arab writing just looks like squiggles to me. I never could figure out what it means. But before I left the Pentagon, I asked Bench if there was anybody around who could translate a short Arabic phrase for me. He said they employed translators and asked what it was. He handed me a piece of paper. I wrote *al Khanjar yaqtil* on it, and gave it back to him.

Bench picked up his desk phone and tapped some buttons. He identified himself and asked for an Arabic translator. A moment later he read out loud what I'd written. He paused while he listened to someone talking at the other end of the phone line. Then he spelled out letter by letter what I'd written on the piece of paper. He wrote down on that piece of paper what'd been said back to him by the translator. He gave the paper back to me. I read it and thanked him. I picked up my stuff, got in my car, and drove back to sunny Florida."

"Good. Now that mystery is solved. What's it mean." Levy picked his pen up again.

"The translator at the Pentagon said it means 'the dagger kills'. But this doesn't make any sense to me because the assassin used a gun....not a knife or dagger...to kill Allan. I can't figure out why the murdering swine said dagger. I never heard of daggers as important symbols to Arabs. Scimitars are...maybe scimitars are, but not daggers. And he used a gun, not a dagger."

Levy wrote on the legal pad.

Hamilton said, "Now tell me what making my patent Special will do for me. Should I tell Major Olson the date and numbers he asked for?"

"Oh, yes. About special," Levy said resuming his lecture. "Well again, I remind you that you won't have a Utility patent until after the Patent Office is through examining the application you now have in your hands. Now it's only an application, not a patent. You don't have the powers and the protection of a patent until after the Patent Office issues your patent. It usually takes about two years."

"Okay, okay," said Hamilton impatiently. "But what does Special mean?"

"Making your application Special is supposed to speed up the process. Standard procedure is for the Patent Office to examine applications in the chronological order in which they receive the applications. When an application is made Special, it is examined immediately as if it were the oldest application they have on file."

"Good enough. I think I understand," Hamilton said. "I guess we want it made Special."

Levy's face indicated they were in agreement.

"New subject," Hamilton said. "There's something else I need to tell you about. Remember the first time we met here. You asked me to sign some kind of a power of attorney in case I die, and who ever's handling my estate can't make up his mind."

"Sure do." Levy picked up his pen.

"You also advised me to make a will leaving my estate to some relative or some charity. And remember I don't have any family or close friends to leave my things and property to. So I went to a local attorney, Sam Fellows. He recommended that I set up an inter vivos trust to avoid the cost and expense of probate when I die. After I die, the trust will give my assets to bounty hunters who kill Arab terrorists."

Levy looked down and began scribbling more notes while he listened.

"My trust will set up specific bounties on the terrorists we know about, and pay the bounty to whoever kills them. We haven't worked out the details of how to verify the identity and cause of death of the dead terrorists. I'm trying to consult… to get help from…the CIA and FBI on those details. You'd think they'd be tickled pink to get some help eliminating the Arab scum. But they're not happy about what I'm trying to do."

Levy looked up and smiled. "I think they regard you as someone poaching in their territory."

"Well, Sam tells me they can't stop me from offering the bounties. So I'm going to test the idea right now by putting a one million dollar bounty on the head of the murdering snake who killed my son. I hope it loosens up some tongues of the people who saw the murderer. We're going to get some publicity from Knoxx News on this. I'll be a guest on the O'Smiley Indicator news show when we work out the scheduling."

"You'll get nothing but encouragement from me on the bounties," Levy said.

"I'm hoping my example will get other people and businesses to put a price on other terrorist murderers. That way private citizens and companies can directly get revenge for friends, family members or employees killed or injured by the terrorists. An army of private bounty hunters not under the control of any government might be more effective than what the government is doing now in wiping out this plague of murdering Arab fanatics."

Hamilton stood and picked up the envelope Levy had given him.

Levy also stood and pointed to the envelope. "Now please go over this final draft and get back to me with any changes you think are needed. Then sign the Declaration document included in the envelope. It identifies you as the inventor of Methods and Apparatus for Producing a Death Ray. The Declaration also secures the benefit of the filing date of the Provisional for the Utility application, so no one you talked to after we filed the Provisional can sneak into the Patent Office and get a filing date ahead of your Utility application." The next day Hamilton returned with the signed declaration. He didn't request any changes, so Rosalind assembled the related papers, which Levy already signed, and mailed the bundle to the Patent Office.

Hamilton shook Levy's hand, walked out and blew a kiss at Rosalind as he went past her desk.

When a return receipt on a post card came back to Levy's office from the Patent Office a week later with the serial number and filing date of Hamilton's Utility application, Rosalind called the inventor and give him that information. Hamilton called Major Olsan at the

Pentagon and gave him the serial number. The Major said he'd have Hamilton's application made Special.

Chapter 24   Fatwas

TWO WEEKS AFTER it was received by the Patent Office, Hamilton's Utility patent application covering the death ray gun was given to Examiner Bennie Tailoren for examination. He called the application file up on his monitor and saw the notation that it had Special status. It was the only Special application assigned to his docket, so he put aside his other work and started reading the specification. The description of the death ray gun was thorough, and the drawings showed it in clear detail. After he read the entire specification and studied every detail in the drawings, Bennie came to the same conclusion as everyone else who read about the invention. He decided the death ray gun could not work because it violated the laws of physics.

Bennie was more thorough than most patent examiners ordinarily were at this stage of the examination process. He was curious to see if there was anything in the file of the Provisional application that might make the death ray appear more feasible. So he brought the file for Hamilton's Provisional application up on his computer terminal. He was shocked when he saw the title.

It actually said the title of the Provisional was *A Death Ray for Murdering Arabs.* He could not believe his eyes and just stared at the screen. He felt the words were both an insult and a threat to his kin and to Allah's jihad. Bennie gritted his teeth and resolved to do everything in his power to deny Mr. Hamilton a patent. When he noticed the name of the attorney who prepared the utility application, Lemont Levy, it sounded Jewish to him. Maybe the Jews were financing this weapon the inventor wanted used to murder Arabs.

Bennie decided to look into Levy's background, so he wrote the attorney's office address in his personal notebook. That evening while Carmina was attending night class, he searched the Internet on his computer for background on Levy. Sure enough when he Googled Lemont Levy's name, he found an article in the *Neighborhood Times* supplement of a Sunday *St. Petersburg Times* identifying Lemont

Levy as one of the members of the *Beth Israel Temple* in St. Pete Beach who was just elected to its Board of Directors. That confirmed Levy was a Jew. Bennie began devising a plan to put fatwas on Hamilton and Levy and to spare Carmina.

A few days later at 8:46 pm Bennie and Carmina were sitting on the sofa facing his brand new thirty-six inch HDTV set. They were eating chocolate covered Dove bars for desert after a dinner of rotisserie broiled chicken and snow peas he bought at a deli on the way home from work. On the TV screen Knoxx News's popular O'Smiley Indicator TV Show was nearing its end.

On the TV screen two men sat facing each other on opposite sides of a small table. William O'Smiley said, "Thank you for staying with us tonight, ladies and gentlemen. On this next segment we have a guest with a very creative idea on how to fight the Arab terrorists. I won't steal your thunder, Mr. Hamilton. Ladies and gentlemen, this is Arnold Hamilton. Tell us what you're doing Mr. Hamilton."

"I'm putting a bounty on the head of an Arab fiend who murdered my son. I'll pay one million dollars to any one who kills the snake who did it," Hamilton said.

"Wouldn't your money be better spent if the bounty hunters captured the terrorist? If they brought him back alive, he could be questioned, and the information he gave up could help capture more terrorists. And maybe what you're starting will snowball and result in a lot of captures."

"Mr. O'Smiley, I respect you enormously. Your show brings out news and points of view the sissy networks won't touch. So please don't be offended when I tell you it's naive to expect a captured terrorist to give up information of value. Part of their training is how to take advantage of American soft heartedness and avoid giving away any useful information. What'd we get from Saddam Hussein? Nothing we didn't already know."

"I'm not offended. Your point is well taken, Mr. Hamilton. They've put so many restrictions on what our intelligence interrogators can do with terrorists it's probably a fluke when we get any useful information. And these are the fanatics who plan on blowing us up, poisoning our water and food supplies, crashing our airplanes, and infecting us with disease germs. And we treat them as if they were entitled to have dignity and some minor comforts in captivity. I'm telling you, Mr. Hamilton, it makes my blood boil. We'd get every useful scrap of information they have if I were in charge." He smiled into the camera, "Which is why I'll never be in charge. Enough about what I'd do. Tell us about what happened to your son. And call me Bill."

"OK. Bill. And, you call me Arnie. Like I said, I've got a personal motive for revenge. An Arab viper murdered my son, Allan. Shot him in the back. Allan never saw the scum who did it. He had no chance to defend himself."

"Where and when'd it happen?"

"In Baghdad last year. Allan was a Marine in a special services unit teaching the Arab kids to play soccer. He'd been a star player in college, so when the fighting was over, the Marines assigned him to public relations. That vermin walked out of a crowd of Arab parents watching their kids play, and then the killer walked back into the crowd and no one tried to stop him before or after he shot my boy."

"What's the assassin's name?"

"Actually we don't know who the assassin was. Nobody in the onlookers could, or would, identify him. But everybody agreed he was an Arab. And he yelled something a few spectators remembered as, "*al Khanjar yaqtil.*"

"What's it mean?"

"The best I've been able to get from any Arabic translator is it means 'the dagger kills.' It's puzzling because the rat used a pistol, not a dagger. I personally think it's a war cry of some terrorist cell. But I'm just guessing. Maybe the rat who killed my boy was just some nut acting alone. But I doubt it. I can't get anyone at the CIA or FBI to admit they know anything about what it means or anyone using it. So I'm offering a bounty of one hundred thousand dollars to anyone who establishes the identity of *al Khanjar yaqtil*, or can explain to me why the murderer yelled it to the crowd."

"Now I'm going to have to use the same word you used for me, Arnie. You're being naive to think a million dollars will get you a terrorist's head, or whatever part of his body you'd have a bounty hunter bring you to prove he got your man." O'Smiley ran his finger across his throat as if he were cutting it. "The standard bounty our government pays is five million, and the last I heard, there was forty million on bin Laden's head. C'mon, Arnie. And a hundred thousand for information explaining a terror cell's slogan, or whatever those Arabic words mean. You're setting yourself up to be taken to the cleaners by some scam artist."

"Bill, I know what you said is probably true. I know this is a long shot, but I—"

"A very long shot."

"But I want to show the families and friends of the victims of these murdering Arab reptiles they're not powerless. They can do something to avenge their loved ones and friend's murders. They can set up bounties to pay to have the murderers murdered."

"You know, Arnie, my first impression is this sounds to me like just another feel good effort wealthy people can talk about at cocktail parties. A gesture that's not going to result in anything useful happening. Say. Where'd you get all this money anyway?"

"I read a book on manias. You know, Bill, like the tulip bulbs in Holland." O'Smiley nods. "Well the dotcom stock craze looked like a mania to me. So I invested the insurance money I got when my wife died in the stocks when they were going up. Then I cashed out and invested every cent I had selling them short when the market was near the top. When the dotcoms crashed, I covered my short sales. Now I want that money to avenge my son's murder. That's what my wife would want to do if she were still alive."

O'Smiley said, "If it were my money, I'd take those spare millions of bucks you've got lying around and donate them to one of the funds that'll help take care of the children of our slain servicemen? That's what I think. Now I'll let you have the last word, Arnie. But no pontificating. That's my job."

"Thank you, Bill. And thank you for making this time available to me." Hamilton turned and looked squarely into the camera, which panned in until his face filled the viewer's entire TV screen. "You people watching this show who've lost someone to these Arab demons can get revenge. Contribute some money, it doesn't have to be a lot, to a bounty earmarked to pay for the murder of an Arab murderer. I've created a web site that is a clearinghouse for information about how you can set up yourself, or just contribute to, a bounty to avenge a murder committed by the Arabs. The site is murder-an-Arab-murderer dot org. It's nonprofit. All the money you donate will go to the successful bounty hunters. Thank you again, Bill, for giving me this opportunity to tell about bounties."

"Very provocative, Arnie. I'd love to hear what they'll be saying about your web site at the State Department and CIA. Actually, now that I reflect on it, Arnie, I think you might accomplish something useful. If all of your efforts result in only one of these assassins being put out of business, it'll be worth it."

The camera panned in on the face of O'Smiley, who said, "And, Ladies and Gentlemen, now for the most ludicrous item of today."

After the TV show came to an end, the name of O'Smiley's odious guest sounded familiar to Bennie, but he couldn't recall where he'd heard the name Arnold Hamilton. And the face...the face that loomed so large...filling the screen of his TV and intruding into his living room like a gigantic, grotesque ogre was etched into his mind. The infidel, Hamilton, called Arabs fiends, snakes, vermin and reptiles, and he was promoting the murder of Arabs with bounties. He even mentioned *al Khanjar*, even though he didn't know what it signified. Bennie was shaken, and it took extra effort from Carmina to arouse him sufficiently to make love to her that night.

The next day Bennie picked up the Death Ray Utility patent application and saw the inventor's name was Arnold Hamilton, the same as O'Smiley's hateful guest. Could it be the same person? It must be the same person. Again he loaded the file for the Provisional application into his terminal. He scrolled to the Cover Sheet and saw the title was what he thought he remembered: *A Death Ray for Murdering Arabs*. The inventor was the same Arnold Hamilton O'Smiley had interviewed.

Bennie thought for a long moment and decided on a different use for the death button he believed the leaders in the jihad would approve. He planned to switch the fatwa from Carmina to Hamilton. But just to be sure the switch was not rejected, he decided not to tell anyone involved in the jihad about the new fatwa target until after the deed was done. And, hadn't the Jew lawyer written up Hamilton's death ray application for murdering Arabs. Well, he'd get another death button and put a fatwa on the Jew lawyer. O'Durea and Muhamed Allah Yatakalan would be proud of him for using his head to change the fatwas to get rid of two significant enemies of Arabs and the jihad, instead of killing a young woman who could do the jihad no harm. He sent an email to O'Durea's web address with a cheerful commentary on the weather and a cryptic remark about a lost black button in need of replacement

O'Durea was annoyed at Bennie's carelessness in losing the death button. But he had a hundred of the buttons, so there was no damage from the loss of one button. He mailed another button in a letter to Bennie's Butlarian Arms address. The letter arrived five days later with the admonition to be more careful, and to destroy the lost button if he ever found it. O'Durea also identified another box at the main post office in Baltimore as the assassin's address for the next thirty days. He told the jihad's assassins, Juan and Pedro, to stay close to the Nation's Capitol because their next hit was going to be somewhere in the area. He failed to tell them their victim was a young woman.

Patent Examiner Bennie Tailoren was now ready to set up the fatwas on the two infidels who sought to cause the murder of his fellow Arab jihadists. He had an official reason for luring Hamilton and Levy to Crystal City where he could arrange for their murders. As did everyone else who learned how Hamilton's death ray gun was supposed to operate, he believed the gun violated the laws of physics if it actually turned light energy directly into a physical force. This simply could not occur. So the death ray gun was inoperative for its intended purpose. Therefore the death ray gun did not satisfy the requirement of the Patent Laws that to be patentable, an invention must work and produce a useful result identified in the patent application.

Tailoren prepared a Patent Office Action, which is a letter from the Patent Examiner who is in charge of a pending patent application requiring some type of response by the inventor or his attorney. The Action Examiner Tailoren mailed to Levy rejected Hamilton's patent application as lacking the usefulness required by 35 United States Code Section 101 because the death ray gun was deemed to be "incredible in the light of the knowledge of the art because it was inconsistent with known scientific principles." He cited the 1963 Appeals Court decision of *In re Citron* as the legal authority for this rejection. The Patent Office Action required Hamilton to bring a death ray gun to the Patent Office and demonstrate that it worked as described and claimed in the patent application.

Levy knew Hamilton had a working model of the death ray gun that could kill roaches, so he did not file arguments contesting the Patent Examiner's rejection of his client's application, as he had the right to do. Instead, he mailed a copy of the Patent Office Action to Hamilton, and asked him to call Rosalind to find a time when they both could schedule an interview in Crystal City with the Patent Examiner to demonstrate that the death ray gun actually worked.

Hamilton was apprehensive because of the ominous tone of the Patent Office's rejection of his invention. But Levy assured him it was routine for the Patent Office to find some reason to reject something about almost every patent application. The Patent Office rules were so complex it is difficult to get every detail correct on the first go round. And the inventor or his attorney is permitted to correct informalities discovered by the Patent Examiner. In this case Levy expected the Examiner to withdraw his rejection after they demonstrated the death ray gun actually killing living creatures.

Rosalind found a morning when Hamilton, Levy and Examiner Tailoren could all be in Crystal City at the same time. Levy was scheduled to argue the appeal of a Finally Rejected application before a three-judge panel of the Patent Office Board of Appeals. The Appeal hearing was at 3:00 pm on a Monday. Rosalind set up the interview and demonstration with the Examiner Tailoren for the morning of the day following the Board of Appeals hearing. She scheduled a morning flight for Levy into Reagan National on the day of the appeal hearing, and reserved a room for him at the Dately Hotel across the street from the Patent Office. Levy planned on flying back to St. Petersburg after the death ray demonstration and interview with Tailoren.

Hamilton decided to stay in Crystal City for several days after the interview to sight see in the Nation's Capitol. Once again, he intended to drive to rather than endure the controversy of trying to get a box of live Florida roaches through airport security. He was staying at the Dately Hotel so he could confer with Levy and walk across the street with him to the interview with Examiner Tailoren. Rosalind told Hamilton he'd have to pass through a security checkpoint at the Patent Office, but it wasn't as thorough as at an airport. The inventor had to show some form of identification with his picture on it.

After she scheduled everything for Levy and confirmed his reservations, Rosalind stuck her head into his office and said, "In all the years I've been with you, that was one of the strangest conversations I've ever had with a Patent Office Examiner."

Levy looked away from his computer. "How come?"

"The Examiner wanted to know where you'd be staying, and for how long you'd be there, and if I knew your room number in advance to your checking in. And he wanted the same information for Hamilton. He seemed annoyed you weren't going to be staying there longer. And he even said he could reschedule the death ray gun demonstration to be held several days before your Board of Appeals hearing, to give you more time in Crystal City. I've never heard of a Patent Examiner being so concerned about an attorney's schedule. I started to ask him why he cared about when you were coming and going, but decided to let it drop."

"You did the right thing in not asking. I want to keep my schedule there short and tight so he won't have the chance to throw some new rejection or technicality at us after we get there and I'm not prepared for it."

Rosalind said, "Well, I have Hamilton's schedule, assuming everything goes well on his drive up there with the box of roaches. And I gave it to, what's siz name...Tailoren. He seemed satisfied one of you was going to be there for a week or more. What does he care how long you'll be around the Patent Office?"

"I could give you some guesses. But I'd just be speculating. But his asking for all the details of our schedules sounds strange to me too. He can always call us on the phone when he has questions or is going to make new demands. Oh, yeah. How about getting us through security."

"I told the Examiner Hamilton would bring live roaches in a shoebox and the death ray gun to shoot them with. He said he'd notify their Security Department to clear the way for the two of you. And another thing I noticed. He talks funny, more formal than we do. Do you think he was born in some foreign country and learned English as a second language?"

"Could be," Levy said. "You already know that many of the Examiners we deal with have foreign accents. But so what."

Rosalind shrugged and turned back to her computer.

After he received their schedules, Tailoren sent a letter to the assassin's Baltimore post office box. His letter gave the names and arrival and departure schedules of his intended victims. It also advised the killers their victims were staying at the Dately Hotel at Crystal City across the street from the Patent Office. He promised to overnight mail the two death buttons together with photos of the targeted infidels he would take on the day of his interview with them.

Chapter 25   Interview

WHEN LEVY FLEW into Reagan National and checked in at the Dately Hotel, there was a message from Examiner Bennie Tailoren asking him to phone him at the Patent Office. Though Levy was irritated at the distraction from his concentration on the appeal hearing, he called and spoke to Tailoren.

Tailoren hoped to have Levy there long enough for the assassins to get him before they killed Hamilton. Novice that he was at being a secret agent, it did not occur to him that the murders of both an inventor and his patent attorney within days of each other would cast suspicion on him because they both contacted him shortly before their deaths.

He told Levy the interview and demonstration needed to be rescheduled for half an hour earlier the next day to accommodate the Security Department, and he asked for Levy's room number in case there were any more changes. Levy told him his room number, reminded him they'd bring the death ray gun and a box of roaches with them, and hung up the phone without pausing to exchange small talk.

At 3:00 pm Levy gave the scheduled oral presentation before the Patent Office Board of Appeals.

That evening Hamilton arrived at the Dately Hotel. They both ate their dinners earlier, Hamilton at a rest stop on I-95 and Levy at the grill in the Dately. After Hamilton was settled in his room, the two men met for a nightcap in the hotel bar. Hamilton assured Levy some of the roaches were still alive, and he brought plenty of batteries for the death ray gun. They agreed to meet for breakfast at 8:00 the next morning to discuss the interview and to give Levy time to check out of the hotel before they left at 9:45 to meet Examiner Tailoren at the security check point of Crystal Plaza Building 4.

The next morning after they were seated at a table and served their breakfasts, Levy said, "Some of these Patent Examiners are quirky, so don't be surprised at anything he says. And always be respectful. Call him Examiner Tailoren. Never use his first name. Some of the procedural points that might come up are very technical and exacting. So don't expect to understand everything he and I talk about. I'll explain it all to you after we leave his office." Levy picked up a bagel, spread honey on it, took a bite and chewed hurriedly. "And like almost all Government operations the Patent Office is politically correct. So don't talk about Arabs being bad people and don't talk about murder or killing anything. Especially not murder."

Hamilton put down his fork and frowned. "I've been brow beaten enough about the word murder not to use it. But isn't killing what my death ray is supposed to do?"

"Yes. That's understood. So leave it unsaid. Let the Examiner talk about killing if he wants to bring it up." The two men resumed chewing in silence.

"Rosalind thought Examiner Tailoren was unusually inquisitive about where we'd be staying and for how long. So humor him if he asks you where you'll be."

After finishing breakfast, they both made pit stops and Levy checked out. He carried his overnight suitcase and brief case with him. Hamilton carried his polished leather suitcase with the ray gun inside, and a Nike shoebox with the roaches. At 9:55 they walked up to the security guard station just inside the entrance of Building 4. Levy was wearing the same, now somewhat rumpled, grey flannel suit, blue oxford cloth button down shirt and solid, navy blue tie he wore the afternoon before at the Appeal hearing. His black loafers were even more scuffed than usual. He pinned his Patent Office identification badge to the outside of the breast pocket of his coat. Hamilton wore dark brown wool slacks, and an open collared white dress shirt under a tan cashmere sweater.

Levy told the guard they were there to see Patent Examiner Bennie Tailoren in Group 3300. The guard extended his thumb and pointed over his shoulder at two men standing behind him. Examiner Tailoren and short, stocky, supervisory guard Arthar Battle were standing next to each other. They walked up to the checkpoint. Tailoren wore a thick, black ski sweater and heavy black wool pants; he scowled at them and introduced himself and Battle. The Security

Department knew what they were bringing with them, so only a cursory look was given at their belongings. The guard on duty winced when he removed the top of the shoebox and activated the roaches into jumping toward him. Hamilton showed his picture on his Florida driver's license and was waved through along with Levy.

Guard Battle, grey haired and ruddy complexioned, wore a blue uniform and kept brushing his palm against the butt of his holstered revolver, as if to continually reassure himself it was there if he needed it.

The four men entered the elevator together, rode up to the third floor, and walked into Examiner Tailoren's office with a minimum of small talk. Carmina knew about the interview, but she wanted no part of it because it involved roaches. She turned her back and looked the other way when she heard the four men walking down the hall toward Tailoren's cubicle. Levy, ever attentive to the mood of an Examiner during an interview, noticed Tailoren rubbing his hands together and massaging the back of his neck. The attorney wondered if the Examiner was already upset about something, or whether he was just nervous about killing roaches in his office.

With four people in the cubicle, there wasn't room for all of them to sit comfortably, so they all stood. Battle moved the visitor's chair out into the hall to provide more room for them to spread out. Tailoren stood behind his desk, and guard Battle stood in the doorway. He continued to massage the butt of his weapon with the palm of his hand. Hamilton stood at one end of Tailoren's desk with his knees against it; he placed the box of roaches near the corner of the desk closest to the office door. The inventor carefully aligned the edges at one corner of the shoebox with the edges at a corner of the desk. Battle inched away slightly.

Levy, standing next to Hamilton and also pressing against the desk with his knees, took a copy of the patent application out of his brief case and laid it open on the desk top. "How do you want the interview to proceed," he said and looked up into the eyes of the taller Tailoren. The glowering look he got back told him Tailoren was hostile to his client's patent application.

"Let's get this interview over with in a hurry by you attempting to kill a roach with this so-called death ray gun." Tailoren spat the words. "And I brought a camera to record the fiasco." He took a small Olympus digital camera out of his desk drawer and held it up.

"Sure," said Hamilton as he gave the Examiner a puzzled look. He removed the top from the shoebox, which caused three roaches to scurry crazily around its periphery and crawl over bodies of two of their former companions lying dead on their backs. He opened his brief case, removed the ray gun and put it down on the desk beside the box of roaches. The bugs calmed down a bit but were now nervously twitching their antennae instead of running around wildly. Hamilton asked Tailoren, "You want to shoot one of them?"

Tailoren shook his head, bent over and flashed a photo of the roaches in the shoebox, causing them to start running around in it again. Then he straightened up and flashed a photo of Hamilton.

"How about you." Hamilton said holding the ray gun out toward Arthar Battle.

"I'll do it, but how does the thing work." Battle said.

"You are the inventor." Tailoren interjected. "You show us how it works." He gestured toward Hamilton and moved to a position from which he aimed his camera into the roach box.

"All right. Here's how it works," Hamilton said. He put a pencil down on Tailoren's desk. "When you turn this laser pointer on, it sends out a laser beam that shows where the gun's aimed." He flashed the laser beam on the desk and moved it on to the pencil.

"That did not do one bit of damage to anything," Tailoren said triumphantly.

"It's not supposed to," Hamilton said. "It's just an aiming tool…to make sure the death ray will hit the target. Watch this." He held the ray gun over the box of roaches. When the laser beam was shining on the back of one of the roaches, he pressed the button on the top of the gun. There was a faint flash of purple light but no sound. The targeted roach was lying broken in half against one side of the box.

"Wow," Battle said. "The ray gun really worked. Say, what's the smell?"

"I shot the biggest one first," Hamilton said pointing at the dead bug with a pencil. "The first one was a Florida Woods roach, and those babies give off an odor that smells something like almonds when you squash them. The others are an American roach and a Brown roach. I brought some of each species because I wanted to be sure some of them survived the trip up here. Did you get a picture," he said turning toward Tailoren.

"No, but I will now." The Examiner bent over and shot a photo of the dead roach in the shoebox, and shot another as he straightened up, this time of the startled Levy. "Pictures of everyone to make the record complete." And he photographed Guard Battle.

Hamilton took a new battery out of his suitcase. "I'll reload the ray gun now." When the spent battery was replaced with a new one, he held the ray gun out to Tailoren with handgrip end toward the Examiner. "Here…you try it."

Tailoren took hold of the ray gun by its handle and, with the gun still pointed at Hamilton, he turned on the laser light which made a red spot on the inventor's chest.

Tailoren put his finger on the trigger button. "What will happen if I pressed this button now?"

"No one knows." Hamilton said. "I've never shot any human being with it. But I do know it won't kill a rabbit or even a mouse because I've tried it on both of them. It hardly did anything to the rabbit I shot with it. It knocked the mouse sideways and stunned it. But it recovered in a few minutes. I think if I'd shot the same mouse several times in quick succession, it'd kill it."

Hamilton made several quick chops with his hand. "Maybe if you hit a person with the death ray in just the right place, like those kill points they talk about in some of the Bruce Lee KungFu movies, maybe you could kill someone."

Tailoren sneered, "But you did not do any of that, so we do not know if it will ever kill a human. I'll try it out now."

"Want me to take your picture?" Hamilton said and reached for the Examiner's camera.

"No! I do not," was the sharp reply from Tailoren. He moved until he stood over the box that now contained two live roaches. The laser pointer remained on so he moved the ray gun until the red spot was on the back of one of the roaches, and pressed the trigger button. There was another faint flash of purple light, and the second roach lay dead, oozing out its custardy innards.

Tailoren handed the ray gun back to Hamilton and picked up his camera. "I will take a few more pictures." He shot half dozen to ten photos in rapid succession, it being impossible for anyone except Tailoren to know for sure what images he captured.

"Want to give it a try, Officer," Hamilton said to Battle as he removed the spent battery and put in a fresh one.

"Sure," Battle said. He held out his hand for the weapon. The guard turned on the laser light, aimed and fired the weapon with the same result. The third roach lay dead in the bottom of the shoebox.

Levy grinned at the dour faced Tailoren, "I believe we've demonstrated that Mr. Hamilton's invention will indeed produce a ray that will cause the death of a living creature. This is exactly what is described in his patent application. Therefore the requirement of 35 U.S.C. 101 has been satisfied and the rejection of the application for lack of utility or inoperativeness should be withdrawn."

Tailoren shook his head, "I want to make sure this is not some kind of trick...that a ray from your contraption is what actually hit those roaches. I have seen enough of the so-called magic tricks to know things are not always what they look like. There are some very complicated paraphernalia magicians can use to fool an audience. How do I know those roaches were real and not just clever props set to explode when you shined a light beam on them."

"Well what do you want us to do now?" the perplexed Levy asked.

"I do not know. It's your show. You have the burden of proof. It is not my responsibility to tell you how to prove your point."

"I have an idea," Hamilton said. "I brought enough batteries for two more shots in case all five roaches survived the trip or in case some shots missed them. Here, I'll hit this pencil." He put a yellow wooden no.2 pencil down on the Examiner's desk. He got down on his knees beside the desk and held the ray gun up parallel with the surface of the desktop. When the red laser light was visible on the center of the pencil, he pressed the trigger button. There was the same dark flash of purple light and the pencil rolled across and off the desktop, falling to the floor.

"There, you saw that," Hamilton said exultantly. "The ray knocked the pencil off your desk."

"That could have been a blast of air you have stored in it," Tailoren said. "I am still not a hundred percent convinced your contraption can shoot out a force wave. It violates the basic laws that the universe operates under."

"I think we've established a prima facie case of operability with the demonstrations we've done so far," Levy said. "But I acknowledge your right to be skeptical. I haven't been able to find a scientific theory explaining how the death ray gets its kick." He punched the open palm of one hand with his fist. "The full understanding of how or why some inventions work sometimes isn't known until years after the invention is in actual use. That's happened time and again for some drugs and chemical reactions. But, never the less, and with no disrespect intended, I request for your immediate supervisor, or at least another patent Examiner to come in here to see the next demonstration."

"Sure you do, but I will do better than that. I will get my boss and I will get my boss's boss too, if they are not tied up right now. I will need them to back me up when I give his patent application a Final Rejection." Tailoren thrust a finger at Hamilton, and walked out of his cubicle.

Ten minutes later two men came back to his cubicle with Examiner Tailoren. He told his immediate supervisor, thirty-four year old Primary Examiner Albert Camden, about the death ray gun interview. Camden insisted that Group 3300 Supervisor Tom Gains be involved because he knew someone at the Pentagon contacted Gains about the weapon. As they were walking back to where the inventor and attorney were waiting, Tailoren told them what happened so far. While they were waiting, Hamilton put a fresh battery into the ray gun.

There wasn't enough space for everyone to be comfortable in the cubicle, so they conducted introductions in the hall. "Everyone who's heard about this patent application has been curious to learn how it works," Gains said. "There've been several death ray patents issued by the Patent Office, but they're all on toys or games. This appears to be the first one that's the real McCoy." He held out his hand to Levy and then to Hamilton. And the formality of introductions continued until everyone was acknowledged. Gains, sixty-two years old, almost completely bald, and wearing brown slacks and an open collared blue sport shirt, took over the interview and was in charge until he left. He walked up to Tailoren's desk and picked up the shoebox of dead roaches. "Something smells funny." He tipped the box to give Camden a look at its contents.

"That smell comes from the biggest roach," said guard Battle, proud he remembered Hamilton's explanation. "It's a Florida Woods roach. They smell like almonds when you squash 'em."

"Thank you, Arthar," Gains said. "That's more than I needed to know. Now, why don't you start, Arthar. Tell me what you saw."

"I shot that one over there," Battle said. He pointed toward one of the smaller roaches with a pen he removed from a breast pocket of his uniform. "I was looking right at it when I pushed the button and the ray gun went off. There was a flash of dark light, but no sound, and something hit that bug and broke it apart. Whatever hit it came from the gun."

"OK," Gains said. "What did you see, Bennie?"

"What I saw was almost identical to what Mr., uh Guard, Battle described. Except I am not sure whatever it was that broke the roaches came out of that gun. These men may have some trick paraphernalia, like they use in magic shows and to make movies. One of them could have manipulated their gadgets to make the roaches explode while the other one distracted me. You know. Distract the audience like they do at magic shows. I cannot say what they did, and I cannot prove it was a trick, but I also cannot explain why the death ray works. And they cannot explain it either."

Hearing this, Levy stuck his head in the office door and said, "We don't have to explain how it works. The Patent Laws don't require a theoretical explanation. All we have to do is disclose how to make a device that produces the result described in the specification and claims. And we just did that. That ray gun killed three roaches." He pointed to the device lying on Tailoren's desk.

"I have an idea," Hamilton said. "I'll make a paper target and tape it to that wall of your office over there. Everyone will stay out of the office except for Officer Battle. That way my attorney and me can't control what happens." He pointed at the guard. "He'll aim and fire the ray at the target, and you'll see what damage it does. You'll see that it'll do enough damage to kill a roach."

"You ever done this before?" Levy asked.

Hamilton shook his head. "No, but I'm sure it'll damage the paper."

"On with the show," Gains said, laughing, while Tailoren stood moping in the background with his arms folded across his chest.

Levy tore a sheet of paper from his legal pad and handed it to Hamilton. On the paper the inventor drew a crude circle with a felt tipped pen and made a bulls eye dot the size of a quarter in its center. He pointed to a dispenser of transparent tape on the Examiner's desk, and he peeled off a strip of the tape when Gains nodded his assent. The inventor tore another sheet from Levy's legal pad and folded it double two times. Then he stapled the target sheet on top of the folded sheet and taped them to the wall at about eye level. The folded sheet held the target sheet about an inch out from the surface of the wall.

"I'm not sure what's going to happen to the wall," Hamilton said. "But I sure don't want to have to pay for painting this office, so I'm hoping the outside sheet will absorb all of my death ray's blast." He handed the gun to guard Battle, and everyone left the room except for the guard. Examiner Tailoren and the two supervisors crowded into the doorway where they could look into the office and observe what the ray did to the paper target. Hamilton and Levy waited in the hall behind them, clearly too far away to control or influence anything the ray gun did to the paper target.

Guard Battle stood against the wall opposite to where the target was hanging, a distance of about ten feet. He activated the laser pointer and aimed the ray gun until the red spot of laser beam was on the bulls-eye of his target. When he pressed the trigger button, there was another dim flash of purple light and a small tear appeared in the bulls-eye on the paper, which fluttered slightly as if it were suspended in a gentle breeze. Also, there was a sound like what is heard when you thump the center of a piece of paper with a fingernail.

"There's no doubt in my mind some force came out of that thing and tore the paper," Gains said. "You agree Camden?" He turned to face his subordinate.

"I agree," Tailoren's immediate supervisor said.

"OK. Withdraw the lack of utility rejection based on inoperativeness," Gains said to Examiner Tailoren. "And get on with the rest of this case. Some of the big brass at the Pentagon want to know whether they'll have to deal with a patented invention."

Tailoren's eyes blazed with his repressed fury. "But I have some more questions for them," he said and glared at Hamilton and Levy.

"OK, ask your questions. Get your answers, but keep this case moving. It's Special and I want it finished one way or another, as soon as possible," Gains said. "I've gotta get back to my office."

"I do too. You can handle this from here on your own, can't you, Bennie?" Camden said. He walked away without waiting for an answer.

Tailoren could not believe his ears. It sounded like he was being ordered to rush the patent application of this accursed infidel through the Patent Office so the American army could find a way to use the death ray against his people. "Come back in here," he hissed through gritted teeth. He went behind his desk and brought the file for Hamilton's patent application up on the screen of his computer terminal.

Hamilton and Levy stood in front of his desk. Guard Battle shuffled out but resumed his position as the sentry in the doorway. He no longer massaged his palm on the butt of his gun.

Tailoren said, "In my opinion this application does not adequately disclose what the lens is. I intended to reject the claims as being based on an inadequate disclosure under 35 USC 112 because there is not enough information to enable someone skilled in the optics arts to make more lenses. And without the right lens, your ray gun can't work."

"But you didn't reject us for inadequate disclosure in the first Office Action, so you or your Primary Examiner Camden must have thought the disclosure was complete," Levy retorted.

"We did not reject for the lack of an adequate disclosure because everyone was so sure you could not make the ray gun work the way the patent specification describes it. Everyone said the death ray defies the rules of physics."

"But we just proved it works and it doesn't matter why it works. A theoretical explanation isn't required. What Hamilton got with his combination of components was an unexpected result. And an unexpected result entitles the inventor to a patent."

"Not if his specification does not adequately tell the public how to practice his invention," the Examiner persisted.

"OK. Lets get down to the nitty gritty of what the specification discloses about the lens. First look at the figures in the drawing," Levy laid two pages on the desk and oriented them to face the Examiner. "The lens in shown in views from its top, bottom, front, back and from each of its sides. And there are two cross sectional views through the center of the lens at right angles to each other. These drawing figures are an adequate disclosure even for a Design patent on the lens. So what's missing?"

Tailoren looked up and glared at Hamilton with hatred in his eyes. "I do not think the specification completely describes what the lens is made of. I think you are holding something back."

"Well, let's see what it does say." Levy turned the pages in front of him until he found what he was looking for. "Here, look at the description staring in the middle of page nine." He pushed the stack of pages toward Tailoren.

Tailoren said, "You hold on to those. Let me see what he said in the papers you mailed to the Patent Office," implying they might be trying to show him a bogus specification now with altered information. "I have page nine on the monitor. So what."

"You see we describe the lens as double-convex glass polished to an optical surface finish. The power of the lens must be at least five diopters. The color of the lens must permit transmission of light rays only from the violet spectrum and below, that is, not more than 400 nanometers in wave length. The center of the lens must be at the center of the plastic tube. The focal length can vary according to where or how far the target is, and that can be altered by putting other lenses ahead of the one on the ray gun. The density of the lens must be at least 3 grams per cubic centimeter. What else do you want?"

"You did not disclose where the glass came from or who manufactured the lens."

"I have a pretty complete workshop with all of the common power tools. I made the lens, cut, ground and polished it myself," Hamilton said proudly. "The glass I used for the lenses I made, and there were several lenses before this one, the glass was cut from all kinds of different glass objects. Some of them like drinking glasses and dishes, I bought from Wal-Mart or Target. Others I got at flea markets."

Tailoren picked up the ray gun and pointed toward its tip. "Where did the glass for this lens come from?"

"This one came from the bottom of a bowl I bought at Ginsberg's gift shop. That shop's located on the Baywalk in St. Petersburg," Hamilton said. "In Florida."

"Ginsberg's, did you say Ginsberg's," Tailoren said, his voice just below a bellow. He leaned over his desk.

"Yes, Ginsberg's. Do you know about the shop?"

"Certainly not. Did they have more bowls like the one you bought or was it unique?"

"At the time I bought it, there was a stack of eight to ten of them on a display table. They all looked alike to me. It, the bowl, had a label on it indicating it'd been manufactured in Israel. So I assume the bowls are widely available in stores here in the US and abroad. The officers at the Pentagon didn't act like they were concerned about finding the right glass to grind lenses for their prototypes of the ray gun."

"Since the glass he used to make the lens came from a commercial product sold over the counter in retail stores, we don't have to disclose the chemical formulation the glass was made from," Levy said. "The disclosure required by the patent laws is complete."

"I do not agree," said Tailoren. "I am going to finally reject the claims, like I said before, as not being derived from an adequate disclosure."

"Look," Levy said. "I can go to Ginsberg's shop and try to find out more about the company that made the bowl Mr. Hamilton used to make the lens if that will help us."

"Counselor, you know you cannot put that information into the specification at this time. It's new matter. Come on," Tailoren crowed, "you know better than that. New matter is never admissible after a patent application has been filed."

"I know it's obviously new matter if it goes into the specification, but I thought it might ease your mind if I got those details into the record in the Remarks section of the amendment I'll have to file answering your rejection," Levy countered. "Anyway, now I'm curious, so tomorrow I'll walk over to Ginsberg's and see what I can find out about the company that made those bowls. Is there anything else you want to know or talk about now?"

"No, not now."

"If you're really serious about making the rejection Final, we'll be seeing you at the Board of Appeals. Let's go Arnold, I have a plane to catch."

"In case something else comes up, where can I get in touch with you Mr. Hamilton?" Tailoren asked.

"The Dately Hotel across the street for the next six days. I'll be in and out. Seeing the sights."

"What room?"

"406."

"And you will be back in your office in downtown St. Petersburg tomorrow, Mr. Levy?"

"Yes, that's right. Call me if you want to discuss this case further."

Levy and Hamilton left the Examiner's office and walked toward the elevators. The two men rode down to the lobby where they took a few minutes for a post mortem before Levy had to catch a cab to the airport.

"Whew. He sure was hostile to my invention, don't you think," Hamilton said.

"Yes he was indeed hostile, but I've seen that many times before. However a few times he did act more belligerent than I've come to expect," Levy admitted.

"How so."

"I sat focused on him when you were doing the talking to see if I could figure out what is his problem. Did you notice how he jumped when you mentioned Ginsberg's shop? And I can't figure out why he needed to know your room number at the Dately."

"Yuh know. All that went right over my head. But now that you've told me what you thought was strange about him, I remember thinking while you were doing all the talking and I was just sitting there listening. Well, I remember I was thinking there was something funny about the way he talked. It sounded formal to me. Like you might hear if you were reading a legal document out loud. Well, maybe not that formal, but more formal than they way we usually talk."

"Could be," Levy said. "I didn't notice it."

They shook hands and parted company forever.

Chapter 26   Murder

AFTER THE INVENTOR and patent attorney left his office, Examiner Tailoren, felt perplexed. He sat in his chair and stared at the drawing of the ray gun lens on his computer monitor. His mind was elsewhere. He was too intelligent to think he himself was the intended victim of a Zionist plot. But there were some puzzling coincidences he couldn't figure out. The Jew lawyer, Levy, the Jew gift shop, Ginsberg's, and the Israeli glass bowl manufacturer. If he possessed any doubts before about putting a fatwa on them all, he resolved them now. The two infidels would die and Ginsberg's shop, the source of the lens material, would be destroyed.

Tailoren wrote down Hamilton's room number at the Dately Hotel and his length of stay, Levy's office address, and the information he had about where Ginsberg's gift shop was located. He took from his desk an express mail envelope he had already addressed with the assassins' Baltimore post office Box, number 317.

He walked to Carmina's desk. "I have to take some personal time to run an errand. I haven't time to explain now, but I'll be back before quitting time," he said to her. She just nodded her head without looking away from her computer terminal. His digital camera hung from his neck by its strap.

Tailoren left his office building and walked to the camera shop in the Crystal Plaza Arcade, where he had three copies made of each of the pictures of Hamilton and Levy. He wrote an identifying name on the back of each photo and also included an explanation of why each infidel was a threat to the jihad. He placed the photos in the previously addressed envelope together with a death button for each of his intended victims.

On a 4x6 note card he gave the location of Ginsberg's gift shop, and described the store as containing a material from Israel the targeted infidels used to construct a lethal weapon they intended for use to kill Arabs. Therefore the fatwas on the two infidels had to be expanded to include Ginsberg's shop. Since only two death buttons were available, Tailoren told the assassins to blow up the shop at a time when it was closed to customers, to avoid the loss of life.

Tailoren walked to the Crystal City Post Office Station in the Crystal Square Arcade, and deposited the express mail envelope containing the death buttons and photos in time to make the day's outgoing mail. The clerk behind the counter assured him of delivery to a box in the Baltimore post office before noon the following day. Proud of himself for shifting the fatwas to real enemies of the jihad, instead of a harmless young woman, he walked back to his office, and looked forward to a night in bed with Carmina.

The two assassins, Juan and Pedro, planned on checking into the Crystal City Dately Hotel after their targeted victims arrived. Although they intended to alter their appearances with disguises and makeup, they did not want anything about them to become familiar to the hotel's employees. So on the day before Levy was scheduled to fly in, Juan had checked into a room at the Shuragon Inn, which was located a block down the street from the Dately. He was well groomed and wore an expensive, well-tailored suit and tie, and highly polished black shoes. Pedro stayed behind in Baltimore so he could open the letter from Bennie as soon as it arrived in their post office box. Then he'd phone Juan and tell him Hamilton's room number, so Juan could request a room on the same floor.

For these assassins, the safest and easiest way to kill a victim was to get the target in a hotel room. Hotel rooms also made it easier to disguise the killing as a sex crime or as kinky sex that went too far. From the schedules given them in the letter from Tailoren, they knew they wouldn't have the information they required soon enough to get Levy while he was in Crystal City. But Hamilton would be an easy target, assuming he stayed at the Dately Hotel during his entire week of sightseeing. They'd get Levy after he went back to St. Petersburg.

During their weeks of training with Gurtenkov at the *al Khanjar* camp, the Russian taught Juan and Pedro how to make electronic pass cards for breaking into the rooms in hotels using these modern keys. The electronic pass cards were like the keys used by housekeeping maids and workers; the pass cards opened the doors of all the rooms on a given floor. Gurtenkov gave the two assassins a card reader-encoder that can make a pass card by reading the information on the electronic key cards for two different rooms on the same floor. So they needed for Tailoren to tell them the floor on which Hamilton's room was located. Juan planned to check into the Dately Hotel after Pedro told him which floor to request. Pedro would drive from Baltimore to Crystal City timing his arrival so he would encounter a different desk clerk when he checked in and requested the floor Juan and Hamilton were on.

The next morning Pedro drove to downtown Baltimore and parked the Blue Pontiac GrandAm in a public lot on High street. From there he walked to the Main Baltimore Post Office at High and Fayette. He went through the doors at nine sharp. He checked box 317 for the letter from Tailoren. The box was empty. He walked out of the Post Office, turned right and strolled down Fayette. When he spotted Elware's Café, Pedro entered the coffee shop, sat in a booth and ordered a cup of black coffee, scrambled eggs and toast. Half an hour later the assassin returned to the Post Office to check the box. Still empty. And so it went until his return at eleven thirty when the express mail envelope was waiting in the box.

Pedro took out the envelope, walked back to his car, got in and closed the door. When he opened the envelope and looked in to view its contents, he was surprised to see two death buttons mixed in with half a dozen photos. This had never happened before. Previously the assassins were given only one target at a time. He thought of phoning O'Durea to confirm that two hits were authorized. But he didn't call because there were two of the death buttons in the envelope. And the last time he called, the Cuban criticized him creating a security by asking about an insignificant detail. OK, he had two death buttons, so they must want two hits.

Juan had already checked out of his room at the Shuragon Inn, and was waiting in the coffee shop of the Dately when his cell phone buzzed. Expecting the call from Pedro, he flopped it open and pressed the answer button. "What," he said.

"406," Pedro said.

"406," Juan repeated.

"Right." Pedro hung up.

Juan finished his coffee, paid his bill and walked into the lobby. He was wearing a blue wool suit and had disguised himself as an older man by coloring his light blond hair with dark grey around the temples and darkening the skin under his eyes. He also put a gold cap Gurtenkov had given him over one of his upper front teeth. He waited until no one was being helped or waiting for service from Janney Hoean, the attractive female clerk behind the desk. He stepped up in front of her and set down his black fiberglass suitcase.

"I want a room on the fourth floor," he said gave her a smile that made the fake gold tooth abundantly visible.

"Floor four. Hummm... let me see. We're not real busy at the moment. Lots of rooms open at this time on a Tuesday," Janney said. She typed into the terminal on the desk in front of her. "Yes, I can give you a room on four that has one queen sized bed. Will that be OK?"

"Good."

"Number 416. And how will you be paying, Sir."

"Debit card, prepaid. Here." Juan handed her a MasterCard. "Charge for three nights. I'll settle up when I know how long I stay here."

"Very good, Sir." She swiped his prepaid card through the reader and tapped in the charge for three nights. "Here is your electronic key card."

"I want two cards."

"Of course, Sir." She handed him a second key card.

Juan took the elevator up to the fourth floor, and when he was in his room, he phoned Pedro. "Me 416," he said

"416," Pedro repeated. He was already driving south on I-95, which he exited at I-495, the Capital Beltway, and thence on it to I-66 and into Crystal City. He avoided the Dately Hotel valet parking service, and left the Pontiac in a nearby public lot. He carried his bag to room 416, knocked on the door, and was recognized through the peephole and let in by Juan.

While the two brothers waited for the desk clerk shift change, Pedro put on his disguise. He had not shaved since leaving Chicago the preceding week, so all he had to do was augment his already abundant whiskers and deepen the dark shade of his skin.

Every half hour Juan went down to the lobby to see if new clerks were on duty at the desk, and finally at 4:00 pm the shift changed. He picked up a house phone and dialed room 416. "Now," was all he said into the phone after Pedro picked up.

Pedro took his suitcase down to the lobby with him and got into the check in line. The hotel was busier now than it had been when Juan arrived. When his turn came, Pedro asked for a room on the fourth floor. The new desk clerk, Fred Purkens, was curious and asked why he wanted to be on that particular floor.

"I'm superstitious," Pedro said. "I had luck getting a prime consulting contract last time I stayed here on four. I'm trying to get another one."

Purkens nodded and said, "We hear that every now and then." He consulted the check-in desk terminal. "I'm sorry, Sir, but there's only one room available on four, and it's our double suite. It has two king sized beds, one each in two rooms connected by a sitting-dining room. It's more expensive—"

"Good." Pedro interrupted before the clerk could finish. "It's what I need to set up a display."

Without waiting to be asked about payment, he handed Purkens a prepaid debit card, and requested two electronic room keys.

Pedro went up to his room and called Juan. The two assassins met and planned the hit on Hamilton. They intended to observe him for the rest of that day and all of Thursday and perhaps Friday, until they knew his routine. Then they could strike during the night on Thursday or Friday, and drive away immediately afterward. They each fed one of their electronic room keys into the card reader-encoder, and it made an electronic passkey for opening the door to any room on the fourth floor.

Hamilton turned out to be an easy target because he followed the same routine each day. He ate breakfast in the hotel's coffee shop at exactly 7:30, and afterward went back to his room to shave and do his morning ablution. At 8:30 he took a taxi across the Potomac into the central part of the Capitol, where he went sight seeing from building to building and monument to monument by walking or taking other taxis. Every evening at 8:00 he ate at Samson's Angus Corral on New York Avenue, and came back to the Dately for a nightcap at the downstairs bar. By 10:30 pm he returned alone to his room.

Thursday when they saw Hamilton enter Samson's Angus Corral at 8:05, the two assassins drove back to Crystal City and parked in the nearby public parking lot. That morning they packed their bags in preparation for a hit Hamilton that night. They loaded everything they brought with them into the trunk of the Pontiac GrandAm. Everything, that is, except the gear they needed to dispatch Hamilton. When they observed their target entering the bar at 9:40, they went up to the fourth floor and used the electronic passkey to enter his room. Wearing gloves, they unplugged every lamp and unscrewed the bulbs of every light controlled by a wall switch. Then they waited on opposite sides of the door.

At 10:15 Hamilton, slightly tipsy from his double bourbon nightcap, opened the door to 406 and walked into the room. It stayed dark despite his efforts to switch on a light. When the door closed behind him, the assassins pounced. A blow to his head stunned him long enough for the pair of terrorists to wrap a plastic clothesline around his neck. They strangled him and in about five minutes he lost consciousness and died.

They carried his body to a bed they had previously disarranged, and removed his shoes, trousers and underpants, which they scattered haphazardly around the room on the floor. They laid him on his back, spread eagled his arms, pull back his knees and separated his legs. They noted with satisfaction the corpse had an erection. One terrorist removed an eyedropper from a bottle and squeezed drops of liquid all over the erection. The scene suggested a kinky sex act that went too far, or a sex crime. They plugged in the lamp cords and screwed the light bulbs into their sockets. Pedro and Juan walked out of the Dately without being observed on the fourth floor that night.

On Thursday April 15, 2004, Bin Nazamunde's assassins ended the life of the father of Marine Sergeant Allan Hamilton, a previous victim of his jihad who had been shot in the back on February 22, 2003.

The assassins went straight to their car and headed south on Route 1, the Jefferson Davis Highway, until it intersected I-95, which they originally intended to drive nonstop for twenty hours to Daytona Beach. However, Juan had become aroused by his participation in Hamilton's murder. He insisted they get on I-64 at Richmond and drive to Norfolk. He anticipated his lust when the assassins were waiting in Baltimore. There he obtained the telephone number of a woman who took care of sailors at the Naval Base. She was available for servicing his carnal need when they arrived, so the assassins were back on I-95 heading south before the first light of day. They took turns driving and sleeping, went west on I-4 across central Florida to I-275, and then south to St. Petersburg, where their next target, Levy, was sleeping peacefully.

Chapter 27   Minimum Bill

THE NEXT DAY Nancia Thorina ran screaming from room 406 at 2:07 pm. The housekeeper entered with her electronic passkey, in accord with Dately Hotel policy, when knocks on the door repeated at intervals after checkout time produced no response.

The Alexandria police were called, and a medical examiner and crime scene techs soon arrived. Hamilton was pronounced dead by Medical Examiner Randolph Florental, and the death was labeled as suspicious. This resulted in the fourth floor being sealed off while the techs scoured and copiously photographed 406 and the adjacent hallway for evidence, much to the annoyance of the hotel's management. Specialists lifted dozens of fingerprints from the room and its door, vacuumed up bags of hair and fiber, and gathered Hamilton's clothes, and the sheets, pillows and cover of the bed on which he had been found. They bagged his stiff body and transported it to the city's morgue.

At that time on a Friday afternoon there were not many guests checked into fourth floor rooms, but police officers interviewed all guests and housekeeping workers on four. None provided any useful information. Six hours later, the fourth floor was returned to the hotel's management, which now had to cope with worrisome reporters and TV crews.

The hotel records revealed Hamilton's Buick had been parked five days earlier by its valet parking service. The car was impounded and towed to a secure police department lot for processing for evidence, and to be held there until it could be turned over to the deceased's next of kin. When a detective asked the hotel management and desk clerks about any suspicious guests or activities, no Dately Hotel employee remembered anything or anyone unusual enough to report.

A day later Medical Examiner Florental pronounced Hamilton's death to be by strangulation, and he had been murdered. There was evidence of sexual involvement at the time of his death. That started the battle over who had jurisdiction. It was not the usual battle between government entities, with several claiming they had jurisdiction over the same crime. This time nobody wanted to be responsible for the case of a tourist from Florida who appeared to be the victim of a kinky sex act that went too far.

That is when William (Minimum Bill) Nollann came to their rescue. William Nollann was the son of Colonel Parlan Nollann, a first generation American of Irish decent. Colonel Nollann's career as a training coordinator for US Army Intelligence and Counter Intelligence took his family to a variety of posts around the world. He was not a field or operating agent, so Colonel Nollann was home for dinner with his family at the end of most days, no matter where they were stationed.

William was born ten years after his sister Alanna. She and their Mother, Finola, indulged him like a living doll because of his happy outgoing disposition. He quickly adapted to the changed circumstances of each different posting and enjoyed meeting new children and making them his friends. When the family was at a given post for several years, William sought and was elected to school class offices. There was talk of his future in politics. But it was not to be. He had little interest in his schoolwork, and only did the minimum required to move up to the next grade. He never played any sport well, but he became the referee or umpire when one was needed. The rest of the time he watched and cheered for his friends.

The Colonel wanted his son to follow in his footsteps into one of the armed services, so he angled to get William into one of the Academies. When he was twelve, to stimulate his interest in a career in the Army, his father started taking William to agent training sessions not involving classified information or violence. The boy's favorite sessions were the witness interviews and the suspect interrogations in which actors were hired to play the persons being questioned by the field agents who were being trained.

At one session when William was fourteen, one of the actors failed to show up. William asked if they had a script or outline for the character the missing actor was supposed to play. When he was told there was a detailed description of what the character was supposed to have witnessed and his motivation, William volunteered to play the part. What did they have to loose? So they let him do it. He studied the script while the other actors were playing their parts and being questioned. William was the last to sit in the witness seat.

He turned out to be a natural actor. He even spoke his part with a different southern accent during a second interview involving the same fact situation. That experience solidified William's thinking about what he wanted to do. He never wanted to be in any of the armed services, and he knew he didn't really have a chance as a politician because he had no stomach for learning about the issues and theories politicians had to talk about. So it was settled in his mind. William Nollann decided to become an actor.

Thereafter he tried out for, and was awarded parts in, school and civic theatre performances open to amateurs. During his senior year in high school William applied for admission to the Yale and Julliard drama schools. But his grades were not good enough. He found a place at the Theatre School of DePaul University in Chicago. Colonel Nollann was disappointed at William's rejection of a military career. But he accepted his son's choice of profession with the knowledge from his own experience that his boy was really not cut out to be a success in any of the armed services.

After graduating from DePaul, William Nollann sought work as an actor in Hollywood. Without any studio connections, and in reality having only journeyman skills as a professional actor, he could only get an occasional bit part. So he moved to New York and tried for parts in stage shows. The outcome was the same. He only got minor parts. And soon he realized he did not like the hours a stage performer had to put in. William longed for regular working hours like he had seen his father enjoying much of the time.

He remembered his first acting experience as a witness in the field agent training program. So the applied for work as an actor with the FBI at their training center in Quantico, Virginia. After about seven months, there was an opening, and William auditioned for it and won the job. While giving his performances, he observed the agents-in-training closely and concluded he would be better than many of them at the interviewing they were practicing.

After working a year at the job of actor, he applied for the position of an FBI agent. The director of admissions to the program had witnessed some of William's acting performances, and he was impressed at his chameleon like ability to instantly change his demeanor, voice and personality. He decided to take the risk and give William Nollann a slot in the Bureau's next training class.

Minimum Bill earned his nickname by being the lowest academically in his Bureau training class, by barely meeting the agent height, weight and strength requirements, and by not being able to shoot straight. No one admits to knowing how William Nollann was able to get into and through the agent training program in view of his shortcomings. But there turned out to be a very good reason for the Bureau to look the other way.

During his training, Minimum Bill exhibited rare talent in the ways he interrogated the actors used as fake witnesses and suspects. And he correctly identified with no errors, which of their statements were true and which were false, in the context of the simulated training investigation; no one had ever been able to do this before William Nollann.

Minimum Bill attributes this feat to his discovery that he has an unusually keen sense of smell. Sometimes odors emanating from a person he is interviewing stimulate a mild form synesthesia, causing him to see a reddish aura or a greenish aura around the person. The reddish aura is associated with truth. The greenish aura is associated with evasiveness or falsehood. Thus, in addition to having the street cop sense of an experienced detective to evaluate a person's body language and demeanor to form an opinion of their truthfulness, Minimum Bill can often smell a lie. So his inability to qualify in firing his weapon was excused by order of the Director of Personnel of the Bureau, and it has been excused each year since then, along with any other Bureau standard Minimum Bill fails to meet.

In April 2004, William Nollann was forty-six years old, and had retained almost all of his light brown hair having flecks of grey around his ears, which lay close to his head. He had a broad forehead, and his rectangular face tapered to a rounded extending chin. His most potent appearance feature was his eyes and the crinkled flesh around them. Beneath thin arched eyebrows matching his hair in color, were a pair of beautiful brown eyes that look like liquid honey. His smile revealed his small white teeth, and deepened the furrows around his eyes, which he can make gleam like small pools radiating sympathy, understanding or pity, as the situation at hand might require. His small lips, mouth and short nose were not threatening in the least. If he had a bushy white beard and side burns, he'd satisfy everyone's image of what Santa Claus should look like.

Minimum Bill was five foot seven and weighed one hundred and sixty-five pounds, with short arms and narrow shoulders. His body was soft and pudgy, and not imposing or threatening. He seldom tried to bully or intimidate a witness or suspect. To induce a reluctant witness to cooperate, he could project an impression of his own helplessness, like the image of a hen-pecked husband. His voice could be deep or soft, and he could utter a stage whisper or a booming oration, as the occasion demanded. He was a natural mimic and always tried to listen to the witness or suspect speaking to someone else before he took over the interview. Then he spoke with a speech pattern and accent close to or matching that of the person he was interrogating.

He continued to hone his skills by talking to strangers during the times he had to spend waiting at places like airports. He found out where people were from and noted their speech pattern and accent. These he tried to imitate more and more as their conversation continued. Most of all he tried to spend time with strangers who also speak a foreign language. He asked them to give him a short lesson in speaking their native tongue. Even if it's a language he has some familiarity with, like Spanish or Russian, he acted as if he knew nothing to find out what the stranger thinks is the first thing he should learn.

These days Minimum Bill works as the FBI's fabled "good cop." He has the reputation of being able to coax a confession out of a marble statute. And his opinion on any one's truthfulness is valued as being worth more than a polygraph test.

To obtain their cooperation in matters of interest to the FBI, the Bureau frequently assigns an agent with special skills to help a local law enforcement agency on a particular case. Minimum Bill had done several of these ad hoc assignments with the Arlington Police, and he was one of their favorite outsiders.

At this particular time agent Nollann was bored out of his skull. He hadn't been involved in an investigation with any degree of interesting complexity for more months than he wanted to admit. And he could be a real pain in the rear by walking around giving a stand up comedian style performance that amused but distracted anyone he was able to corner. He pleaded with his immediate superior, Glenn Johns, Director of Special Services, to let him get involved in something difficult.

So when the news of Hamilton's murder reached him, Johns called Sidney Phillips, his liaison in the Arlington detective squad, and asked if he'd like to have Minimum Bill's help. Phillips was elated. He knew the agent had some skill at public relations, and he figured he could keep the news media off their backs. Because even when he didn't have anything of substance to give them, Minimum Bill knew how to send the reporters away thinking something he had told them was worth printing.

"How can the Bureau justify getting involved in this case? It just looks like a sex crime," Phillips said.

"Do you remember the guy who set up bounties on terrorists?" Johns asked. "He was interviewed on the O'Smiley Indicator Show a few weeks ago."

"No. I can't keep track of all the crackpots O'Smiley talks to."

"Well your victim wasn't a crackpot. During the TV interview he talked about what I think is a really worthwhile effort to get individual citizens involved in avenging terrorist murders by putting their own bounties on the terrorist's heads. That will be my basis for getting Minimum Bill in on this case. We can say we suspect terrorists may be involved in getting the guy…Hamilton…in Hamilton's murder. You need to send me a request for help giving that as the reason, and I'll complete the paper work over here."

"Wonderful, I'll have a fax coming out of your machine within an hour."

Phillips didn't expect to solve Hamilton's murder anyway. The physical evidence from the crime scene was worthless. There were so many fingerprints and so much hair and fiber from all the guests who had been in 406 that nothing stood out enough to identify any worthwhile leads. And Hamilton seemed to be as much at fault as the perpetrator by putting himself in a situation where he was likely to get hurt.

Nollann spent the next two days, Saturday and Sunday, going over the crime scene evidence, coroner's reports, and the reports of the interviews with the hotel's employees and guests. The only lead of substance was the business card of Patent Attorney Lemont Levy, which was found in Hamilton's wallet. Apparently Hamilton paid cash for everything except his hotel bill and bar charges because they found no credit card receipts among his belongings.

Chapter 28   Reconnoitering

THE AFTERNOON THEY arrived in downtown St. Petersburg, the assassins, checked into separate rooms in the Hopten Inn on Beach Drive. The inn was easy walking distance from the law office of Lemont Levy, Patent Attorney, on the second floor of the Commerce Building on Second Avenue North. Their investigation of the downtown area also revealed Ginsberg's gift shop only a block from the patent attorney's office. They decided to blow up the gift shop early in the morning of the day when they were going to kill Levy, so the police would be distracted and focusing on the explosion and resulting fire.

That night the two assassins investigated the area around Levy's office. While Juan acted as a lookout, Pedro put on a pair of plastic gloves and picked the outside door lock in less than three minutes. He walked up the stairs to the second floor. The lock in the door to Levy's office was even easier for him to open. He used a small penlight and looked around the office.

The attorney's desk calendar showed he had scheduled a tee time at noon on both Saturday and Sunday. On Levy's desk he found a sheet from a memo pad giving the schedule of a cruise his wife, Susan, was taking. They were in luck. She was scheduled to be gone during the coming week, so they could take Levy down in his home. And they could make it look like he was having a sexual encounter while his wife was away. But to be sure, when the attorney's office opened on Monday, they needed to confirm that his wife had not changed her plans and was out of town. From the local phone book they learned Levy's home was an apartment on the third floor of a high-rise condominium in the housing community surrounding the Gardenia Golf and Country Club.

The Gardenia housing development is gated, with a guardhouse on each of the two streets leading into the subdivision. It is impossible to drive a motor vehicle into the development without having an access sticker on the windshield or stopping and registering with a guard. However the development is wide open to foot traffic. There are many places where a person can walk in without attracting attention. And no guard checks on nonresidents who walk in and out.

So on the day after their arrival in St. Petersburg, at a time when Levy was scheduled to play golf, the assassins parked their car in the lot of a minimart adjacent to the Gardenia development. Juan and Pedro dressed like golfers in shorts, saddle oxfords, colorful shirts and bill caps embroidered with the logos of golf club manufacturers. Pedro carried a grey, rectangular duffle bag having the Titleist logo prominently displayed on its top. When they walked into the development, no one paid any attention to them.

The assassins sauntered around Levy's high-rise condo building and found the rear entrance to be the most promising. It was in a secluded alcove shielding the door from view on three sides. The door could only be seen by someone walking or driving a car across the street bordering the condo's landscaped grounds, which included trees and shrubs partially obscuring the rear door from the street.

Pedro went back to their parked car, opened the trunk and removed a case of lock picks, which he put into the bag he'd been carrying. The two assassins ambled off in different directions, but ended up at their prearranged destinations fifteen minutes later. Juan stood where he could act as a lookout observing the alcove in which the condo's rear door was located. Pedro was already in the alcove working his picks in the door lock, and soon had the door open.

The rear door opened into a stairwell, which was intended as the exit route from the building in case the electricity went off during an emergency and shut the elevators down. So much the better for the assassins. Pedro phoned Juan and gave him the prearranged signal that he was in the condo. Juan walked around the condo building and meandered around in sight of the front entrance.

Pedro walked up to the fifth floor, then back down to the third floor; he learned the stairwell doors were the same on all floors. Levy's condo was an end unit on the third floor adjacent to the door of the stairway through which Pedro had just entered. He walked back and forth in the hall on the third floor. The door to each of the ten condo units on the floor was in its own alcove, and thus was hidden from anyone walking in the hallway. There was another stairway at the opposite end of the hall, which meant he and Juan could enter and leave the third floor from opposite ends of the building if they chose to do so.

The assassin knew he could hear anyone entering the hall by opening the door of their apartment or by arrival of the elevator at the third floor. This made him confident he was alone in the hall, so he inserted picks into the lock in Levy's door. He turned the picks moving the lock to its open position. But he did not push the door open because just then he heard the elevator door open on the third floor. He removed his picks and casually walked through the exit door and down the stairs he had just come up.

On Monday morning Juan called Levy's office. When Rosalind answered the phone, he asked her if Mrs. Levy's had a cell phone he could reach her on because he had not been able to contact her on her home phone, and he had an appointment with her he wanted to confirm. Rosalind told him there must be some mistake because Mrs. Levy was on a cruise and would be out of town for the rest of the week. He thanked Rosalind and said he'd call Mrs. Levy at home in a week to reschedule the appointment. Good, that confirmed there was only be one victim to murder, and he was going to be by himself. This would be an easy hit.

The assassins decided to plant the bomb in Ginsberg's shop and set it off before dawn the next morning. They planned on killing Levy Tuesday evening when he returned to his apartment from work. His desk calendar had not shown any scheduled activity for Tuesday after work.

Chapter 29   Friends

THE NEWS OF Hamilton's death reached the St. Petersburg news media by the time the Arlington police made inquiries about his next of kin. So Levy was aware of his client's murder when Nollann phoned him on Sunday evening to set up an interview at the Bureau's field office at 500 Zack Street in Tampa. Levy pledged his cooperation, and was waiting there the next day at 3:20 pm when Nollann walked in after his morning flight arrived from Dulles.

A secretary guided the two men into a small, windowless interview room on the sixth floor, where there was just enough space for its grey metal table and two barely upholstered chairs. Nollann asked if he could record their conversation, and he plugged in and turned on a small tape recorder when Levy nodded his assent.

Levy put his briefcase on the floor beside his chair. "Mind if I get comfortable," he asked.

"Not at all," Nollann said, and Levy took off his corduroy sport coat having leather patches at its elbows, and sat there in a short sleeved lime green golf shirt and chinos waiting for the agent to begin.

Nollann undid the top button of his white dress shirt, loosened his tie and removed the coat of his dark blue wool suit. "So far as we know, you're the last person we can identify who Mr. Hamilton was with before he was killed. Please tell me where you were during the past week." He gave Levy a friendly smile, and placed a yellow legal pad on the desk.

"Lemme see. A week ago Sunday I drove my wife, Susan, to the Tampa Port docks. She got on a cruise liner for a trip around the Caribbean and on to Mexico. She'll be back here in four days, and I'll pick her up at the same place." Nollann began writing on the pad. "I came back to my golf club, the Gardenia, played nine holes and had supper at the pool grill. Susan and I try to coordinate our travel schedules so we're both away from home at the same time."

Nollann looked up and smiled. "I know how that goes."

"First thing Monday morning," Levy continued, "I drove to the Tampa airport. I flew to Reagan National, and checked into the Dately Hotel. Then I walked across the street and presented oral arguments before the Patent Office Board of Appeals concerning Finally Rejected claims in a pending patent application. Hamilton arrived that evening and we met to discuss our interview on Tuesday with Patent Examiner Bennie Tailoren. We had the interview with Tailoren as scheduled, I took a cab to Reagan National, and flew back here."

Nollann stopped writing and asked, "What time did you part company with Hamilton?"

"About 11:15. My plane left at 12:40. Tuesday night I ate dinner at the club again and went to bed. Wednesday I took the day off, went over to the club after breakfast and hit balls on the range until 11:45, when three of my friends arrived, and we teed off and played eighteen holes. The guys scattered after we were finished playing. So I came home, put on my shorts, and jogged for an hour around the course. Then I had a hot shower and heated up a frozen pizza in the oven." Levy paused until Nollann raised his eyebrows. Levy gave the agent a questioning glance. "Are you sure you want me to tell you all of these little details?"

Nollann said, "Just get us through Thursday night when Hamilton was murdered." He had already concluded Levy was not involved in Hamilton's murder. The closed atmosphere in the small room enabled Nollann to inhale the undiluted essence emanating from Levy. Momentarily, he had shut his eyes and focused his concentration on what he breathed in. His synesthesia was activated by the purity of Levy's vapors. When he opened his eyes, the red aura he saw around his subject told him this man spoke only what he believed to be the truth. He made the snap judgment this was a person who's honesty he could bet his life on. He'd never spent any time with a patent attorney before, so he decided to try to engage his companionship for the evening. Nollann was sure he could learn something new and interesting from Levy.

Levy continued, "OK. Thursday morning I went to my office after breakfast, and worked there until noon when I went to Three G's deli. I stopped by Ginsberg's gift shop to check on something and then I went back to work in the office until 4:30 when we closed it down for the day. I drove to the club, chipped and putted on the practice green for an hour, and went inside for dinner. My paralegal, Rosalind Katz, was with me while I was in my office, and I signed chits at the club for dinner and the drinks. Then I went home, had a shower, got a glass of wine and watched reruns of *Law and Order* on TV. At 11:30 I went to bed."

"Can anyone vouch for your whereabouts from the time you left your club until midnight on that Thursday?"

Levy frowned, thought for a moment, smiled and said, "I got a call from my daughter, Rachael, around ten. She forgot her Mother was on a cruise and wanted to ask her for some recipe. We only talked for about three minutes."

Nollann put down his pen and smiled reassuringly. "Good enough. You're in the clear, but I have to make the record of your alibi complete, so why don't you give me Rachael's full name and telephone number."

Levy reached over and wrote them down on Nollann's yellow pad.

"You were never really a suspect. Now what can you tell me about Hamilton and who might have killed him or wanted him dead."

Levy looked perplexed. "I've been wracking my brain from when I first read he'd been killed. I can't think of any person to suspect. But, you know, we only had a business relationship: attorney-client. I never had anything to do with him socially. We had one business breakfast and one business lunch. That's it.

Of, course, and you already know this next thing I'm sure. He was on the O'Smiley Indicator TV show promoting the idea of private citizens putting bounties on the heads of Arab terrorists, and an Arab terrorist murdered his son."

Nollann nodded his head and said, "The possibility of terrorist involvement is why I...the FBI...is investigating this murder."

"Well, he also has this inflammatory title on his Provisional patent application. He called his invention A Death Ray for Murdering Arabs."

Nollann looked surprised. "The Patent Office permits a title that provocative?"

"No. Not on a regular Utility patent. But the title was just on a Provisional patent application. Do you really want me to give you a lecture from Patent Law 101 explaining all of this right now."

Nollann shook his head, "Not now." He thought the Patent Law 101 lecture would be a perfect topic to get Levy talking about himself that evening. "Can you give me any documentary evidence showing Hamilton used the 'Death Ray For Murdering Arabs' title? It might lead to something...to a motive."

Levy didn't answer and stared down at the floor. A bit later he said, "Let me think out loud a moment. Ordinarily the Patent Office Filing Receipt with the title is covered by the attorney-client privilege until a patent issues, then the information becomes public. But Hamilton has been giving copies of the Filing Receipt to his friends to let them know he's trying to avenge his son's murder. He told me he was doing this. So he erased the privilege by showing the Filing Receipt around and giving copies of it away." Levy beamed and reached for his briefcase. "Sure, I can let you copy the Filing Receipt. I have it here in a file folder."

"Getting back to the people who Hamilton interacted with, do I understand you as saying you know nothing about his family and next of kin, and friends."

"Oh, I know all about his family and his son, the one murdered by the Arab terrorist. He told me all about himself when I first started working on patenting his invention."

"I'd like to hear everything you know about him, and his family, and his friends and business associates. In other words please identify everyone you know who knew him or was involved with him in any way."

For the next forty minutes Levy told Nollann everything he knew about Hamilton, including the death of his wife and his high hopes for Allan. Levy also explained Hamilton's determination to get revenge against the Arabs for Allan's murder, and how the drive for revenge led to Levy's involvement with him in their efforts to patent his death ray.

"What's the death ray gun look like?" Nollann asked.

"Like the ray guns they used in the old Buck Rogers movies. Or like one of those futuristic toy water guns."

Remembering what he'd been shown by the Arlington police, Nollann nodded his head. "So a death ray gun is what that plastic thing was they found in the trunk of Hamilton's car. Does it really work? Could he kill people with it? That gun might lead us to the motive for his murder."

"Well, the ray gun works well enough to kill roaches. Hamilton demonstrated that several times. And that will be good enough to get him a patent on it. But it isn't powerful enough to kill a human being in its present configuration. Like I told you a few minutes ago, Hamilton got Colonel Bench at the Pentagon interested in the ray gun. He demonstrated it for them by killing some roaches. You want Bench's phone number? I can get it out of my file." Levy reached into his open briefcase.

"Please do. And I'd like to have your file now so they can make a copy of it for me to read tonight." Nollann pointed toward the closed door.

"I don't know about that. The patent application is supposed to be kept a secret until it or the patent is published by the Patent Office. And there may be some security restrictions from the Pentagon. Major Olsan, who works with Colonel Bench, sure got the Patent Office to move fast on this application."

"I'm sure I can get a subpoena, if you refuse to cooperate." Nollann saddened his eyes and took on a hurt look.

"No, no. I want to cooperate in every way I can," Levy quickly blurted. "But this is a new one for me. I'm not sure where the attorney-client privilege ends in this situation. How about if I give you everything in my file except the patent application itself? I don't know what good that'll do you anyway. You already have the only embodiment of the death ray gun."

"That'll do for now. If we need to get the written details of the ray gun out of the patent application, we'll get a subpoena and whatever backing we need to get you off the hook for giving them to us. Or maybe it will be easier just to get them directly from the Patent Office."

Nollann put down his pen and folded his hands in his lap. "Now let's turn to some delicate aspects of this case. What do you know about Hamilton's sex life, and what about his sexual orientation?"

Levy frowned and shook his head. "You're asking me if he was gay, aren't you?"

"Yes, that along with everything else you know about him." Nollann smiled encouragingly.

"Well, first of all, I truly don't know anything about his sex life. But what I can tell you is this. Hamilton was always a perfect gentleman whenever we were together. He never made salacious remarks about any woman we saw or told any off color jokes. From my very limited dealings with the few gay people I've met, my very strong impression is Hamilton was straight. What happened that makes you ask?"

"I can't give you any details." Nollann broke eye contact. "However I can say the *Washington Post* reported yesterday there was a sexual angle to Hamilton's murder. That's unofficial, of course. Does that stimulate your thinking?"

"No. I've told you all I know about Hamilton and sex. But I'd really like to hear more about what makes you interested in this."

Nollann ignored the query and turned off the tape recorder. "That wraps this session up." He pointed at Levy's briefcase. "Please give me all of the papers in your file you don't think are privileged, and I'll have someone here copy them. Since we're both batchin' it tonight, let's go out to dinner together. On the flight down here, I saw an ad in a travel magazine for Ruthie's Broiler Steak House somewhere here in Tampa. I've been to the one in Chicago, and let me tell you, their steaks are the best I've ever eaten. So let's go there if we can find the place."

"I know where it is. It's at the International Mall, not far from here. But I'll only go on one condition. That place is expensive, so it'll be Dutch treat." Levy handed Nollann a stack of papers he had been gathering from his file while they were talking.

"Agreed." Nollann walked said and out the door with the papers Levy just handed to him. He returned in several minutes with a folder containing the copies he wanted, and handed the originals back to Levy.

"I'm ready to call it a day. I had the receptionist make 7:00 pm reservations for us at Ruthie's Broiler, and she confirmed my reservation for tonight at the Clarentown Hotel down the street from here. In the mean time, is there a nice place around here where we can go for a beer? I'm parched."

"Let's take your car and mine too and drive over to the Mall." Levy pointed over his shoulder. "There's lots of bars over there and there's plenty of parking. When the evening's over, I can zip on to I-275 and home, and you'll be near downtown Tampa and the Clarentown. I'm driving an old white Cadillac parked in the lot across the street. I'll come out of the lot and turn south on Zack."

"Lead the way. I'll be following you in a tan two door Chevy parked in a Bureau slot on that same street." Nollann removed his tie and draped his coat over his arm.

Twenty minutes later the two men were seated facing each other in a booth at Tigar's sipping beers from a pitcher of Sam Adams they were sharing. Without revealing much about himself, Nollann used his charms to induce Levy to talk about himself and his lifestyle. Not that the G-man had anything to hide. He just wanted to indulge his pastime by collecting all he could from this man in what Nollann considered an exotic profession. After all how many people could stomach the rigors of both engineering and law school. To Nollann the mind set that accomplished this was incomprehensible.

Levy told of his early childhood and growing up in Duluth, and of being steered by his parents and uncles into studying engineering at Cal Tech simply because he could get into that prestigious institution. And of learning that working as an engineer bored him, so when he gained the opportunity to go to law school on the GI Bill, he took it and became a patent attorney. And how over the years he developed his skills until he became what his peers called a "wordsmith", with the ability to select the perfect words and phrases making his client's inventions appear different from everything else that has ever existed. He also gave Nollann his Patent Law 101 lecture.

Nollann continued to deflect questions aimed at him, except he revealed that after completing college, he too changed his occupation from actor to detective for reasons somewhat similar to Levy's for getting out of engineering.

At 7:00 they drifted across the mall to Ruthie's Broiler and Levy continued talking about patents while they enjoyed their meals. Nollann had a rib steak and Caesar salad, while Levy had a filet and garden salad. Neither had desert, but over coffee Levy revealed that he considered himself to be an amateur detective. And he really wanted to help solve the mystery of his client's death.

Levy said, "I average reading almost a book a week, and the majority are mysteries. Actually I read very few of the books. Almost all of them are audio books I load into an iPod. I carry it with me everywhere."

He demonstrated the little MP3 player for Nollann, who placed the speaker buds in his ears while Levy scrolled to a John Sandford mystery. Nollann was intrigued and listened for several minutes before removing the tiny speakers from his ears and handing them back.

Nollann shook his head. "It's an interesting gadget, but it's not for me. It's too distracting for me. I like to hear what's going on around me...what people are saying. I need to have my ears open."

Levy wound the speaker cords around the iPod and put it into his pocket. "To each his own. But please let me help you with this case. I already told you I was trained to be a CIC (Counter Intelligence Corp) agent at Ft. Halabird. I use some of the things I learned there every now and then."

Nollann raised his eyebrows. "How so?"

"Well, while Susan is gone on her cruise, one of our neighbors we traded keys with...we trade or give our neighbors duplicates of our condo keys in case one of us looses their keys and is locked out or in case of an emergency and someone needs to get in to help. What happens is I think our neighbor who has our key has been snooping around while neither of us is around. She's more likely to snoop when

Susan isn't around because Susan'll notice if anything's been moved. That kind of thing, something out of place, goes right past me. But I'm suspicious of her. So, I remember being taught to put a small piece of paper or string between the door and the jamb that will fall out if the door is opened. I've been doing that with a piece of paper since the day Susan left."

Nollann chuckled. "Catch anyone?"

"No. Not yet. Maybe I've read...er listened to...so many mysteries I've become paranoid."

"I'd say you're suspicious, not paranoid." The look on Nollann's face became serious. "Being suspicious is not a bad thing. I wish your client, Hamilton, had been more suspicious. He might be alive today. He certainly wouldn't have let himself get put into the position we found him in."

Levy sensed an opening and probed, "What position would that be?"

Nollann wagged his index finger reproachfully, "I've already told you more than I should've. Let's drop it there. And I'm bushed from the flight down here, so let's settle up with Ruthie and get out of here and go to bed. I've got a long day tomorrow starting with an interview with Sam Fellows—"

"I know about him." Levy interrupted, "He's executor of Hamilton's trust and estate. Thank goodness he is, or else I'd be holding the bag by myself trying to figure out what to do with Hamilton's patent application."

"After we meet at his office," Nollann resumed, "Sam'll give me the keys to Hamilton's house to see if I can find anything suggesting a murder motive, or his sexual activities, or leads to more people who knew the guy. What I find there'll probably keep me here for a couple more days."

After paying their restaurant bills, the two men walked to their cars, which were parked side by side. Nollann climbed into his car, lowered the window, and said, "Lemont, I've enjoyed your company more than I can tell you now. And I've been thinking about what you said about wanting to get involved with us in figuring out who killed Hamilton."

Levy leaned toward the open window and nodded his head enthusiastically.

"Sometimes, I have a thought that's so farfetched it's nothing more than an impression. I can't always put it clearly into words. I need someone to bounce what I'm thinking off of. Someone I call tell a hunch, or a thought or an impression. Someone with no background in the case. Sometimes what I'm thinking is so weird I'm ashamed to tell my thoughts to any other agent. I'll be looking for a fresh unbiased view of events and of my reasoning. Can I enlist you, Lemont, when I want to talk to someone who's out of the law enforcement loop? I think you may be just the kind of person I've been looking for." Nollann held his hand out the car window.

"I'd be honored and flattered to have the chance to help you and the Bureau," Levy said. He grabbed the agent's hand and pumped it energetically. "Remember I'm a patent attorney and a lot of times we hear weird things from inventors. Can you imagine how surprised I was when Hamilton told me he'd invented a death ray gun for murdering Arabs? So I won't be startled by anything you say. And if we're going to have a continuing relationship, you need to know my friends call me 'Lem'."

"Then Lem it shall be, henceforth and forever more. And my friends call me 'Bill'." Nollann grinned as he drove out of the garage toward the road back to downtown Tampa and the bed he was looking forward to in his room in the Clarentown Hotel. Minimum Bill decided he should wait until the next time they met before revealing his complete nickname to his new friend.

Chapter 30   Escape

WHILE NOLLANN AND Levy were dining at Ruthie's Broiler, the assassins were planting a bomb in Ginsberg's Gift Shop in downtown St. Petersburg. Earlier in the day, Pedro walked through the shop looking for a place to hide the bomb. "How late're you open?" he asked.

"The shop closes at 8:00 pm," a clerk said.

Pedro hadn't shaved since the assassins left Crystal City. He wore tan shorts, a tan sport shirt, dark sunglasses and a dark blue straw hat having a wide brim with an orange band around the crown, and a cluster of yellow feathers held in the band. He didn't attract any special attention. He looked like just another of several dozen lookers who wandered through the shop every day.

He found sitting on the floor near the rear of the shop, a large grey and ochre Raku urn having a removable lid. Pedro lifted the lid and looked in. He estimated the space inside the urn to be about one cubic foot, ample room for the bomb and pint bottle of gasoline to act as accelerant for the resulting fire.

At 7:45 that evening Juan, wearing a light blue business suit, black tie and black shoes, and a man's conventional felt hat walked into Ginsberg's Gift Shop. He had the same fake gold tooth in his mouth he'd used when he checked into the Dately Hotel in Crystal City.

Marsha Ginsberg was the only person on duty in the shop at the time. Her employees left when their workday came to an end at 6:00. She was a thin, short woman of forty-seven with shoulder length jet black hair and close set dark blue eyes in her bony square face. She wore loose fitting, heavily embroidered ankle length shifts that made her body look heavier than it actually was. The floppy sandals on her bare feet revealed toenails painted a variety of gaudy colors she intended, with her funky clothing, to give the impression she was an artist.

Juan began systematically picking up, pondering, and returning craft objects and gifts to the open tables on which they were displayed. As he meandered toward the rear of the store, he observed, sitting on the floor, the grey and ochre urn Pedro had described to him earlier. Juan slowly wandered through the display tables back to the front of the shop. Pedro, who was sitting on a nearby bench holding a newspaper, could see him through its glass windows. Juan removed his hat, which was their signal that the urn was sitting where Pedro had seen it earlier in the day.

Pedro, now cleanly shaved and wearing tan slacks, an open necked pale blue sport shirt, and a brown tweed sport coat, but no hat or sunglasses strolled into the shop. He was carrying black leather, open topped satchel, inside of which was a grocery store bag containing the bomb and plastic bottle of gasoline.

About five minutes before the store was scheduled to close, Pedro was standing next to the urn, and Juan had a small brass kaleidoscope in his hand asking the shop owner about the craftsman who'd made it. With Marsha Ginsberg distracted by Juan, Pedro took the lid off the urn, removed the grocery bag from his satchel, and lowered it into the urn. Then he put the lid back on the urn. He waved goodbye, smiling as he walked out of the shop and disappeared from sight. Juan completed the purchase of the kaleidoscope, paying in cash. He gave Marsha a wide smile revealing the fake gold tooth, and he too walked out of the shop and into the night.

Ten minutes later, Marsha Ginsberg emptied the cash register into a brief case, turned off the lights, locked the front door, hurried out the rear door of the shop, and drove to her two-bedroom house in Lakewood Estates. She planned to come back to her shop early in the morning to total up the day's receipts and order any items of stock that were sold out.

In her kitchen she opened a can of sockeye salmon, which she ate cold on a bed of romaine lettuce, seasoned only with pepper and lime juice. She poured a glass of merlot from a previously opened bottle she had kept in her fridge, and sat down on her couch. She found the place where she had stopped reading the evening before in a novel by Chaim Potoc. She was happy with her life.

Lemont Levy ended the evening he'd spent with William Nollann feeling very good about himself. You always feel good when you've spent a lot of time talking about yourself, and what you think you've accomplished in life, and what you like to do. And Minimum Bill had an easy time of it getting Levy to talk about himself.

Now Levy was walking down the hall to his condo apartment wondering if the scrap of paper he'd left on the doorjamb had fallen on the floor, signaling that their neighbor, Urmah Hamsey, had been inside snooping around. As he took out his key and inserted it in the lock, he saw the scrap of paper was not on the floor. When he opened the door he saw the paper flutter out. Urmah had not been inside. As he reached down to pick up the scrap, Levy thought this was truly a waste of his time. So what if she came in and snooped. She wouldn't steal anything, and he and Susan had nothing to hide. And what'd he do if the scrap of paper were on the floor when he got back one day. Go down the hall and yell at Urmah. Nope. That wasn't his style. But if he did catch Urmah snooping, he'd tell Susan about it when she got back from the cruise, and she'd handle it. Right. Susan'll figure out a way of getting the message to Urmah without causing a confrontation and ruining the very convenient arrangement the Levy's had with their neighbor. He decided he'd put the scrap of paper back when he left for the office tomorrow.

While Marsha Ginsberg lay sleeping peacefully, at 3:00 am the next morning, Pedro dialed the number of the cell phone he had left in the urn in her shop. That phone was wired to set off the detonator for the C4 in the urn. When the phone rang, the blasting cap detonated and the bomb exploded. The bottle of gasoline vaporized and the fire spread throughout the shop. Bin Nazamunde's terrorists brought an end to Marsha Ginsberg's successful, happy way of life.

The next morning when Levy was walking out the door of his apartment, he had second thoughts about hiding the piece of paper in the doorjamb. He'd forgot to tear the corner off a page of the morning paper, and he didn't want to go back into the apartment. So he locked the door and backed away starting to turn and walk down the hall.

Then he stopped and turned back to the door. Then he turned away from the door again. Then he turned back toward the door. He laughed out loud as he remembered a Jimmy Durante routine where the comedian paced back and forth across a stage, like Levy was now doing right now, while he sang something about not knowing whether he wanted to go or wanted to stay.

Frustrated by his own indecisiveness, Levy stood facing his door and rammed the key into the lock. He twisted the key as hard as he could, flung the door open and stomped into his foyer. The door slammed shut behind him in response to the force from the automatic closure fixture attached to it inside of the apartment. He picked up a newspaper from the recycle bin and tore the corner off a page. He held the door open while placing the paper scrap between the door and jamb, and then he closed the door on it. While locking the door with his key, he shook his head again wondering at how he wasted his time by putting a scrap of paper in there.

It's a good thing he put it there. It would save his life.

Levy found out about the bombing when he arrived at his office. Police were everywhere questioning people, and the street in front of Ginsberg's shop was sealed off with yellow crime scene tape. Thank goodness the alley he used to get to the parking place with his name on it was still open. He parked and walked toward the taped off area where he found Rosalind shaking her head and crying. She and Marsha Ginsberg were friends.

"Who could do a thing like this?" Rosalind said and wiped her eyes. "Thank God no one was hurt. But poor Marsha. That shop was the center of her life. And it made her a good living. She built up the business from a hole in the wall store in Clearwater to the best location over here in our downtown. I wonder if she'll have the will to start over again."

Levy put his hand on her shoulder. "I didn't watch the TV this morning. When'd it happen?"

"Last night, uh, early this morning at about 3:00 am. I'd like to help Marsha if I can." She pointed in the direction of the devastated shop. "Will you survive the day without me?"

He messaged her shoulder reassuringly. "Go and take as many days as you want to, and call me if you think of anything I can do."

"Thanks, you're the best boss there is." She brushed his cheek with a light kiss and hurried away in search of her friend.

Levy lingered for half an hour talking to others he knew who worked in the vicinity. Everyone was shocked such a crime could occur in sleepy downtown St. Petersburg. He went to his office and let himself in. He had trouble concentrating on the appeal brief that was the next work on his schedule. So he spent the morning and early afternoon on routine chores like bringing his follow-up lists and billing records up to date. Then he backed up the files he'd created during the previous day. And finally the went to the Patent Office web site to find out if they had changed any rules or procedures affecting his work.

At 3:30 he gave up and drove to the Gardenia Golf and Country Club parking lot. Ronny recognized his car when it first entered the lot. So by the time Levy had parked and walked to the pro shop, his clubs and a large bag of yellow range balls were waiting for him on a golf cart. He tipped Ronny a buck and drove the cart over to the range. He tried to relieve his frustrations from the unfruitful day by pounding drives toward the fence at the far end of the range. An hour later he'd had enough of hitting balls. But he was still too upset to go over to the practice green to chip and putt. His nerves were shot, so the light touch needed to practice his short game just wouldn't be there. He had, however, worked up a good sweat by swinging his clubs as hard as he could in the bright afternoon sun. So he returned the golf cart to Ronny and drove to his assigned parking space in his condo building's garage.

The two assassins had checked out of the hotel and were waiting for Levy in his apartment. They wore ski masks, gloves and white coveralls having the BEST PLUMBERS embroidered in large red letters on the back. They wore the coveralls to absorb any blood or body fluid expelled or excreted by their victims. Juan held a twelve-foot length of plastic clothesline in his hands. Pedro held a blackjack he used to stun their victims. The assassins had left the condo building's rear door slightly ajar, but looking like it was closed, because the door tended to stick shut, and they might have to leave in a hurry. They also left the third floor hall door at the entrance to the stair well partially open to facilitate a speedy exit from the building.

Levy got out of his car and walked to the nearest entrance from the parking garage. He inserted his key in the door switch and turned it, opening the door. He walked through the lobby and went to the bank of resident's mailboxes. He opened the box for 310 and retrieved the day's mail. He chatted about the weather with another resident of the condo building whose name he didn't remember. The two men walked to the elevator and rode up together while continuing with inconsequential small talk. Levy got off first, and his companion with the unremembered name continued riding up to the tenth floor.

Levy was curious about what was in the day's mail. And he was frustrated because he'd not been able to open any of it, since he felt an obligation to be courteous and talk to his neighbor. He focused on the pieces of mail in his hand as he walked down the hall to the door of his apartment. Absent-mindedly he took out his key and pushed it into the keyhole and turned it to the right, moving the lock to its open position. As he was about to push the door open, he glanced down at the floor by his left foot and saw the triangle of newspaper he'd wedged between the door and jamb laying on the rug. He removed his key and stepped back from the door, astonished that Urmah had actually gone into his apartment.

When he looked up again, his suspicions aroused, Levy noticed that the peephole in the door was dark. Ordinarily, on any sunny day, and this day was brilliantly sunny, the afternoon sun shining on the inside of the door made the peephole behave like a tiny flashlight emitting its beam into the hall. Someone inside of the apartment was blocking the sun from shining on the door. Obviously, it was Urmah Hamsey.

She had stayed in his home past the time when she knew he usually returned for the day. As his anger at her impertinence built inside of him, Levy pushed his key back into the lock and yelled, "Urmah, I know you're in there." He hoped he'd hollered loud enough for his neighbor across the hall to hear him.

Fully alert with his adrenalin surging, Levy flung the door open and started to walk in, but stopped in amazement at what he saw. Two men wearing ski masks, gloves and white coveralls were standing in his foyer. The taller of the two was standing about five feet beyond where the end of the door was swinging. He held a length of rope the ends of which dangled down to the floor from both of his hands. The shorter man was just beyond the edge of the inwardly moving door, which he had to catch in one hand to hold it open before it could be swung shut by the automatic closure mechanism. Levy was so surprised he stood motionless for an instant. During that moment the nearest assassin, while holding the door with one hand, raised the blackjack in his other hand over his head as he took a step toward Levy, who was still standing motionless in the hall just outside of his doorway.

Realizing he was being attacked, Levy threw the handful of mail he was holding into the face of the advancing attacker. This caused Pedro to miss Levy completely with the descending blow of his blackjack and to make him momentarily loose his balance as he bumped into the retreating target. Levy turned and with two steps was at the stair door. He was surprised to find the door sufficiently open that he didn't have to turn the knob. He just pushed it and it opened. As he dashed into the stairwell, he heard to door click shut behind him while Pedro was recovering his balance and turning to chase him. The delay while his pursuer had to turn the doorknob and push the heavy fire door open gave Levy a head start of half a floor of stairs. As he ran down the stairs, he heard the stair well door open again, and the sound of the footsteps of his attacker following rapidly on the stair behind him.

He heard someone yell down the stair well from above them, "Ruslan. Nyet. NYET."

The sound of the following footsteps slowed and stopped, as Levy reached the building's rear door and burst through it into the bright sunlight. He ran around to the front of the building and out into the middle of the street where he stopped to catch his breath. No one followed him out of the building. He stood a moment to collect his thoughts. His keys were hanging from the door lock, unless the robbers stole them along with whatever else they were taking. Since he didn't have his keys, he had to call someone to buzz him back into the building. Then what. Go back to 310. Not without the police, or several of his neighbors going with him.

So Levy walked up to the front of the building where the intercom used to buzz visitors in through the front door was located. He dialed the number of his golfing companion, Nat Prader, and briefly told him what happened. He asked Prader to call the Gulfport police and report the break-in and attempted assault, which he did when Levy hung up the intercom. Then Prader came downstairs and out of the building. The two men sat on a concrete bench at the entrance waiting for the police to arrive.

Prader was a decade younger than Levy, but no longer worked because he was in poor health. He was overweight and had been weakened by diabetes the doctors had trouble keeping under control. But Prader was available for golf at any time. Now he was wearing a tee shirt under a heavy cotton black sweatshirt and matching sweat pants and sandals.

Four minutes later a squad car drove up and parked in front of the building. Dell Stome, a deeply tanned police officer with a black walrus mustache, got out and came over to Levy. The statement Levy gave to officer Stome included a description of what the intruders were wearing and his recollection of one of them yelling "Ruslan. Not yet. Not yet."

After Levy answered all of his questions, Officer Stome and the two civilians went into the building and rode the elevator to the third floor. They went into the hall, and Stome motioned for the other two to get behind him. He drew his Beretta and walked to 310. Levy's keys were still in the door lock, and his mail was strewn haphazardly in the doorway alcove. With his weapon raised to eye level in front of him, Stome pushed the door open, stepped in and turned from side to side. Levy caught the door as it was swinging shut, and he and Prader walked into the entrance foyer. Stome quickly went from room to room and within a few minutes declared the apartment secure, as he holstered his side arm.

The door had not been damaged, which made Officer Stome suspicious of Levy carelessly leaving his door open when he left that morning. The apartment was in the same condition as when Levy had left it. The TV's, computers, cameras, camcorder and stereo components were all there. A search of his and Susan's jewelry boxes and his secret hiding place for cash under their bed revealed nothing had been stolen. In fact the intruders had not moved or disturbed a thing. So Levy concluded to his dismay, and Stome agreed, though not officially, the motive for the home invasion was to kidnap Levy. They believed the length of rope the intruder held was for tying him up. Who and why anyone wanted to hold him, of all people, as a captive were beyond Levy's comprehension.

Officer Stome said, "My incident report will identify the crime as a home invasion without damage or theft, but with an attempted assault on the owner by two unknown intruders wearing ski masks and white coveralls. Mr. Levy, I have to warn you this crime won't support a claim on your homeowners insurance policy. That's usually the first thing people ask me about when their residence is broken into."

"I'm not worried about insurance. But what if they come back. I don't have a gun to defend myself with," Levy said in a shaky voice.

"We'll keep a close watch on the building tonight. Before I leave, I'll check on all the entrance doors to make sure they close properly." Officer Stome said goodbye, handed one of his cards to both Levy and Prader, and told them to be sure to phone him if they thought of anything else the police should know about.

Chapter 31   Failure

HEARING JUAN'S SHOUT, Pedro stopped chasing Levy down the stairs, and waited for a few seconds to think about what he was doing. Then he ran back up the stairs to where his brother was standing on the third floor landing. The two assassins never before failed to kill their target on their first try, and Pedro was overcome with the urge to finish to job. He was afraid if they failed to carry out any assignment, he and his brother wouldn't be rewarded by having their parents smuggled into America. Juan's recognition that this attempt had already failed exhibited better judgment because Levy was out of the building before they could catch him. And killing him out in the open where the murder could be witnessed was out of the question.

So the assassins retreated back into Levy's apartment where they removed the coveralls and ski masks, and stuffed those garments into their Titleist bag. They were wearing shorts and logoed golf shirts under the coveralls. They put the golfer's bill caps on their heads and walked out of Levy's apartment. The letters Levy had thrown at Pedro were now on the floor and scattered out into the hall. Pedro pushed them back into the door's alcove with the side of his shoe so they wouldn't be visible and attract the attention of someone walking in the hall.

The two assassins walked to the exit door at the opposite end of the hall from where they had entered. They went down the stairs and into and through the parking garage, and finally out on to the street. They didn't attracted attention from a couple who were parking a car as the two men strolled by, waving cheerfully to them. They split up and walked different paths back to their own car.

During the walk back to the car, their moods reversed. Pedro calmed down and started planning their next move, while Juan began to panic. This was their first screw up and he wanted to keep it a secret from O'Durea until they finished the assignment by killing Levy.

When they were in the car driving away, Juan said, "Let's buy a rifle and shoot him in his car tomorrow. When he's driving back from work. Just pull up along side of Levy and shoot him. And then drive off."

"No way're we gonna take anyone out in the middle of a street," Pedro said. "We can't do anything like that without Gurtenkov's permission. Don't you remember anything from our training? We'll phone O'Durea, and tell him what happened and ask him what to do next."

They drove on to I-275 going north. While they were passing through Tampa, Pedro called O'Durea on one of their prepaid cell phones. The Cuban picked up on the sixth ring and answered with a "Yeah."

Pedro recognized his voice and gruff tone. "We got the infidel inventor Hamilton and blew up the Jew gift shop." Then, sheepishly, he admitted, "But the Jew lawyer got away. How long you want us to wait before we go after the lawyer again."

"What're you talking about," O'Durea bellowed. "You were not authorized to kill two men and blow up a shop. Your target's one young woman. Did you get her?"

Pedro was dumbfounded. "He mailed two death buttons to our box in the Baltimore post office with photos of two men, and a letter telling us to blow up the Jew gift shop. We haven't been told to blow up any shops before, but everything else was the way you told us it should be. We had two death buttons for two hits and we had several pictures of each of the two male targets. So we thought the hit on the shop must be something you wanted us to do. Gurtenkov taught us how to put together the bomb we used.

We don't question who or what our targets are. You and Gurtenkov trained us to follow orders without asking any questions. Are you giving us different orders now? Can we ask questions now? Should we go after Levy, the Jew lawyer?"

Pedro's account of the bungled assassination momentarily stunned O'Durea into silence. Recovering his voice, the Cuban barked, "No not now. Maybe we'll have to kill the Jew lawyer another time. Your orders and the procedure haven't changed. Drive back to Baltimore. Someone'll send you the death button and photos of your next target. It'll be someone in the DC area." He ended the call abruptly.

O'Durea was furious when Bennie Tailoren's deceit finally sank in. He sent an email signaling Tailoren to call him using one of his prepaid cell phones. Before going to work the next day, Tailoren made the call.

Without revealing his anger, O'Durea asked Tailoren if he'd sent the two death buttons directing the assassins to kill an inventor and his attorney and a letter telling them to blow up a gift shop. Tailoren proudly admitted doing all of those things.

"Why them?" O'Durea asked. He knew he'd have to make a complete report to Gurtenkov.

"The infidel Hamilton invented a death ray gun he wanted used to murder Arabs. Those were his exact words, a death ray gun to murder Arabs. The Jew lawyer was helping him get a patent on his death ray gun. And the death ray gun worked. They demonstrated it for me."

"Are you telling me they actually killed someone with a ray gun," O'Durea said with disbelief.

"No. No. They killed cockroaches with it. A ray emitted from their gun killed the roaches. I saw it happen several times. These two men were true enemies of Allah's jihad. They deserved to die. The innocent girl who helped me didn't deserve to die. She can't hurt Arabs like those two infidels could hurt us before I had them killed."

O'Durea realized Tailoren didn't know Levy was still alive, and he intended to keep that fact away from the wayward agent. "What about the gift shop. Why'd you have 'em blow it up?"

"Ginsberg's shop was the inventor's source of a critical material for his death ray gun. The glass he used to make the lens for concentrating certain light rays into the lethal death ray. And the glass for the lens of the death ray gun they intended to use to murder Arabs was made in Israel. Made in Israel. It was a three part conspiracy against Arabs I decided I had to stop, once I thought of a way to have all three parts of the conspiracy eliminated. Please report the success of my mission to Muhamed Allah Yatakalan. I know he'll be pleased with what I've accomplished."

"I'll tell him what you've done," O'Durea said. He reflected bitterly: *But it won't be in any context you've imagined.*

It was 8:30 pm in Riyadh the next day when O'Durea was finally able to get Gurtenkov on the line. The Russian had just finished a big steak dinner followed by a slice of whipped cream pie for desert. He was enjoying a Cuban cigar and a tumbler full of single malt scotch when the phone in his apartment rang.

After O'Durea told him of Tailoren's insubordination, Gurtenkov's rage made O'Durea's anger seem like a mild pique. He ordered O'Durea to have the insolent agent killed. He collapsed on a sofa fearful his rage might precipitate an apoplexic stroke. Then he withdrew the death sentence and told O'Durea he'd call him back in a little while after he had a chance to calm down and think out more clearly what they should do.

Half an hour and another tumbler of scotch later, Gurtenkov phoned O'Durea. This time the Cuban picked up on the first ring.

"I knew something like this was going to happen," Gurtenkov said worriedly. "You can't send an inexperienced agent, by himself, to do undercover work among people he hates in a foreign country. It doesn't matter that his assignment to get information out of the Patent Office was nonviolent. Something was bound to go wrong. The honey trap was a mistake. We should've used baksheesh."

"Or not had him go for the Top Secret clearance," O'Durea said. "How many Top Secret inventions can there be. If he doesn't go after Top Secret, he doesn't need the girl's help, and we don't have to push him into the honey trap."

"That's it! Going for the Top Secret clearance was the only mistake," Gurtenkov said with unconcealed relief. "Sami Insien insisted Tailoren needed the higher clearance because it gave his computer hackers additional Patent Office access codes. That clarifies my thinking. It wasn't my fault. It was Sami's fault. I'll take it up with bin Nazamunde first thing tomorrow." Then he hung up the phone.

Not until 2:00 pm the next day could Gurtenkov get everyone bin Nazamunde wanted present into their overlord's plush office. Three men sat on tan, leather-covered chairs they pulled up to the edge of bin Nazamunde's massive rosewood desk. Sami Insien was his persona of an executive in charge of a team of computer software developers. He was wearing an open necked, crimson sport shirt, faded blue jeans and sneakers but no socks.

Abu Wagdy was his same old self: sly fixer and thug doing bin Nazamunde's dirty work and dressed in the same style of clothing as his boss. This day they both wore traditional ankle length gowns. Gurtenkov, nattily attired in a grey wool suit and yellow tie, told the stunned assemblage what had been done by Bennie Tailoren, previously known to them as Hamde Jawade.

The immediate reaction of bin Nazamunde and abu Wagdy was such insubordination must be punished in a way making an example of the miscreant to deter others involved in the jihad from similar behavior. Gurtenkov agreed with this assessment; he was pleased because bin Nazamunde momentarily forgot it was he who insisted on sending an inexperienced agent to America without a partner. The Russian told them he could have the assassins eliminate Tailoren in a way resulting in media coverage they could preserve and display at the training sessions for future secret agents. Bin Nazamunde agreed to this and told Gurtenkov to proceed at once before Tailoren could do something else that might expose their conspiracy in America. That was the end of it, thought Gurtenkov.

And then Sami spoke up. He had not said a word during the preceding discussion. Looking directly into bin Nazamunde's eyes with his possessive gaze, he said in a rapid voice of elevated pitch, "I beg to disagree with this group's conclusion and ask you to hear my reasons."

Gurtenkov stood and indignantly blurted, "But bin Nazamunde's already decided—"

Bin Nazamunde silenced him by shooting his hand up. "Tell us what you think," he said and looked down at papers on his desk to free his eyes from Sami's mesmeric grip.

"Tailoren's too valuable to eliminate until we can infiltrate a replacement for him into the United States Patent Office." Sami punctuated his words with rapid hand movements, and his eyes darted from one of his listeners to another. "The entry codes he's given me enabled us to earn almost fifty million dollars for the jihad in the short time he's been in America."

"I've been impressed by your upsurge in stock trading profits," bin Nazamunde said as he cautiously raised his eyes from his desk. "How does Tailoren contribute to your success?"

"The access codes Tailoren gives to me each day enable our computers to scour the pending patent applications for key words which alert us to inventions that could possibly bring great profits to the companies owning the resulting patents. In particular, drug companies, small computer software developers and originators of unique computer hardware or hardware components can become extremely profitable when they get a key patent.

We learn of favorable actions by the US Patent Office approving critical claims in pending patent applications we've targeted. Our advantage is that we learn a patent's approved before the company or the company lawyers receive the favorable information. This gives us the opportunity to buy their stock before the company's executives and other insiders can load up on it. And, of course, the American public will be the last to know a valuable patent has been approved."

His voice dripping skepticism, abu Wagdy asked, "How can you find out what's going to happen before the patent attorneys representing the companies owning the patent applications know what's happening?"

Sami gleefully replied, "There's a delay of several days between the time when a Patent Examiner enters a favorable Action into the Patent Office's central computer and when the letter advising of the favorable Action is printed and mailed to the patent attorney handling the application. Add to this the time lag while the letter from the Patent Office is being delivered to the patent attorney by US mail. It gives us plenty of time to buy the company stock before the good news gets out."

"And why is this Tailoren so important to you," bin Nazamunde said. "You've already broken their security code."

"They frequently change the codes. Yes, I know what all of you are thinking." Sami looked briefly at each in turn. "The United States Patent Office uses Microsoft Windows based software, so we will be able to penetrate any defenses they set up. But analyzing changed access codes takes time and reduces our advantage of knowing what's going to happen before the patent owner knows he will get a patent. That's why we need to have our own agent in the Patent Office keeping our computers up to date every day after every change in their access codes. It eliminates the delay we'd suffer if we had to break every code change.

Let us give this examiner, Bennie Tailoren, another chance. From what you said, Gurtenkov, he thought eliminating the inventor and his lawyer removed a threat to the jihad. This proves he's loyal to the jihad. And he was clever enough to fool those supervising him in the way he acquired the death buttons, and directed the assassins to their targets. The failures were in his lack of training and the lax supervision by those controlling him. Bennie Tailoren deserves another chance."

Gurtenkov bristled at Sami's criticism of the way he was running the secret agent program in America. But he was smart enough to let the issue fade into the background as they concentrated on the details of what Tailoren had to do to redeem himself. The Russian said, "O'Durea told me he believes Tailoren is romantically attached to the woman who helped him get the Top Secret security clearance. As you know, she was the target we intended for the assassins. I'll order Tailoren to arrange her assassination. If he refuses, we'll kill him. And, anyway, we need to find another source of the access codes Sami uses."

"He won't refuse," Sami said. "I'll talk to Muhamed Allah Yatakalan and ask the Grand Imam to speak to Tailoren over the Internet on the iSight camera linkage. The Imam will convince him the woman is a threat to the jihad and must be eliminated."

Gurtenkov and abu Wagdy looked at each other and rolled their eyes.

Bin Nazamunde was too focused on the potential loss of profits to notice Sami's display of his insanity. He changed the subject. "Gurtenkov had the right idea. We need to acquire another source of the access codes. The profits from our penetration of the Patent Office's computer system are too large to let them depend on one person. Abu Wagdy, I order you to find to find another informant for us in the Patent Office. Baksheesh will probably be your best approach. Does everyone know what I expect them to do next?" Without waiting for answers, bin Nazamunde waved his hand toward the office door and picked up a file of papers from his desktop.

Chapter 32   Sawed-off

GULFPORT POLICE OFFICER Stome failed in his effort to reassure Levy he was safe. Levy vowed to himself that the very next day, he'd buy firearms he could use to protect himself and Susan. And he'd talk to Nollann. Kidnapping was a federal offense and he wanted Nollann and the FBI involved in finding out who was after him.

"What do you use to protect yourself with, besides a kitchen knife?" Levy asked Ned Prader, who remained standing with him in his apartment after Stome left.

Prader thought a long moment before answering. "I'll only tell you this because you're a close friend, but I've got a Remington 12 gauge, double barreled, sawed-off shotgun."

"Aren't those guns illegal?" Levy took a step back and gave his friend a quizzical look.

"You bet they're illegal. They've been illegal since 1934, when Congress passed a law covering sawed-offs and machine guns."

"Then where'd you get it?"

"You already know I grew up on a farm in Kentucky." Levy nodded. "Well, my uncle, Elwinn Prader, was county sheriff, and he got hold of guns used in crimes and he confiscated some others. He passed some of them around to his brothers. So one day he gave the sawed-off to my Dad. He told Dad he took it when they raided a whiskey still. I inherited it when my Dad died. Come on up and I'll demonstrate how intimidating the thing is."

They rode the elevator up to Prader's apartment on the sixth floor, He went into his bedroom, and Levy followed. Prader reached under his bed and pulled out the Remington.

"Just watch this," Prader said. He pointed the sawed-off toward Levy and chambered a shell, which produced a loud "kerchunk."

"Ok, Ok," Levy whined as he felt a surge of pressure in his bladder. "I see what you mean. The sound of chambering a round is enough to protect you because everyone knows if it's fired at him at close range, he's dead. There's no chance the gun'll miss, is there."

"You got it." Prader pointed the shotgun at the floor, ejected the shell and slid the weapon back underneath his bed. "How about staying for dinner, Lem. I told Rosealee what happened to you before I went down there to be with you, and she said to ask you to eat with us tonight."

Shaking his head, Levy said, "Thanks, but I'm too upset to eat any time soon. I've got to go home and sit down and figure out what this is all about. I'll thank Rosealee on my way out."

Sitting at his desk back in his apartment, after drinking two glasses of red wine on an empty stomach, Levy had calmed down enough to make plans. The next day he'd phone Sam Fellows, the executor of Hamilton's estate. He'd get permission to use Hamilton's workshop tools, and he'd buy a 12 gage double-barreled shotgun. He'd cut the gun down to a sawed-off length with Hamilton's tools. Levy intended to it carry around in his car and have it with him at the office, so the gun needed to be short enough to fit under the car seat and in his desk drawer.

For his home, he'd buy two of the smallest single barreled shotguns he could find, one for him and one for Susan. They'd keep one gun on each side of their bed. Susan wouldn't be upset at having the guns around because she hunted quail and ducks with her Father's shotgun when she was growing up in rural Missouri.

When news of the bombing and the resulting fire reached the Tampa field office, Minimum Bill Nollann was still there, scheduled to interview people associated with Hamilton. He'd obtained their names from Sam Fellows. These days a bombing was assumed to be the work of terrorists. So the local police contacted the FBI.

The phone in Nollann's room at the Clarentown woke him at 7:00 am with a call from Tampa Field Office SAIC (Special Agent In Charge) Thelma Grasse. She told him the Bureau's headquarters wanted him to represent its Terrorist Task Force on the bombing which occurred early that morning in St. Petersburg. Not much was known at the field office, so there weren't any adequate answers to his questions except that no one had been injured by the blast.

Grasse told Nollann to cancel all other appointments and concentrate on the bombing. He shaved, got dressed in a suit and tie, grabbed a quick breakfast at the hotel coffee shop, and drove to the scene of the bombing. He saw that the St. Petersburg police and the fire department had the scene and the gawkers under control.

Nollann read the statements the police had taken from the first spectators on the scene after the explosion, and he got a preliminary estimate of the size and location of the bomb from the sergeant in charge of the bomb and arson squad. He also read Marsha Ginsberg's statement.

Reid Bensen was the sunburned, eager, young police officer assigned to assist Nollann at the crime scene.

"Is Ms. Ginsberg still nearby so I can interview her myself?" Nollann asked.

Bensen pointed to two women inside the crime scene tape who were standing side by side so close to each other their hips were touching. It looked like they were leaning against each other. "She's the one with the long black hair," he said.

Nollann stepped over the tape, walked up to the ladies and introduced himself, showing his FBI creds. He folded his wallet containing the creds, and put it into his hip pocket. His infallible memory for names told him Ms. Ginsberg's companion, Rosalind Katz, worked for his new friend, Lem Levy. He reached out and took Marsha Ginsberg's frigid hand into his two warm hands. He gave her his most sympathetic face with his own tender brown eyes seeming moist with tears and asked, "What can the FBI do to help you, Marsha?"

She thought a moment, leaned forward, put her free hand on Nollann's shoulder, her head on his chest and started crying. Then Rosalind Katz started crying, so Nollann reached over with the hand that was on top of Marsha's and patted Rosalind on the shoulder. After about a minute, the two women regained their composure. Rosalind suggested they walk across the street to the garden outside of the Commerce Building where Levy's office was located. There they could sit on benches under the trees, and Marsha could ask for any help she wanted from the Bureau, and Nollann could ask his questions.

They sat in the dappled shade from the Ficus tree; a light breeze was blowing. Marsha's grief was turning to rage. "The first thing the FBI could do for me is catch the fiend who destroyed my store and force him to tell me why he did it."

Trying to reassure her, Nollann exaggerated. "That's exactly what I've been assigned to do by the Director's office in Washington." He removed a pen and small l brown notebook from his suit pocket and started asking her his questions. After receiving no information of value from the usual questions which were essentially the same as those the police detective had asked Marsha, Nollann asked one that often paid off for him. He said, "Marsha, please tell me the most unusual thing you saw or that happened yesterday, even if it has no relation to your store or to the bombing."

She eyed him doubtfully, thought for at least a minute and then replied, "I saw a well dressed man with a big, conspicuous, gold front tooth. My customers and the people I associate with have porcelain crowns if they have a tooth or teeth that's got to be crowned. I think of lowlifes and, I hate to sound elitist when I say this, but the lower classes are the ones who cap their front teeth in gold that's conspicuous. This man was genteel in every way, and he bought a relatively sophisticated gift for, he said, for his daughter."

Nollann stopped taking notes and mused: *An amateur's disguise trick, if this guy turns out to be involved.* To Marsha, he said, "Please go on. Tell me everything you can about the man and what he bought."

, "What he bought. It was a small brass kaleidoscope. It was hand crafted by Meyer Ashter. His shop is in Hayward, Wisconsin. He paid cash so I don't know his name. He was my last customer of the day." She paused a moment, started crying again, turned to Rosalind and said, "He was my last customer forever."

"You'll rebuild your business," Rosalind encouraged. "You'll have the insurance money to start over with."

"What time did the gold tooth man come in and make his purchase?" Nollann asked after she stopped crying.

"Right before I closed, at about 7:45. And he walked out almost exactly at 8:00. Then I emptied the cash register and walked out the back door myself."

"Please describe what he looked like."

"Tall, almost, but maybe not quite six feet. Caucasian, but with a good tan. Well dressed. Did I say he was wearing a suit and tie?"

Nollann shook his head, jotted some notes and prompted her. "Hair color and eyes? Can you pick his picture out of a mug book?"

"I'm sorry. I can't...I don't...remember," she mumbled. "All I can remember is his nice suit and tie, and the gold tooth."

Curses, the disguise worked, Nollann fumed to himself. "Was anyone with Mr. Gold Tooth?"

"No. He was definitely by himself. But, wait a minute, after he came in, another man came into the shop and walked to the back. He left while Mr. Gold Tooth was paying me for the kaleidoscope. This person didn't buy anything."

"Tell me all you can about this other man."

"I hardly saw him at all. Most of the time Mr. Gold Tooth was standing between me and this other person. I do remember he was shorter, not as well dressed. He had on casual clothes. Maybe he was Hispanic. I have some recollection he was dark, not Caucasian."

Nollann wrote this down, then closed his notebook. "Could you identify his face in a mug book?"

"I'm not sure. I don't think so," she said hesitantly. Then her face brightened. "But now I remember his ears. Yes. His ears stuck out from his head like cup handles."

Nollann opened his notebook, jotted this down and said, "It's been our experience at the Bureau that looking at mug books stimulates people to remember things they didn't think they knew." He turned his face to look directly at her and gazed at Marsha with his most pleading eyes. "Please do this as a favor to me. Go with the police sergeant and look at the mug books. You'll feel better because you'll know you did everything those of us trying to solve this crime wanted you to do to help us." He gave her a big smile.

Of course Marsha Ginsberg did what Nollann asked her to do, but she found no one she recognized. Looking at mug books was a waste of time.

The breeze had prevented Nollann's synesthesia from working. But his perceptive powers told him Marsha Ginsberg was telling the truth and knew nothing about the bombing. Her body language and the stroking gestures Rosalind Katz gave Marsha Ginsberg revealed to Nollann she too had nothing to do with the destruction of her friend's shop.

The morning after Levy had been attacked, he called Sam Fellows, who told Levy he hadn't sold any of Hamilton's power tools. Actually, Fellows hadn't even had time to hire someone to tally a complete inventory of the dead inventor's possessions. He gave Levy permission to use Hamilton's tools. He could pick up the keys to Hamilton's house and garage at the office. Levy thanked him and told Fellows he'd come by to get the keys soon after lunch.

He drove to a Field gun store, bought a double-barreled Remington twelve gauge and a box of shells. He also bought two single barreled 410 Junior shot guns and a box of shells for them. Even though he knew the one for the Remington was going to be too large, he bought carrying cases for all three weapons.

Levy drove to Sam Fellows' office, met the tall, gangly, elegantly dressed lawyer for the first time and mused: *I can understand why Hamilton told me he never sweats no matter how hot it is. He's all skin and bones. He's got no flesh to hold in his body heat.*

After picking up the keys at Fellows' office, Levy drove to Hamilton's house in Brandon. Fellows told him Nollann was coming to Hamilton's place in the afternoon, and he could leave the keys with the FBI agent. Levy nodded, but was so focused on his objective of arming himself he wasn't paying much attention to what anyone said to him.

Levy parked his car in Hamilton's driveway and let himself into the house with a key Fellows had given him. He walked through Hamilton's kitchen into the garage, where he found a band saw with a metal cutting blade, and a table saw with a ten inch crosscut blade. Perfect tools for what he intended to do. He returned to his car and took the gun case with the Remington out of the trunk. Once inside the garage again, Levy removed the shotgun and laid it on the bed of the band saw.

He pondered: *I've never committed any crime before, except speeding and jaywalking when I'm in a hurry. And everyone does that. Do I really want to do this?* Shouting a resounding "Yes," he pressed the switch starting the band saw, and reached for the shotgun. Then he shut the machine off. He tried to remember how long the barrel was on Ned Prader's gun. He'd been so intimidated by having the loaded weapon pointed at him he hadn't examined it closely. He thought a minute and decided his gun barrel should be two inches long.

He started the band saw up again, turned the gun upside down on the bed and pressed the side of one barrel into the blade. The cutting went slowly. The barrels were made of hardened steel, and the saw blade wasn't new. He shut the saw off, and looked around for an oilcan or something he could use as a cutting lubricant. He remembered a patent application he prepared many years before covering a petroleum derivative used to speed up metal cutting and extend saw blade life. He found an oilcan containing an oily lubricant. The can had a lever he could press to squirt oil out of its snout. It was just what he needed.

The cutting went at a much faster pace after he doused the gun barrel with oil at the point where it met the saw blade. Soon he had the major length of the two barrels separated from the rest of the gun. He found a tattered shop rag hanging on a nail and used it to wipe the excess oil and metal saw dust from the gun.

When Levy looked up, he saw William Nollann standing in the doorway connecting the kitchen and the garage. The stress Levy was under and his eagerness to arm himself with a weapon had caused him to forget Fellows told him Nollann was coming to Hamilton's house.

Nollann was staring at him with alarm showing on his face. "I'm not exactly sure what I see happening in here," he said accusingly.

"And I'm not going to walk into the garage to get a closer look. Lem, I don't want to have to read you your rights just as we are becoming friends. But whenever I see a crime being committed, I have to do my duty. So put away whatever you're working on and come in here where we can talk." He turned his back on Levy and walked into the kitchen.

Levy hastily put the shotgun and the barrel portion he'd just sawed off into the gun's carrying case. He wiped off the band saw, swept up the metal shavings on the floor and put them into a garbage can. He didn't need to use any more of Hamilton's tools. He had a rasp and a saber saw back at his apartment. So later on, he could file off the serial number and cut the gunstock off below its pistol grip to the size he wanted. He looked around to make sure he'd put everything back in its place, walked through the door into the kitchen, smiled and held his hand out to Nollann.

"What's going on with you?" Nollann said. He shifted his gaze from Levy's eyes to avoid giving his friend another accusing look.

"You heard about the kidnappers, didn't you," Levy said. "I'm still shook up about it."

"I was completely engrossed with Ms. Ginsberg and the store bombing yesterday and this morning, and just got away from her case. When I asked Sam Fellows for the key to Hamilton's house, he told me you were already here. So I drove here and saw your car parked in the driveway. I haven't heard about any kidnapping. Tell me what happened, and what it has to do with you." He pointed toward the garage. "And I still do not want to know what you were doing out there. Now what do you know about a kidnapping."

"I thought the FBI was involved in all kidnappings," Levy said. "Well, I'm not sure the Gulfport police reported it as an attempted kidnapping, but I'm sure it was." He pulled out a kitchen chair and sat down.

"The FBI will not be automatically involved. Certain conditions have to be met. If you weren't transported anywhere or held captive, you wouldn't have been kidnapped. So the Gulfport police wouldn't automatically contact our Tampa field office. Now tell me what happened to you." Nollann sat facing Levy across the kitchen table.

"Here's the way it happened. Tuesday, yesterday, when I got home from work, I was about to open the door to my apartment. I noticed the signal I'd left to alert me my neighbor's been snooping told me someone had been in my apartment. I already told you about the trick of putting a piece of paper between the door and jamb I learned when I had the CIC training at Halabird." Nollann nodded, his expression serious. "The piece of paper was on the floor in the hall outside of my door. And the afternoon sun wasn't shining through the peephole in the door, like it should've been. So I knew someone was waiting by the door inside my apartment."

Levy pointed his thumbs at his chest. "Now I know to run downstairs and call the police if it ever happens again. But yesterday I thought it was Urmah…I won't tell you her full name. The nosey neighbor. I thought she had trapped herself inside my place during one of her snooping escapades. So I threw the apartment door open.

Two men wearing ski masks, gloves and white coveralls were inside waiting for me. One was holding a length of rope they were going to use to tie me up. For an instant I just stood there too stunned to move. The other kidnapper, the one not holding the rope, he grabbed the door with one of his hands before the closer could swing it shut. He had a blackjack in his other hand, and he tried to hit me with it. Like this." Levy swung his right hand as if to blackjack someone.

"I was holding the day's mail in one hand, and I threw it in his face when he came at me with the blackjack. I threw the mail instinctively. I didn't even think about doing it. I know the mail spoiled his aim, and that's why he missed me. He let go of the door and stumbled into me. He was off balance because he'd swung wild with the blackjack. But he didn't fall down."

"It looks like the paper in the door jamb trick paid off," Nollann said encouragingly.

"It sure did. I came to my senses and turned and ran into the stairwell. That fire door is usually hard to open, but this time it wasn't closed all the way. Something was holding it partially open."

"Your assailants might have left it partially open to speed their escape," Nollann speculated.

"Well, I was able to just push the door open and run on to the stairs. The door closed completely behind me by the time the kidnapper regained his balance and got to it. So he had to turn the knob before he could push the door open. That gave me a head start of half a flight of steps. I heard him start running down the steps after me. Then someone, it must have been the other kidnapper, yelled down the stairwell 'Ruslan, not yet, not yet.'

What he yelled doesn't make any sense to me." Levy lifted his eyebrows and shrugged. "I read an article in the *Wall Street Journal* about a plane the Russians make, the world's largest cargo airplane. They call it the Ruslan. So what does it mean when one kidnapper yells to another 'Airplane name, not yet, not yet'? It must be some kind of code word because the kidnapper chasing me stopped running down the stairs. I went out the rear door of the building and ran around to the front entrance. They didn't chase me or come after me. So I had a neighbor call the local police. I guess their incident report will confirm what I just told you."

Finally Nollann's expression became friendly. "I have some thoughts about what happened to you that differ from your conclusions," he said "But I haven't time to get into it with you now. I'm on a tight schedule and need to finish up this afternoon going through Hamilton's things. I might get some new leads here, so I've got to go over the place thoroughly. I'm flying out of here first thing tomorrow morning. Can we get together again for dinner tonight. I'd like to brainstorm my ideas about this case with you, Lem. You told me you'd be willing to talk." He stood up and started to walk out of the kitchen.

"Sure." Levy's face beamed. "I really want to hear what you think, Bill. But I'm through here and don't want to wait around here all afternoon, so you come to my club, Gardenia, and be my guest tonight. It's steak night, and I was going to go there by myself and have a filet or prime rib, if they haven't sold out by the time I get there. The steaks aren't as good as at Ruthie's Broiler, but they're still plenty good. Anyway the Gardenia is only about twenty minutes past where you'd turn off to go to Ruthie's Broiler at the International Mall. What time should I make the reservations for?"

Nollann extended his hand for Levy to shake. "OK. I'll be your guest this time, but next time it's on me. I may be working here into the evening, so can we make it at 8:00."

"It's a deal. Here's how you get there." Levy wrote the directions on a sheet of notebook paper, handed it to Nollann, stood and left Hamilton's house.

Chapter 33   Suspect

AT 6:20 NOLLANN phoned Levy and told him he'd finished going through Hamilton's place. "I can leave for the Gardenia right now," he said. "Can you meet me there in about forty-five minutes? And can I leave Hamilton's keys with you to return to Fellows?"

Levy answered yes to both questions.

At 7:15 the two men sat side by side at a table looking out of the tall windows at the picturesque eighteenth hole of the Gardenia Golf Club, which is bordered on its south side by one of the residential canals slicing into the waterfront areas of Pinellas County. Nollann removed his tie when he learned they were not required attire in the club's main dining room. Both men sipped glasses of house cabernet, while the prime rib dinners they ordered were being prepared.

For a few minutes they commented on the display of busy energy of a tractor drawn rig gathering up brightly colored balls from the driving range. And the last foursome hurrying to finish while there was barely enough light to see where their balls landed. They were completely at ease with each other.

Nollann began, "Here's what I think is going on. You understand, this is just my hunch. What happened at your apartment yesterday was not an attempted kidnapping. It was an attempted murder."

"My God," sputtered Levy. "I—"

Nollann held up his hand, before Levy could say more. "I'm going to guess the perps were Russians. Ruslan is a fairly common male name in Russia. And I think the one who yelled said 'Nyet, Nyet'. That translates from Russian as 'no, no' which makes more sense than the 'not yet, not yet' you thought you heard."

"Yes. That makes sense to me now," Levy agreed. "I thought he yelled 'not yet, not yet' but if I were in a courtroom under oath, I'd have to say I think he said that. But I'm not a hundred percent sure. If I'd testified he yelled 'not yet' my testimony might break down under cross examination."

"Now I'm going to take you into my confidence and tell you what the crime scene looked like where we found Hamilton's corpse." Nollann leaned toward Levy. "You've got to keep everything I tell you now in complete confidence. If you're the student of crime novels you claim to be, I'm sure you already know why."

Levy nodded, and took another sip of his wine.

"Hamilton was strangled with a piece of clothes line that was probably the same kind as the piece of rope you saw in the home invader's hands. Hamilton was on his back lying on the hotel bed, completely naked. His trousers, socks, shirt, boxer shorts and shoes were scattered all over the room, as if he had flung them off in a big hurry."

Levy grimaced. "The poor guy," he said.

"Hamilton had an erection, and there was female saliva on his organ. The woman's DNA is not on record anywhere in the system. There were no signs of a struggle in the room and no defensive wounds or bruises on his body. His tox screen came back negative except for a couple of shots of bourbon he drank just before he was killed. His charges at the Dately Hotel bar confirmed what he drank and when he drank it." Nollann paused and took a sip of wine.

"In the room there were dozens of fingerprints from Hamilton, the cleaning staff, and previous guests. Only two prints showed up in our database. They were from people who'd been guests in 406 a week or two earlier, and they both had iron clad alibis for the night Hamilton was killed.

No one's been able to come up with a motive for anyone to murder Hamilton. It looks like it could have been kinky sex that went too far. Or it could have been a murder they carefully staged to look like an unfortunate outcome to some kind of rough sex act. Lem, what do you think about what I've told you so far. Any ideas about motive?"

Their salads arrived while Nollann was talking. Levy put down his fork, wiped his mouth and said, "One thing jumps out at me. The crime scene must have been staged after Hamilton was killed."

"Why do you say that?" Nollann lowered his fork before taking his first bite of salad.

255

"Hamilton was a neatness freak. He wouldn't have been able to stand it having his clothes scattered around the room. I bet you found everything else of his neatly hung up or arranged carefully."

Nollann nodded enthusiastically and began munching his salad.

"Hamilton even lined up the corners of his suitcase or shoebox with the corners of any desk he put them on. I saw him do this both times he demonstrated his death ray gun by shooting roaches with it. If he knew his clothes were jumbled everywhere in his room, I think he'd be too uncomfortable to participate voluntarily in any kind of sex act. Of course, like I told you the first time we talked about him, I really don't have any actual knowledge of his sex life. But that's what I think."

"Anything else." Nollann sipped his wine.

Levy picked up his fork and started eating his salad again. In between bites, he said, "I can't articulate it yet. But there's something here I know must be the key. Let me think a few more minutes."

Nollann nodded and both men ate in silence until they had finished their salads. A busboy picked up the empty bowls. Levy looked out the window into the fading twilight and noticed his own reflection staring back at him in the now darkened glass. He brushed back his hair with his hands.

A few minutes later, the waiter arrived with their dinners. Nollann had his prime rib cooked medium but blackened. Levy's was rare. They continued to eat in complete silence for almost five minutes, which attested to the degree of comfort the two men felt in each other's company.

All of a sudden, Levy's eyes opened wide. He put down his fork and steak knife. He choked down the bite of meat he'd been chewing, and wiped saliva from his lips with a napkin.

"Bingo!" he exclaimed, and slapped the top of the table with the palm of his right hand. This sloshed some of the wine from his glass on to the white tablecloth. "There's too much here for this to be one big coincidence. I know you detectives don't believe in coincidences. The sleuths in the novels I read say there's no such thing as a coincidence. Sandford's Lucas Davenport, Burke's Dave Robicheaux, and James's Adam Dalgliesh all taught me when there's been a murder, there are no coincidences."

"Enough already about the fiction," Nollann admonished with amusement. "Out with it."

"It's the Patent Examiner controlling Hamilton's patent application who's behind all this," Levy said excitedly. "He's the only common link to all of the crimes. Except, right now I can't remember his name. But I can get it from a file in the Powerbook back at my apartment when we're through with dinner. It has to be him."

Nollann smiled at his cohort's enthusiasm and said, "Slow down a minute and tell me about the coincidences."

Feeling jubilant at his sudden insight, Levy chugalugged his wine and held his goblet up, signaling the waiter to bring a second round. "The bomb that blew up Marsha Ginsberg's shop ties it all to the Patent Examiner. Hamilton bought the glass for the lens in his death ray gun from Marsha's shop. There are only four people in the whole world who know where the lens glass came from. Hamilton, but he's dead, me and my paralegal, Rosalind Katz, and the Examiner. He's the common link. I'm sure Rosalind didn't have anything to do with this."

"I agree with you. I met her yesterday when I interviewed Marsha Ginsberg, and I'm sure she'd never do anything to hurt her friend."

"The Examiner was unusually hostile to Hamilton's invention. But I can understand his attitude, for legitimate professional reasons. But only up to a point. We can't explain how the death ray gun produces the force that kills the roaches. It defies the laws of physics, the laws of nature. And the Examiner gave us a hard time about that, as he should have done. It was his job to make us prove the death ray gun worked the way the patent application said it worked. And we did that."

Levy gulped some wine and continued eagerly. "But the Examiner wouldn't accept our demonstration as being on the level, until his boss forced him to. The Examiner insinuated we were trying to trick him with gimmicky props like stage magicians use. That goes beyond what an Examiner's supposed to be concerned with."

Nollann looked skeptical. "But where's the motive. Why would a Patent Examiner conspire to murder an inventor, conspire to murder his patent attorney, and finally plot to blow up a shop selling some component of his invention? I know the invention is a death ray gun, but even if the Examiner's a pacifist, that's not what you'd expect him to do."

"Speaking about motive, here's another possible factor," Levy said. "I know you're already aware of Hamilton's anti-Arab crusade. His interview on the O'Smiley Indicator TV show and all that." Nollann nodded his head. "Well, the title for the Provisional patent application, remember I told you what it is during my Patent 101 lecture." Again Nollann responded with a nod. "Well remember the title for the Provisional patent called the invention A Death Ray Gun for Murdering Arabs. I told you that when we met in the FBI field office on Zack Street."

Nollann pursed his lips and thought a moment before asking, "Are you telling me the Examiner's an Arab?"

"No, I don't think so. Now I remember his name. It's Bennie Tailoren." Levy frowned and cogitated. "That doesn't sound like an Arab name to me."

"Does he look like he might be an Arab? People can change their names."

"Now that you mention it, he did look like he had a an unusually dark tan for a DC area resident at cherry blossom time. But he was clean-shaven. No beard or any facial hair. And he is handsome. Yeah, I guess I can describe him as tall, dark and handsome."

"That settles it. I mean him looking dark," Nollann said. "Patent Examiner Bennie Tailoren is now a suspect. I'll find out what I can about him when I get back to DC tomorrow. But the motive is still up in the air, in my mind, because the two perps who came after you were probably Russians. Why would Russians care if Hamilton wanted to kill Arabs? Unless possibly they could just be assassins for hire who belong to the Russian mob. This is all just speculation. I don't think we've figured out the motive yet."

Levy glanced around the dinning room. "It looks like the busboys are starting to close this place down now, so let's finish our food and call it a night here."

"Lem, I'd like for you to show me the scene of the crime in your apartment, and then I'll get on the road back to Tampa before I get sleepy."

Levy signed the dinning room chit for their meals, and they went back to apartment 310 in the tall building where Levy lived. Nollann looked around Levy's apartment for about ten minutes, declined the offer of a nightcap, shook his friend's hand and drove back to the Clarentown in Tampa.

The next morning Levy told Rosalind about his meeting with Nollann, and his own suspicions about Examiner Tailoren being the common link in all three crimes. He told her the kind of things the FBI agent asked about Tailoren. She reminded him of how nosey Examiner Tailoren was about the hotel room where he and Hamilton were staying and the length of their stay there. And Levy remembered her impression that the Examiner spoke like a foreigner for whom English was not his native language, and Hamilton had the same thought. Levy phoned Nollann's office and gave these impressions to someone who said he'd pass them on to Minimum Bill after he got back around noon.

Levy asked, "Why do you call him Minimum Bill?"

"It's a nickname he's earned, but you'll have to get the whole story from agent Nollann."

Nollann's flight touched down at Reagan National at 12:20 pm. After deplaning, he spent thirty-five minutes on the phone with an assistant whom he asked to get him the Patent Office's personnel file on Tailoren and any other information about the Examiner in their records. The assistant told Nollann the impressions about Tailoren Levy had phoned in to his office that morning.

Nollann drove straight to the Crystal City Dately Hotel, showed his creds and asked to speak to the manager. He wanted to interview the desk clerks who were on duty during the week of Hamilton's murder. This was quickly arranged, the hotel's management being eager to cooperate in getting the crime solved and the press out of their hair. In response to Nollann's question, the manager looked at the records and confirmed no plumbers had worked for the hotel on the day of Hamilton's murder, nor had anyone else wearing a white coverall.

Janney Hoean, one of the desk clerks who worked the day shifts, was now on duty. The manager took her place behind the desk and she went with Nollann into the manager's office and closed the door. They sat facing each other in the upholstered visitor's chairs on the same side of the manager's desk. Nollann had a copy of her statement in the case file with him. He reviewed it with her to see if he could jog her memory into revealing something she'd overlooked. Ms. Hoean had nothing new to add to her statement.

Finally Nollann gave her his most understanding smile and made his final request. "Please tell me about the strangest thing that happened while you were behind the desk during the week of the crime, even if you're sure it had nothing to do with the crime."

She thought for a full minute. Then shook her head, and said, "There wasn't anything strange going on that week. I'm sorry."

But Nollann persisted. "Just tell me anything different you saw or that happened that week, even if you wouldn't call it strange. Anything. Tell me about something."

"OK. Let me think." She closed her eyes a few moments. Reluctantly, she said, "I can tell you this thing happened. When one guest smiled at me, I saw a big gold tooth in the front of his mouth. I haven't seen anyone with a gold front tooth since my Grandfather died."

Nollann internalized, *Gotcha.* "Tell me all you can about the person with the gold tooth," he said.

"It's been too long, and I've waited on so many guests. I can't remember anything about what he looked like except the gold tooth." She looked perplexed, and then brightened. "But, oh yes, he was a white man." After another pause, "And, oh yes, he had grey hair." Nollann smiled and nodded encouragingly. "Oh yes, now I remember something. He was the guest who asked for a room on the fourth floor. Now I do remember that," she said proudly. "Do you think he was involved in killing our other guest, uh, Mr. Hamilton?"

"Don't know. Would you please check the registrations and find out more about Mr. Gold Tooth?" Nollann said with his most appreciative look. "You've already been very helpful."

Janney Hoean beamed. She returned to the front desk and checked the hotel guest registrations. She found that a Mr. Alfred Elleart checked in during her shift at 12:15pm on the day before Hamilton's murder and she gave him room 416. Elleart paid three days in advance with a debit card from MasterCard, and gave his home address as 228 Manchester Road in Wilmington, Delaware. He claimed he had no car to park in the hotel's lot.

Remembering Marsha Ginsberg's statement, Nollann said, "One more question, please. Do you remember anyone with ears that stick out?" She shook her head and turned to give her attention to a guest checking in.

Nollann phoned the information on Elleart in to his office for investigation. As he had expected, a search of all data available to the FBI revealed no record of a person named Alfred Elleart, and no such address as Manchester Road in Wilmington. But at least he had some testimonial evidence indicating one of the men who'd been involved in bombing the Ginsberg shop had asked for a room on the same floor as Hamilton. The gold tooth ploy had backfired on Gurtenkov's pupil.

Nollann had to wait until the shift change at 4:00pm to talk to Fred Purkens, the clerk who had been behind the desk on the next shift. While he'd been talking to Janney Hoean, his office obtained some of the information about Bennie Tailoren. They read Nollann what they had gathered so far. Nollann was pleased to learn the suspect worked across the street from where he was now waiting for the Dately Hotel shift to change. So he asked his office to arrange for him to make a security check of the building where Tailoren worked, without indicating the Examiner was the subject of an investigation. He wanted to hear Tailoren talk to see if he sounded like a foreigner.

An informal security check was set up. Twenty minutes later Nollann walked across the street to Patent Office Building 4 and was met at the entry check point by supervisory guard Arthar Battle. The

FBI agent reviewed visitor check-in procedure and pronounced it adequate for the equipment they were using. He asked if he could walk the halls to see if anything in need of correction caught his eye. Guard Battle was confident everything they were doing was secure, so he agreed to walk around with Nollann wherever the agent wanted to go.

Nollann knew where Tailoren's office was located. When he and Battle arrived in the hall just outside of his suspect's office door, Nollann stopped and said, " Whew. I need to rest for a minute or two to catch my breath."

Tailoren was on the telephone conducting an interview with some inventor's attorney. Nollann leaned against the wall. He eavesdropped and noted Tailoren's speech pattern didn't sound like someone who lived in the Midwest almost all his life. He used less slang and fewer contractions, and in general sounded more formal. Nollann speculated English might be Tailoren's second language. This deepened Nollann's suspicions and convinced him to have Tailoren put under part time surveillance.

When Nollann returned to the Dately Hotel for the interview with Fred Purkens, he learned Purkens had traded shifts with another clerk and was not going to be on the job until the following day at the 4:00 pm shift change. It was just as well. It had been too long a day already, and Nollann was ready to return home for an evening with his wife and children. But he left a message with the manager he'd return tomorrow to meet with Purkens.

Nollann spent the next day catching up on paper work and writing a report of his trip to St. Petersburg. Soon after shift change time he arrived at the Dately Hotel for the interview with Fred Purkens. It was almost a complete waste of time. Purkens had no memory of the time period around Hamilton's murder. His mind was a complete blank for the answers to all of the questions Nollann posed. He could not remember anyone at any time looking different or strange enough to mention, like someone who had a prominent gold front tooth or ears that stick out. Recalling a remark made by Janney Hoean, Nollann asked, "Do you remember if anyone specifically asked for a room on the fourth floor?"

Purkens said he did recall that happening, but he couldn't remember anything about who requested the fourth floor. He couldn't even say whether the person was male or female, Caucasian or another color, young or old, or whether it happened during the time period Nollann was asking about. Nollann reviewed his notes from the interview with Hoean and saw the man with the gold tooth had requested the fourth floor on the day before Hamilton was murdered.

He asked Purkens to get him the guest registration information for everyone given a fourth floor room during the period starting two days before the murder until the day after the murder. Mentally he gave himself a kick in the pants for not having thought of asking for the information sooner. A search of the Bureau's records the following day revealed that another of the fourth floor guests gave a bogus name and fictitious address when he checked in on the day before Hamilton's murder. So that confirmed, in Nollann's mind at least, two assassins working together had killed Hamilton.

Director of Special Services Glenn Johns turned down Nollann's request for surveillance of Bennie Tailoren. There was no evidence linking the patent Examiner directly to any of the crimes. The Bureau's investigation revealed he was at work at the Patent Office in Crystal City on the days before, during and after the murder, the attempt on Levy and the bombing. Before he was willing to assign the significant resources required for surveillance, Johns wanted more than the weak circumstantial evidence from Nollann indicating Tailoren was part of a conspiracy to murder Hamilton because the inventor was anti-Arab. Nollann's plea that surveillance might lead to the discovery of other members of the gang of murderers fell on deaf ears.

So Nollann called on his liaison with the Arlington detective squad, Sidney Phillips. There were no big cases in his unit's docket at the time, so Phillips agreed to help Nollann. "I've got two new candidates for promotion to detective, Abe Meldman and Tyler Jackson," Phillips said. "I'd like to give them some surveillance experience. But they won't be available over the upcoming weekend, or for the first half of Monday."

Nollann replied, "Tailoren will be working all day Monday in building 4 of the Patent Office in Crystal City. So your team of two detective candidates can latch on to him when he leaves work at around 5:00pm. They can watch until the lights are out in his apartment and make a note of anyone who enters or leaves the place. Then they can go back to their other duties and connect with him when he leaves for work on Tuesday morning. I'll fax you a copy of the picture of Tailoren we got from the Patent Office personnel files and his description."

Chapter 34   Witch

AFTER THEY DECIDED to give Patent Examiner Bennie Tailoren a second chance, abu Wagdy, Gurtenkov and Sami Insien stopped in bin Nazamunde's outer office. Abu Wagdy faced Sami; "We need to work together to identify possible replacements for Tailoren within the Patent Office. Can you find out what they pay each of the employees who know the access codes? And can you find out if any of them appear to be living beyond what their salary allows; can you check on their automobile registrations, home addresses, vacation properties, boats, airplanes, criminal records, bankruptcies, credit cards, bank accounts, email, and brokerage accounts?"

Beaming with confidence, Sami replied, "The names of all of the Patent Office employees we might want to hire are listed in their computer files. My staff of computer hackers can easily crack out the type of information you want about those people. I'll have a list of potentially vulnerable patent Examiners and supervisory personnel back to you in a few days." Four days later he handed abu Wagdy a file folder with the names, addresses and personal information of six Patent Office employees who might be willing to take baksheesh.

Bennie Tailoren was elated by what he expected to be the favorable aftermath of his coup de grace eliminating two enemies of the jihad. Obviously he could not tell Carmina anything about what he'd done. But his high spirits were abundantly apparent to her when they left the Patent Office after work on the day after the bombing of Ginsberg's shop was reported in the Capitol news media. He insisted they catch a cab and go directly to The Shekel, an expensive restaurant featuring Middle Eastern cuisine. A belly dancer entertained the diners while they sat on mock animal skin rugs on the floor among plush cushions. This was the first time he gave any hint he liked anything having an Arab flavor. Carmina was surprised and delighted. Her beau had never expressed any definitive interest in where they went out to eat, always deferring to her choices. This was progress she thought—a step in the right direction.

The meal and entertainment at The Shekel were a resounding success. Bennie ordered appetizers for them, and Carmina was even more surprised at his knowledge of the cuisine. He selected humus and stuffed grape leaves for appetizers, and lamb stew for his main dish. Carmina ordered shish kabob. The meal came with baklava for desert. Again Carmina was surprised when Bennie ordered Turkish coffee with his desert. She stuck with conventional decaf and a snifter of brandy, which she lingered over as they watched the belly dancer gyrate among the reclining diners. Carmina wondered if this was going to be the night he gave her the present he was concealing under the bed in the leather tube.

Back at his apartment they stripped, jumped on to his bed and had two rounds of the energetic sex that was now routine for them. Then they slept peacefully in each other's arms.

Neither could know it was the last time.

When they returned from the Shekel, Bennie did not check his computer for email. So he was not aware of the message from O'Durea telling him to be ready for an iSight conference with Muhamed Allah Yatakalan during his lunch hour at noon the next day. Before leaving for work, he saw the message, and it elevated his already high spirits. He anticipated the Grand Imam himself wanted to praise him for his service to the jihad. All morning long he bubbled with joyful expectation, and was unable to concentrate on searching the Patent Office database for prior art revealing the invention disclosed in the application he was examining.

He told Carmina there was something he wanted to do back at his apartment, and he left for lunch a little ahead of schedule. Back in his apartment he was pacing nervously in front of his Powerbook, which was already booted to iSight with an invitation to talk keyed to the Imam's image in his directory. An alert sounded, summoning him to the computer, and the face of Muhamed Allah Yatakalan wearing a gold trimmed turban appeared on the computer's screen. Bennie sat down in a chair placed in a location where the iSight camera on his desk focused on his face and beamed it to the Imam.

"Greetings, your Holiness," Bennie said, thereby violating the protocol by speaking to the Grand Imam before he had been spoken to.

The Imam's stern countenance alerted him their conversation would not go as he anticipated. From eight thousand miles away, the Imam's bottomless black eyes sought to take possession of his will power. Speaking slowly and hypnotically in the deep sonorous voice of his Imam persona, Muhamed Allah Yatakalan said, "Bennie Tailoren, you are a valuable asset to Allah's jihad. The information you give us from the infidel's Patent Office is vital to our work. We must continue to get their access codes.

There is another serious task you must do for the jihad. The infidel woman who knows how you got the Top Secret security clearance must be silenced forever. She is a threat to you. The jihad cannot risk losing you. You must cooperate with the warriors who we will command to take her away forever under my fatwa."

Bennie turned his head away from the computer screen to avoid looking at the Imam's face and being captured by his eyes. "But she knows nothing of what I do for the jihad, and she's devoted to me. She will never do anything to hurt me," he protested.

"Turn your head and look at me," the Imam demanded. "You have feelings of affection for her, do you not?"

Still not looking at the Imam, Bennie said, "I am fond of her, she brings joy into my life. I am happy with my existence on earth for the first time in my life. I no longer yearn for death and a martyr's reward in paradise. But I know I will never be able to marry her because she is an infidel. But for now I am content to just live with her." He added defiantly, "I will not help anyone kill her."

"You speak blasphemy when you reject Allah's will," the Imam raged. "But I understand what happened to you. I will guide you and tell you how to redeem yourself in Allah's sight."

Bennie turned his head and looked inquiringly into the Imam's hypnotic eyes.

The Imam continued in a less condemning tone, "The infidel woman is a witch. She has erased your faith and captured your will. She works for Satan to deprive Allah's jihad of your unique skills. You are the only warrior the jihad has ever found who is qualified to do what you do for us in the Patent Office. Allah gave you the genes and skills to do this work for His jihad."

Bennie felt his will to resist ebbing. He shifted his gaze, searching for the outline of the dagger on the Imam's chest, to free his will from capture by those eyes.

"Now it is your duty to Allah to repay Him for the blessings He has bestowed on you. You must work with the other warriors to banish the infidel witch to hell where she belongs. The feelings of joy the witch tempts you with now will endure for only an instant, but your rewards from Allah in heaven will last for eternity."

Changing his voice to a beseeching tone, the Imam implored, "Hamde Jawade, tell me you will do what Allah demands of you."

The unexpected use of his real name and the Imam's supplicating demeanor dissolved what remained of the young man's resistance. "I will do what Allah command's for the jihad," he said gritting his teeth with determination.

A smile lit the Imam's face. "Good. O'Durea will contact you with the details of the fatwa. Continue your relationship with the witch and all of the other infidels you must endure to do Allah's work. The sacrifices you are making will be tallied up and you will be redeemed and rewarded." The Imam broke the connection and his face dissolved into the computer screen.

Bennie hurried back to the Patent Office so as not to be late from lunch, picking up a chocolate covered nut bar on the way for his noon meal. Carmina was sitting at her desk when he arrived, so he stopped and gave her a perfunctory neck rub on his way to his own office. It didn't feel the same to her as his previous neck rubs, a little rough, and he didn't linger until she shook her head to indicate she'd had enough. She figured something was distracting him, but she reveled in this attention he showered her, which the other women in the office were sure to notice. The rest of the day Bennie avoided Carmina, pretending to be busy with some work he needed to finish up before the weekend.

At the end of the day on Friday, they ordinarily met for a drink across the street at the Dately Hotel bar. Carmina ordered either a glass of chardonnay or a vodka martini. Bennie drank nonalcoholic beer. If she ordered a glass of chardonnay, it meant she wanted to go home and spend Friday night by herself or with some lady friends. If she had a vodka martini, it always meant she wanted to go back to his apartment and hop into bed with him. This time she ordered a glass of chardonnay.

Carmina could tell from his body language and shifting eyes that Bennie didn't want to spend any time with her. She suspected one of the other women of luring him away from her. She was afraid this might happen. When Bennie said he wanted to leave their weekend plans open for now, she feared the worst. He promised to call her before noon on Saturday so they could make their plans for the weekend. She quickly gulped her chardonnay, gave him a peck on the cheek and hurried of to the subway for the ride to her apartment. She hoped he'd have a rotten time with the hussy he'd be with that evening.

Bennie was thankful he could be alone. He needed to convince himself he was doing the right thing. Once he was back in his apartment, he pulled the leather tube out from under his bed, zipped it open and removed his prayer rug. He oriented the prayer niche on the rug toward Mecca, knelt down on it and prayed for Allah's guidance for the first time since his first night in bed with Carmina.

As he softly murmured phrases in Arabic praising the greatness of Allah, words spoken by the Grand Imam Muhamed Allah Yatakalan kept pulsating in his ears like the words of a song endlessly repeated on a faulty record disk, *"The information you give us from the infidel's Patent Office is vital to our work. The infidel woman is a witch. She erased your faith and captured your will. She works for Satan to deprive Allah's jihad of your unique skills. You are the only warrior the jihad has ever had who can do what you do for us in the Patent Office."* His feeling of dedication to the goals of the jihad returned with a burning intensity, and his fondness for Carmina evaporated in a flash like a drop of water spilled on a the glowing coil of a hot plate.

His attitude toward Carmina changed from her fun loving swain, Bennie, to the predator for Allah's jihad, Tailoren, who was capable of any action aimed at achieving the jihad's goal of ridding the earth of infidels and heathens.

Half an hour later, while he was putting a frozen pizza into the microwave for his dinner, his cell phone rang. The message of his willingness to cooperate in eliminating Carmina traveled fast from Muhamed Allah Yatakalan to Gurtenkov to O'Durea. To avoid another fiasco, the Cuban called him to discuss the details of the hit.

Tailoren was surprised at how calmly he could talk about Carmina's death. She was, after all, only an infidel woman, and Muhamed Allah Yatakalan convinced him she exerted some evil power over him, depriving him of his judgment. Perhaps her evil powers came from her Native American heritage. After all, the people called Indians originally were heathens until missionaries converted them into infidels. His predator attitude against the witch deepened.

"Everyone in Group 3300 knows we're sleeping with each other most nights of the week," he told the Cuban. "I will be the number one suspect when something happens to her, just like the surviving spouse is the first suspect the police evaluate when a married person is murdered."

"Yeah, we already thought of that. I'll tell you the way we'll give you an alibi," O'Durea said. "When's the next night she'll be able to sleep at your apartment?"

"Tomorrow night, Saturday."

"Good. You'll need to take Monday and Tuesday off. The assassins will be disguised as plumbers."

"But plumbers do not work on weekends," Tailoren protested. "And plumbing repairs are the landlord's responsibility. Not mine."

"Just listen and stop interrupting me," O'Durea rebuked. "Plumbers work on weekends when there's an emergency, and no one'll know whether you called'em or the landlord called'em. I'll have a small dose of the date rape drug Gamma Hydroxy Butyrate (GHB) delivered to you tonight."

Tailoren continued to protest, "But I'm not going to rape her."

Exasperated, O'Durea plowed ahead, "Don't be surprised when some kid knocks at your door and hands you a plastic bag with some white powder in it. You don't have to pay him anything for it. You'll put the GHB into her glass of champagne, and she'll drink the drug and fall asleep. The plumbers'll tie her up and stuff her into a water heater box they'll take with them when they leave your place. Replacing your water heater is the reason you give for the plumbers coming to your apartment, if anyone asks.

You'll leave after she falls asleep and drive to Atlantic City for a three-day vacation. That's why you'll take Monday and Tuesday off. Use your credit card, and leave big tips so waiters'll remember you. That'll establish your alibi. You don't need to know the rest of the details, but you'll be in the clear when you go back to work on Wednesday."

"She'll be suspicious about the champagne," Tailoren objected. "I have never bought any before, and I only drink non-alcohol beverages. What reason do I give her?"

"First of all you buy non-alcoholic champagne," O'Durea said. "There are lots of brands. You buy an expensive brand. Tell her you want to celebrate a special gift you have for her. Make it mysterious. Have the champagne bottle already open when she gets to your apartment, and have the GHB already in one of the wine glasses. Stand between her and her glass when you pour the champagne because the powder will cause her wine to fizz more than yours will at first.

Promise to give her the gift after you've toasted it together. She probably knows something has changed between you two. Women are sensitive about these things. So tell her you want to redeem yourself for being distracted and neglecting her."

"This is too complicated," Tailoren shouted. "I am not an actor. She will know I'm lying."

"Temporarily, she'll hold off any of her doubts about you. It won't take you long."

"OK, what next," he mumbled with resignation.

"You call the plumbers just before or just after you make the champagne toast and she drinks the drug. The GHB will only keep her asleep a short time, and all traces of it will leave her body by the time the police find her dead."

Hearing the word 'dead' kindled a feeling of remorse, but Tailoren squelched it by remembering the stern face of Muhamed Allah Yatakalan staring at him from his computer screen.

"I'll set the operation up with the other agents," O'Durea continued. "Don't you contact them until the night they take her away. They'll be waiting in a rented van close to your apartment at 6:00 pm, the time we've schedule for her abduction. You tell her you have to make a call to make sure her surprise will be ready, and then you walk away from the table. I'll give you their number to call. You enter it into your cell phone so all you have to do is press one button to dial it. You won't speak to them. Just dial their number, let the phone ring five times, and then end the call. If she asks about why you didn't speak to anyone, just say the line was busy.

She has to be asleep when the plumbers arrive. And you will already be gone from your apartment, on your way to Atlantic City, when they take her. Leave the apartment rear door open when you leave. And turn the alley light on outside the door. That'll be the signal you're gone. The plumbers'll lock your place up when they leave. You won't see them, and they won't see you. Do you have any questions?"

"No questions, but I have bad feelings about this," Bennie muttered, barely audibly.

O'Durea gave him the assassin's number to enter into his cell phone, and the plans for the abduction and murder of Carmina Burneta were complete.

Chapter 35   Switched

IT WAS STILL early in the evening on Friday. Tailoren expected Carmina to be at her apartment even if she planned to go out with her lady friends. So he decided to call her and ask her to come to his place Saturday at dinnertime, to preempt any chance she might schedule something that would foil the plot against her.

Carmina was at home, and she was delighted to hear from him and to hear the melancholy tone of his voice. She guessed his liaison with the other woman fell through or turned out badly. And it made her so happy she said she'd take a cab back to his place and spend the night there. She was not happy when he quickly turned down her offer of sensual bliss.

In a monotone, he slowly mumbled, "I am planning a present for you, and I want it to be a surprise. I am afraid I will give the surprise away if we are together tonight."

His tone of voice didn't sound sincere or enthusiastic, as it was the night when they went to dinner at the Shekel. Instead he sounded worried and evasive. The way he expressed himself was so unlike his usual manner of speaking it put Carmina on her guard. But she hoped that finally he was going to give her whatever the fabric thing was he'd been hiding in the leather tube under his bed. Her curiosity outweighed the apprehension she felt from the way he sounded, so she agreed to come to his apartment at 5:30 Saturday afternoon. But her suspicions were still aroused and she was determined to find out what changed her lover's attitude.

At 11:20 Tailoren was in bed in his pajamas trying to lull himself to sleep by reading a Proust novel. There was a sharp knock on the alley door at rear of his apartment. He jumped out of bed, fully alert, and grabbed the aluminum baseball bat he kept leaning against the headboard. In his bare feet, he walked to the door and turned on the outside light. Through the glass pane on the door, he could see standing in the dim light, a pale, thin young man dressed in an open leather jacket and wearing a cap with the bill turned the wrong way.

He wore a tee shirt with *Gravity Sucks* imprinted on it. Tailoren remembered O'Durea told him the drug was going to be delivered to him that night. He put down the baseball bat and opened the door.

The young man's pockmarked face lit up with a smile. He handed Tailoren a plastic bag containing about a tablespoon of the date rape drug. He said, "Half this's enough to knock 'er out for a hour or two of fun. It's a little salty. Ya need to disguise the taste with sweet pop. If you're up for a second round, give 'er the other half. Wish I'd a dad like yours to buy me stuff in'n emergency. It sure cost'm a bundle. Hav'uh great weekend." He turned and walked away. Tailoren shook his head and shut off the light.

After ending the call to Tailoren, O'Durea dialed the emergency number he'd set up with the two assassins. Juan answered the phone and let the call continue when he recognized O'Durea's voice. The Cuban gave him the details of the hit on Carmina Burneta, and made him repeat them so he was sure there'd be no slip-ups. He described what their victim looked like, and told Juan they didn't need a photo in this case because their victim would be drugged into unconsciousness when they got to her in Tailoren's apartment. He told Juan to hand the phone over to Pedro, and he repeated the details to him. O'Durea made Pedro repeat them back to him. He told the two assassins to discuss the details with each other and to call him back if they were not in complete agreement about everything he told them. Then he ended the call.

Juan was overjoyed with their new assignment. Only once before was their victim a woman, and they murdered her as soon as they caught her alone in her house. But this time they'd kidnap their female victim, and hold her prisoner for two days. She'd be in his power. Considering all of the violent crimes he committed, surprisingly, Juan never assaulted a woman sexually. But he thought about it many times. Sure, he paid a call girl to pretend he was defiling her. But it was only mildly erotic because they both knew it was pretend. But this was going to be the real thing. He fanaticized about what he could do before it was time to kill their captive.

Early in the morning on the third day they held Carmina, they planned to strangle her and dump her body beside the road on Rock Creek Parkway. She was sure to be discovered soon after her death. This would establish Tailoren's alibi because he was going to be in Atlantic City at the time she was killed. And, finally, Juan would fulfill his carnal fantasies.

At 5:45 Saturday afternoon, Tailoren was fidgeting around his apartment. He wondered where Carmina was. Did his demeanor spook her? Or was she just a little late, like several times before. He put two wine glasses on the counter in the kitchen beside the refrigerator. The opened bottle of champagne was on the cocktail table in the living room with a bowl of Cheesebangies, Carmina's favorite junk food.

Tailoren divided the GHB into two doses like the drug deliveryman advised. The dose he was going to use was in a spoon hidden under a paper napkin on the kitchen counter. The rest of the drug was in his pants pocket in the plastic bag in which it came. He didn't plan on molesting Carmina after he fed her the drug. When he was sure she was asleep, he'd turn on the alley light and leave for Atlantic City in a rental car he picked up earlier in the day. His packed suitcase was already in the trunk of the car. And he had a reservation at the Elhamber Casino.

Tailoren left the apartment door unlocked, so Carmina arrived and let herself inside before he realized she was there. This startled him, but he smiled and moved quickly to embrace her. They kissed each other on the lips without their usual passion, and moved apart. He took Carmina's light blue coat and draped it over a chair in the entrance hallway, and she hung her purse on the chair by its strap. They forgot to lock the door. She sat on the couch and picked up a Cheesebangie, plopped it into her mouth and looked at Tailoren expectantly.

"Oh, I forgot the wine glasses," he said, reaching for the bottle of champagne.

"Leave the bottle here and just bring the glasses in here," she said.

But Tailoren kept on moving and took the bottle in his hand. "No. You wait here. Leave everything to me." And he walked out of the living room into the kitchen.

This take-charge behavior was so unlike him; her suspicions were even more aroused. In the past he always let her be in command whenever they were doing anything relating to food or drink, except, of course, paying for it. So she decided to sit and wait for a minute to see what he did next.

Tailoren walked into the kitchen and glanced back to make sure Carmina was not following him. Good. She was still sitting in the living room. He took the paper napkin off the spoonful of drug, emptied the powder into one of the wine glasses and poured in a little champagne. He was surprised at how much it fizzed. He stirred the drink with his finger, and wiped it on the paper napkin. He let the bubbles settle down and poured in more until the glass was full. When he poured champagne into the other glass, he noticed it didn't fizz as much as the doped drink. He prayed to Allah that she would not notice.

Allah was not listening.

Waiting by herself while Tailoren took over her job made Carmina impatient. She stood up and walked toward the kitchen just as Tailoren was picking up the two wine glasses. He was moving slowly trying not to spill the bubbling liquid.

"Here. I'll take mine," she said reaching out her hand.

He hesitated a moment longer than he should have looking into the glasses he was holding to make sure he gave her the one with the drug.

"OK, here you go," he said with strained cheerfulness. He put the glass into Carmina's hand, turned his back on her and returned to the kitchen to pick the champagne bottle up off the counter with his free hand.

The things Tailoren was doing were making Carmina more apprehensive by the minute. As she walked back into the living room, she noticed how quickly the bubbles in her glass of champagne diminished. It was almost flat by the time she returned to the couch, ready to sit down. But with her back still to Tailoren, who was just now emerging from the kitchen, she took her free hand and dipped her forefinger into the champagne, and put it into her mouth. It didn't taste like any champagne she ever drank before. It tasted faintly salty. She sat down on the couch.

Maybe it tasted funny because it was non-alcoholic, or maybe it was because of the salt on her finger from the Cheesebangies. But the wine was definitely different, and until their relationship was resolved favorably, she was wary of drinking something that didn't taste right.

Carmina deliberated: *What's going on with you? Are you afraid he's going to drug you so he can take advantage of you and have sex? You know you'll let him do it if he wants to. So calm down and maybe he will too.* She smiled up at him as warmly as she could under their present tense circumstances.

Tailoren sat down beside her and put his glass on the cocktail table next to hers, while he absentmindedly clutched the champagne bottle in his right hand. She knew something was on his mind distracting him. She noticed the champagne in his glass still effervescing vigorously, while the wine in hers was definitely flat. She couldn't figure out what was going on, but that settled it. She was not going to drink the champagne in her glass. She'd tump the glass over and spill it out if she couldn't think of any other way to avoid ingesting the liquid. She reached out and filled one hand with Cheesebangies.

Then Tailoren noticed he was still holding the champagne bottle, so with an embarrassed laugh the plunked it down with a thud on the table beside the wine glasses. The vibration made the liquid in the glasses slosh around briefly, which made the effervescence of his and the flatness of hers all the more apparent to her. He didn't notice the difference.

Tailoren lifted his glass to make a toast. "Here's to us," he said.

Carmina stuffed some Cheesebangies into her mouth causing her cheeks to bulge while she chewed. She held up a finger on her free hand signaling she didn't want to drink a toast while her mouth was full of food.

Tailoren drained his glass, picked up the bottle and poured himself another drink, which fizzed briskly in his glass. He was concerned because it was now past 6:00 pm, the scheduled time of her abduction, and she was just sitting there slowly chewing on those accursed Cheesebangies.

Carmina was down to the last Cheesebangie in her hand. She decided to knock over her glass of champagne when she finished munching on it and no longer had an excuse not to drink the wine.

Just then Tailoren stood up and said, "I've got to make a phone call to schedule a surprise for you. Now when I get back, I expect to see your glass empty." He walked toward the kitchen.

She smiled and nodded. "You betcha."

When he was out of sight in the kitchen, Carmina picked up Tailoren's glass and drank its contents. It did not taste salty. She switched glasses with him by sliding hers over on the cocktail table to where his glass had been sitting. She took the bottle and filled up the empty glass in front of her and drank it down half way.

In the kitchen Tailoren pressed the buttons on his cell phone sending the signal alerting the assassins their target was about to be unconscious. Then he walked back into the living room with a smile on his face. He was puzzled as to why Carmina didn't ask him why she didn't hear him talking on the phone, but let it pass. It didn't matter any more. Their relationship would soon be over forever.

"Let's drink the toast," she said and held up the half filled glass.

Eager to get the full dose of the drug into her, Tailoren picked up the glass she'd switched with his and clinked it against the one she now held. "To us," he said and drained its contents in one continuous quaff.

"To us," she repeated after she drank hers. Carmina wondered what would happen next. It didn't take long for her to find out. Tailoren filled their glasses again and they drank a second toast to themselves. He was so agitated he hadn't noticed one of his glasses of champagne tasted salty.

They sat there talking about where to go out for dinner, with Carmina doing most of the talking in between mouthfuls of Cheesebangies. They finished off the bottle of champagne. Within ten minutes Tailoren's speech began to slur and he said he felt sleepy. He put his head back on the couch and closed his eyes. It never occurred to him he'd taken the drug intended for Carmina. In another five minutes he was fast asleep and snoring lightly.

It was obvious to Carmina that he'd put a sleeping potion in her drink, but she couldn't think of any reason why he'd want to drug her. He must have some hidden agenda, and she didn't want to stay around to find out what it was. She was disappointed he hadn't given her the gift as promised. She was so sure it must be the beautiful fabric something-or-other, whatever it is, in the leather tube under the bed. She decided to unroll the thing in the tube before she left to see what it was.

Her curiosity almost cost her life.

The two assassins were becoming concerned something was wrong. Half an hour passed since they got the signal the girl was taking the drug. She should be out cold, and Tailoren should be in his car driving to Atlantic City by now. But the alley light was not turned on. Maybe he forgot to turn it on when he left. It wouldn't surprise them if Tailoren screwed something up. They decided to investigate.

Juan drove the van into the alley and left it with the motor running near the rear door of Tailoren's apartment. They looked in through the glass pane on the door but saw no one. All the lights were on, and he rear door was still locked. Pedro took out his picks and inserted them into the lock. It was a simple tumbler design and he could open it with a few pushes and a twist of the picks. But he decided to knock first. He gently tapped on the glass.

A few minutes earlier, Carmina grabbed another handful of Cheesebangies and walked calmly into the bedroom. She pulled out the leather tube with her empty hand and sat down on the bed to finish eating up the tasty morsels. Realizing crumbs and salt soiled her hands, she walked into the bathroom to rinse them off. She wiped her hands on a towel and returned to the bedroom.

The leather tube was on the floor. She picked it up and put it on the bed. Carmina pulled the zipper all the way open and removed the rolled up fabric. She unwound it on the bed and stared in puzzlement at the three by five foot thing; it was apparently a rug of some sort. She turned it over and realized she was now looking at its underside.

So she turned it back over so the topside was face up. There was an abstract design on it and some writing in a strange language she'd never seen before. She concluded that if this were a present for her, Tailoren had unbelievably poor taste, and she could do without the thing. She rolled it up again and tried to stuff it back into the leather tube. But it wouldn't go. So she decided to leave it for him to put back when he woke up.

As she walked back toward the living room, Carmina heard Pedro tapping at the back door. She was still wondering why Tailoren attempted to put her to sleep, and she was mad about it now. Maybe whoever was tapping knew the answer. So she stuck her head into the kitchen to see if she could find out who was at the back door.

Pedro could see her clearly in the lighted house, but she could not see him in the dark alley. As quietly as he could he, pushed the picks into the door lock, moved them in and out twice feeling them slide the tumblers into place. He twisted the picks disengaging the lock and started to push the door open.

As the back door started to open, Carmina walked briskly toward the front door. Both assassins wearing ski masks and gloves came through the door toward her. They expected their target to be unconscious so they did not put on white coveralls. Juan said, "It's her." And they ran toward the girl.

By now Carmina was terrified. She grabbed her purse by the strap on which it was hanging, but went past her blue coat and left it draped over the chair. She easily beat her pursuers to the front door, which had not been latched after she came in through it earlier in the evening. She turned the handle, pushed the door open and dashed into the entrance lobby of the building. Several people stood by the elevator waiting for its doors to open. Carmina did not look back at her pursuers even though she was out of harm's way once she was among other people in the lobby.

Pedro led the charge after their target, but he stopped short of the front door. Juan was concerned about what might happen if they failed to carry out two assignments in a row. So he opened the front door slightly and peeked out to determine if there was any chance of catching her.

Short, plump Tonie Dender was standing by the elevator watching the scene unfold. She saw Carmina, obviously distraught, run out of the apartment door, and, as fast as she could go, out of the building and into the street, where she waved frantically and yelled for a cab cruising by. This would provide some juicy gossip for her and her friends about the handsome young man in apartment 1 C. Mrs. Dender also saw Juan in the ski mask peeking out the door for only a few seconds, but never the less she definitely saw him. She raised her hand to her mouth and gasped, as the assassin quickly closed the door. She had another tidbit to toss into the gossip blender for her friends to puree.

The assassins knew O'Durea and Gurtenkov expected a complete explanation. So they lingered in Tailoren's apartment to learn whatever they could about what went wrong, even though their training and instincts told them to leave immediately. They noticed Tailoren's body on the couch as they went by it the first time. Now they returned to the couch to see if he was still alive. With his head laid back on the top of the couch and his mouth open, Tailoren was snoring loudly now. Juan shook him while Pedro went into the kitchen and filled a pitcher with ice cubes from the freezer and poured water into it. Tailoren did not respond to Juan, so Pedro started pouring the ice water slowly on his face and chest. He opened his eyes and stared at them with a dazed expression on his face.

"What happened?" Juan demanded.

"Swished glazzes wi' me. D'witch swished glazzes," he mumbled and fell back to sleep when Pedro stopped pouring the ice water on him.

It was all the assassin's needed to hear. They made sure they left nothing behind and went out the back door to the idling van. They drove straight back to Baltimore and returned the van to the rental company. Every fifteen minutes they tried to get O'Durea on the phone. Eventually, at 9:30 pm he answered with his usual, "Yeah."

Pedro told him about the fiasco, with Tailoren asleep on the couch, and the girl escaping out the front door when they picked the lock and entered and tried to catch her. "We woke him up briefly by dousing him with ice water, and he said the witch switched glasses with him. Those were almost his exact words."

"Anybody see you," O'Durea said.

"Only the girl, and Tailoren. And he was so groggy he fell back to sleep when we stopped pouring ice water on him. We had the ski masks on." Pedro purposely failed to tell O'Durea that Juan's masked head might have been spotted when he peeked out the door of Tailoren's apartment to see if they could catch the girl.

"Be ready to go back and get that screw-up Tailoren," O'Durea said.

Chapter 36   Aftermath

AS CARMINA RUSHED out the door of the Butlarian Arms, she saw a cab pulling away from the curb on the opposite side of Clark Street. She dashed out into the street, waving one arm and yelling, "Taxi, taxi, taxi".

The driver saw her and stopped. She fumbled the door open and heaved herself into the rear of the cab, reached around, slammed the door and depressed the door lock. Only then did she look out the cab's window to see if the masked men had pursued her out of the building. Seeing none, she started to cry and whimpered with relief.

"You OK, lady?" the cabbie asked.

"I'll calm down....in a few minutes," Carmina said between sobs. "My boyfriend tried to drug me and two masked men tried to catch me. Now take me to the nearest police station; please...hurry."

"Sure thing, lady." The cabbie drove off toward the Franconia Road Police Station in nearby Alexandria.

Even though it was a Saturday, it was still early and the officers were not busy responding to accidents and petty crimes. Carmina rushed up to the Duty Officer, and put her elbows on the desk he was sitting behind. "I want to report a break in by masked men, and an attempted drugging by my boy friend and an attempted abduction by the masked men."

Behind the desk, Arnie Saul, grey haired and overweight, was a veteran police officer with twenty-six years of service. He'd seen and heard almost everything an officer of the law ever heard or saw. He raised the index finger of his right hand and looked at Carmina carefully. Her eyes were not dilated, and she was tastefully dressed, though a little disheveled. But you never know. Without saying a word, he reached into a drawer in front of him, took out a Breathalyzer and walked around his desk to where Carmina was now standing, glaring impatiently with her arms folded. "Please, Mam," he said, "Let's get you in the clear first thing, so please put a few breaths into this." And he handed the device to her.

Without hesitation, Carmina poked the tube into her mouth and puffed continuously until Officer Saul reached over and took it from her. He looked at the zero on the round dial, and walked back to his chair and sat down. "Is anyone injured or hurt?" he asked. She shook her head vigorously. "When did all of those things happen?"

"About half an hour ago. It might not be too late to catch the masked men. Please send a patrol car to apartment 1 C of the Butlarian Arms condo in Crystal City. Oh, dear, I've gotta go right now." She turned her back on him and walked as fast as she could to the ladies room.

When she returned to the desk, Detective Henry (Hank) Frank was standing beside Officer Saul talking about the shad run in the Potomac. A tall, well-built red head with sparkling green eyes, Frank only recently received his gold detective shield. It was really a slow night to have a detective involved at this early stage of investigation. He introduced himself and escorted Carmina into an interview room. With her permission he put a small tape recorder on the table between them and turned it on. He opened a pad to take down his own notes and impressions.

The first thing Carmina said was they should send a patrol car in case the masked men robbed Tailoren or did anything to him. Frank told her they'd get to that in a few minutes. Ten minutes later, Carmina had told the detective the complete history of her relationship with Bennie Tailoren and the details of his attempt to drug her but she switched their glasses, and the break in by masked men and what she could remember about what they looked like. One was tall and one was shorter, but not real short, and they wore black ski masks and gloves.

She also confessed to helping her former lover get a Top Secret security clearance which might be improper. She repeated Tailoren's story of a high-ranking friend at the FBI walking his SF-86 through the screening procedure. At this point Hank Frank picked up the phone on the desk in front of him and asked Arnie Saul to send a car over to Tailoren's place to see what was going on. He didn't want any loose ends if the FBI was going to be involved because some one got a Top Secret security clearance by fraud. Carmina asked them to get her light blue coat off the chair in the hall and bring it back for her.

After Carmina told detective Frank everything, and he was reaching to turn off the tape recorder, she shook her head and pointed at the recorder. "I forgot to tell you this before." Visibly embarrassed, she said, "I hope you won't think I'm stupid for not remembering it sooner."

"Please tell me everything you know. You never know what'll be important to solving a crime." Detective Frank reassured her, "Nobody's going to laugh at you, whatever you tell us."

"OK, when the masked burglars started coming toward me in Bennie's apartment, one of them said 'It's her.' I heard him say it clearly. There's no doubt in my mind he said 'It's her.' So they must have known I'd be there, if I was going to be the one they were after."

Detective Frank thanked Carmina for her help. The police gave her a ride back to her apartment in a squad car. The officers searched her apartment and the surrounding area, but found nothing suspicious. So Carmina went in and spent an almost sleepless night. The next morning was Sunday, and she booked a flight to Spokane, and called her parents and told them she'd be coming home for a while. They were delighted and said they'd meet her flight and drive her home.

Tailoren awoke with a start about 7:15pm. The inside of his mouth felt parched and tasted like burned toast. His shirt and hair were wet. He vaguely remembered someone pouring something on him and talking to him. He swayed when he stood up. Still lightheaded from the drug, he staggered around in his apartment. He saw the open back door, closed and locked it and went to the front door and locked it.

Carmina was nowhere in sight, but her light blue coat was still draped over the chair in the hall. He thought she might come back for it, and then he could give her the dose of GHB that was still in his pocket. The assassins could take her away like he planned with O'Durea. He reached into his pocket and took out the plastic bag with the second dose of GHB. He was looking at it in his hand when there was a knock at his door.

"Who is it?" He walked toward the door with the bag still in his hand.

"Police. Please open up."

Realizing he was holding an illegal drug, Tailoren stumbled into the bathroom, lifted the lid on the toilet, dropped in the bag and pressed down on the handle. He turned toward the door and yelled, "Just a minute."

He staggered back to the door and opened it for veteran police officers Howard Roan and Gill Nelson. Tailoren's delay in answering and the sound of the toilet were familiar events telling them he was flushing down illegal drugs. They accused him of getting rid of his stash, and he denied it. They did not believe him.

While Roan walked through the apartment making sure the intruders were gone, Nelson told Tailoren they were sent to investigate a break in by masked men reported by a young woman. Tailoren told them there was no break in, but his former girl friend drugged him and robbed him.

Roan said, "What'd she steal?"

"I don't know. I just woke up from some drug she gave me."

Nelson was a thirty-two year old African American with a full head of coarse black hair. He and Tailoren looked around the apartment to determine what was missing.

Roan, a tall, slim forty-one year old with thin brown hair graying at the temples walked out into the building's entrance lobby to canvas the residents for witnesses to the break in. The arrival of the police and the flashing blue light on the police car attracted the attention of the building's residents. When Roan asked if anyone in the lobby knew anything about a break in, two women told him to look up Toni Dender in 4B. She'd seen the whole thing.

Roan rode the elevator up to the fourth floor and walked down the hall to a door marked with a B. He knocked and was greeted warmly by a short, grey haired woman he guessed was about sixty. She was wearing a yellow bathrobe and matching fuzzy slippers. In reply to his question about a break in, she told him about Carmina's frantic exit from 1C, and the tall man in a black ski mask she'd seen peeking out the door right after the young girl fled.

Roan asked, "Are you sure about what you just told me you've seen."

She raised her right hand and said, "I can swear on a bible I saw a man in a black ski mask for just a few seconds when he peeked out of the door. But there's no doubt in my mind about what I saw."

Roan got her telephone number and thanked her as he wrote down the substance of what Toni Dender told him.

All Tailoren could find out of order was his prayer rug stuffed part way into the leather tube. "See," he said to Officer Nelson, "she was going to steal the piece of art."

Nelson unrolled the rug and looked at it form both sides. "Looks like a Moslem prayer rug to me," he said. "And she didn't steal it because it's still here."

Flustered because he didn't expect a black Virginia police officer to recognize a prayer rug, Tailoren insisted, "I'm sure I am going to find some cash missing. But I don't want to press charges against her. Let her go, Officer. I am willing to forgive her."

Nelson groused to himself: *Mighty generous of you, you lying scumbag. I wish we'd caught you with the dope you flushed down the toilet.* He closed his notebook, picked up Carmina's blue coat off the chair in the hall and walked out of the apartment.

When Nelson and Roan returned to the station, they reported what they found to detective Frank. He accepted their opinions about Tailoren lying about everything, in particular since Mrs. Dender's statement corroborated what Carmina told him about the burglars wearing black ski masks. And her blue coat was on a chair in the hall like she said.

Frank walked into the office of shift commander Ben Blake and reported, "We might have evidence of a violation of security regulations the FBI will want to know about. A young woman has all but confessed to being involved with her boyfriend in fraudulently getting him a Top Secret clearance. Nelson saw a prayer rug in the guy's apartment suggesting he might be a Muslim. His name is Bennie Tailoren."

That was enough for Lieutenant Blake. The possibility of a Muslim getting a bogus Top Secret clearance by fraud demanded immediate attention. Blake phoned the Arlington police department's FBI liaison, Sidney Phillips, at his home and told him what his men found out. Phillips thanked Blake. He remembered agreeing to a surveillance of Tailoren for Bill Nollann. He picked up his phone and called Glenn Johns, his contact at the FBI.

After listening to Phillips, Johns said, "I'd like to have a synopsis report faxed to me right now for immediate entry into our data base on terrorist activity. Have a full written report delivered to my home in the morning, even though it'll be Sunday."

Phillips promised Johns it would be done as he requested

Then he added, "I'll put two more items on my list of chits I can cash in for favors from the FBI in the future."

Johns chuckled, "For sure."

By Sunday afternoon all information from the Arlington police was entered into the Bureau's database. The first thing that popped out was no SF-86 had ever been filed seeking a Top Secret clearance for anyone named Bennie Tailoren. So if the Patent Office records showed Tailoren having Top Secret clearance, it was obtained by fraud. The second noteworthy item was that Tailoren's name appeared in the file of an investigation of possible terrorist activity resulting in a murder at the Dately Hotel in Crystal City, and in St. Petersburg relating to an attempted murder and a the bombing of a shop.

Minimum Bill Nollann was the FBI officer assigned to these cases, and he was notified by Glenn Johns. Nollann reminded Johns of his request for surveillance of Tailoren, rubbing in the fact he'd been turned down. He confirmed the part time stake out by the Arlington police he'd arranged with Sidney Phillips. The two debated whether they should get a warrant for Tailoren's arrest because of the security clearance fraud. But they decided to keep him under surveillance for a few days to see if it would reveal anyone else working with him.

They decided not to change the surveillance presently scheduled by the Arlington police because Johns did not have any agents he could spare on such short notice. But he could get Bureau agents to take over the surveillance work by Tuesday afternoon when Tailoren left work. Nollann agreed to follow Tailoren when he left his office for lunch on Monday and Tuesday in case he met with someone. He called Phillips, asked for the Arlington police stakeout to begin at 3:30 pm, and was assured it could be arranged.

Chapter 37   Setup

TAILOREN WENT INTO a panic after the police officers left his apartment. He knew he'd screwed up royally, but he didn't know what to do next. Apparently the police were not going to arrest him, or they would have already done so. He tried to call O'Durea to ask him what he should do, but the Cuban was not answering his phone. The rental car with his packed bag in the trunk was parked outside, and he had a reservation at the Elhamber Casino. So he shut out the lights and walked out of his apartment, locking the door as he left. He drove to I-95 with the intention of taking it north to Camden where he could get to the Atlantic City Expressway toll road. By 11:00 pm he was checked into his room at the Elhamber. He kept dialing O'Durea's number on his cell phone and the Cuban eventually answered.

"What happened to you?" O'Durea asked.

Tailoren gave his version of the evening's events, emphasizing Carmina tricked him by distracting him until she could switch glasses with him and feed him the drug. "She must really be a witch, like Muhamed Allah Yatakalan told me, because she knew which glass had the GHB in it," he said.

O'Durea recognized the folly of trying to pull off their plot when the key operator was an inexperienced amateur who didn't know he should put the drug into a glass he could keep track of because it had a flaw, blemish or stain making it look different in some way. He made a mental note to include this advice with his instructions the next time an agent under him needed to drug their target. "Where are you now?"

"I drove up to Atlantic City like I was scheduled to do. I used my reservation at the Elhamber Casino. I thought it'd be less suspicious if I went on this trip as planned. What should I do now?"

O'Durea was silent as he pondered telling Tailoren to stay there at the Elhamber. It might be easier for the assassin's to take him down in his hotel room in the same way they got Hamilton by checking in and getting rooms on the same floor, and making an electronic pass key with the encoder. But he hadn't been able to get hold of Gurtenkov, and he knew it might be days before they could get bin Nazamunde to make a decision. Though he doubted it, there was some possibility Sami might persuade them to give Tailoren still another chance. The assassins could always get the girl some other way. So he decided to tell Tailoren to check out of the Elhamber on Sunday and go back to his apartment, and return to work on Monday as if nothing happened. Tailoren thanked him and they ended the call.

O'Durea stayed up and kept trying to get a call through to Gurtenkov. He knew the Russian disconnected his phone when there was a girl with him and also when he wanted to sleep off his night's indulgences. Finally, on Sunday at 10:00 am in Riyadh, the Russian reconnected his phone and the call went through. Though slightly hung over from the half liter of single malt scotch he consumed the night before, Gurtenkov was in high spirits because the tall, thin, blond call girl performed so athletically in bed with him. She was gone, but he was still aglow with his reverie of the night before.

O'Durea began, "We expected too much from an unskilled amateur." He gave Gurtenkov the explanations of the failed kidnapping he'd heard from both the assassins and Tailoren.

Gurtenkov's good mood kept him from flying into a rage, as he'd done when O'Durea told him Tailoren authorized the hits on Hamilton and Levy. "Keep the assassin's primed for action because either or both Tailoren and the girl will have to be eliminated," the Russian said. "I'll take the matter up with bin Nazamunde as soon as I can." He recognized there was the danger Tailoren might be arrested and be coerced into telling what he knew about the *al Khanjar* operations. He might also alert the US Patent Office that Sami's hackers were entering their supposedly secure files.

Gurtenkov called bin Nazamunde's office and learned he was enjoying a weekend with his family in his penthouse at his resort at Jubail on the Gulf of Oman. His next call was put through immediately to bin Nazamunde when Gurtenkov told the concierge a misadventure by an associate might cause the loss of a financial opportunity. He knew anything threatening income would get bin

Nazamunde's attention. He explained why Tailoren's arrest might result in the Patent Office shutting off the information Sami was using to generate large profits.

Bin Nazamunde ordered Gurtenkov to find abu Wagdy and the two of them to get in a company helicopter and fly to the resort at once. At this time Sami, in his persona of Muhamed Allah Yatakalan, was at the *al Khanjar* camp indoctrinating the latest group of the jihad's terrorists. He didn't want to take the time to fly the Grand Imam back to Saudi Arabia. Bin Nazamunde had the thirty-inch, high definition, LCD monitor in the conference room set up with an iSight camera so the talking face of Muhamed Allah Yatakalan could be with them during their deliberations.

At 2:00 pm bin Nazamunde was sitting in his high backed black leather chair at the head of a massive rosewood conference table inlaid in a random pattern with circular ebony disks of different sizes. Gurtenkov and abu Wagdy were sitting in low backed white upholstered chairs facing each other on opposite sides of the conference table. The LCD monitor was on the table between them with the flat screen toward bin Nazamunde. The face of Muhamed Allah Yatakalan was on the screen looking at bin Nazamunde. Sami packed a seventeen-inch Powerbook and all the peripherals he might need before he morphed into the Grand Imam. He turned on iSight and pressed bin Nazamunde's icon in the directory. So now bin Nazamunde's face was on the screen of Muhamed Allah Yatakalan's Powerbook.

Gurtenkov went over what happened the night before. He recommended sending the assassins to get Tailoren and the girl. Bin Nazamunde agreed when Gurtenkov explained why Tailoren's arrest might jeopardize the profits Sami was making from the information he takes from the Patent Office's files. He wished Sami were in his computer executive persona, instead of the persona of Muhamed Allah Yatakalan.

"What will Sami say about the loss of our agent in the Patent Office?" bin Nazamunde asked. Gurtenkov and abu Wagdy just shrugged their shoulders.

But Muhamed Allah Yatakalan spoke up. "I talked to him before I flew here to the camp. He told me he gave the names and financial information of some Patent Office employees to abu Wagdy, and he can get by with the access codes he now has for about a week without loosing any significant opportunities for profitable security trades."

Abu Wagdy nodded in agreement. "That's the same thing Sami told me. I'm working with Caspare Ouiment at your AraSuz bank. He'll hire a stockbroker in Paris, who'll hire a stockbroker in Quebec City. The Canadian will travel to the United States to find out if any of the Patent Office employees on our list is willing to help with what we'll claim is a securities buying scheme. We'll offer the Patent Office employee two thousand dollars in cash for each week he gives us the information we ask for. After one of them accepts some payments, he'll get used to receiving the weekly baksheesh, and we will have him in our power for as long as we want to use him. It works that way all over the world." The others at the table nodded in agreement.

"What happens after a week without our inside agent giving Sami the codes?" bin Nazamunde asked. "Are we out of the securities business until we get to some other Patent Office employee."

"Not necessarily," Muhamed Allah Yatakalan said. "If Sami starts cracking their codes right now, he may be able to fill in the gaps by the time all the ones he has become obsolete."

Gurtenkov looked from one to the other. "What choice do we have? We can't take the risk of Tailoren exposing our operations." No one objected. "Is it agreed then?" The others nodded their heads. "I'll tell O'Durea to have the assassins take out Tailoren Monday after work. That way Sami will be up to date with the latest access codes Tailoren gives him on his last day. Also, I'll call off the hit on his girlfriend. She's already done all the damage she can, and it's too risky because the police will be trying to protect her." Everyone indicated they were in agreement.

"That is all for today," bin Nazamunde said. He stood up and walked out of the conference room.

Gurtenkov called O'Durea and told him to go ahead with the hit on Tailoren. But not to take him out until after he came home from

Charles Kaplan

work on Monday, so he could make sure Sami possessed the latest Patent Office access codes. O'Durea called the assassins and the hit was set up for after 5:00 pm on Monday. He told them to be waiting for Tailoren in his apartment when he got home from the Patent Office. O'Durea cancelled the hit on Carmina.

Before he could exit from iSight on his Powerbook, Muhamed Allah Yatakalan noticed Tailoren's icon blinking in the directory. He scrolled the cursor over to the blinking icon and pressed down on his mouse. Tailoren's face appeared on the computer's screen and his own face appeared on the screen of Tailoren's computer. This time Tailoren remembered not to speak until he was spoken to.

"The failure of the operation yesterday has been discussed," Muhamed Allah Yatakalan said. "Your work is so important you must go back to the Patent Office tomorrow and continue to give us their latest access codes."

Tailoren whined, "I am afraid because I have failed the jihad. I feel like hiding somewhere until I can leave this land of infidels and return to Saudi Arabia."

"No. You must stay there and do your work in the Patent Office," the Imam said emphatically. "We will protect you. The men who came after the girl will protect you like bodyguards. They are your friends. Make sure O'Durea knows where you are at all times, and send us the latest codes before you leave work tomorrow." His friendly facial expression concealed his treachery.

"Thank you." Tailoren's relief was evident on his face. "That makes me feel safer. I was afraid the men who came after Carmina might be sent to harm me."

"No. That will not happen. You will be safe with them."

"But what about the girl. You were right. Carmina is a witch. She read my mind. Did the agents get her and silence her. I am afraid she will betray me if they did not silence her."

"She will be taken care of. Do not fear her. We will protect you from her. And now I must get back to the Gold Room. Goodbye." He shut down his computer.

Tailoren was finally at ease, so he lay down on his bed and relaxed for the first time since awakening from the drug induced sleep. Muhamed Allah Yatakalan deceived him into thinking he was safe at last. He walked to work Monday morning feeling confident he was in the clear from the police because if Carmina told them anything about what he had done which they considered illegal, they'd have already arrested him. And Muhamed Allah Yatakalan promised him the jihad planned to protect him from harm.

He was relieved when he passed Carmina's desk and saw she wasn't sitting there. He'd not heard from her since she left his apartment. He assumed the assassins took her away and silenced her forever.

Tailoren thought maybe he'd start paying attention to some of the other infidel women who were flirting with him. He was somewhat attracted to one girl who was almost as chubby as Carmina. That could wait until another time. Today he needed to find the time to send all of the latest Patent Office access codes to Sami's hackers. He hadn't brought his Powerbook with him, so he'd have to go home at his lunch break to get it done.

Nollann was standing in the lobby of Building 4 at noon when Tailoren stepped off the elevator. He followed the Examiner out the door and down the street to the Butlarian Arms. The day was sunny and mild, so Nollann enjoyed walking back and forth outside while he waited for the subject of his surveillance to reappear. Nollann walked through the front entrance of the Butlarian Arms and into the lobby. He took a leisurely stroll through the lobby to kill some time and to see where the door to apartment 1C was located. He paused outside of it for a moment and listened. He heard nothing. Then he walked out of a side door located down the hall from 1C and observed the side door was closer to 1C than the door at the front entrance. When he was outside the side door, he checked it and found it was unlocked.

Nollann sauntered around the side of the building to the alley at its rear. He walked down the ally past an unmarked door which must be the rear entrance to 1C because of where it was located. He glanced through the glass pane on the rear door as he went past it. He saw nothing moving inside the apartment. He turned around and walked past the rear door going in the opposite direction. Again he saw nothing occurring when he peeked in through the glass pane. He walked out of the alley and stood where he could see both the side door of the building and the rear door of the apartment, in case Tailoren left through one of them. If his subject came out the front entrance, he had to pass Nollann as he walked back to the Patent Office down Clark Street.

Inside his apartment Tailoren turned on his Powerbook. First he used Safari to access his email. There was a message from Sami's hackers establishing the new web address he must use to communicate with them. The hackers changed the address for incoming email every thirty minutes. It took him less than fifteen minutes to send the US Patent Office's current access codes to the jihad's web address. He looked at the list of other messages in his email inbox and was relieved to see there was nothing from Carmina. This reassured him the jihad's assassins had silenced her. He turned off his PowerBook and walked out of his apartment, locking the door behind him.

Tailoren left the building through the front entrance and walked back to the Patent Office. Nollann saw him as he came around the building on to Clark Street. Tailoren entered Building 4 and stopped at the concession counter in the lobby. There he picked up a granola energy bar having a center of unsweetened chocolate. He ate the bar for lunch as he rode the elevator up to the third floor. He hadn't noticed the short, pudgy man who followed behind him until he passed the building's security checkpoint.

Nollann left Crystal City and drove back to his office. He would accomplish nothing by waiting outside of the office building where Tailoren worked. He needed to get the evidence he already possessed into a condition usable by a Bureau attorney to get a warrant for Examiner Tailoren's arrest. He hoped to get authorization to detain Carmina Burneta as a material witness. He decided to call the contact numbers in her personnel file after he finished assembling the evidence. He planned on returning to Crystal City before 5:00 pm to make sure the stake out was in operation.

Chapter 38   Slaying

THE TWO ASSASSINS planned on arriving in Crystal City about 4:00 pm on Monday. They expected considerable activity on the streets from people leaving the places where they worked, so the killers would not be as noticeable as at the times when the streets were nearly empty. They intended to park the rental van on the street as close as they could get to the Butlarian Arms. They could walk the rest of the way and go into the alley behind apartment 1 C. They believed they were less conspicuous because they were disguised as plumbers wearing their white coveralls embroidered with a plumbing company name and carrying a grey metal toolbox. Tradesmen were usually required to use apartment rear entrances. But two men dressed in casual or business clothes in the rear alley might attract attention. They planned to remove the coveralls after Tailoren was dead, put them in the toolbox, and leave by the front door of his apartment.

The assassins arrived in Crystal City on schedule at 4:15. They considered themselves lucky when a Lincoln pulled out of a parking space on Clark Street about half a block from the Butlarian Arms. Juan picked up the toolbox and they walked along Clark until it intersected the alley on to which Tailoren's rear door opened. They didn't notice the two men sitting in a late model, black Ford parked across from the front entrance of the building they intended to break into.

And the detectives, Meldman and Jackson, in the Ford didn't pay any particular attention to them. It was the time of day when tradesmen finished their work, left the buildings they were working in and walked on the street. These two plumbers were not carrying any bulky or heavy materials that would make them want to park directly in front of the building where they were working. The assassins' disguise had worked, so far.

From where the black Ford was parked, the detectives could not see the two plumbers in white coveralls turning into the alley at the rear of the building. Jackson, a large, well built African American who was a Terrapin linebacker at the U of M five years earlier, picked up a copy of the case. Neither of them had looked at anything in the file. Jackson sifted through the papers without reading anything and then put the file down to talk about the Orioles prospects for the season with Meldman, a short, thin veteran officer in his early fifties.

Jackson picked up the file again and began to read it with his full attention. At this time Meldman noticed a person looking like the picture of Tailoren and fitting the description Nollann gave them. The man was walking down the street toward where they were parked. He nudged Jackson with his elbow and tilted his head in the direction of the walker.

Jackson put down the file and looked in the direction Meldman indicated. He saw Tailoren and nodded his head. "It's him all right."

Meldman nodded in agreement. They watched as Tailoren entered the building through the front entrance. Jackson picked up the file and continued reading. Suddenly he looked up and turned to Meldman. "Didn't two guys in white coveralls walk past us about half an hour ago?"

Meldman slowly nodded his head, "Yeah, I think I remember them."

"Where'd they go?"

"I didn't pay any attention. Why'd you ask?"

"In the file here, there's a record of an interview with some patent attorney and he says he was chased by two guys wearing white coveralls and black ski masks he thinks wanted to kidnap him," Jackson said.

"Well the guys I saw weren't wearing black ski masks," Meldman chortled.

A moment later Nollann drove by in his own Buick station wagon. He intended to be there before Tailoren arrived at the Butlarian Arms, but was delayed by a traffic jam going over the Theodore Roosevelt memorial bridge. He cursed himself for not checking out a Bureau car having a siren he could have used to bypass the traffic clogging the bridge.

Jackson recognized Nollann and opened the street side door of the Ford and waved furiously at him. Nollann jammed on the brakes stopping his car in the middle of Clark Street. "What's up," he asked, as Jackson stepped up to the passenger side window of Nollann's car that was now sliding open.

Jackson blurted anxiously, "Is it important if we saw two guys in white coveralls walking down the street about a half hour ago?"

"Where'd they go?" Nollann's voice was foreboding.

"We don't know," Jackson said apologetically.

"Where's Tailoren," now Nollann sounded apprehensive.

"He went into the building through the front entrance. He hasn't come out. So I assume he's still in his apartment," Jackson said.

Nollann left his car in the middle of the street with its engine running and jumped out. "Come with me," he yelled over his shoulder as he ran toward the side entrance of the Butlarian Arms building.

As Jackson ran around Nollann's car, he shouted for Meldman to follow them and sprinted after Nollann. He was faster than the FBI agent so both men arrived at the side door at the same time. Nollann grabbed the handle, turned it and said a word of thanks the door was not locked. He ran in and stopped in front of the door to 1C.

"Kick it in!" he barked at Jackson.

"But," Jackson said, "we don't have a warrant."

"You kick it in now or I'll shoot it open," Nollann exclaimed. He fumbled in his suit pocket for the Black Widow .22 he carried, reluctantly, because Bureau regulations required him to be armed.

Jackson obeyed and gave the door a violent kick at the level of the lock, springing the latch out of its recess. The kick left Jackson off balance, so Nollann was the first to enter Tailoren's apartment.

He'd seen a lot in his fifteen years as an FBI agent, but what Nollann saw at that moment caused his mouth to fall open. Standing less than ten feet in front of him were two men, one tall and one shorter. They were wearing black ski masks and white coveralls. In one of their gloved hands each of the assassins held one end of a length of white clothesline wrapped around his palm; the other hand gripped the clothesline above the palm. The clothesline was wrapped around the neck of Bennie Tailoren, whose tongue hung out of the side of his mouth. His face was splotched with purple. Blood ran from his nostrils and one corner of his mouth. Tailoren's fingers were wrapped around the rope on either side of his throat. Apparently he was struggling to loosen the strand that was garroting the life out of him. The killers were using the rope to support his body and keep him standing upright on his feet.

The unexpected bursting through the door by the FBI agent and police officer startled the stranglers momentarily. The taller killer was a sadist who enjoyed the act of strangling his victims. He was turned on sexually by their helpless struggles. He tried to prolong their agony by letting up occasionally on his end of the rope to let them get a gasp of air. This always annoyed his shorter partner who wanted to get the job over with and get away from the crime scene as quickly as possible. The sadistic killer was on the side of their victim closest to Nollann. The other killer was on the side closest to the rear door of the apartment.

Hoping to finish off his victim, the tall killer gave the end of the rope he was holding a final heavy tug. This sadistic move cost him his life, because he gave the last pull on the rope at the same moment his partner let go of his end and started running toward the alley door at the rear of the apartment. This caused the tall killer to loose his balance and take two stumbling steps in the direction away from the rear door and toward Nollann. It also gave Nollann the time to he needed to flick his Black Widow's safety off. By the time Nollann had his weapon up and ready, the tall killer regained his balance and was stepping over Tailoren's body, which was slumped on the floor between him and his escape route.

"Stop there, I'm FBI," Nollann shouted as he raised his weapon and pointed it at a live human being for the first time in his life. When the killer stepped over Tailoren's body and started to run toward the rear door, Nollann started pulling the trigger. The deafening sound and flash of the first shot caused him to flinch and close his eyes. But he kept on pulling the trigger until all five rounds in the cylinder were fired and all the weapon did was click.

Then Nollann opened his eyes to see if he'd hit anything. At the range of less than ten feet and the target six feet tall, even Minimum Bill couldn't miss. The first .22 WMR (Magnum) slug hit the killer in the left side of his chest, bounced off of a rib, went through one lung, nicked his heart and lodged in the other lung. His heart continued pumping. Internally he was bleeding profusely. His blood was flowing into his lungs and he was drowning in it. The other four rounds fired from Nollann's Black Widow were embedded in the walls and ceiling of the apartment.

Nollann felt his right hand shaking. He looked at it and saw he was still gripping his pistol so tightly the trigger was pulled all the way back to the rear of the guard.

By now Meldman was in the apartment with his Glock drawn. Nollann yelled, "Put it away, and call for ambulances. Hunt around and find anyone who can give these men medical help. The shots must have attracted somebody. See if anyone has medical training. We need to get whatever information we can from them before they die. Now move fast."

Nollann dropped down on his knees and bent over Tailoren's body. He put his face inches away from the dying young man. He looked into Tailoren's closed eyes. "Can you hear me, Son?" He put on his most sympathetic face with tears starting to form in the corners of his soft brown eyes. Tailoren's eyes flickered open. Nollann's smile beamed down at him. Projecting confidence he didn't have, Nollann said, "Hold on, Bennie. You're gonna make it. You'll live if you can hold on until a doctor gets here." But he knew it wasn't true. A victim of strangulation often dies of a heart attack. And Tailoren's vital signs, shortness of breath, beads of sweat on his forehead and trembling left arm and hand, indicated he was having a heart attack. It was more than likely going to be fatal.

In an indignant tone, Nollann demanded, "Who did this to you, Bennie?"

Tailoren's lips moved and Nollann put his ear so close it almost touched them. In a hoarse voice he barely whispered, "Imam lied, set m'up." He started coughing and closed his eyes.

In a softer tone, Nollann pleaded, "Bennie, tell me who did this to you."

Tailoren opened his eyes briefly and mumbled "khanj, khanj" and then lapsed into silence.

Remembering what he read from the file on Hamilton, Nollann said, "Do you mean *al Khanjar* did this to you."

Tailoren nodded his head without opening his eyes.

"Are you a Muslim?"

Again Tailoren nodded his head keeping his eyes closed, as his entire body began to tremble.

"Where is *al Khanjar*?"

But Hamde Jawade, the fake Bennie Tailoren, was dead.

Nollann stayed on his knees and scampered over to where the tall killer was lying on the floor. He bent over the killer, as he'd done with Tailoren. Once again putting on his most sympathetic look, he pleaded, "Tell me why you did this. You will die in peace if you confess your crime."

The killer looked at him and started to laugh, but stopped when it made him spit up blood. He sputtered through the blood in his throat, "Muslims don' confess. Go to heaven if I kill for jihad. Ruslan alive?"

It sounded like a question, so Nollann said anxiously, "Are you asking me if Ruslan is alive?"

The killer nodded his head.

"First tell me if you're Russian."

The killer barely shook his head and whispered, "Chechen."

"Is Ruslan your partner?"

The killer gave a barely perceptible affirmative nod.

"Yes he's alive," Nollann told him even though he didn't know if what he said was true.

The killer smiled and started coughing up more blood.

Nollann continued with his questions. "Who else have you killed? Did you kill the inventor, Hamilton? How many have you killed?" But the killer did not answer. He lapsed into unconsciousness and died before medical help could reach the crime scene.

Although the aura of each dying man was barely perceptible to Nollann, his synesthesia told him they both had been truthful.

As soon as Pedro ran through the rear door into the alley, he took off his ski mask and threw it to the left, the direction opposite to the one he intended to run.

Jackson saw Pedro escaping and noticed the "Best Plumbers" logo on the back of the fleeing killer's white coveralls. He didn't needed to hear any orders from Nollann, and started chasing the escaping killer when Nollann stopped firing his weapon. Jackson recognized the danger of moving anywhere in the direction Nollann was pointing the weapon until he stopped pulling the trigger. He was forced to guess which direction the assassin turned when he fled out the rear door into the alley, and he guessed wrong. Jackson saw the ski mask on the left hand side of the door so he ran that way.

When Pedro rounded the corner of the building, he realized his ruse had worked. His pursuer went the wrong way. So he stopped, squatted down beside a dumpster and took off his cap and the white coveralls. He lifted the lid of the dumpster and dropped them inside. Then he calmly walked down the street to where he parked the van, got in and started the drive back to Baltimore. At this moment, for the first time, he wondered whether his older brother had been wounded or shot dead.

Jackson soon realized he'd turned the wrong way in his chase of the fleeing killer, so he ran back into the alley and picked up the ski mask. At least they had the killer's DNA, he thought, because there were sure to be hairs, or dandruff or skin cells inside of the mask.

Meldman was on the phone calling police headquarters, so help was arriving in all directions. Jackson returned to Tailoren's apartment. Nollann straightened up and stood. He swayed slightly as the blood rushed from his head. He told Jackson he was turning the crime scene over to the Arlington police. As he spoke, officers were searching Tailoren's apartment. They found the prayer rug rolled up in its leather tube, four prepaid cell phones, and an Apple Powerbook having an iSight camera plugged into its firewire port. They photographed the prayer rug and took the Powerbook and cell phones to the crime lab for analysis.

"I'll going outside to prepare my statement," Nollann said to Jackson. He walked out to his car, which was still parked in the middle of Clark Street. Meldman had turned the motor off and left the keys in the ignition. Nollann turned the key starting the engine, made a U-turn and pulled over to the curb in front of the entrance to the Butlarian Arms. He closed his eyes, put his head back on the car seat and tried to slow his breathing and pounding heart. Soon the adrenalin stopped surging into his blood stream and he started to calm down. He opened his eyes, picked his notebook up from the passenger seat, took out his pen and began to write.

By 8:30 pm the bodies were removed, the crime lab techs departed, and apartment 1C was sealed off with yellow crime scene tape. A search of the alley and dumpster found the fleeing killer's cap, and white coveralls with the "Best Plumbers" logo.

After Nollann statement was typed up and signed, Arlington police Captain Collins assured him the investigation of his shooting a fleeing murderer was going to be perfunctory. When he handed his statement to Captain Collins, he put his large hand on Nollann's shoulder and said with a grin, "Maybe we'll change your nickname from Minimum Bill to Deadeye." Nollann smiled weakly, still too shaken by the experience of firing his Black Widow and killing someone to enjoy the glory he was getting from the way he handled the case.

After he returned the rental van, checked out of the motel and was on I-40 driving back to Chicago, Pedro phoned O'Durea and told him what happened. Pedro's voice began shaking as he neared the end of his narration. "They got Zaindin."

"You mean Juan."

"Yes, my brother, Zaindin. They shot him. I think they killed my brother."

"Don't worry. The jihad will get you another partner."

Even the normally cynical Pedro was dismayed by the callousness of this remark. He had to stop talking for a moment to regain his composure; his initial impulse was to curse O'Durea and the jihad.

"Are you still there?" the Cuban asked.

"Yes." Through gritted teeth Pedro raged, "I don't want another partner. I want revenge. I blame the Jew lawyer who got away for causing this."

"Was he there? Did he come in with the FBI agent?"

"No. But I believe if we killed Levy in his apartment, Zaindin would still be alive."

O'Durea didn't see any logic in Pedro's reasoning, but he realized the assassin was too upset to be rational. So he changed the subject. "Did you leave any evidence at Tailoren's apartment to link you to the murder?"

"I got the gloves and ski mask and white coveralls with me in a plastic garbage bag," Pedro lied.

"Get off the interstate at Frederick and dump them in a trashcan at some truck stop. When you get back to Chicago, move to a suburb where no one knows you. Gurtenkov will begin searching for your new partner."

Struggling not to sob, Pedro murmured, "I don't need a partner now. I can garrote them and blow them up without help." Although he would never know why, his hunch was correct. If they had killed Levy, Tailoren would not have been put under surveillance and Minimum Bill Nollann would not have stumbled in on them strangling him. And his brother, Zaindin, would still be alive.

Chapter 39   PAM

SOMEHOW THE *WASHINGTON Times* managed to get a copy of Tailoren's photo from the Patent Office personnel files. His face was on the front page of the Tuesday edition of the newspaper along with the other pictures of the crime scene their photographer was able to snap from outside the crime scene tape as the bodies were being removed. Tailoren's photo also appeared on the Tuesday morning news broadcast of WTTG in their coverage of the murder and shooting.

Early in the afternoon a phone call came in to the Arlington police from Mrs. Pamella Henderly, a young lady living in Annapolis. She claimed she knew Bennie Tailoren and the man shown in the newspaper and on TV was not Tailoren. The person Tailoren listed as his next of kin in the Patent Office records turned out to be fictitious, so the police were interested in hearing from anyone who claimed to know the victim. The call was shunted through to detective Hank Frank. He asked the caller to come in to the station and bring any evidence supporting what she was telling them. Frank scheduled an interview for 10:00 am the following morning at the Franconia Road station. The detective went up the chain of command and sent the substance of Mrs. Henderly's assertion to Nollann, who he invited to attend the interview.

The next morning, a silver Chevrolet Tahoe drove into the Franconia Road station lot and parked in a visitor's slot. A slender, but shapely young woman stepped out, locked the car and walked into the station. Pamella Henderly, aged thirty-one, had shoulder length brown hair she parted on the left side of her long narrow face, which ended in a pointed chin. She had blue eyes, a straight nose and a wide friendly smile. Wearing brown dress slacks, a peach colored sweater, and low-topped cordovan boots, she walked in carrying a manila envelope.

When she identified herself, the police officer at the desk told her she was expected. He stood and escorted her to an interview room at the end of a hall. In the room four chairs with padded seats and metal backs were pulled up to a grey metal desk. She sat down and waited patiently for the detectives to arrive. A minute or two later Hank Frank walked in, introduced himself, and he was followed by William Nollann, who displayed his FBI credentials. Frank took out a tape recorder and asked for her permission to use it.

Pamella Henderly nodded her assent, removed two newspaper clippings from her manila envelope and began talking. "I don't know who this man is," she held up the picture of Tailoren printed in the previous day's *Washington Times*. "But he's not Bennie Tailoren. He looks a little like Bennie. He could possibly fool people who didn't know the jerk very well. But he doesn't fool me."

She held up the second newspaper clipping. "This is from a Sunday nuptial section of the *Waukegan News Sun*, and it shows the real Bennie Tailoren. If you look closely, you can see there's a tattoo on the wrist of the hand he's holding up. His right wrist. And if you look very closely, you can see the tattoo has 'PAM' in the middle of a heart made from rosebuds. See where the news story says Bennie Tailoren is displaying the tattoo with the name of the girl he is engaged to marry."

Frank took the clipping, looked at it and nodded. He passed it to Nollann, who studied it without comment.

She continued indignantly, "I never agreed to marry that turkey. Why...uh...he's the type of jerk who yells 'Freebird' at a rock concert."

Frank nodded his head and chuckled. Nollann frowned, not understanding the insult.

"One date is all I ever had with him. I never wanted to see him again, but he became obsessed with me. My name was Pamella Brown before I married Avery Henderly. By the way my husband is a gunnery officer teaching at the Annapolis Naval Academy." Her pride evident from her smile.

"Well, Bennie the nerd went around humming the tune from Tom Hall's song *Pamela Brown* talking about all the good times he had with Pamella Brown. You're familiar with the song aren't you?"

Frank shook his head negatively, but this time Nollann smiled and nodded his head affirmatively.

Charles Kaplan

"Ruining my reputation by insinuating I fooled around with him," she said angrily. "I never even kissed the jerk." She snatched up the clipping showing Tailoren and jabbed it with her finger. "He was such a pest, a torment. Calling me all the time…stalking me," her voice quivering with rage. "I took the first decent job teaching elementary school I could get and moved away from Waukegan. My job turned out to be in Annapolis where I met Avery." She paused to get her breath.

In the closed room Nollann's synesthesia indicated she was telling the truth. He said, "Well it looks like everything turned out OK for you in the end, didn't it." He gave her his you can trust me smile and body language. "But I have to share something with you, Pamella. May I call you Pamella?"

She nodded her assent but gave the agent an inquisitive stare.

"The Bennie Tailoren who was murdered yesterday has a tattoo on his right wrist; it has PAM surrounded by a heart made of rose buds. This can't be a coincidence. The facts are too unusual, the strange name Tailoren, the word PAM, and the heart shape made from rose buds. The dead man in the morgue just has to be Bennie Tailoren."

She placed the two clippings side by side and studied them. "Now you're making me wonder."

"Nobody's come by to look at the body and identify it," detective Frank said. "Are you willing to do that to help us get it off our list of things to be done to close this case. But I have to warn you. It won't be a pleasant sight."

"Sure, but I'm not going to say it's Bennie if I don't recognize him. If I don't believe it's really him," she crossed her arms defiantly.

Detective Frank had a police cruiser brought to the front of the station. He, Nollann and Mrs. Henderly got into the cruiser, and Frank drove them to the Fairfax County morgue. Once the detectives identified themselves to a clerk, they were escorted into a cold room where the bodies were stored in the stainless steel drawers of a large green metal cabinet. The clerk consulted a list of names he picked up on the way to the storage room and walked over to drawer 17D. He slid the drawer all the way open exposing the full length of Bennie

308

Tailoren's pale body, which was covered by a sheet of white plastic drawn up to his chin leaving only his head exposed.

Pamella Henderly took one look and said, "It's not him. It's not Bennie Tailoren. There is absolutely no doubt in my mind. I don't know who he is but he's just not Bennie. Look at this picture." She laid the clipping from the *Waukegan News Sun* on the plastic just below the chin of the corpse.

"That picture is several years old, and this body has been traumatized. You can't expect him to look exactly like an old picture," detective Frank said.

"Let's take a look at the tattoo," Nollann said. He pulled the plastic off of the right arm of the corpse and turned the hand over revealing a tattoo with the word PAM surrounded by rose buds arranged into the shape of a heart. "See. It's just like you described it to us. That proves this is Bennie Tailoren."

She shook her head and said confidently, "Bennie's tattoo was different. The letters were taller and thinner, not short and squatty like these are. And the heart didn't crowd the letters like this one does." She pointed with her finger. "See, these rosebuds almost touch the stem of the P and one leg of the M. On Bennie's tattoo, there is a definite space between the letters and the rosebuds because the letters are taller and thinner, like I just said. This proves what I told you before. This body's not Bennie Tailoren, and I'm not going to sign anything saying it is." Pamella Henderly put her hands on her hips and glared stubbornly at the two detectives.

"Wait a minute," Frank said. "I'll get a magnifying glass and we'll take a closer look at the tattoo in the clipping."

The clerk brought them a 3.5x Zeiss magnifier. Each of them took a turn looking at the tattoo in the clipping. But the even the magnified image was still too small and dim to verify what she was saying.

Nollann pulled the plastic sheet back over the body. "We're not going to settle who this really is this morning," he said. "Let's go back to the station and let Mrs. Henderly get back to her family. We'll contact the *Waukegan News Sun* to see if they kept the negative or can give us a better copy of his picture."

During the ride back, Nollann turned toward Mrs. Henderly and asked' "Do you know if Tailoren was a Muslim. That dead man in the morgue told me he was Muslim just before he died."

Smiling for the first time since they left the morgue, she said, "I'm sure Bennie Tailoren was not a Muslim when I knew him in Waukegan."

Waukegan News Sun could not help them solve the mystery of the corpse's identity. They only had a paper copy of the image they'd published. Enlarging their image did not enhance its quality. So the search for the corpse's identity ended there.

Chapter 40   Post-Mortem

THREE WEEKS AFTER the person calling himself Bennie Tailoren was murdered, Levy checked into the Dately Hotel in Crystal City the night before he was scheduled to represent a client at a morning hearing before the Patent Office Board of Appeals. He called Nollann and gave the agent his schedule. They decided to meet in the evening to discuss the murders. The Hamilton murder and Ginsberg bombing were still listed as unsolved crimes in the records of the appropriate police departments.

The two friends decided to order from the hotel's room service menu and eat in Levy's room. Nollann brought two bottles of merlot with him. Both removed their coats, ties and shoes. They lounged in their socks on upholstered chairs they pulled up to a low table at one end of the room. A container of ice and a bottle of wine sat on the table. Levy inched his toes up over the edged of the table, and slouched in his chair.

"Let's start with Bennie Tailoren," Nollann said. "We'll keep calling him Tailoren for now, although Mrs. Henderly told us she was sure the corpse is someone else. I interviewed her, and I think she was telling us what she believed to be true, even though the corpse had a Pam tattoo like the one she said the real Bennie Tailoren had."

Nollann gave Levy a conspiratorial look. "Now remember. This is all off the record."

Levy opened his mouth feigning astonishment and nodded solemnly.

"Here's what we do know about Tailoren. He was highly intelligent and had a scientific education. He told me he was Muslim. There was a Muslim prayer rug in his bedroom. So I think we can conclude he was a Muslim. But Mrs. Henderly was sure the Bennie Tailoren she knew was not a Muslim.

Our lab has been working on his Powerbook. They learned he was sending the Patent Office's access codes to a lot of different

Internet addresses. But they can't find any relationship for those Internet addresses."

Levy interrupted, "My two granddaughters are computer hackers. They claim they can crack into any Internet web site or address."

"Do you actually believe your granddaughters can solve a computer problem that's been baffling the FBI's experts?"

Levy shrugged. "Who knows. Let's not get side tracked on that right now."

Nollann nodded and went on, "Tailoren tried to drug Carmina Burneta. She's the girl who helped get him a bogus Top Secret security clearance. Two men wearing black ski masks tried to catch her in Tailoren's apartment. Just before he died Tailoren told me an Imam set him up to be killed. He implied his death has something to do with *al Khanjar*."

Nollann looked at Levy as if he expected a question. When none came, he resumed, "I interviewed Miss Burneta last week when she came back to work. No one's tried to kidnap or hurt her since the incident in Tailoren's apartment. So it looks like the assassins aren't after her any more. She was clueless about every thing important to these cases. She didn't know the rolled up fabric in Tailoren's bedroom was a prayer rug. She didn't even realize he was a Muslim until I told her. She told me she knew no reason to think Tailoren had taken over somebody else's identity. All she could say for sure about him was he was very nice to her until the day before he tried to drug her. And," imitating Groucho Marx by twitching his eyebrows, "she said he was great in the sack."

Levy grinned and twitched his eyebrows back at Nollann.

"One of the men who murdered Tailoren told me he, the killer, was Muslim. He also said he was a Chechen. He asked if his partner, Ruslan, was killed."

"Ah ha," Levy interjected, "One of the men who chased me called his partner Ruslan."

Nollann nodded. "And you told me they wore black ski masks, gloves and white coveralls, and one of them held a length of rope in his hands."

"That's right. They did," Levy confirmed.

"Hamilton and Tailoren were both strangled with a piece of rope. The two men I saw strangling Tailoren were wearing black ski masks, gloves and white coveralls."

"Three times, the same M.O. Right?" Levy inquired.

"Two times for sure," Nollann said. "We got the DNA of the escaped strangler from the ski mask and clothes he left behind. From something Marsha Ginsberg told us, we think his ears stick out. And analysis of the dead strangler's DNA revealed that the two stranglers are brothers."

"That means the one that got away is also a Chechen," Levy quickly blurted.

Nollann nodded and chuckled at his friend's enthusiasm. He paused to open the bottle of merlot on the table, and filled their glasses.

"Here's something else you don't know," Nollann continued. "A man with a conspicuous gold front tooth asked for a room on Hamilton's floor the day before he was murdered, and a man with a prominent gold tooth was in the Ginsberg shop the evening before it was bombed. The day before Hamilton's murder another man asked for a room on Hamilton's floor. Both registered under fictitious names."

"See. It was the same killers and M. O. three times," Levy persisted.

Nollann tented his fingers. "Here's what I can infer from what we know. The two men who came after you were the same ones who strangled Tailoren. They were probably the same ones who strangled Hamilton. A man with a fake gold tooth was involved in Hamilton's death and the Ginsberg bombing. Tailoren, a Muslim, was enraged by Hamilton's anti-Arab efforts and he fingered Hamilton for assassination. He put out a hit on you because you're Jewish and were helping Hamilton; and Ginsberg's shop was bombed for the same reasons. The girl, Ms. Burneta, became a target because she knew Tailoren got a fraudulent security clearance. When Tailoren screwed up the hit on Burneta, he became the assassins' target because she would turn him in. And his handlers were afraid Tailoren might tell us what's going on, in order to save his own skin. What do you think, Lem?"

Levy put down the glass of wine he'd almost emptied. "I see two possible flaws in your deductions, Bill. You already convinced me the man who was after me yelled 'nyet' rather than 'not yet'. And nyet is a Russian word. And Ruslan is a common Russian name. But the dying strangler told you he was Chechen. If he lied about one detail, doesn't that taint everything he told you?"

"He didn't lie," Nollann said. "Most Chechens speak Russian, and Ruslan is a common name in Chechnya too. So I don't think he was lying."

"OK. I'll agree the dead strangler probably told you the truth. I was just trying to be the devil's advocate." Levy laughed and paused to sip some wine "The other flaw is I believe Mrs. Henderly was right. The man you saw being murdered wasn't the real Bennie Tailoren. The real Bennie Tailoren was a small town Midwesterner; he wouldn't convert to Muslimism and join a cell of secret agents."

"I agree," said Nollann. "But we don't have any evidence as to who the false Tailoren really was."

Levy continued, "The stranglers and Tailoren must have been working together at one time on the same mission until Tailoren screwed up the hit on Ms. Burneta. And they are all Muslims; even the strangler who got away because his dead brother was a Muslim. So we have a group of Muslims working together, killing Hamilton who was anti-Arab, and trying to kill me because I'm a Jew helping Hamilton."

"Here's what I think." Levy twirled his glass around, paused to contemplate the swirling wine, then drank it down. "There's an Arab-Muslim jihad with plenty of money backing it. The jihad has financed a secret cell of terrorists in our country. Some of the terrorists have infiltrated the Federal Government. The terrorist cell includes assassins who kill people who get in their way. And the cell can steal the identity of American citizens and use the stolen identities to conceal their secret agents. They even go so far as to copy the tattoos of the people whose identity they steal."

Nollann's facial expression indicated he agreed. He lifted the wine bottle and filled Levy's glass again.

Abruptly Levy jerked his toes off the table and shot to his feet, spilling some wine on his shirt. "Oh my God," he exclaimed. "It just occurred to me. There's still a fatwa out there with my name on it."

Epilogue

THE PATENT OFFICE approved the Hamilton patent application covering his death ray gun because the inventor proved that the ray the gun emitted could be used to kill living creatures. But the scientists working for the Pentagon were never able to develop the weapon into something the armed forces could use. The single ray gun Hamilton constructed actually did violate the laws of physics and could not be reproduced or scaled up to a more powerful version. Hamilton's unique gun was an abnormality that only worked because the specific materials the inventor cobbled together functioned synergistically as an anomaly for which there is no scientific explanation.

Hamilton's Trust donated his ray gun to the weapons collection at the Smithsonian.

Sequel

In the sequel, *A PATENT ON GREED*, bin Nazamunde's agents continue to clash with Lem Levy and Minimum Bill Nollann. The story begins when an inventor comes to Levy with a gadget that increases auto mileage to 250 miles per gallon. Because of the potentially astronomical profits such an invention might produce, the characters display various degrees of greed.

The US President backs a free lance assassin, called The Ghost, who attacks the jihadists, and in the end, the villains pay for their crimes.

Acknowledgements

I thank my children, friends and relatives for their continual encouragement. More specifically, I thank Carol Towne and Jack Draper for scouring the manuscript for errors; Ed Niederhofer, Steve Marshall and Beth Kaplan for reasoned criticism; Miriam Jones for character emphasis recommendations; Austin Jones for advice on describing mental illness; and Bob Casagrande for spotting inconsistencies. Insights and advice from Suzanne Fischer Staples helped me avoid some of the mistakes of a neophyte author. Thanks are also due to early readers Susie and Stu Mulligan, Barbara McClellan, and Laurie Park, for plowing through immature drafts, and to Karen Flowers for her undiminished enthusiasm from the inception of this endeavor.

But the most thanks go to my wife, Sara, who shared my excitement for the project, who attacked every draft with a proofreader's eye, and who never tired of hearing about my struggles.

Printed in the United States
52852LVS00003B/52-93